Unforgettable Mistakes

Also by Nikki A Lamers

The Unforgettable Series
The Unforgettable Summer (#1)
Unforgettable Nights (#2)
Unforgettable Dreams (#3)
Unforgettable Memories (#4)
The Unforgettable One (#5)

Home Duet
Dreams Lost and Found (#1)
Finding Home (#2)

**Looking for Clean Contemporary Romance?
Read books by Nicole Mullaney**

Ivy & Mistletoe
The Maltese Holiday
Deck the Heart
Magic in Mount Holly (Coming November 2021)

Or books by Character Ethan Dulane
Ethan Dulane is a character created by
Nicole Mullaney and Candy Cain
for the films and books below

Joy & Hope

Unforgettable Mistakes

The Unforgettable Series #6

By Nikki A Lamers

Copyright

Frey Dreams an imprint of Nikki A Lamers

ISBN 978-1-951185-09-01 (paperback)
ISBN 978-1-951185-10-7 (ebook)

Cover design by Jessica Scott, Uniquely Tailored

Table of Contents

Unforgettable Mistakes *1*

Also by Nikki A Lamers *2*

   The Unforgettable Series 2

   Home Duet 2

Unforgettable Mistakes *3*

   The Unforgettable Series #6 3

Copyright *4*

Table of Contents *5*

Chapter 1 ....*8*

Chapter 2 ....*16*

Chapter 3 ....*23*

Chapter 4 ....*32*

Chapter 5 ....*41*

Chapter 6 ....*48*

Chapter 7 ....*56*

Chapter 8 ....*64*

Chapter 9 ....*74*

Chapter 10 ....*81*

Chapter 11 ....*91*

Chapter 12 ....*99*

Chapter 13 ....*108*

Chapter 14 ....*115*

Chapter 15 ....*122*

Chapter 16 ....*130*

Chapter 17 ....*139*

Chapter 18 ....*146*

Chapter 19 ....*154*

Chapter 20 ....*162*

Chapter 21 ....*170*

Chapter 22 ....*178*

Chapter 23 ....*186*

Chapter 24 ....*195*

Chapter 25 ....*204*

Chapter 26 ....*214*

Chapter 27 ....*223*

Chapter 28 ....*233*

Chapter 29 ....*242*

Chapter 30 ....*251*

Chapter 31 ....*262*

Chapter 32 ....*270*

Chapter 33 ....*278*

Chapter 34 ....*288*

Chapter 35 ....*297*

Chapter 36 ....*306*

Chapter 37 ....*314*

Chapter 38 ....*322*

Chapter 39 ....*331*

Chapter 40 ....*339*

Epilogue *347*

Acknowledgements *355*

Connect with the Author *357*

About the Author *358*

Chapter 1

Amy

I sit on the cold hardwood floor, trying to hear what my parents are arguing about this time. I cautiously scoot closer and place my back against the wall, right next to the small opening of my bedroom door. I pull my knees up to my chest and wrap my arms protectively around them, holding on tight. I hate when my mom and dad fight, but they seem to fight a lot lately when they think they're the only two around. I just wish I could do something to stop it. "That happy little girl upstairs is the only reason I'm still here right now," Dad grumbles, his voice almost deadly.

I bite my lower lip, letting the tears roll down my cheeks, while I attempt to hold back my sob. I don't want him to leave.

"I'm so sorry. It was a mistake and I wish I could go back and change it, but I can't. I'll do anything to make it up to you, Jim. Please," Mom pleads.

"Anything?" he questions.

"A...anything," she stammers.

"Then prove it," he demands.

"I will," she replies, weakly.

I quickly scamper to my bed and curl up in a ball on my side. I put my hand over my ear closest to the mattress and use the pillow to help cover the exposed one in attempt to block out the sounds of my mom and dad arguing. I gasp, startling myself awake at the memory.

I blink my eyes open, taking in the familiar sights of Matt Young's tan bedroom. At the bottom of the bed, a long, worn, dark blue wooden dresser is pushed up against the wall, with a large mirror above it. Pictures stick out haphazardly from the edges of the mirror, reminding me of my history with Matt. He has pictures of him with my best friend Bree and me when we were younger. I've known both of them nearly my whole life, although Bree just a little bit longer.

I grew up next door to Bree in Massachusetts. For the longest time, we were inseparable. She's my opposite in looks and so much more. She has long, chestnut brown hair and soft brown eyes, compared to my long, wavy, platinum blonde hair and pale blue-grey eyes. She's three inches taller than me at 5'6" and she has a lean build, while I have a big chest and I'm visibly stronger from cheerleading. Bree was never allowed to do any activities or sports growing up because her parents were too busy with work, while cheer for me was engrained in my soul. I needed the outlet. Bree loves the quiet, while I like the noise of people all around me. I had a need for parties, boys, popularity and taking chances, while Bree always seemed content staying in the background and supporting those she loved. I'm the one who's always seen as smiling and energetic and trying to rub off on those around me. At least it's that way as long as you're on my good side.

In the summers Bree would leave me for a couple weeks to go visit her grandmother in Maine. I hated when she would leave me. It felt like a betrayal, no matter what the reason. Our last summer before senior year, we both tried talking her parents into letting her stay here with me. We wanted to spend our last summer as high school students together going to parties and hanging out when I wasn't at cheer camp. That didn't work out how we wanted though and she inevitably left for Maine, while I stayed here with cheer and Matt.

While in Maine, she wouldn't stop talking about this guy she met, Christian, so I was surprised, but thrilled when she came home early. Unfortunately, I saw less and less of her, even though she lived across the street and

9

still claimed I was her best friend. I went to parties, while she stayed home to help take care of her mom. Then the following year, when it was time to leave for college together, I left alone. Her mom passed away and she missed our whole freshmen year. By the time she started the next year, I had new friends, a hot new boyfriend and she was finally moving in with me, like we planned.

I grimace at the picture of the group of all of us together, including Christian. I don't even want to think about him.

I glance at the next few pictures of Matt and his best friend Blake. Blake is tall, lean and firm, with short sandy brown hair, spiked slightly on top and chocolate brown eyes. Blake didn't move into town until our junior year of high school, but him and Matt became close fast, probably because of baseball. They're both incredibly good. Blake's a good guy, but he always watches out for Bree first, then Matt, before me. I know Matt can take care of himself, but I hated always being on the bottom of the list.

I notice a few pictures of him with other girls, but it doesn't bother me. We have a strange sort of relationship. Matt has always been there for me. He's pulled me out of trouble more than once and he always comes to my rescue whenever I need a date or just a friend and I do the same for him. The poster behind me, where the headboard would be probably bothers me more than the girls tucked into the mirror. The poster is a picture of a dark haired, dark eyed, perfectly tanned model. She's dressed in a yellow string bikini, standing near the waves, posing on the beach with her back arched, arms out and chest up. I grimace, believing I couldn't look like that if I tried.

I heave a sigh and roll over, letting my eyes fall on Matt's naked, broad, muscular back, leading down to his narrow waist. His short, dark brown hair is a mess from both sleep and my fingers. I smile to myself, as I remember tracing the dark lines and curves of his relatively new shoulder tattoo with my tongue last night. It's a design one of his friend's made for him, curving around his shoulder and then shoots out like black fire down his upper arm and at the top of his back and chest. The way it connects to the edges of the phoenix he got a couple years ago on his upper back, makes it hard to decide if the bird is being consumed by the flames or rising from the ashes, but I guess that's the point. I can easily admit he's hot as hell and makes my heart race uncontrollably. We have insane chemistry in bed, but that's all it can ever be for us, a really good fuck when we both need it and of course an irreplaceable friend. I don't know what I'd do without him.

He rolls over and blinks his gorgeous emerald green eyes open. He sees me and gives me his panty-melting smile. The same one he uses to get girls into bed all the time. "Morning," he rasps. His barely awake, deep, gravelly voice rumbles through me, giving me shivers. He reaches for me and cups my ass, pulling me into him. I barely get out a squeak, before he covers his mouth with mine and I instantly melt into his kiss. His tongue pushes inside my mouth and tangles with mine. I run one hand through his hair as the other slowly makes its way down his hard chest. I can't let this go too far this morning. I have too much to do, but he feels so damn good!

Matt

I don't know how this woman riles me up like this, but I cant' get enough of her. I trail one hand up her spine and weave it into her soft blonde hair, while the other hand begins to roam around the front and between her legs. She whimpers as my thumb sweeps over her heated folds, over the top of her thong. I push it over to the side and slip my finger inside her already wet, swollen pussy. Her head falls back from my lips and she gasps, whispering my name, "Matt." She breathes harshly as I curl my finger, caressing the spot that drives her fucking crazy with need for me. "I...I can't," she stammers. She exhales harshly, as her back arches towards me, making me smirk.

"Do you want me to stop?" I taunt.

"No, don't stop," she whimpers.

I slowly kiss a trail down her neck, licking and gently sucking as I keep curling my finger inside of her. I move down to her breasts and begin cherishing them. I'm both an ass and a breast man and Amy has perfectly overflowing handfuls of both. My tongue sticks out circling her breast and then gently sucking her taut nipple into my mouth, as her hand tangles into my hair. I release her breast with a pop and give the other side the same treatment. She tugs on the ends of my hair as my finger curls faster and I rub my thumb over her clit in the same motion. She pulls my hair harder, moaning as her walls begin clenching my finger, over and over again, before she collapses beneath me with a satisfied smile. "Mm, what a way to wake up," she groans in appreciation.

I chuckle softly and insist, "I'm not done with you yet."

She giggles and then shakes her head, as if shaking herself out of orgasmic bliss. "Yes, you are," she declares. She grabs her phone and glances at the time, her nose scrunching up in annoyance with what she sees. She heaves a sigh and mumbles an apology, "I'm sorry, Matt. I have enough time to help you out," she offers. She nods down at my dick, now as hard as stone.

I grimace at her response, knowing in five minutes she'll be gone and I'll be rubbing it out in the shower for relief. I love waking up to her in my bed. Of course, she always has to ruin it by taking off for her real life or doing something else to remind me that we agreed to just be fuck buddies. At the time, that's exactly what I wanted, but now I don't think that was my smartest decision. I don't think that's what I want anymore and every day this whole thing between us seems more and more fucked up. It's not like we're each other's dirty little secret. Everyone pretty much knows we hook up regularly and we do bring each other as dates to many different places, but we both date other people and she's not my girlfriend. She hasn't been since high school. Then again, even in high school we'd claim we weren't boyfriend and girlfriend. Even I don't know the fuck why anymore.

True, I've known Amy since kindergarten. She's always been that cute, spunky girl that everyone wants to be friends with, date, or in some cases be just like her. Then she grew up and holy fuck she became hot as hell, with a sexy attitude to go along with it. I'll admit, the first night we hooked up, we had both just broken up with someone and we hung out together a lot. I'm not even sure who started it, but we both sure as fuck finished it. Ever since then, she uses me as a fucking booty call and I have to admit, I do the same. But I have to be more careful than her about when and how often I do now, for more than one reason. She seems to think we can't be together, although, I'm not exactly sure why. But I'm almost positive it has something to do with her parents. They never liked me. She acts like it's because we've known each other too long. I may have agreed with her at one point, but I don't know how long I can continue doing this, while I watch all my friends get married and start families. It's not like I've ever said any of this to her and I honestly don't know if I ever will. Maybe if she really stays this time, I'll consider it.

She reaches for me and I grab her wrist, holding her back. I sigh in resignation and hold her hands above her head as I press my lips to hers, savoring the sweet kiss. I lean back and paste a smile on my face. "You do what you need to do," I insist. "You don't just take care of me quick," I warn.

"Matt," she pleads, frowning at my comment. "You know it's not like that," she proclaims.

I smirk and tease her, "I know you'd miss my big dick if I didn't fuck you."

She blushes a beautiful shade of pink and rolls her eyes. "True," she murmurs.

"I'll just have to show you how much I appreciate having you back in town again next time," I tell her.

She smirks and teases, "I thought that's what you did the last few nights."

I chuckle softly and shake my head. I give her a look, letting her know what I think of her comment. "You've only been back a week," I remind her. "I have so much more to show you," I taunt, trying to keep my tone light.

The corners of her mouth curve up and she sighs happily. She lifts her head and brushes her lips across mine. The sound of her phone ringing breaks us apart almost instantly. She feels around on the bed for it and picks it up. She glances at the screen and hits ignore, as she scrunches up her face in annoyance. "I really have to go, Matt," she grumbles. "I'm sorry," she repeats.

I press my lips to hers again and roll off her, attempting to act like its no big deal. I grab a black t-shirt off the floor and quickly pull it on over my head as she gathers her own clothes and pulls them on. She walks over to the mirror and runs her fingers through her hair.

14

Then she reaches into the pocket of her jeans shorts and opens a small, round, plastic container of mints. She pinches one between two fingers and pops it into her mouth. "I'll see you later," I mumble.

Then she turns to me with a smile and says the words I hate, "I'll text you." The same words I've given to numerous women and she's given to the assholes her parents expect her to date. But I'm nothing like the other assholes she dates and I expect to be treated as such.

I grind my jaw, fighting my cringe. I give her a stiff nod, before I turn around and stride to my bathroom without looking back. When the fuck did I turn into such a pussy? I heave a sigh and run a hand through my hair in irritation. "I think it's time for a run," I mumble to myself. I need to do something to work off my frustration and I fucking hate going to the gym on my day off. If I do, I end up working anyway and that's not what I need today.

Chapter 2

Amy

I grab my keys off the end table in my apartment, which is really only a studio apartment above my parents' garage, not including the kitchen I have to share with them. I keep a mini-fridge and microwave in here, so I don't have to go into the house for every little thing, but it still sucks, knowing I no longer have my college apartment with Bree to go back to, now that we graduated from the University of Southern Maine. Plus, my mom and dad gave me time to find a job up there they thought was the right fit and that didn't work out too well for me, so now I'm back home, living in a semi-private space on my parents' property.

It appears very similar to what my room looked like up in Portland. I have my white four-poster bed, white night stand on each side, and my white dresser up against the wall with a large mirror overhead. In the corner to the right of the dresser, I have a full-length mirror and the door is to the left of the dresser, stepping out onto stairs on the side of the garage. On the wall opposite the dresser there's a pale pink curtain with long-stemmed darker pink flowers decorating the front, where my dad had shelves, hooks and a bar installed to use as my closet. I have a fluffy pink rug on the floor on each side of the bed, matching the accents of my white, pale blue and raspberry pink comforter. Then at the opposite end of the room from my bed, I have a pale tan couch with throw pillows in sage green with a cream pattern as well as chocolate brown pillows with the same cream pattern. Next to the couch, I put a small end table and then a yellow armchair with a white daisy pattern next to that, making the seating an L-shape. In front of the couch, but against the wall sits a small black entertainment center with a 36" flat screen TV. Then to the right of it I have the mini fridge and a shelf with the microwave, while to the left, a door to my small bathroom. I don't have anything on the walls yet, but I'm just happy to have everything unpacked.

I glance down at my outfit one more time. I have a white jumper on with a deep V in the front and small, silver buttons down to my waist. I pulled a silvery-grey blazer on over the top, giving it a professional touch. I smile to myself, satisfied and pull out my phone to snap a quick selfie. I grin and press the camera button a couple times before I skim through the pictures. Happy with the results, I pick one to post on all my social media platforms. Then I add a quick message. "Off to my first interview. #Kissforluck #Interviewinstyle #Jobsearch." I sling my matching white purse with a silver buckle over my shoulder before I turn towards the door. My silver heels click on the wide plank wood floors as I step outside. I pull the door closed behind me and cautiously descend the stairs. I walk up to my Black BMW 3 Series my dad bought me as a graduation present and slip in behind the wheel, onto black leather seats.

My cell phone rings just as I start the car. I pick up my phone and smile as my dad's face lights up the screen. I get my thick, blonde hair and blue eyes from my dad. He's a big man and used it to his advantage in sports when he was younger. He played football all through high school and college and he's still able to use his connections to drum up business. He's in medical equipment sales and provides clinics, hospitals, doctors' offices and specialty care centers with a variety of things, such as pacemakers, respirators and so much more. My mom on the other hand gave me her height, without her lean frame. I guess I get my curves from dad's side of the family. I'm also really good at faking it because of her, so I can't say she never gave me anything.

"Hi, Dad," I answer, cheerfully.

"Hi, Sweetheart. Are you ready for your interview?" he inquires. He got me in for an interview today with one of his friend's marketing companies.

"Yes, I'm ready," I promise. "I was just about to pull out of the driveway when you called," I inform him.

He chuckles softly. "That's great, Amy. Drive safe and good luck," he encourages.

"Thanks," I murmur. "I love you!"

"Love you, too," he replies, before he disconnects the call.

I start my car and pull out of the driveway and turn towards Boston. We don't live too far from the city and I quickly pull into a parking garage and find a spot on the roof. I grab my phone and notice I missed a text while driving. I unlock my screen and find a message from my mom, making me grimace. "Good luck at your interview. Don't mess it up! These people are important to your father. He really stuck his neck out for you," she reminds me.

I heave a sigh in irritation. "Thanks for the luck, Mom!" I reply, bitterly, knowing she's already shaking her head in disappointment. She's usually passive-aggressive with me. It's almost like it's her way of reminding me dad said he only stuck around because of me and she's been paying a penance. She's both grateful and hateful because of it. Technically, I'm not supposed to know anything about that, but she's aware I do. She made sure of it. She even made it seem like if I mess up, it'll be my fault if he leaves. I love my dad, so I've always been afraid to take that chance, even if I don't believe it's true. Then again, most of the things she's pushing are just things he wants for me because he wants me to be happy or he wants the

18

best for me. How can I complain about something like that when he would do anything for me?

My phone sounds again, but I ignore it, as I step out of my car and slip my purse over my shoulder. I take a deep breath and push my shoulders back. Then, I stride towards the elevator to make my way to the building for my interview with complete confidence. At least that's what I'll look like on the outside, but on the inside my stomach is filled with chaos and taunting the rest of my body in hopes it will play along.

Matt

I get back from my run, still feeling wound up, but I don't feel like running anymore. I slip my air pods back into their case and drop them on the kitchen counter as I walk by. I reach up with my right arm and pull my t-shirt over my head. I roll it up in a ball and toss it into my laundry basket in the corner of my room on my way to the bathroom across the hall. I turn the water on and shut the door behind me out of habit, even though I live here alone. I set my phone down on the sink before I kick my shoes off and pull off my socks, abandoning them on the floor. Slipping out of my shorts, I step into the shower. I gasp at the shock of cool water on my skin and then exhale slowly, as I step forward. I drop my chin to my chest and stick my head underneath the steady spray.

As the water warms, my muscles loosen and my body begins to relax. Without my consent, my mind wanders back to this morning when I first woke up with Amy in my bed. I love her perfectly curved and plump ass cheeks. Some of my favorite days are when I wake up and I'm able to just reach out and grab her ass and pull her into me. I easily give in, knowing it's pointless to hold myself back. Why the hell would I even want to? I reach down and grab my already hard cock, or still hard would be more accurate. I plant my left hand on the wall as I stroke it in long even strokes. I picture the way her perky round breasts fit in my hands and her nipples stand at attention with just a look from me. I love the sweet and salty taste of her skin as her body heats from every touch, lick and kiss I place on her body as I make my way down to the even sweeter taste of her pussy.

I groan, stroking myself a little faster as I think about what I would do to her right now if she were standing in front of me. I'd make her pay for leaving me hard and wanting. I'd turn her around and bend her over just enough, so she looks like she has her sexy ass up towards me. I'd stroke her cheek gently, before giving it a light smack. Then, I'd bend over her and place her hands on the wall and tell her not to move. I'd run my hands slowly down her body, pinching her nipples, as I nibble at her neck. Then, I'd nudge her legs apart and circle her pussy with the tip of my cock before I thrust in hard, making both of us groan in both surprise and pleasure. Then, I'd grab her hips low, my thumbs digging into her ass cheeks, as I pound into her. "Fuck," I groan as my balls squeeze tight, just before my orgasm hits. I pump my dick, until I drain it completely, letting the evidence of my weakness to mere thoughts of Amy wash down the drain with the water.

I heave a sigh, not feeling much better. Grabbing my shampoo off the small shelf, I squeeze a small amount into my hand. "Not exactly how I thought things would go today," I grumble to myself and begin washing my hair.

A few minutes later I step out of the shower and quickly dry off, before I pull on a gray t-shirt, black boxer briefs and olive-green cargo shorts. I quickly brush my teeth and then slip my phone back in my pocket. I stride out of the bathroom and make my way towards the kitchen for something to eat, when I hear my cell phone ringing. I pull it out of my pocket and glance at the screen, seeing my buddy Brett's face light the screen. He's one of the few friends I have who's still single, like me. Brett is about five feet, eleven inches with more of a runner's build; thin, strong legs, especially calves. He has black hair and hazel eyes that appear more gold to me. I hit the green answer button and mumble, "Hey, Brett. What's up?"

"Matt," he replies, dragging out my name as if his mind is elsewhere. "What are you up to tonight?" he questions.

I shrug, even though he can't see me. "Nothing. Why?" I prod.

"I was thinking of hitting Bro's tonight," he informs me. Bro's is a relatively laid back, but extremely popular local bar. It has booths along the walls with black leather seats and golden oak tables. The bar itself is in the middle of the room in a square, with the same wood on the bar top. Then around the bar, there are a few tables scattered haphazardly, making sure to leave plenty of room for the standing room only patrons. The back of the bar has darts and a few pool tables, while the bathrooms are in the back left corner. It's popular for their great deals on beer and their simple appetizer and burger menu. They even offer free beer on your birthday, but only in one of their special birthday mugs.

"I'd be up for that," I respond. I know I can't sit around and wait to find out what Amy is up to later. That's probably the last thing she would want from me.

"Great," he mumbles. "I need a drink and I need to get laid," he murmurs.

"Yeah, you do," I joke.

"Fuck you," he replies and then laughs. "I've had a long fucking week, man," he mutters.

I'm sure he has. He just finished his second year of law school at Boston College. He's doing an internship over the summer, so he doesn't have the free time like he used to. Then again, instead of going to bars, we used to be the ones having all the parties. Now it's easier if we just go out for drinks, especially if either of us wants to find a woman to hook-up with or even date. Most of our friends are in serious relationships and I don't feel like hanging out with a bunch of couples, without prospects when I'm still single. Bree and Christian's wedding was strange enough. I still have the house for parties, but I don't think the cleanup is worth it anymore. I'm sure he feels the same way, besides having the need to let off some steam. "I'll meet you there at 9?" I propose.

"Sure, then we can catch up before it gets too loud," he acknowledges.

"Great. Later," I reply. I end the call and slip my phone back in my pocket.

My stomach growls and I open the refrigerator to look for something to eat, but find the shelves nearly empty. I heave a sigh as I close the door. I swipe my wallet and keys off the counter instead and stride out towards my truck. I love my dark blue GMC Sierra. Not a lot of people drive pick-up trucks around here, but I love mine and it works for me.

My cell phone rings again as I slip in behind the wheel and shut the door. I pull out my phone and glance at the screen. My dad's face stares back at me and I grimace. I immediately drop my phone in the cup holder instead of answering. My parents are low on my priority list right now. It's not like I've ever been high on their priority list, so why should I start giving a shit now? I start my truck and buckle my seatbelt, before I back out of my driveway and head to the store.

Chapter 3

Amy

I walk through the glass doors into Kirst Marketing with a smile on my face. My eyes narrow briefly as I step into the extremely bright entrance area. I take a second for my eyes to adjust, staring at the large white divider wall leading towards the back, where I assume all the offices and conference rooms are located. Four framed posters are mounted vertically on the wall and spaced evenly. The first one is blue and white as if your head is up in the clouds, with the word, "Dream," written on it in a bold script. The second is black and white stating, "Write," in a typewriter font. The third is a scramble of colorful jigsaw puzzle pieces saying, "Create." The last one looks like a rainbow of colorful sticklike figures, and declares, "Explode." There's a tall black desk centered directly in front of me, shaped in a half moon. Then behind me four black leather armchairs sit against the wall, two on each side of the glass entryway, with a small black table in between.

Suddenly, a man behind the desk looks up at me, sitting a little taller as he quickly assesses me. He appears to be a few years older than me with neatly trimmed dark brown hair, coffee brown eyes behind wire rimmed glasses and flawless chocolate brown skin. I can only see his upper half, but he appears to be wearing a cobalt blue suit filling it out nicely, with a white button-down shirt, but no tie. Offering me a bright smile, he politely greets me, "Good morning! May I help you?"

Pushing my shoulders back, I return his smile as I approach the desk. "Hi, I'm Amy Stone. I have an interview with Mr. Kirst at 11am," I announce.

He arches his eyebrows in challenge, but doesn't comment. Instead, he grins a little wider and offers encouragement. "Well, Amy Stone, it looks like you're right on time and you look fabulous. You'll do great. I'll let Mr. Kirst know you're here," he states.

"Thank you," I reply, gratefully.

He picks up the black office phone on his desk and broadcasts, "Your 11am appointment is here." He pauses, listening, before he comments on something else, "Of course, thank you." He hangs up the phone and immediately directs his attention to me. "Mr. Kirst will be right out," he apprises me.

"Thank you," I reply, smiling.

A good-looking guy, appearing close to me in age, steps out from behind the wall and lets his eyes fall on me. He's about five-feet, ten inches, with dark brown hair styled perfectly and swept up to his right. He has soft brown eyes and a square jaw. He straightens his broad shoulders underneath his black suit, white shirt and a dark gray patterned tie. I watch as his eyes quickly scan down and then back up my body. Tilting my head to the side, I arch my eyebrow in challenge, waiting for him to acknowledge me. His eyes finally meet my gaze and the corners of his mouth twitch up in amusement at the look on my face. "Miss Stone," he states, with a nod of his head. He steps towards me, holding his hand out for me. He waits until I reach forward, before he grasps my small hand in his strong one. "I'm Mr. Kirst," he informs me.

My eyes widen in surprise and a gasp slips out before I can stop it, making him laugh softly. I take a deep breath and push my shoulders back, before I smile and respond to his introduction. "It's nice to meet you Mr. Kirst. I apologize for my reaction. I was led to believe you were," I hesitate momentarily before I reveal, honestly, "older."

He chuckles, his smile softening his features. "I get that a lot," he claims. He stares at me, still holding my hand, before finally releasing it and nods towards the back. "Why don't you come with me," he suggests. He turns around and saunters around the wall, not once looking back to see if I'm trailing behind him.

I follow as he ushers me past a maze of cubicles, a wall of doors and windows leading to several conference and meeting rooms, as well as what appears to be bigger offices all along the back wall. We stop at an office in the back left corner, with huge picture windows overlooking the outskirts of Boston. "Wow," I murmur, "You have an incredible view."

"Thanks," he forces a smile, "but the best view is the office on the other side. My dad occupies that one," he concedes. I nod my head as understanding washes over me. Mr. Kirst handed me off to his son. I turn and face him, leaning back in a black leather desk chair with an L-shaped black maple desk in front of him and matching book shelves behind him with a black and white photo on the water's edge centered on the wall in the middle of it. He cocks his head to the side, awaiting my response.

"So, do you know anything about me? Or was this interview just thrown at you at the last minute?" I inquire, attempting to hide my bitterness.

He shrugs in response, "Does it matter?"

"Actually, it does," I declare, defiantly.

He sighs and leans forward, resting his elbows on the edge of his desk. "Look," he begins, "I get where you're coming from. I'm working for my dad," he emphasizes his point. "But since you'd be working with me, I'm the one making the decision about you either way," he reveals. "So, why don't you have a seat," he reiterates, nodding towards the black leather chairs across from him.

I bite the inside of my cheek to stop myself from flinching. I step in front of his desk and slowly lower myself down to the edge of the leather seat. "Did you get a chance to look at my portfolio?" I prompt.

"I was just perusing it before you arrived and I have to say, you seem to have a strength in design and digital marketing," he admits.

I feel a small sense of pride sink in with his words and murmur, "Thank you."

"But," he begins, "you still have a lot to learn with target audience, print marketing and market research," he proclaims. I pinch my lips tightly together and nod my head stiffly in acknowledgement. "Why do you want to work here?" he probes.

"It would be a great opportunity for me to acquire experience working with a company like yours and I would put everything I have into it," I state robotically.

He laughs in response. I quirk my eyebrows in confusion and he mumbles under his breath, "I think we may have more in common than you think."

"What?" I question.

He shakes his head and waves away my inquiry. "We should have plenty of time to figure that out later. We have some long hours and late nights, but if you're willing to work for it, for me," he emphasizes, "I have a place for you here," he finishes, vaguely.

My eyes widen in surprise and I clarify, "The internship?"

He shrugs his shoulders and nods slowly. "It could lead to a permanent position if you really throw yourself into it," he announces.

"That's it?" I mumble under my breath.

"Excuse me?" he prods.

I paste a smile on my face as my stomach turns. I don't feel the excitement I know I should be feeling.

"Thank you," I reply. "I'd love that," I claim, hoping I sound sincere.

I stand holding my hand out across his desk. He grasps it and squeezes gently as he tugs me a little closer, making me exhale harshly in surprise. "Let me take you to dinner to celebrate," he requests, making it sound more like a demand.

"Um...I...I don't know," I stammer, awkwardly, which isn't like me at all. I grit my teeth and try again, "I just mean I need to check my calendar."

He looks into my eyes and then nods his head in acceptance, before releasing my hand. "Give me a call by three today and let me know," he instructs. He opens the top desk drawer and reaches in, pulling out a business card. He holds his hand out, offering me the card. "Here, this card has my personal cell. Put it in your phone," he advises. "You're going to need it."

I nod in acceptance and mumble, "Thank you, Mr. Kirst."

He walks around the desk and stands directly in front of me with a cocky smile. "Call me Preston." I gulp down the lump in my throat and nod my head. He chuckles softly and walks towards his office door, opening it and gesturing for me to exit.

"Thank you for the opportunity," I reiterate.

"I'm looking forward to a lot of opportunities with you," he utters. I can't decide if his words feel welcome, creepy or make me horny. I'm going to have to keep my head on straight with this guy. He's definitely someone who's used to getting what he wants.

I stride towards the exit, feeling his eyes practically burning a hole through me most of the way. I step around the barrier to the front and instantly feel my body relax. I smile and wave at the man behind the front desk. "Thank you," I repeat. Pushing the glass door open, I step into the hallway, immediately making my way down in the elevator and back out to the parking garage.

I pull my phone out of my purse as I stalk towards my car. I quickly tap my dad's number and wait for him to pick up. "Sweetheart," he answers, adoringly. "How'd the interview go at Kirst?" he inquires, almost immediately.

I nod my head, even though he can't see me. "It went well, I guess. I met with Preston Kirst," I inform him.

"That's great! Preston is a good kid," he declares. "He's really smart and he's set up to take over his father's company some day," he reveals what I already assumed.

"I don't know if I'm really a good fit there, Dad," I admit.

"What do you mean, Amy? You just said the interview went well," he reiterates my earlier statement.

"It did. I just think that he might be more interested in me than in me working for him," I concede.

"Would that be such a bad thing?" he probes, making me wince.

"I don't know," I grumble.

He heaves a sigh and I hear the rising tension in his voice. "Amy, I'm not telling you to marry him or even date him, but you're going to have to get serious about your future sooner or later. Don't you think it's time?"

"Dad, I'm not even sure that's really what he wants. It's just a feeling I had," I grumble, knowing I'm right about him. "And I am serious. I just want to be hired for what I can do," I emphasize.

"Did he not have anything good to say?" he pushes, his voice laced with concern.

"No, he did. He said I seemed to be strong at design and digital marketing," I admit.

"Well, there you go," he states, his pride evident. "Cut the guy a break. It sounds like maybe you're being a little too harsh on him," he proclaims. "Isn't that what you don't want him doing to you?" he reminds me.

I scrunch up my nose in annoyance. "You're right, Dad," I mumble, reluctantly. "He wants to take me to dinner tonight to celebrate."

"You should go," he insists. "You two would make a great couple. I've known his dad for a long time and he's a good man. I remember Preston when he was younger and he's a good kid. I've never heard anything but good things about him from other people too, both personally and in business," he enlightens me.

"Okay, I will," I concede. I believe it's the right thing to do even though I'm not exactly sure what I think of him yet.

"I have a meeting in a few minutes Amy," he informs me. "Have fun on your date."

"Thanks, Dad. I love you."

"I love you too," he replies and then disconnects the call.

I slip in behind the wheel with a groan. Then I flip my cell back over and call his phone before I have a chance to change my mind. "Preston Kirst," he answers after the second ring.

"Hi Preston, it's Amy Stone," I announce.

"Amy," he rasps my name, sounding pleased with my phone call.

"I just wanted to let you know my calendar is clear and I'd be happy to go to dinner with you tonight," I state, formally.

"Excellent. I'll pick you up at 7. Dress nice," he declares. Then he disconnects the call before I have a chance to respond.

I huff in irritation and glare at my phone. I don't like being told what to do, but I do want to dress for wherever he's taking me. Groaning, I mumble to myself,

"What the hell did I just get myself into?" I drop my phone into my purse before I start my car and buckle my seatbelt. I pull out onto the road and an image of Preston crosses through my mind. I admit he's hot, but he definitely knows it with his cocky attitude. My mind flashes to the smile on Matt's face this morning in bed, causing my heart to skip a beat and bringing a grin to my own lips. I stop and quickly shake him out of my head, knowing what my parents think. Preston is the kind of guy they want me to end up with, so I need to make an effort with him.

Matt

I finish putting away my groceries and close the refrigerator, before I grab my phone and send a text to Amy. "Going to Bro's tonight with Brett at 9. Meet us for a drink." I pause then ask, "How'd the interview go?" Then, I slip my phone into my pocket and walk down the hall towards my room. My phone pings, alerting me to a text.

I pull it out and the corners of my mouth tug up in a grin the moment I see Amy's name on the screen. "Interview went great! I got the internship and a date, so I'm not sure if I'll make it to Bro's," she replies.

I scowl at the screen grumbling, "Fuck me." I pocket my phone and stalk the rest of the way to my room. I change into faded jeans and a black V-neck t-shirt, suddenly feeling anxious. I run my hand through my hair and grab my laptop. I need to keep my mind busy until I take off. I can check my email and do some more research on starting up my own gym locally. Before I get too far into it, I send another text to Amy. "Have fun," I declare, bitterly. At least it's over text, so she won't know my true intentions. I drop my phone on the table, listening as it clatters to a stop. It goes off again and I ignore it, focusing on my research instead. I need to start having more realistic expectations for my future and at least this is a start.

Chapter 4

Amy

I run my hands over my hips, relishing in the feel of the smooth silk of my sleeveless, pale mint green dress. The neckline falls in a rounded V, accenting my already full breasts, as the material loosely follows the curves of my body stopping with a short hemline. I glance up at my hair, pushing it back over my shoulders, so it falls in smooth waves down my back. I reach for my gold and opal teardrop necklace and clasp it around my neck. Then I slip on my silver two-inch heels and buckle the straps crisscrossing over my toes and again at my ankle. I pucker my lips adding a pink blush glossy lipstick to my plump lips, before giving myself one last glimpse in the mirror. "I guess I'm ready," I mumble.

I grab my phone and glance at the time before slipping it into my small silver purse and spinning for the door. The last thing I need tonight would be for him to walk up to my parents' front door thinking I live there. Who knows what kind of crap my mom would spew.

I pull the door shut behind me and begin to descend the stairs just as a sleek, silver, Audi R8 pulls into the driveway and comes to a stop. Preston opens his door and steps out of the car with a broad smile on his face. He's wearing a black suit again, but he has a light blue button-down shirt on, letting me know he changed for the occasion. He watches me as I approach him with a hungry look in his eyes. I slow as I get closer and he steps away from the open driver's door. I steel myself as he reaches out, letting his fingers run down my arm from my shoulder to my fingertips. He grasps my hand and with his other hand, nudges my hips, urging me to spin for him.

I turn in a slow circle and he grins in approval. "You look gorgeous," he rasps.

"Thank you," I reply with a smile.

"I'd love to see you in blue next time with those diamond eyes of yours," he informs me and leans down placing a kiss on the corner of my mouth.

I gulp down the sudden lump in my throat and attempt to ignore what feels like a half-assed compliment. Was his kiss to soften the blow? I give myself a mental shake and remind myself to stop judging before I even know him. Instead, I step back and arch my eyebrows in challenge, "Next time? You're pretty confident." He smirks in response. "Let's get through tonight first," I emphasize.

He chuckles softly and ignores my comment. He puts his hand out, gesturing towards his car and prompts, "Ready?"

"Yes," I confirm.

Escorting me to the passenger side, he opens the door for me, waiting as I slip inside, lowering myself onto the soft black leather seat. He slams the door shut behind me, causing me to believe he can be a gentleman. I watch as he strides around the front of the car and slips in behind the wheel. He quickly backs out of the driveway and pulls onto the road. "So, Preston," I begin, "Where are we headed?"

"You'll see," he answers with a mischievous grin. "So, do you live above the garage?" he asks, instantly changing the subject.

"Yes, it's my parents' house. I just moved back to the area and they have an apartment above the garage they usually rent. So, I'm living there until I decide what I'm going to be doing," I inform him.

"You're not sure if you're staying?" he prods, sounding more curious than anything.

"No, I'm pretty sure I am, but I'm not sure what I'll be doing for a job after the internship is over, so I don't want to get into a place long term until I know where I'll be working and what kind of money I'll be making," I explain.

He nods his head thoughtfully. "Makes sense. You were in Maine before?" he questions.

"Yes," I concur, keeping it simple. "What about you? How long have you been working for your dad?" I inquire.

He flinches, but almost instantly masks his reaction. "It's hard to find a job in marketing when your father is their competition," he discloses, causing me to soften. He glances at me, and offers me a shrug like its no big deal, but I understand what it's like. I open my mouth to ask him more when he announces, "Here we are."

I glance through the windshield as he pulls up to Valet at the Kingdom Hotel. My heart jumps up to my throat and my spine stiffens. "What are we doing here?" I snap.

"We're here to eat," he replies, playfully.

I nod and take a calming breath, forcing myself to relax. I unclip my seatbelt just as the valet opens my door for me. He holds his hand out and I take it, allowing him to assist me with climbing out of the car as I stare up at the tall, elegant building in front of me. "I've heard they have really phenomenal food at Le Bisou," I murmur.

"You've never been?" he prods.

I shake my head, "No, I've lived in Maine for the past 5 years. This place is too new," I remind him.

"Well, then, let's go," he declares, offering me his arm. I wrap my hand gently around his arm and smile up at him. "Do you know what Le Bisou means?"

"The kiss," I reply, confidently. "I always liked French," I admit.

His answering grin is nearly salacious, as we step inside the front lobby. I turn away, admiring the high ceilings, with elaborate carvings, thick ivory columns and ivory and blackwood couches, coffee tables and chairs that appear more elegant than comfortable. We turn to our left, my heels echoing on the white marble floors. Stepping up to the podium he announces, "We have a reservation under Preston Kirst."

The tall, lanky, dark haired woman nods her head and smiles wide. "Yes, Mr. Kirst. Your table is ready. She reaches down underneath the podium and pulls out two black leather menus with gold writing on the front with the name of the restaurant. "Right this way," she urges.

Preston gestures for me to go first and his hand momentarily falls to the small of my back. She guides us to a back corner with a small round table for two, draped with an ivory tablecloth and a window overlooking a park. Preston nods at her in approval as he pulls my seat out for me, angling it to get the best view. I smile up appreciatively as I sit down. He scoots his chair next to mine, instead of across, before he sits down, his knees bumping against mine. "Is this okay?" he prompts.

"This is beautiful," I mumble.

He stares at me with a small smile on his face. "Yes, it is," he agrees.

I bite the inside of my cheek to stop myself from rolling my eyes. Oh, boy. Well, at least he means well, I think.

My phone pings with a text alert, with another immediately following, causing my fingers to twitch, wanting to reach for it. Preston glances down at my purse, before returning his gaze to me giving me a small nod. "You can check your phone if you need to," he offers.

I force a polite smile and mumble, "That's okay. I'm here with you."

My phone pings again, causing me to grimace and Preston to laugh. I meet his gaze and his eyes are alight with amusement. He nods his head again in encouragement. "Go ahead. Now I'm curious," he prompts.

I hesitantly pull my phone out of my purse and glance at the screen, seeing my friend Carrie's name. "It's from my friend Carrie. We were in cheer together back in high school," I explain.

The corners of his mouth curve up in a smile and he clarifies, "You were a cheerleader?"

"Yeah," I murmur and nod my head mindlessly as I open her texts, full of curiosity.

"Looks like your boy is having some fun tonight," she declares. Followed by a picture of some slutty red head all over Matt, making my blood boil. I hate seeing this shit, even though I have no right. Her last text comes through "I'm down at Bro's with some friends. Come and join us," she requests.

I quickly reply, "I'm on a date."

"Everything okay?" Preston inquires.

I lift my head and meet his eyes, full of concern. I give him a reassuring smile and inform him, "Yes. Some of my friends are out for a drink at Bro's tonight and they just wanted me to come down and join them," I reveal, honestly.

He nods in understanding. "Bro's?" I smile in answer. "Why don't we go down there for a drink after dinner," he suggests.

My eyes widen in surprise and I prompt, "Really?"

He laughs and nods in agreement. "Yeah. A nice dinner and casual drinks with your friends?" he prods. "We are celebrating your new job tonight and I'm going to keep you pretty busy after tonight."

I bite the inside of my cheek, wondering if I should really bring my date to the same bar where I know Matt is right now, but I can't exactly tell him that. "Okay, sure, that sounds good," I stammer.

He grins in satisfaction. Obviously pleased with himself. I open my mouth to take it back when the waiter steps up to our table with a polite grin, causing me to snap my mouth closed. I guess I'll figure it out later.

Matt

"I'm so ready to be done with this shit," he grumbles. He shoves the plate of what's left of the chicken wings away from him.

"One more year," I reiterate.

"Thank fuck," he mumbles. "When will Blake be down for a visit?"

I shrug my shoulders, "Not sure. I guess it depends on Liz and his family. I'll let you know next time he's around," I promise. A waitress steps up to the table placing two fresh beers down for us. I smile in appreciation and mumble, "Thanks." Then I immediately put the amber bottle to my lips and gulp down half the beer before I set it down on the table in front of me.

"Thirsty?" Brett taunts.

I shrug in response. He stares at me momentarily through narrowed eyes, before he questions, "How's Amy doing?"

I huff a humorless laugh and nod my head in recognition. "Same as always," I reply, attempting to keep the bitterness out of my voice. "I told her to come by to have a drink with us, but she's out on a date tonight with some asshole, so she's not sure if she'll make it."

He nods his head in understanding and takes a drink of his own beer, just as a group of five women walk into the bar, laughing loudly and definitely dressed up for a night out, pulling both of our attention. "Are you up for some fun tonight?" he smirks.

"Fuck, yeah!" I agree. "It's your turn," I remind him.

He nods in agreement, "So it is." We clink the longneck of our bottles in a toast, before I down the rest of my beer and slam the empty bottle on the table as he does the same.

"Let's go," he grins as we both slip out of the booth and saunter towards the women lined up at the bar. It's early enough that there's still plenty of room around the bar to order a beer, but we step up right next to the group of women, still placing their order with the bartender. "Can you add two pints of what's on tap to that?" Brett adds. The bartender nods in agreement and instantly turns away to get the beers.

Predictably, all five heads turn towards us in response. "Aren't you supposed to be buying us drinks?" a petite blonde challenges him. She's all his, she reminds me too much of Amy.

He steps closer to her, invading her space and declares, "There's five of you and only two of us. I'm sure we could handle all of you, but," he shrugs.

She bursts out laughing right in his face. "You're crazy! Why can't you pay for your own beer?" she pushes. "You're a grown-ass man."

He smirks and informs her, "I'm a sexy one too, but I'm too busy finishing my last year of law school to get a job that really pays." Her eyes widen in surprise and I fight to not laugh out loud. "How about you buy the first beer, hang out with me and I'll take care of you the rest of the night," he proposes. She barely hesitates before she nods in agreement and slaps the money down on the bar for our beers.

He grabs his beer in one hand and reaches for the woman's hand in the other. He pauses whispering to me, "Looks like it's your turn to pay the tab tonight," he announces, clearly winning our on-going bet.

"Yeah, yeah," I grumble and shake my head.

"What's your name?" I hear him ask as he saunters towards the pool tables in the back, tugging her along with him.

"So, are you as much of an asshole as your friend?" a sultry voice prods, garnering my attention.

I turn around, chuckling at the question, as I take in the woman standing in front of me with her three other friends. She's tall and thin with big breasts and fire-red curly hair. She's dressed in a simple black miniskirt and a gold tank top with spaghetti straps. She's sexy and the opposite of Amy, so I grin wide. I shrug and reply, "Depends."

"On," she prompts.

"If you think you can handle me," I taunt.

She crosses her arms over her chest, pushing her breasts up even further as she looks me up and down. Then she laughs and smirks at me, letting me know she caught me staring. "Oh, I can handle you alright," she mumbles playfully. She walks by me, with her three friends following and strides for the pool tables. Stopping, she spins on her heels and tilts her head to the side, staring at me with her emerald green eyes. "You coming?" she dares.

I reach for the beer on the bar and take a huge gulp, before I casually stroll behind. I reach the back and lean against the wall by the pool tables, content to watch for now. The red head steps up to me and asks, "Got a name?"

"Matt," I state.

"Matt, I'm Ember," she announces.

"Like fire, fitting," I mumble.

"Oh, you have no idea," she laughs. "Up for a friendly game of pool?" she suggests.

I hesitate for only a moment before reacting. "Absolutely."

Chapter 5

Amy

"Are you sure you want to do this?" I repeat, glancing over at Preston.

He slips off his suit jacket and carefully lays it down over the back seat before he turns towards me with a smile. "I'm positive," he confirms. He bends his arm and unbuttons his cuff before rolling his sleeve to just below his elbow. Then he repeats the process on his other arm. "Let's go," he urges.

"Wait," I request. I lean towards him and reach out with both hands, unbuttoning the top button of his shirt and then one more. "There," I declare, with a gentle pat to his chest.

I start to pull away when he grasps my wrists with both hands and presses his lips to mine, causing me to gasp in surprise. He takes that as an invitation and pushes his tongue inside my mouth. I kiss him back reflexively, before pulling back and pasting a smile on my face. "Now, I'm ready," he mumbles.

He climbs out of the car and I grumble to myself, "Fanfuckingtastic," before I push my own door open. He steps in front of me and reaches his hand out to assist me. I grasp it and climb out of the car. My heart begins to pound and I feel my body heat with anxiety. I take a deep breath, trying to pull myself together. I don't want to take a step inside with anything but my usual confidence. I pause, forcing myself not to dig my heels into the ground. "Wait," I repeat, just before he opens the door to Bro's. He stops and looks at me, arching his eyebrows in question. "Um...can I...do you...do you mind if I get a selfie of us for my blog?" I stammer, not able to come up with another excuse.

He chuckles softly and nods in agreement, mistaking my anxiety about bringing him here tonight for nerves because of him. "Of course," he grins.

He wraps his arm around me and pulls me close. I quickly dig out my phone and tap on the camera before I hold it up in front of us. I snap the picture and type out a caption. "Out celebrating my new internship!" I post it and slip my phone back into my purse.

He leaves his hand low on my hip and guides me towards the door, pulling it open. I reluctantly step inside with him right behind me, his hand immediately returning to my hip as I quickly scan the room. My eyes almost instantly find Matt back by the pool table. He's standing with his arm around a redhead, tilting his head down as she whispers something in his ear. He throws his head back and laughs, making my stomach flip at the sexy sight. He steps away from her and saunters around the pool table. He glances up just before leaning down to take a shot and his gaze crashes into mine. He visibly flinches as Preston's arm falls to my shoulders, before tearing his eyes away.

"Do you see your friends?" Preston inquires.

"Um, not Carrie," I reply honestly.

He glances towards the pool table critically before looking back at me, but thankfully he doesn't say anything. I force myself to scan the rest of the room and quickly spot Carrie's short, pixie-styled brown hair. "There she is," I announce.

Preston lets his hand slide down my back and clasps my hand as I lead him towards Carrie and a few other familiar faces. Carrie turns just as we reach her, her hazel eyes lighting up as she spots me. She throws her arms around me and happily declares, "Amy, you came!" I reach up, since she's almost seven inches taller than me and return her hug with my free arm. She pulls back and

42

glances over my shoulder at Preston, noticing our joined hands. She smirks and proclaims, "And you brought a hot date."

Preston chuckles and releases my hand to shake hers. "I'm Preston," he introduces himself. "And you must be Carrie," he continues.

She nods and proudly announces, "That's me." She turns towards the rest of the group standing with her, including two men, both tall with dark hair and eyes and three women, all of which I believe I went to high school with, but I don't remember their names. Two have dark brown hair and one has hair as black as night, but all of them as beautiful as Carrie. "And this is everyone else," she states. She looks back at me and informs me, "We all work together at Vice Corp."

I nod in acknowledgment, although I don't remember what she actually does now. I haven't really seen her since I left for Maine. "It's been a long time," I emphasize.

She nods in agreement as her friends begin talking amongst each other again. "Yes, it has," she concurs. She turns her eyes to Preston asking, "So, how did you two meet?"

Preston begins, "Well," but pauses almost instantly. He pulls his phone out of his pocket and glances at the screen lit up with an incoming call. He lifts his head and gives me an apologetic look before he claims, "I'm really sorry Amy, but I have to take this." He gives my hand a squeeze as I nod in understanding. He leans down and whispers in my ear, "Thanks." Then, he places a kiss on the corner of my mouth before he drops my hand and turns away. He strides back to the front door and slips out of the bar to take the call.

I exhale slowly as he disappears. Almost instantly, I feel all the tension leave my body. "How do you find all the hot men you date?" Carrie questions.

I laugh in response and shake my head in amusement. "We're going to be working together at Kirst Marketing," I reveal.

"Working together?" she prompts, with wide eyes. A slow grin covers her face and she murmurs, "That could be trouble."

I force a smile and nod my head in agreement, "Yup."

"Wait," she mumbles and glances towards the door and then back to me. "Preston," she repeats. "Is that Preston Kirst?" she inquires, her eyebrows nearly hitting her hairline.

I feel my face heat in embarrassment. There's a small group of men that garner a lot of attention around here and he's one of them. I nod my head in acknowledgement and mumble, "Yeah."

"Oh, so he has a hell of a lot more going for him than just being hot. You don't say no to that man," she declares. She takes a sip of the red drink in her hand and a slow smile spreads across her face. "Speaking of hot men," she murmurs mischievously, "you aren't dating Matt anymore?"

I attempt to gulp down the sudden lump in my throat, as I shake my head in response. "We never really were," I answer.

She giggles and rolls her eyes dramatically. "Are you sure about that?" she challenges.

"We've always been close, but I guess sometimes we were a lot closer," I concede. My eyes automatically drift over to the pool tables, just as the redhead runs her hand down Matt's hard abs, making me grimace. "I think I'm going to go say, Hi," I mumble. Carrie says something in response, but I don't pay attention to her words as I turn towards Matt, my feet moving without my consent.

Matt

Of course, Amy struts in here looking hot as hell in that fucking dress. It's like I could feel her the moment she walked through the door and the second my eyes found hers, I could feel my body heat with desire. Then that asshole had to put his arm around her, like he was claiming her. We've always dated other people, but we don't rub it in each other's faces. She threw all that out the window the moment she walked in here with him. What the fuck was she thinking? She knew I was here hanging out with Brett. I invited her, not her fucking date.

"You're really tense all of a sudden," Ember observes. She runs her hands over my shoulders and down my back. Then she slips under my arm and steps in front of me, letting her hands roam my chest and abs. "Your muscles were hard before, but you feel different...stressed," she assesses, hitting the nail on the head.

"I'm good," I claim, leaning back against the wall. I know I'm not fooling anyone, but I don't care.

She smirks and trails her fingers back up and around my neck. "I just bet you are," she mumbles, almost inaudibly. She pushes up on her toes and kisses my jaw, making me wish her touch made me feel like Amy's does. "The twitch in your jaw is telling me that's not the case," she asserts.

I flinch and open my mouth to retort, but I'm interrupted as Brett calls out, "Asshole, you're up!"

I breathe a sigh of relief and reply, "Coming."

I rest my hands on Ember's waist and gently move her to the side. "Excuse me," I mumble as I step around her. Then I grab my cue and add chalk to the tip as I assess the table, attempting to shove Amy out of my thoughts.

"Heads up," Brett warns, nodding his head with a flick of his chin at something behind me.

I feel light pressure of her fingers on my back, making me aware of exactly what he was attempting to alert me about. "Hey, Babe," Amy announces. Her fingers trail down my arm as she makes her way around the pool table. She places her hands on the edge and leans towards me over the table, waiting for me to lift my head and meet her gaze.

The corners of her mouth curve up in a small smile and her blue eyes sparkle with mischief. "Amy," I mumble, narrowing my eyes on her. "Where's your date?" I push.

She leans her hip against the pool table, ignoring my question. "You said I should meet you and Brett here when I was done with my meeting," she emphasizes. I grind my jaw in irritation, knowing she wasn't at a fucking meeting.

"You didn't tell me you had a girlfriend," Ember comments. I see her out of the corner of my eye, with her arms crossed over her chest and glaring at me.

"I don't," I reply, maintaining my glower on Amy.

Amy leans over the pool table, her cleavage on display for me. "I'm sorry I had to leave so early this morning," she tells me loud enough for Ember to hear. She runs her teeth over her lower lip, knowing it drives me crazy.

"It's not a problem," I emphasize, attempting to let her know I don't need saving. "I'm just fine on my own," I reiterate.

She disregards my comment and repeats her apology. "I'm really sorry though, Matt. Let me make it up to you," she mumbles. She pushes up onto the pool table

46

and reaches all the way across it. She weaves her hands into my hair and tugs my head towards her. She covers my mouth with hers and kisses me hard.

I hear Ember mumble, "Fuck this," just before I hear her retreating footsteps.

Amy pushes her tongue into my mouth and I let her, savoring her sweet taste as our tongues begin tangling for control.

"If you're not playing, get off the fucking table," Brett demands.

I reluctantly pull back from her lips, staring at her as we both catch our breath. "I didn't need to be saved," I insist.

"Didn't you?" she challenges.

Instead of arguing with her I repeat my earlier question. "Where's your date?"

She shrugs and leans back with a smirk. "He had to step out to take a call or something," she replies, with a wave of her hand like it's no big deal.

I nod my head in acknowledgement, pissed off she brought her date here and then proceeded to fuck up my night. I walk by Brett and hand him my cue before I stalk around the pool table towards her. I grab her hand, clasping it tightly, before I turn around, tugging her along with me.

"Where are we going?" she prods.

I ignore her question and keep moving. My body vibrates with both anger and lust. She wants to save me, fine! But she's dealing with the consequences right now!

Chapter 6

Matt

I clasp Amy's hand tightly as I tug her towards the bathrooms. The women's bathroom door opens and I notice a small group of women standing in front of the mirrors touching up their make-up and washing their hands. I push the men's bathroom door open just as a tall guy steps out and strides past us without a word. I glance inside, not seeing anyone in the open area. So, I tug on Amy's hand and she pulls back, slightly hesitant. I turn and look down at her, arching my eyebrow in question.

"Matt, I'm not going in there," she declares.

"There's no one in there," I insist.

"Did you check the stalls?" she reminds me.

"I will after you come with me," I proclaim.

She grimaces and steps inside, the door swinging closed behind her. I reach behind her and hook the latch, locking the door. "What are you doing?" she prods.

"Amy," I sigh her name, "we're going to talk about what happened out there. Aren't you supposed to be on a date?" I reiterate, hating how she walked in with that asshole.

"I am on a date," she declares. "He's outside on the phone," she restates, pursing her lips in irritation.

I laugh humorlessly and shake my head. "Then why were you fucking with me?" I demand.

"I was helping you," she repeats.

I turn on her and plant my hands on either side of her head, caging her in. I lean down, my lips barely a breath from hers as I look into her darkening eyes, her chest heaving up and down. "Helping me?" I repeat, my disbelief clear. She nods her head wordlessly. "Are you sure you weren't being..." I pause, attempting to come up with the right way to say it, "selfish?"

Her eyes widen and her face reddens, in anger or embarrassment, I'm not sure. "Matt," she begins, ready to argue.

I shake my head, refusing to listen. I do that enough when it comes to her. "You think you can do whatever you want, with whatever asshole you want, but I don't get the same fucking respect?" I challenge.

She whimpers and restates, "I thought you wanted me to save you from her."

"No," I argue. "You didn't want me to have her," I claim, trying to force the truth.

"That's not true," she pleads.

"I thought we had an agreement," I grumble.

"What?" she rasps, as if confused. I grimace and shake my head in annoyance.

"Are you sure you didn't just come here to tease me in this dress?" I demand, changing direction. "You knew I would lose my mind seeing you in this," I rasp.

She arches into me, practically begging for my touch. "Matt," she whispers.

I let one hand fall from the door and trail my fingers down her jaw, to the soft skin of her neck, down her collar bone and over her breast, pausing on her nipple and making her groan. "You're practically falling out of this dress. You knew when you leaned over the pool table that I wouldn't be able to resist." I allow my hand to move down her body, over her hip and skim my fingers across her skin at the hem of her dress. "And this," I emphasize, "I only need to push this dress up a couple inches to know you're just as wet for me as I am hard for you."

"What did you want to do about it?" she taunts, breathily.

The corners of my lips tug up with her words. "I wanted to bend you over the pool table and smack your sweet ass for torturing me. Then I wanted to fuck you right then and there," I reveal, honestly.

She inhales deeply and looks up at me, defiantly. "Then what are you waiting for?"

"Fuck," I grumble, my hips instinctively push forward, towards her hot center. I slide my hand between her legs and slip my fingers underneath her thong finding her dripping. "You're soaked," I groan.

She reaches down and cups my dick, straining through my jeans to get to her. "Punish me," she requests.

I flip her body around, so her front is pressed to the door, pushing my front into her back. I lean down and whisper into her ear, my voice husky, "Are you sure?"

She turns her head so she can see me out of the corner of her eye, a small smile pulling at the corners of her lips. "I trust you," she claims, causing my heart to skip a beat and my body to heat with unrelenting desire.

I pull her dress up, her silver thong barely noticeable, leaving her round cheeks exposed. I caress the smooth skin, before I smack her ass, the sound echoing against the tile walls and making her gasp. I crouch down, running my hand lightly over the almost instant red spot in the shape of my handprint, before treating it with a lick and a kiss. "I like seeing my mark on you," I admit. She moans and I return my hand to between her legs. I push her thong to the side, running my fingers along her swollen folds.

"Just rip it off," she pleads.

I shake my head and stand up. "If you're leaving with that asshole, you will be wearing these," I declare. I snap the small strip of fabric, making sure she knows there's no room for argument. I spin her back around and cover her mouth with mine, in a deep consuming kiss. I

50

tangle my hand into her hair, holding her to me as I lick and taste every spot in her mouth, claiming it as mine. She wraps her arms around me as she returns my kiss with urgency and need, driving me to the edge.

I slowly release my cock from my jeans, not able to focus. She wraps her hand around my shaft the moment it springs free dragging a groan out of me. I release my hand from her hair and pull a condom out of my back pocket. I rip the package open with my teeth and she reaches for it, rolling it over me. "Please," she begs, guiding me to her center.

"Wrap your legs around me," I demand. She instantly complies, sinking down onto my dick as she does, causing both of us to groan. I put one hand under her ass to hold her up and the other against the door for leverage as I drive into her. She gasps for breath, her nails digging into my back as my hips move harder and faster, wanting to possess every single inch of her. "I'm not going to last," I rasp.

"Neither am I," she whimpers, as if giving me permission to let go. I push her into the door and thrust into her as deep as I can go, over and over again, wanting her to see stars. She moans that sexy as hell sound of orgasmic bliss as her walls begin squeezing my cock, milking it and pushing me over the top. I drive into her a few more times, emptying myself, as she holds on, her head dropping to my shoulder with exhaustion.

Moments later, I let my head fall into the crook of her neck and inhale deeply. Loving her sweet scent of vanilla and coconut, mixed in with sweat and sex. She begins to lower her feet and I give her ass a firm tap. "Not yet," I warn.

She barely waits a moment before she reminds me, "I'm sorry, Matt, but I should get back…" she trails off, both of us knowing how her sentence ends.

I grind my jaw and sigh in defeat. I lean back and she slowly lowers herself to the ground, my dick slipping out of her in the process. I wait a few seconds to make sure she's steady on her feet before I roll the condom off and step away, tossing it in the garbage. I tuck myself back inside my jeans and wash my hands as she smooths down her dress.

She steps up next to me and glances in the mirror, smoothing out her hair the best she can. I watch as she reaches into her purse and pulls out a tube of lipstick, reapplying it to her kiss swollen lips. I don't want her going home with anyone else. She should be coming home with me. "Amy," I begin, her name a plea on my lips. She looks up at me expectantly. A loud banging on the door interrupts us almost immediately. "Fuck," I grumble.

"Open the fucking door! I have to take a piss," some loud asshole slurs through the door.

Amy looks at me and grins mischievously, "That was incredible. You," she emphasizes, "can punish me anytime." She grasps my arm and pushes up on her tiptoes, giving me a chaste kiss. "I guess we'll have to talk later," she states, gesturing towards the door, shaking from the pounding on the other side.

I grimace and heave a sigh, nodding my head in agreement. I paste a cocky smile on my face and proclaim, "Too much of me and I'll ruin you for anyone else."

She giggles and spins on her heel. I follow and reach over her to unlock the door. I don't want the drunk guy on the other side to run into her or give her a hard time. The second the door is unlocked, I wrap Amy around the waist and spin her out of the way as it flies open. I set her back on her feet and she pats my chest in appreciation. She smiles and waves as she weaves her way through the bar. I run my hand through my hair in irritation. "What the fuck does she do to me?" I grumble to myself. I stalk back towards Brett, already talking with two new women. I need another beer.

Amy

Preston pulls into my driveway and puts the car in park, immediately turning off the ignition. "You don't have to walk me to my door," I insist.

He chuckles and steps out of the car, ignoring me. "Great," I mumble. I heave a sigh as I push the door open, just as he reaches my side. He holds his hand out for me and I take it, allowing him to assist me out of the car.

He puts his hand on the small of my back, guiding me forward. "Thank you for dinner and everything," I croon, appreciatively. I stop at the bottom of the steps leading up to my apartment and turn around.

"I'm walking you all the way to your door," he insists. He moves into my space when I don't immediately move, causing me to lose my footing as I turn around. "Whoa," he utters as he wraps his hand around my waist, catching me. I grimace and bite the inside of my cheek. I continue walking up the steps and his hand slides down to the hem of my dress, pausing before it falls away.

We reach the top landing and I spin around, facing him. "Thank you, again, Preston," I repeat.

He reaches under my chin and nudges my head up until I meet his gaze. "I had a good time tonight," he claims.

"Me too," I mumble. I feel a flash of heat consume my body as images of what Matt did to me in the bathroom run through my mind.

Preston mistakes my reaction for wanting him. He leans towards me, sealing his lips over mine. He flicks his tongue inside and moves in a slow, methodical rhythm I attempt to match, knowing I have to give him a chance.

His hand moves over my hips and he gives me a gentle squeeze as he presses his body into mine. He pulls back and I smile up at him. "I'll see you tomorrow," he reminds me.

I nod my head in acknowledgement. "I'll be there at 9am."

"Eight," he corrects. "So you can fill out all your paperwork in Human Resources first," he explains.

"Got it," I agree. "Bye, Preston." He steps back and I quickly pull out my keys and unlock my door. I force another smile as I pull my door open and disappear behind it, immediately closing and locking my door.

I sigh heavily and pull my phone out of my purse before I drop it on the table. "Why can't a guy like Preston turn me on the way Matt does just by looking at me?" I ask myself, as I fall back onto my bed. Preston is the kind of guy I should be with. He's the kind of guy my parents want for me. According to my parents, after what happened to Matt's brother, dating Matt was one of the worst things I could do to them. I know I can make this work with Preston. He's perfect for me and he's definitely hot. I just have to change my mindset. I'm sure he can make me feel those things too.

I grab my phone and hold it above me on my bed. My blonde hair is fanned out around me and I pull my dress down just a little bit near my chest to straighten it out. Then, I paste a dreamy smile on my face and snap a picture. "This works," I mumble to myself. I quickly type out a caption. "Home from an epic night out. Looking forward to next time," I state and tap post before I change my mind. Preston will think this is meant for him, while Matt will be the only one that knows the true meaning of my post. I drop my phone on the bed next to me and drape my arm over my face as I close my eyes.

Sometimes I just wish things could be different. I wish I could be different. I want that feeling that everyone else seems to get. The feeling that tells you you're in love and he feels the same way about you. The feeling that tells me I'm good enough and he'd do anything for me. The happy feeling that makes your heart race, makes your palms sweaty and makes you lose control. It's something you feel deep down into your soul. I wish it could be Matt for me, but that's not possible. He's not the one. He can't be.

Chapter 7

Amy

I've spent the last four hours with HR filling out all my paperwork, followed by a company orientation and struggling to stay awake. The old guy leading it needs to retire. He's not very good with technology. Isn't this a marketing company? Don't you have to be good with tech to work in marketing now? I don't get it, but I'm just an intern. My opinion wouldn't matter...yet. I heave a sigh in annoyance as I push my chair back from the table and watch as the small group of people walk out of the conference room.

I begin gathering my things and pull my phone out of my purse. I quickly snap a picture of myself with a disgruntled look on my face. Then I type a quick caption. "That feeling you get when you know your questions won't make a difference. At least I can look good doing it." I slip my phone back in my purse and grab the orientation folder off the table.

"So, what are your questions?" Preston asks, from just over my shoulder. I bite the inside of my cheek to stop myself from making a face. I can't believe he's looking at my phone. What if that was private? I need to watch what I'm saying from now on, my blog included.

I take a deep breath to calm myself down as I stand up with my folder in hand and slip my purse over my shoulder. I spin on my heel and face him, pasting a bright smile on my face. "I have some questions on the tech programs you use. I just don't think Mr. Simms is the right person to ask," I rephrase.

He pauses, staring at me, before he chuckles softly and nods in agreement. "You may be right about that," he mumbles. A smile spreads across his face. "Well, that's the perfect opportunity for us to spend lunch together, don't you think?" he proposes.

"Of course," I instantly agree.

"Let's order and have lunch in my office," he suggests. I nod in acceptance and fall in step beside him. He leans down towards my ear as we're walking and whispers, "You're right though, you look damn good doing it."

I pinch my lips tightly together, attempting to keep my irritation to myself. I was posting it for the world to see, it shouldn't matter he saw it. We stop at the desk right in front of his office. A beautiful woman with light brown hair and eyes looks up at us. She glares at Preston and then turns to me, smiling. "Hi, you must be Amy. I'm Polly," she introduces herself, holding her hand out for me to shake.

Grasping her hand, I reply sweetly. "Hi Polly."

"I'm Preston's assistant if you need anything," she informs me, as she gives him a look of disgust.

I arch my eyebrows in surprise and Preston grumbles, "She's also my sister. Ignore her."

I giggle, suddenly amused. "Ah, I see."

He ignores my comment and informs her, "Polly, we need you to order lunch for us and let me know when it's here."

She hands us a menu without saying a word. We look it over and give Polly our order before we slip inside his office. "She's nice," I begin, wanting to hear his reaction.

"She's annoying, but our dad wants us working together. She just started at the beginning of the summer, so she still has a lot to learn," he reveals.

I nod in acknowledgement and move to sit in one of the chairs across from his desk. "Not today," he states. He wraps his arm around my waist and guides me to a black walnut, rectangular table, pushed up against the wall with four matching chairs surrounding it, two on the same side. He pulls out a chair for me to sit down and I lower myself into the seat. He sits down next to me, but on the short side of the table. "Ask away," he offers.

Taking a deep breath, I dive into my questions and he answers several of them before his sister storms in without knocking, holding a brown paper bag with our lunches. Scowling at her, he reiterates, "I said to let me know when it's here."

"I'm sorry," she apologizes instantly.

He shakes his head in annoyance. "I don't want to be disturbed until I tell you. Amy and I are going over some things," he emphasizes.

She gives him a fake smile and spits out, "Yes, Sir." Glancing at me, she grins with a glint in her eyes and informs me, "Oh and Amy, flowers were just delivered for you. I put them on your desk. Here's the card." She holds out a small sealed white envelope. I reach up and take it from her, slightly stunned. Who would send me flowers?

"You can leave now," Preston demands, dismissing her. She rolls her eyes and stomps out of the office, slamming the door on her way out. "I'm sorry about her," he apologizes. "Who are the flowers from?" he questions.

"I don't know," I mumble.

"Open it," he encourages.

I hesitate for just a moment before I slip my finger under the flap of the envelope and tear it open, with Preston watching my every move. I pull the card out and read it silently, "Good luck on your first day. ~ Matt" My heart skips a beat at the kind gesture.

"Who's it from?" he probes.

I shake my head and reveal, "Just a friend."

He clenches his jaw and nods his head in acknowledgement. "A friend," he grumbles. He stands up and leans over me, planting a hand on the armrest on each side of my chair. The corners of his mouth curve up, but he gets a look in his eyes that makes my stomach roil and not in a good way. He rasps, "Anything for a friend, right?"

My eyebrows draw down in confusion, as I try to figure out his intentions. I straighten my shoulders and feigning confidence I declare, "Right."

He suddenly pushes his hand into my hair and crashes his mouth into mine. He plunges his tongue into my mouth, kissing me urgently, almost possessively. His free hand falls between my legs and he squeezes the inside of my thigh. He pulls back and mumbles, "Are you sure you don't have a boyfriend?" he questions, searching my eyes for clarification.

"I don't," I confirm.

"I don't know if you working here is a good idea," he admits.

I feel the blood drain from my face, instantly thinking about what my dad would say. "Why not?" I prod, with false confidence.

He smirks. "I don't know how I'm going to keep my hands off you during the day," he answers.

I don't know how to respond, so I don't say anything. Did the flowers from Matt bring this on? It's like he flipped a switch. He pushes off the chair with a grunt. "I'm going to go get us drinks. Polly seemed to forget those. I'll be right back."

I nod my head and wait until he steps out of his office before I pull my phone out of my purse and send a quick text to Matt. "Thank you for the flowers!"

Matt

I smile down at my phone. Happy she got them. I wonder if the asshole she works with saw them? I chuckle to myself just thinking about it. "You're welcome. Call me after work to tell me about your day."

"I will," she confirms.

I nod in satisfaction and move to set my phone down when it rings. I glance at the screen and smile at the sight of Blake's image flashing on the screen. I tap answer and put the phone to my ear. "Hey, Man!" I greet him.

"Hi, Matt. How are you?" he mumbles.

"Good. I just got home from the gym," I reveal.

"So, working hard. Are you any further on your own plans?" he prompts.

"I'm working on it," I state vaguely. I don't really want to go into everything I still have to do right now.

He knows me well and changes the subject. "What are you up to this weekend?" he questions.

"Nothing," I reply. "Are you coming down for a visit?"

"Yeah, Liz and I are coming down to see my family. Christian and Bree are coming too. Aubrey has been asking to see her since they got married, so of course Bree feels bad. She's bringing pictures down to share with her and we'll do a small little celebration with her at the home," he explains. Aubrey is Blake's little sister and she's lived in a home since I've known him. His whole family was in a car accident when he was little and she has lifelong repercussions from it. "We thought we could all get together Saturday night before the four of us have to head back to Maine on Sunday. Amy too," he adds as an afterthought.

"Hell yeah, I'm in," I declare. "I can talk to Amy about it, unless Bree is mentioning it to her."

"I'm sure she will, but give her a head's up. Bree has had a lot on her mind and I know she wants to see Amy," he reiterates.

"Alright," I agree. "How's everything else going?" I inquire, pushing the conversation away from Amy. I know we'll talk about it when he's here and right now, that's soon enough for me.

"Good Matt, really fucking good," he sighs, happily. "I'll fill you in this weekend."

I nod my head even though he can't see me. I'm glad things are going so well for him. He deserves it. Most of his life he's dealt with so much shit. He always puts everyone he cares about first and would do absolutely everything he can into helping and protecting them. It's one of the things I admire most about him, but I don't need to tell him that. I guess both of us had bullshit we've had to deal with and that's one of the reasons we became so close so fast. Of course we had sports, but recognizing someone who's trying to escape from something came easy with each other. We knew when to talk, when to give each other a beer and when to leave it the fuck alone. More than anything we provided each other an escape. Of course, I had Amy, while him and Bree were really close, but that's another tragedy in itself. "Sounds good," I respond.

"And I expect an update from you too," he adds.

There's not much to tell, yet, but I mumble my agreement. "Sounds good. Tell Liz and Bree I'm looking forward to seeing them," I proclaim.

"I will," he agrees. "See you Saturday," he repeats.

"Looking forward to it," I claim, just before I disconnect the call.

I immediately pull up Amy's name and send her another text. "We have plans on Saturday," I state, leaving no room for argument. I chuckle to myself, wondering how long it will take for her response to come through, knowing my message will irritate the fuck out of her.

My phone beeps with her reply before I even set my phone down. "You don't tell me what to do!" I grin, staring at the dancing dots as I wait for the rest of her message.

"Why? What's going on Saturday?" she rephrases.

"Blake and Bree will be home visiting and want all of us to hang out," I state.

"Just them?!?" she clarifies. Her excitement is palpable, even through a text.

I shake my head in amusement and then grimace, knowing I have to disappoint her. I hate seeing her disheartened, but I don't have a choice. "No, Liz and Christian are coming too," I reply. It's not like she really cares if Liz comes or not, but Christian is another story altogether. That whole situation puts me on edge, especially watching her anxiety increase when he's around. She's really good at covering it up for everyone else, but I know her too well. She's had a few years to deal with it and after everything Bree went through, Amy would never say anything. She acts like none of it bothers her and in a way, I don't think it does. I think what really bothers Amy is the fact she thinks she wasn't good enough, when in reality it never had anything to do with her. I guess it's hard to believe when Christian wasn't the first guy to treat her that way. Honestly, it's hard to believe he's the same guy when I see him with Bree. They really are perfect for each other. I guess I just don't want Amy to feel any pressure when it comes to hanging out with our friends. Those are the times she should be able to relax, have fun and be herself. I've always loved that side of her.

"Okay," she finally responds. "We'll talk details later."

I set my phone down and open my laptop. I turn it on, wanting to keep my mind busy. I open up my business plan and take a look at the numbers. "I'm almost there," I mumble to myself. Just a couple more weeks with a full calendar of personal training sessions and that should take care of it. I'm so fucking close.

Chapter 8

Amy

I step out of the closet behind Bree, with a smile on my face. We stand back to back, posing in front of the mirror and checking out our reflection. We're both dressed up in dresses that are way too big for our twelve-year old bodies; hers is red and mine, blue. We both have mismatched beaded costume jewelry around our necks and wrists, as well as oversized clip-on earrings. "I love the blue on you," Bree compliments.

"Thanks," I reply. "You look fabulous in anything," I insist. She rolls her eyes at me dramatically and we both instantly burst into laughter. I glance out the window and gasp at the darkening sky. "What time is it?" I ask. My whole body tenses and my heart begins beating out of control. I'm suddenly overwhelmed with anxiety.

"It's a few minutes after eight," she answers.

"Oh, no!" I scream. I quickly begin taking off all the jewelry and setting it down on the dresser, before I slip out of the dress. "I was supposed to be home at six for dinner. My dad is leaving on a business trip tonight," I explain, my panic clear in the tone of my voice.

"Go," she urges. "I'll clean up," she offers.

"Thank you," I mumble, giving her a quick hug in appreciation. Then I spin on my heel and run downstairs and out the front door of Bree's house. I glance at the street, grateful there are no cars in sight as I sprint across the road and in through the front door of my house.

"Mom, Dad! I'm sorry I'm late. I lost track of time," I blurt out, loudly.

Dad strides into the foyer, letting his small suitcase roll behind him. "Why didn't you call?" dad questions. "We were worried about you," he states, not giving me the opportunity to answer. "I thought you were playing outside with Bree and then you're just gone," he continues.

"I was playing with Bree, but we went inside for a while," I explain.

Mom steps into the entryway and gasps. "I thought her parents weren't home yet. You're not supposed to be inside her house when just her nanny is home."

"I'm sorry," I apologize with tears in my eyes. "I didn't think it was a big deal," I claim.

Dad shakes his head and a look of pure disappointment covers his face, causing my heart to sink. "I have to go Amy, but this isn't over. You have to be more responsible. Your mother will take care of your punishment." He opens his arms and I run to him, wrapping my arms tightly around his waist. "I love you, but I'm very disappointed in you right now," he declares.

My tears flow freely as I squeeze him tighter and whimper another apology. "I'm sorry, Dad."

He gives me a kiss on the top of my head and mumbles, "I know, Sweetheart." He leans down towards mom and gives her a chaste kiss, before he gently removes my arms from around his waist. "I have to go before I'm late, but I'll be home at the end of the week," he advises.

"I love you, Dad!" I call as I watch him walk out the front door.

"Do you have any idea what you did tonight?" mom probes. "You ruined dinner the same night your father was leaving," she emphasizes.

"I'm sorry, Mom," I repeat. "I didn't mean to be late."

"Of course you didn't mean to be, but you were late, Amy. It's like you don't even try for this family!" she exclaims. She begins pacing back and forth in front of me, her hands shaking in anger.

"I do try, Mom. I did my best," I plead.

She stops and steps closer to me, glaring down at me. "Your best isn't good enough! It's never good enough! If your father doesn't come home, it would be your fault! Try harder!" she screams.

I flinch and my heart drops into my stomach at her words. My whole body aches as I helplessly wipe my tears off my cheeks, but they continue to rapidly fall. I open my mouth, wanting to defend myself hoping to make myself feel better. "I try harder than you," I declare defiantly.

Mom gasps, her face instantly turning a deep shade of red in pure anger. Before I have a chance to react her hand swings, forcefully connecting to my cheek with a loud slap. The sound echoes off the walls, while her power behind it knocks me completely off-balance and I'm barely able to stay on my feet, left with my ears ringing.

I blink my eyes open with a gasp, startling myself awake. I look at my surroundings and breathe a sigh of relief, allowing a few tears to fall. I slowly sit up in my bed, rubbing my cheek as if my dream were real. Then again, it was real, it just already happened. That was the first time my mom ever hit me, but definitely not the last. I take a deep breath and exhale slowly to calm my anxiety. I haven't had one of those nightmares in a really long time, but then again, I haven't lived here in a long time. I need to shake it off. "At least it's Saturday," I mumble to myself. I glance at the time, my eyes widening in surprise, realizing I already slept half the day.

The rest of the workweek passed by in a blur. Preston was working on a project with one of their big clients, so I didn't really see much of him. I had the luxury of staying in the office every day in my little cubicle and studying current projects and clients as well as some old ones, to give me an idea of how they do things here. Of course that's in between running all the small errands for any of the project managers and their team members. I seem to spend most of my time in the copy room or at the coffee shop around the corner. In other words, I've been bored out of my fucking mind. It's not like I want to be one of them some day, but I can't quit either. Maybe if I finish the internship, I can do something I want to do. Or at least I can do something where I have a little bit more control. I understand starting at the bottom, but starting at the bottom of a company I have no motivation to go anywhere in doesn't feel right.

I heave a sigh and pull out a silvery blue tank top with spaghetti straps I just received in a large box from a clothing company. They sent me a bunch of clothes and accessories for sharing and promoting them on social media. I'm always getting something for free because I have such a huge following, which helps because I love clothes and everything that goes along with it. I match it with a pair of white short-shorts, going for the cute, but casual look. Then I slip on a pair of white sandals with a wedge heel and a small silver buckle on the top near my toes.

My phone rings and I pick it up, glancing at it to see who's calling. I grimace at the sight of my mom, filling up the screen. It's not like I can ignore her when I live above their garage. She knows I'm home. I take a deep breath before I tap answer and put my phone to my ear, attempting to keep my distaste out of my tone. "Hi, Mom."

"Amy. Your father and I have been waiting for you to come talk to us about your week," she murmurs, accusingly.

"It was a long week, Mom. I didn't get home until almost nine last night," I reveal.

"Well, it's Saturday," she states the obvious. "Come over now," she urges. I don't respond immediately, attempting to come up with a way to get out of it. "Dad wants to talk to you," she adds. She knows exactly what to say for me to give in.

I heave a sigh and relent, "I'll be over in five minutes."

"Great," she mumbles. She disconnects the call before I have a chance to change my mind.

I slip my phone into my pocket and grab my keys and my purse. I want to be ready to leave when Matt or Bree texts me. I lock up my apartment and trudge over to my parents' house. I walk through the back door and right into the large open kitchen. It's decorated with oversized white cabinets, adorned with silver knobs and handles, matching the top-of-the-line stainless steel appliances. The speckled granite countertops have a mix of white, tan and shades of grey. There's an island in the middle with a huge farm sink and space for six people to sit atop bar stools on the opposite side. A huge farm table with seating for twelve sits in front of windows lining the back wall and overlooking the back yard. I don't know why we need so much space for just us, but what do I know.

I find my dad sitting at the end of the table peering down at some papers, as usual. He looks up as I close the door and gives me a loving grin. "Hi, Dad!" I declare. I return his genuine smile and stride right over to him and into his embrace.

"Hi, Sweetheart. How are you?" he questions, as he releases me.

I sit down next to him and reply, "I'm tired, but good."

"So, your first week went well at Kirst?" he prompts.

My mom strides in and sits down next to my dad and across from me. "Don't let me interrupt," she murmurs. "Answer your father," she commands and waits for my response.

I clasp my hands together and lean on the table, keeping my focus on my dad while I talk. "It went well. I mostly ran errands and did little tasks for all the project managers. Besides that, I did some research on a bunch of their projects," I explain, keeping it simple. "Everyone seems nice," I add, shrugging my shoulders.

"That's wonderful," he proclaims, grinning proudly.

My stomach twists in response. I have to put all my efforts into this job, even if it's just for him. I don't want to disappoint him.

"I heard you and Preston went out on a date," mom announces, interrupting my thoughts.

I force a smile and nod my head in confirmation. "Yes, he seems like a good guy," I reply, vaguely.

Her eyebrows arch in challenge and she informs me, "Well, he seems to be very fond of you. His father called and spoke to dad early this week."

My eyes widen in shock and I glance at him for confirmation. He nods his head and concurs, "He did. He said Preston couldn't stop talking about you."

A lump suddenly forms in my throat. It's not that I don't like him, it's that I wish there were more between us. But I guess that's what real relationships are like. It's not about the chemistry; it's about the commitment and finding a partner who's a good fit. Then we can build on that. "That's sweet," I mumble, pasting a smile on my face.

"Why don't you invite him to have dinner with us tonight?" Mom suggests.

I grimace, knowing what her reaction will be to my response, even before I say it. "I have plans tonight," I enlighten her.

Her eyes narrow and she inquires, "What plans?"

"Bree and Christian are in town and so are Blake and Liz," I begin.

"So, Matt will be there," she interrupts.

I bite the inside of my cheek, barely stopping myself from rolling my eyes. "Yes, Mom," I grumble through my teeth.

"Careful," Dad warns, causing my stomach to twist.

I take a deep breath and exhale slowly. "Matt will be there. He's Blake's best friend," I emphasize.

"But you're not his date?" Mom pushes.

I heave a sigh and lean back in my chair, crossing my arms over my chest. "No, Mom. Matt is not my date, nor are we dating. We're friends," I emphasize. "What do you have against him anyway?" I probe.

I watch a look pass between my parents, before their gazes return to mine. "Amy, it's not that we have anything against him," my dad begins. His phone rings, interrupting when he's finally about to give me more. He glances at his phone and grimaces. He lifts his head, his eyes apologetic. "I'm sorry, Sweetheart, but I have to take this," he proclaims.

I nod in acceptance and glance down at the table as he stands and walks away with his phone in hand. "You don't want to get involved with the Young's," she argues. The look on her face shows obvious distaste.

"Why?" I ask, for what feels like the millionth time.

She shakes her head and insists, "They're trouble." "You just have to trust us on this."

I scoff at her comment. "Trust you?" I challenge. I shake my head, knowing she's not going to give me anymore. I push my chair back and stalk towards the back door. "Whatever you say, Mom," I sarcastically retort.

"Amy," she warns.

I keep walking and mutter, "Tell dad I said, bye." I let the door slam shut behind me and descend the four steps to the patio. I stride right to my car and slip in behind the wheel. I start my car and pull out of the driveway, turning towards Matt's house, without even thinking. Hopefully he won't care that I'm early.

Matt

"Okay, Blake," I agree. "I'll pick Amy up and we'll meet you at the diner in an hour," I confirm.

"Great," he acknowledges. "Later, Matt."

"Bye," I state and tap end to disconnect the call. I send a quick text to Amy to let her know the plan, before I drop my phone on the kitchen counter. I take a step towards my room when a knock sounds on my front door and I change direction. I pull the door open and my eyes widen in surprise. "I just texted you," I mutter.

Amy gives me a crooked smile and arches her eyebrow in trepidation. "Is it okay that I'm here now?" she questions.

I nod in affirmation. "You can show up on my doorstep anytime," I affirm.

"Anytime?" she prods, skeptically.

I smirk in response and she rolls her eyes. I gesture for her to come inside and she takes a step towards me. I shut the door and lean back against it, crossing my arms over my chest. I let my eyes skim over her body, my stomach clenching at the sight of every luscious curve. I return my gaze to hers and flinch at the look on her face. "Is everything okay?" I prompt.

She scrunches her nose up in displeasure and then heaves a sigh. "Yeah, I guess," she grumbles, not bothering to hide her mood.

"What's wrong?" I push.

She shakes her head in annoyance and reveals, "My parents happened." She shrugs and restates, "Well, mostly my mom happened."

"Okay," I mumble dragging out the word. I push off the door and take two steps towards her. She offers me a timid smile and closes the distance between us, wrapping her arms tightly around my waist. My arms reflexively close around her, attempting to protect her from whatever is hurting her. "Do you want to talk?" I inquire. I want to know what's going on, but I know better than anyone, you can't push her to do something she's not ready to do. She shrugs in response. I tighten my hold on her and lift her up, just enough that her toes are off the floor and carry her over to the brown leather couch. I flop down, twisting her onto my lap. My chest tightens as she leans her head on my shoulder without a fight. I run my hand up and down her arm in a soothing motion, hoping she'll start talking.

She inhales deeply and exhales slowly, before she starts speaking. "I just don't understand," she mumbles.

"What don't you understand?" I quietly prod.

"What my mom has against you," she mumbles so softly, I almost don't hear it.

I flinch as if she punched me, even though I always assumed that might be the case. I've worked my ass off to make something of myself and they still have a fucking problem with me. Of course they do. Anyone who knows what happened with my brother seems to put the blame on my whole family, even me. I force myself to relax enough that she hopefully doesn't feel the tension inside me. "I'm guessing it has something to do with what happened to Grant," I admit.

She pushes back and looks me in the eyes, her eyebrows drawn down in confusion. "You mean your brother?" she questions.

I nod my head in confirmation and croak, "Yeah."

"That doesn't make sense," she mutters. She's right, but nothing about that situation made sense. "What really happened to him?" she probes. "I was so young at the time, my parents sheltered me from the whole thing. I've heard rumors, but you've never talked about it. Not really," she claims.

I sigh and hold her a little closer. I push my face into her hair and take a deep breath. The scent of vanilla and coconut and Amy give me a sense of calm. "I will tell you everything, I promise, but can't we talk about it tomorrow?" I propose. She glances at me out of the corner of her eye and I quickly explain my partial reasoning. "It's a long, hard story and I don't want to get into it right before we walk out the door. We're supposed to meet everyone at the diner soon," I announce.

She places her palm on my cheek and looks into my eyes, as if she's trying to read their truth. She finally smiles sadly and nods her head in agreement. "Okay, Matt," she murmurs.

"Thanks," I rasp, appreciatively.

She leans forward and presses her lips to mine in a soft, tender kiss, making my heart skip a beat. She slowly lets her hand slide down to my neck, but maintains the sweet kiss, never pushing for more. Her mouth moves in a slow rhythm in time with mine, saying so much more than words ever could. She gently pulls her lips away and rests her forehead against mine, with my heart now pounding like a hammer up to my throat. She knows just what I need without me even saying a word. I'm supposed to be the one comforting her and she ends up caring for me. This woman will be the death of me. I reluctantly loosen my hold and remind her, "We should go."

"Yeah," she agrees, before she gives me another sweet kiss. I'm so screwed, especially if her parents really hold what happened with my brother against me. Will I ever have a chance?

Chapter 9

Amy

We walk into the diner and I immediately spot all four of our friends seated in the back corner booth. Bree's long chestnut brown hair and soft coffee brown eyes light up as they meet mine. I squeal in excitement and run over to them. Bree stands up just in time for me to throw my arms around her, knocking her back onto the booth. She laughs as she returns my hug. "I'm so happy you're here, Bree!" I exclaim.

"I missed you," she replies.

I reluctantly release her and she steps around me to Matt, giving him a hug as well. She's wearing cut off jean shorts with a white sleeveless button-up shirt tied at her waist. Liz stands up with a smile. She's beautiful with her dark brown wavy hair, green eyes and a few freckles over the bridge of her nose she attempts to hide with make-up. She's always nice to me, but she wasn't around yet when I messed up and felt like I lost everything. Looking back, I have so many regrets, especially with how I treated Bree. I'm grateful she never gave up on me, but then again, nothing about our situation was normal. Plus, it's not like you can change how you feel just by telling yourself to do so.

Liz gives both Matt and me a hug, before Blake steps up from behind her, as he pushes his sandy brown hair out of his chocolate brown eyes. He hugs me and then turns to Matt. They shake hands before pulling each other into a one-armed embrace with a firm pat on the back. I glance over at Christian and he gives me a polite smile, not the brilliant one he's known for that makes anyone on the receiving end melt. His bright blue eyes meet mine, as he runs his hand through his messy-styled, light brown hair. "Hi, Amy," he says, nodding in greeting. I reply in kind, grateful as Matt steps up and places one hand on my back in support, while he reaches towards Christian with the other, shaking his hand. "Good to see you Matt," Christian states.

"You too," he replies.

I sit down next to Bree, sliding in to the curved red leather booth to make room for Matt right next to me. I exhale slowly as Matt's body heat calms my anxiety. You'd think I would be over it all by now and I am, but maybe not in the way everyone thinks. For me, it's the inadequate feelings that consume me whenever I see Christian. I know we were never meant to be. I don't crave him or wish he were mine. Sometimes I even wonder if I ever did. What I do wish is that just once I would be enough. I want to be the one the perfect guy takes home to meet his parents. I want to be the girl that same man fights for and the one that the same man would do anything to keep. I don't want to be the sidepiece. I want to be the one who's more than good enough for a good man.

Matt looks at Blake and asks, "How's Aubrey?"

Blake's face lights up as he talks about his sister. "She's good. She got some of her friends at the home to help her decorate one of the gathering rooms to celebrate Bree and Christian's wedding," he announces.

"It was so sweet," Bree praises, the pride clear in her voice. "She had white streamers everywhere and she made some signs and delicious cupcakes," she explains. She smiles brightly, Christian watching her with complete love and devotion. I want someone to look at me the way he looks at her. Is that really so hard?

"So, Amy, how did your new internship go this week?" Bree prods, refocusing my attention.

Although, I appreciate her asking, I mumble, "It was fine." Then, I shrug, like it's no big deal, hoping she'll let it slide for now. "What about you, you haven't even really told me about your honeymoon," I remind her.

She grins and begins telling me all about it, making my heart hurt. I am happy for her. I don't know if I've ever seen two people more in love than the two of them. I know she deserves this more than anyone. I love her after all. She's like a sister to me, but sometimes even with how much I love her, it's hard to accept because she has the kind of love I may never have with any man. But feeling that way only causes me to feel guilty all over again. It's like my reminder to tell me how happy I am that she's here, that she's okay and it's good her and Christian finally have each other back. I have no doubt in my mind they're both better together.

The waitress steps up to our table and we all place our orders, before returning our attention to catching up with our friends. Matt slips his hand over my knee and gives it a light squeeze in support. I think he's the only one who really understands what I feel like when we're all together. Plus, he doesn't judge me for it.

"So, Liz and I have some good news to share," Blake begins, draping his arm across the back of the booth behind her. He looks at her and grins from ear to ear. Then he turns back to us and announces, "I proposed and she said, yes."

Liz's cheeks instantly turn pink as she grins and nods in agreement. She holds her left hand out, adorned with a princess-cut diamond solitaire for us to see. My heart jumps up to my throat as everyone begins hugging and congratulating them both. "Congratulations," I say, automatically. I paste a smile on my face as Liz tells us about the proposal.

Matt

We sit back down and I smile across the table at my best friend. "I'm really fucking happy for you," I reiterate.

He grins wide as Christian, Blake and myself all start talking about the upcoming football season, while the girls' conversation drifts towards wedding planning.

I glance down at Amy sitting quietly by my side. She's smiling and nodding in agreement, while Liz asks Bree a bunch of different questions about planning a wedding. I wonder if Amy even knows what she's agreeing to. I wrap my arm around her and give her a light squeeze as I pull her a little closer to my side and place a kiss on the top of her head. She looks up and smiles in appreciation as she meets my gaze, causing my chest to ache at the flash of pain in her eyes. "Thanks," she mouths the words to me. I nod my head in understanding, wanting to do everything I can to make her feel better. She should be enjoying this time.

I know what's going through Amy's mind right now, even if I don't truly understand it. But as she likes to tell me, I tend to look at her through rose-colored glasses. I can't help it. I want her to see what I see in her. I notice her insecurities practically consuming her thoughts, as her eyes slowly dull throughout the night. I hate that for her. She's incredible and any man would be lucky to have her in their life. It's the assholes she's been dating who haven't been worthy of her. She deserves so much more than she's been getting. I just don't see why I can't be that man for her. I know her parents aren't my biggest fans, but if they would give me a chance, I could prove to them how much I would cherish her, be there for her, support her and love her. I know how amazing she is and I would make sure she's treated with the love and respect she deserves.

"So Matt, when are you guys going to actually be together and not just do this?" Blake blurts out. He glances back and forth between Amy and me, fighting a grin and interrupting my thoughts. "Hmm?" he probes, arching his eyebrows in challenge.

Both our eyes widen in surprise at his outburst. I knew this was coming, but now? What the fuck is he thinking? "What?" I prod.

"Seriously?" Amy questions. All of a sudden, she bursts out laughing, causing me to flinch at her reaction.

"Thanks a lot," I grumble, irritably.

She grins and pats me on the cheek playfully, before kissing me on the corner of my mouth in attempt to placate me.

"Well, you guys are each other's back-up plan," Bree, taunts, reminding me of our long ago promise.

She's right. I smirk and mumble, "I forgot about that."

"I didn't," Bree adds, playfully.

"Wasn't that in like seventh grade?" Amy inquires.

"I think it was fifth," Bree corrects. "We were out on the playground for recess at the time," she explains her reasoning.

Amy chuckles and nods her head in agreement, grinning at the memory. My stomach turns for a different reason and I take a deep breath, watching her closely. "That's right!" she exclaims, her eyes sparkling with sudden mischief. "And didn't Shane try to say the same to you and you said, "No way, boys are gross!" she imitates a young Bree.

Bree blushes and nods her head, as Christian joins in the laughter. "You tell 'em Bree," he comments, clearly enjoying the story.

"Well, I obviously don't think that anymore," she proclaims, glancing in his direction.

Christian leans in and presses his lips to Bree's, sneaking in a quick kiss from her and deepening her blush even further. "Obviously not, Wife," he emphasizes.

She blushes a deep shade of red and if we weren't in this booth with them, they'd probably be all over each other. Bree clears her throat and quickly diverts her attention back to Amy and me. "You two are perfect together," she claims. She glances in Blake's direction, as if asking for his help.

I direct my gaze towards Blake and arch my eyebrows in question. Did they plan this attack? He chuckles, obviously amused by my reaction. Then he meets my gaze and shrugs his shoulders, as if confessing. I chuckle and shake my head in amusement. Of course they did. Although, I'm sure it was Bree's plan, Blake knows how I feel about Amy and would happily urge it along. It would help if I could get Amy to see things my way.

I glance at Amy, knowing this isn't a conversation she'll willingly have in front of our friends. This is something we need to talk about without their meddling, no matter how good their intentions. I'll help her with a change in conversation, for now. But this conversation is far from over. I plan on coming back to it when we're alone and I won't let her brush it off so easily then. I need to go there, even if it's only for my own sanity. "So, are you guys up for a fire after we eat?" I propose.

"At the park?" Blake questions.

I shake my head in response. "No, it's just the six of us, so why don't we go to my place?" I suggest.

"Like old times," Bree mumbles.

"Yeah, except you're married," Blake emphasizes.

"And you're engaged," she reiterates.

He laughs, amused with her response. Then he glances at Liz before he mumbles his agreement. "Sounds great, Matt."

"Absolutely," Bree concurs.

Amy nods and scoots a little closer to my side, just as the waitress arrives with our food. "Thank you," we all murmur our appreciation. I drag my hand over Amy's shoulders as I return my hands to my lap, preparing for my food.

"Let me know if you need anything else," she mumbles as she sets the last plate down in front of me. "Enjoy," she adds. She spins on her heel, walking away.

"Oh, Blake," I mumble, "I almost forgot to mention, but Brett was asking for you. You too, Bree," I add.

"How is he?" Blake asks, curious.

"He's good. We went out together last weekend," I mention. I notice Amy's cheeks turn pink as she looks down at her turkey sandwich, like it's the most interesting thing in the room. She's probably remembering our encounter in the bathroom. I grasp her hand and give it a squeeze, deepening the color on her cheeks even further. I fight a smile as I continue. "He wanted to come see you while you were here, but he has a huge case he's working on for his internship at the law firm and can't get away. I guess they have court on Monday," I declare. "He says he'll have to catch you next time."

I glance at Amy, reluctantly releasing her hand. She slides it to my knee giving it a squeeze, warming me both on the inside and out. I grab a fry and hold it out for her, laughing as she bites it from my fingers with a smile. Then I dig in to my own burger, happy to finally see her a little more relaxed and a little more herself tonight.

Chapter 10

Matt

I peer over the flames of the fire pit, watching Amy's head fall back in laughter as she talks with Bree and Liz. She catches her breath and finishes off the beer in her hand. "So how are things going with you two," Blake prompts, pulling my attention back to him.

I readjust in the Adirondack chair, so I'm facing him. "She's barely back a couple weeks," I remind him.

"And," he prods.

"And..." I pause, taking a quick glance at Christian. I know anything I say in front of him could get back to Amy. He's not really one to gossip, but him and Bree tell each other everything. "And we're spending a lot of time together, but she also went on a date last week with some stuck-up asshole," I mutter, not hiding my irritation.

"You need to talk to her, Matt," he encourages.

"I'm aware," I mumble, "and I will."

I take a sip of my beer as we all glance in the direction of the girls. "Can I ask why you two aren't together?" Christian hesitantly inquires. I look over at him, surprised he's saying anything. He never asks. He shrugs and explains, "It's just Bree has told me you guys have sort of been on and off since high school. Now that she moved back, why aren't you together?"

I take a deep breath and exhale slowly. His question is logical. He's right. "Circumstances?" I state as more of a question. I grimace at my own response, knowing its bullshit. I look at her as I answer, "I'm honestly not even sure anymore."

She turns her head as if she can feel me staring at her. She smiles and turns her head back to the girls. I watch as she says something and they nod in agreement before all three stroll around the fire towards us. I reflexively hold out my arms for Amy. "I have room right here," I encourage.

She grins and lowers herself onto my lap, wrapping her arm around my back and leaning into me. "Hey handsome," she murmurs.

I grin and reply, "Hi, beautiful."

She giggles happily and kisses the corner of my mouth in appreciation. I love her playful side. When she's like this, it's almost as if she has no worries. Then again, the beer may have helped with that a little bit. I may have to keep a close eye on her tonight to make sure she's okay, although I don't believe she's had too much to drink. I just want to keep it that way, so we can have a good night.

Christian stands up with Bree in his arms. He places her feet on the ground and spins her around so they're both facing us, keeping his arms around her waist. "We're going to take off. We have to head out early tomorrow to get back," Bree explains.

"Yeah, my brothers aren't thrilled I took another weekend so soon after our honeymoon, even though things were kind of slow this weekend," he admits. Then he glances at Blake and adds, "But we wouldn't have missed today for anything."

"Thanks," Blake murmurs, appreciatively. Him and Liz stand up and he glances at me. "He's our ride." Christian doesn't drink, so he's the designated driver. I'd offer for them to stay here, but I want Amy to myself tonight.

"Amy, are you coming with us? We can drop you at home," she offers.

"No," I blurt out, before she has a chance to answer. "Amy's staying with me," I add.

She looks up at me and arches her eyebrows in challenge, but her broad smile gives her away. She wants to stay with me. We both stand up and quickly say our goodbyes to our friends. I immediately pull her back into my arms as they walk around the front of the house to leave. I settle back into the chair with her in my lap.

"We're not going inside?" she prompts, surprised.

"We will in a few minutes," I reply. I just want to hold her close for a few minutes and watch the fire die down. She lets her head fall to my chest as she relaxes into me. I reach up and mindlessly run my fingers through her soft hair. "Did you have fun tonight?" I ask.

I feel her smile before she responds. "I did."

After a few minutes I hear her sigh deeply and burrow further into my chest. "Are you cold?" I inquire, rubbing my hands up and down her back.

"No," she whispers.

My heart sinks just a little, knowing something's wrong. I continue rubbing my hand up and down her back, attempting to soothe her. "What's going on in that sexy head of yours?" I probe. She laughs humorlessly, causing me to wince. "Amy," I push.

She sighs heavily and then she ponders, "Is that all I'll ever be?"

My heart skips a beat and I cautiously prod, "What do you mean?"

"Sexy, pretty, a hot piece of ass, a one-night stand," she elaborates.

I feel my blood begin to boil with each word she utters. "What the fuck," I grumble, startling her. I spin her around so she's facing me. I place one hand on each side of her face, cradling her in my hands while I wait for her to look me in the eyes. She hesitantly drags her gaze to meet mine. "You are so much more than that. Yes, you're fucking gorgeous and sexy as hell, but you're smart, determined, fierce, I fucking love that about you," I insist, only revealing the first few.

She grimaces in response, not believing me. "But then how come I'm never good enough?" she complains.

My chest aches, realizing what this is really about. "That's not true. You were attracted to the guy, but I would argue you never had real feelings for him. He was a challenge because you knew he was so deep in love with her. He was desperate to not be in pain anymore. He tried to move on thinking she was lost to him forever, but she was in just as much pain as him. They were meant to be together," I emphasize the words I've been too afraid to say to her out loud for so long. She pushes me and stumbles as she stands up.

"Don't you think I know that?" she yells down at me. "They should be together. I wouldn't have it any other way," she concedes. "But it wasn't just him, Matt! It's every fucking guy I date. Over and over again I put myself out there to these...guys," she declares and scrunches her nose up with distaste. I don't miss the fact that she didn't say what type of guys either, but I ignore it for now. "I'm always good for tonight, but never for tomorrow," she vocalizes, her irritation and hurt thick on her tongue.

I stand up and look down into her eyes. "Not with me," I proclaim, begging her to see the truth in my words.

She stares up at me, breathing heavily, appearing slightly stunned. I see in her eyes that she's hit her limit with this conversation, but I'm not about to let her retreat into herself thinking the worst. Instead of saying anymore, I close the distance between us and crash my lips into hers. I weave my fingers into her hair and tip her head up, as I lean down, moving my lips in a slow, seductive rhythm, as she meets me beat for beat. She parts her lips and I slip my tongue inside, searching for her tongue and coaxing her out to play. I nearly breathe a sigh of relief as she returns whatever I give and more. I slow the kiss and pull back for just a moment, knowing we need to move this inside. She falls back on her heels, tearing her lips away from mine. I maintain my hold on her cheeks as I look into her eyes emphasizing, "You're incredible!"

"Let's go inside," she urges.

Momentarily searching her eyes, I nod my head in agreement. "I'll dump a bucket of water on the fire and I'll be right in," I advise.

She pushes up on her tiptoes and presses her lips to mine, before she drops back on her heels with a smile on her face. "Hurry."

I chuckle softly and quickly stride to the side of the house where I keep the bucket and hose, and heed her advice. I'll tell her everything tomorrow. I have to; it's time she knows how I really feel.

Amy

I run into Matt's bathroom and pull out the pink toothbrush I leave here. I quickly brush my teeth and then slip out of my shoes. I peel off my top and shorts, before I lay down on his bed in nothing but my matching black lace bra and thong. He walks through the door and freezes, slowly taking in the sight of me. His gaze sweeps over my body like a soft caress, giving me goosebumps and bringing a smile to his face. "Took you long enough," I taunt, earning myself the sound of his low chuckle.

He stalks towards me, as if I'm his prey. "Looks like I'm just in time," he rasps. He grabs my ankle and gives it a light tug, causing me to fall back onto the bed. He crawls over me, licking and kissing his way up my body. He starts at my ankle, to my knee, to the inside of my thigh, my breath becoming heavier with each kiss. He skips up to my stomach and I groan in protest. He chuckles in response, before he kisses me between my breasts and then continues to my shoulder and my neck. I reach up and sneak my hands underneath his shirt, trailing my fingers across his taut abs. He pushes up and reaches one arm behind his head, ripping off his shirt. He lowers himself back towards me and looks into my eyes. My heartbeat speeds up in anticipation. "You're so much more than beautiful," he rasps. "So much fucking more," he emphasizes, causing my heart to skip a beat.

"Matt," I whimper. He finally presses his lips to mine, completely devouring me. I slide my hands over his back, one moving up into his hair to pull him closer. We've barely started and I feel like I can't get enough of him.

His tongue tangles with mine, urging me to slow down with soft sweeps and then a twirl. He tears his lips away from mine and begins to kiss a slow sensual path over my jaw, down my neck and over my collarbone as he slips my bra strap to the side. His lips move down to my breast. He pushes the fabric away, letting my breast spring free. My nipple tightens eager for his touch. His hand skims over it, before he cups my breast, nudging it towards his lips. His tongue juts out, swirling its way around my nipple, before he covers it with his mouth, heating me to my core. My body reflexively arches into him and he releases it with a groan. "I love the way you react to me," he praises. My hands continue roaming over his firm body, while he moves to the other side, giving my other breast the same treatment. He releases it with a pop, before his hand slips behind my back, letting my breasts spring completely free. "Better," he mumbles, as he tosses my bra to the side.

"What about you?" I prompt, tugging at the waistband of his jeans.

"In a minute, I'm busy," he replies, his voice laced with amusement. He places a kiss at the bottom of my ribcage.

"Hey," I complain. I reach out to smack his ass, but he's already too low and I connect with the bare skin of his back.

He glances up at me with a smirk and arches his eyebrows in challenge. Then he looks down and continues kissing a path down my body. He kisses me just above my warm center and I gasp for breath, as heat floods my body. He slips the thong down my legs and tosses it on the floor. Then he sticks his tongue out and firmly licks my folds. "Fuck," he gasps, "you're so ready for me." I whimper in response, not able to do anything else. He takes a deep breath and covers me with his mouth, making me groan. His tongue barely strokes a few times, before I feel like I'm about to lose control. He gently sucks me into his mouth and I scream, arching towards him, not being able to hold it in. Suddenly, he releases me, pushing away and off the bed before I have my release.

"Matt," I pant, barely able to force his name from my lips.

"Patience," he grins, mischievously. He kicks off his jeans and black and white striped boxers, his long, hard cock springing to life.

"Boxers?" I question, arching my eyebrows in surprise. He usually wears boxer briefs.

"Sometimes," he shrugs. Then he walks over to his nightstand and opens the drawer. He reaches inside and pulls out a condom.

I roll towards him and grasp his thick shaft, causing him to groan, while his eyes practically roll to the back of his head. I love that I'm able to do that to him. He grasps my wrist and pleads, "Please, I want to be inside you."

I move my hand up and down before releasing him and placing my hands on his chest. I kiss him in the middle of his chest and slide my hands up and around his neck as I pull his head down to my lips. I kiss him hard, pressing my body to his as he lowers me back to the bed. I bend my knees and attempt to pull him closer with my feet. "Give me the condom," I demand. He holds it out, already open. I pull out the condom and move my hands down to his dick, slowly rolling it on. I reach his base and move my hand around giving his full balls a light squeeze.

"Fuck, Amy," he grunts. He pulls my hand away and traps both of my hands above my head, holding them there. He looks into my eyes as he adjusts himself at my entrance. "Ready?" he prods. He looks at me as if he's asking for so much more than sex.

I huff, as my heart skips a beat. I nod my head in response, not able to speak any words. He pushes inside me in one hard thrust. I gasp and close my eyes. He holds himself, buried deep inside me. "Look at me," he urges. I attempt to move, but he doesn't allow it, holding me in place. I reluctantly open my eyes and look deep into his. I see everything I've always wanted to see in them, as he begins to move inside me, maintaining eye contact. He moves in and out at a torturously slow pace, staring into my eyes and giving me more than he ever has. My heart beats erratically as I struggle for breath, every miniscule movement almost too much for me to handle. I've never felt so much. He begins to pick up the pace, never allowing me to break our connection. My hips move up to meet his, thrust for thrust, our overheated bodies moving in perfect sync.

My core feels like fire as a tingling sensation increases in strength. "Matt," I whimper, "I can't..." I stammer.

"Let go with me," he encourages.

His words send me over the edge. I feel my insides begin to spasm, squeezing his cock, over and over again and I'm no longer able to keep my eyes open. He lets out a loud groan and buries himself to the hilt inside me, as my body continues to spasm. I feel his release as my body begins to finally come down from my epic orgasm. My insides clench once more, as Matt finally drops his head to my shoulder. He still holds himself above me enough not to crush me as we both gasp for breath, our bodies slick with sweat. He finally lifts his head and stares into my eyes. "I..." he begins, but quickly snaps his mouth shut. "You are incredible," he insists.

My heart skips a beat as I look at him. This feels like so much more. This feels like love. My breath catches in my throat at the thought. Am I in love with Matt? I can't be. My parents would never let us happen. He gives me a chaste kiss and pulls out of me, leaving me feeling empty as he pushes up off the bed. He ties off the condom and tosses it in the garbage, before he disappears into the bathroom. I take a deep breath as I listen to the water run, knowing he'll be back any second. I need to just enjoy tonight. I can worry about my parents tomorrow, but I feel a painful gnawing in my gut, telling me I'm treading dangerous waters.

I force a smile as he walks back into the room with a warm washcloth. He makes his way over to me and takes care cleaning me up. He tosses the washcloth towards his laundry basket in the corner and climbs back on the bed with me. He slips in behind me and wraps his arms around me, pulling my back close to his front. He kisses me just behind my ear and whispers, "Are you alright?" I nod my head, still not able to speak. He lets his head fall to the pillow and pulls me tighter. I lay awake in his arms, not wanting to be anywhere else, but also not wanting to miss a second of it. I listen to the sounds of his breathing slow and eventually even out, telling me he's asleep.

Chapter 11

Matt

I lay awake watching her as she sleeps, wrapped in my arms. I can't believe I almost told her I loved her last night. I know that would terrify her and send her running, even if I believe she feels the same. I can tell her how I feel, but I need to take a cautious approach. I gulp down the lump in my throat, my nerves already getting the best of me, but I have to do this. Last night was like nothing I've ever experienced before. That was so much more than just great sex. I don't care what she claims. I can't hold myself back anymore by denying the truth.

She begins to stir, whining, "No."

I run my hands over her hair, in attempt to soothe her. "It's okay, Amy," I encourage.

She squirms out of my arms like she's trying to get away from me. "No, please," she pleads.

I loosen my hold and attempt to gently wake her, "Amy, wake up. You're having a bad dream."

She screams at the top of her lungs and grunts, "No!" startling me.

She sits up in bed appearing frantic, "It's okay, it's okay, you're okay," I ramble, hoping to calm her and not sure what kind of dream did that to her. She looks at me with wide frightened eyes, gasping for breath. She sees me and I see the relief in her eyes the moment she realizes where she is. She throws herself into my arms and my arms immediately wrap protectively around her, wanting to give her every comfort. "Are you okay?" She nods into my chest holding on tight. "Are you sure?" I prod anxiously.

She takes a deep breath and exhales slowly, loosening her hold around me. She finally lets her hands fall to her lap. Her cheeks turn slightly pink as she peeks up at me, a little sheepish. "I'm sorry," she apologizes.

I shake my head and insist, "There's nothing to apologize for."

"I had a bad dream," she admits, scrunching her nose up in distaste.

"I figured. Are you going to tell me what it was about?" I probe.

She looks up at me, hesitant. "Will you hand me a shirt?" she requests. I reach down and grab my black t-shirt from the floor along with my boxers. I pull my t-shirt over her head and she slips her arms through the holes. I pull my boxers on as I watch her scoot against the wall and pull her knees up to her chest, wrapping them protectively around her. I sit down next to her, but turn so I can see her face. I place my hand on her knee in comfort and gently move my thumb in a slow, soothing circle. She leans towards me without even realizing it. I wait quietly, hoping she'll open up.

She heaves a sigh and shakes her head in annoyance. "It's stupid," she claims. I shake my head, and open my mouth to argue, but she speaks first. "It was just me having a fight with my mom," she quietly concedes.

"Are you fighting with her a lot?" I push. She shrugs her shoulders, giving me an answer without saying anything. "What were you fighting about?"

She grimaces and mumbles so quietly I almost don't hear, "You." My stomach churns, with anxiety, knowing this could be both good and bad. "I don't want to talk about it," she blurts out, desperately. "Please," she begs meeting my gaze.

My chest tightens seeing the pain in her eyes, making me hesitate, unsure what to do. A tear runs down her cheek and I reach out, brushing it away with the pad of my thumb. "I don't like seeing you in so much pain. I think we should talk about it."

"I will, just not today," she claims.

I heave a sigh and nod my head, relenting. "Okay," I murmur, "but I'm here when you need me and we will finish this conversation."

She nods in agreement and pastes a smile on her face. "Thanks," she murmurs. "So, what are you up to today?" she asks.

"Hanging out with you?" I propose.

She laughs and nods her head in agreement. "Okay." She loosens her hold around her legs and stretches out on my bed, suddenly appearing relaxed. "It was really good to see everyone last night," she proclaims.

"Yeah, it was," I mumble my agreement. I don't know if this is the best time, but I promised myself I would talk to her today, so here it goes. "So, you know how everybody was joking about us being each other's back-up plan?" I inquire.

She glances warily at me from underneath her eyelashes and murmurs, "Yeah?"

"Well," I hesitate briefly, "what do you think about it?" I probe, attempting to get a feel for what she's thinking.

"What do you mean what do I think about it? Lots of people joke about that kind of thing and a lot even do it," she claims and shrugs like it's no big deal. "So, do you have to go to the gym today?" she asks, changing the subject.

I sit up and move to the end of the bed. I put my feet on the floor and look at her, knowing I need to watch her body language closely. "I just told you I was hanging out with you today," I remind her and she winces in response. "I want to know what you personally think about our back-up plan in relation to you and me," I reiterate.

She grimaces and looks away, causing me to flinch. That's not the reaction I was going for. "I don't know if we'd really be a good idea," she grumbles, awkwardly.

I breathe in and exhale, focusing momentarily on my breathing, attempting to stop myself from saying something I'll regret in response to her reaction. I speak softly, but firmly as I challenge her remark. "Why would you say that? What is so wrong with you and me? We have fantastic chemistry, we always have. Sex with you is always off the charts. We have fun together outside the bedroom too," I argue.

"Yeah, like on the kitchen table, or up against any solid wall," she jokes.

I shake my head and blurt out, "You know that's not what I fucking meant!" I grind my jaw in irritation with her for making our relationship a joke and myself for taking her bait. I gulp hard, attempting to push my heart back where it belongs. "You've always shared things with me you couldn't even share with Bree. We can talk about anything; we laugh together and we love doing the same kind of shit together. We even take each other as our plus ones when we need one and we have a good fucking time together," I remind her.

I watch as she nods her head in agreement. Her expression goes from acknowledgement, to pained, before finally ending with acceptance. She takes a deep breath and squares her shoulders before she turns and looks me in the eyes. "You're right," she concurs, briefly giving me peace. I see a shift in her eyes causing my heart to stop and my blood to rush to my ears as it begins beating again. "But that's all it can ever be with us Matt, fun. We can't be together," she claims. "We would never work," she emphasizes.

"Are you fucking kidding me right now?" I ask, demanding an answer. I stand up and pace away from the bed before I spin back around and close the distance between us. "Why Amy? Tell me why!" I stress. "The real answer," I grunt.

She flinches at my tone. I don't raise my voice to her, ever, but this fucking hurts. She looks into my eyes and I see so much pain in them, so much regret. She opens her mouth and then closes it. Then she opens it again and whispers my name sounding desperate, "Matt."

"I want to be with you! Please, just be honest with me for fucking once!" I plead.

I see it the moment she makes a decision and concedes to her internal debate. Her shoulders sag and she stares at my chest as she speaks. "I can't do that to my parents, especially my dad."

My whole body tenses. I gulp down the lump in my throat, as tiny pinpricks feel like their attacking every inch of my insides to take me down. "What do you mean you can't do that to them?" I rasp.

"They expect me to end up with a certain type of guy," she replies softly. She's so quiet I'm surprised I hear her at all, but I do. I hear every fucking word. She would do anything for her dad and I don't fit into that mold. "You, specifically, they warned me against and I can't disappoint him," she whimpers. She looks away, wiping a stray tear that escaped without her consent.

I nod my head slowly, processing her words. I decidedly take a step back from her, silently fuming. I look at her and shake my head in both realization and utter disappointment, as I feel my heart breaking in two. "So, miss high and mighty, that's really all I am to you after everything we've been through?" I know I sound like a pussy right now, but I don't give a shit. "You're always so fucking concerned about how everyone treats you and yet here you are, acting like you're too good for me," her eyes widen at my words. I point at myself and remind her, "I'm the guy who has always been there for you when you felt like you were all alone. I'm the guy that has always gone out of his way to help you and support you. Your parents wouldn't want that for you?" I contest.

She looks at me with tears in her eyes and stutters, "I...I...Matt...I..."

"Why do you always date assholes you try to fix into a decent human being, instead of going for a decent fucking man in the first place...like the one standing right in front of you?" I challenge, glaring down at her.

"Matt," she gasps, shocked at my outburst.

I shake my head in disbelief as tears fall from her eyes. She could make sure neither of us are hurting right now. She just doesn't want to or have the courage to do so. Either way, I can't fucking do this anymore. "You know what Amy, fuck this...I'm done being your fucking doormat," I grumble.

She straightens slightly and prods, "What do you mean?"

"You were never going to give me a chance," I conclude. "It doesn't matter how good I am for you or how good we are together. Only their opinion matters," I state. I see the truth in her eyes causing me to feel like she's crushing my heart in her clenched fist. "I can't do this anymore," I mumble, feeling completely defeated. I run my palm down my face and over the center of my chest, attempting to dull the painful ache. It feels like I just ran a fucking marathon.

"You can't do what?" she asks, sounding slightly panicked.

"This," I emphasize, throwing my arms back and forth between us. "Find another fuck buddy since that's all I am to you. I need to move on and find someone who actually fucking respects me," I proclaim. "Good fucking luck!" I announce. I pivot on my heel and storm out. I hear her calling after me, but I quickly stalk to my truck as if I don't. I'm fucking done. I get in behind the wheel and slam the door. "Unfuckingreal," I grumble to myself as I start my truck and quickly back out of the driveway, leaving her to vacate my house on her own.

Amy

I flinch as the door slams, tears streaming down my face. Did he feel the same way about me? I shake my head, knowing it doesn't matter. I just ruined everything. It looks like I finally did it. I finally did what my parents wanted me to do and it feels like the only thing I succeeded in doing was breaking us both. I've never hated myself more than I do in this moment. I hear the screech of his tires as he pulls away from his house, causing the damn to break and I begin to sob, uncontrollably.

I don't know how long I sit there crying, but when my tears subside enough, I know it's time to get up. I wipe my face and take a deep, shaky breath, before I force myself to stand. I wander around his room and begin collecting my things through my blurred vision. Out of respect for him, I shouldn't be here when he comes home. I slip on my underwear and shorts. I pull my arms out of his shirt to put my bra on before I put it back on. I need to take him home with me somehow. I stuff my shirt into my purse and walk into the bathroom. I glance in the mirror and grimace at my reflection. My eyes are red and swollen and the blue appears dull. I turn on the faucet and splash my face with cold water, before switching it off. I slip on my shoes and glance at his room one more time, remembering how perfect last night was for me. I'll remember it for the rest of my life, but that kind of life is not meant for me. He had it all wrong, he's the one who's too good for me. I turn away and trudge out the front door trying to hold myself together.

I glance over at my car sitting in the driveway, next to the empty spot Matt's truck just vacated. I'm grateful I came over early yesterday, or I'd be doing the walk of shame all the way across town. Goosebumps prickle my skin. The chill in the air telling me summer really is coming to an end, just like my life. I slip in behind the wheel and send a quick text to Matt. There's so much I want to say, but none of it is fair. So, I simply state, "I'm sorry," knowing it's not even close to enough. Nothing will ever be enough. I hurt so much, but I deserve this pain and so much more. I warrant all the pain that comes my way after this.

Chapter 12

Matt

I glance at my phone and see another text from Amy. I open it and read, "Please talk to me." I leave the message on read and close it without responding, like I have been all week. I've thought about blocking her number, but I can't do it. I just need some space for a little while, so I can move on. I can't do that if I hear her soft voice or see her beautiful face right now. This is the way it has to be for now. It won't be forever. I slip my phone back into my pocket, knowing I'll need it for my next session.

I saunter up to the desk in the gym, not knowing who the client is that scheduled the spot for my last session of the day. "Hey Kim," I greet the woman behind the desk. She's twenty-four and currently in her last year of grad school for physical therapy. She's a great asset to have around here, but she loves to work behind the desk so she can use times that we're slow to study. She's tall and thin with long black hair. She has it pulled back into a high ponytail, showing off her dark, flawless skin and brown eyes. She's stunning.

She glances in my direction and arches her eyebrows, as if asking why I'm bothering her. "Your new client just arrived. She's putting her things in the locker room," she informs me.

"Thanks," I mumble. She keeps looking at me, as if she's waiting for me to say something. I heave a sigh and lean down next to her. "Is there something you want to ask me?" I probe, more curious than anything. I reach for my water bottle and when she doesn't say anything, I touch it to my lips and tip it back to take a sip.

"I'm just trying to figure out if you've already fucked her or if she's coming here to fuck you?" she blurts out, honestly.

I gasp in surprise, spitting out some of my water on the floor. "Excuse me?" I prompt, feigning innocence.

She rolls her eyes and mumbles, "Don't pretend like you don't know what I'm talking about. Half the women who schedule a session with you want to fuck you or have already and the other half want to or just want to dream about it."

I give her a cocky smirk and lean a little closer to her. "So, is that what you do all day?" I tease. I love giving her a hard time, but mostly because I know she can take it.

"Ew," she mumbles, pursing her lips in disgust.

I huff a humorless laugh and mumble, "Thanks."

She chuckles and shakes her head. "What do you expect? Men are assholes," she elaborates. "And besides, it's not like you need an ego boost," she claims.

I laugh and shake my head in amusement, "You're definitely not helping my ego."

She shrugs like she doesn't care. "I'm not trying to." Then she sighs and maintains, "I think I'm better off avoiding men for a while."

I nod my head in acknowledgement and claim, "I'm not just any man."

She rolls her eyes again and requests, "Leave it alone, Romeo. I think you're going to have your hands full with your new client."

She nods towards the women's locker room just as a tall, thin, beautiful woman steps out. She has slightly rounded hips and full breasts, smashed down with a marbled teal sports bra, leaving about an inch of her belly bare, before her charcoal workout pants skim down her legs like a second skin. She has long dark brown hair pulled up into a high ponytail and her eyes widen momentarily the moment she spots me behind the desk. I watch as she approaches, attempting to place her, but I honestly have no clue. As she walks towards the desk, I realize her eyes are a soft, amber brown. She has high cheekbones and a button nose. She offers me a small, hesitant smile and murmurs, "Hi, Matt."

Ah, fuck. She knows who I am. "Hi," I reply. She looks familiar, but I can't quite figure out why. She looks at me expectantly. I want to flip through the papers to find out her name, but I don't want to be obvious.

"Vanessa signed up for six private training sessions with you, over the next two weeks," Kim reveals, saving my ass.

I glance at her and she smirks in response. "Thanks, Kim," I mumble under my breath.

I step around the desk and offer Vanessa a wide smile. "You ready?" I prompt.

"Sure," she mumbles.

"Let's go loosen up, while you tell me a little more about your exercise routine and what your goals and expectations are for these sessions," I instruct. She nods in agreement and I reach for my iPad, before I guide her towards the back by the mats. I easily lead her through a few warm-up stretches, as I ask her several questions and record everything on a form I designed to keep track of it all and help develop the perfect plan for each individual. I attempt to focus on her workout, but my mind keeps wandering, trying to figure out how I might know her. "Have you been here before?" I finally ask.

"No, not really," she responds, "This is only my second time here. Last time I did the basic training on the equipment," she elaborates.

I grimace with her response; almost positive that couldn't be it. "Let's head over to the treadmill and do a

101

little cardio. Her eyes narrow on me as we make our way over to a row of treadmills. I stop at one and begin pushing buttons, trying to ignore her glare. I stop and blurt out, "Did I do something to offend you?"

She laughs humorlessly and shakes her head in annoyance. "Seriously?" she prods, her disbelief clear.

"What?" I push, needing to know who she is at this point. Especially since I'll be seeing a lot of her the next couple weeks.

"Do you really not remember me?" she prompts.

My mouth drops open and my breath gets stuck in my throat momentarily, feeling trapped. "I...I..." I stammer.

She rolls her eyes and shakes her head. "You really are an asshole," she mumbles, as she steps onto the treadmill. I press start and set the speed and incline mildly at first. "I met you at Bro's, last week I think," she enlightens me. My heart skips a beat, hoping I didn't do anything with her and then not even recognize her. "I was with Ember," she reveals and I breathe a short-lived sigh of relief. "The redhead that was all over you before the blonde practically jumped you on the pool table," she elaborates. I feel the rare occurrence of my face heating in embarrassment. I've learned not to let most shit bother me, but I hate when my personal life spills over into the gym. It's one of the reasons I know I'm ready for a commitment. I hate mindless hook-ups. I want to date one woman, be with one woman. It just took me a while to realize it will never be Amy. "You didn't exactly make the best impression," she declares.

"Thanks," I grumble, irritated with myself. I don't blame her for thinking I'm an asshole. She's right. I kick up the speed and incline, just a little bit.

"Was the blonde your girlfriend?" she questions.

"What? Amy?" I ask. I grimace as her name passes through my lips. "No," I answer.

"An ex then?" she clarifies.

I heave a sigh and run my hand through my hair in frustration. Amy is the last thing I want to be talking about right now. "Something like that," I grumble, irritably. "Look, I can find you a different trainer," I begin.

"No," she interrupts, shaking her head in refusal. "I heard you're the best. That's why I'm here," she proclaims. I hesitate for only a moment before she interrupts my thoughts. "I'm sorry. I'll stop bugging you about women and what you choose to do with them," she claims, the look on her face revealing how much she hates my choices.

I shake my head and clarify, "Not women, just my ex."

She gives her head a firm nod in agreement and claims, "I can do that. Thanks."

I shake my head and insist, "You don't need to thank me. Besides, you were right," I proclaim the same words I was thinking earlier. She arches her eyebrows in question. "I was an asshole the other night," I concede. "I'm sorry." She offers me a small smile in appreciation and I increase both the incline and speed. "How about we start over?" I propose.

"I'd like that," she concurs, not even sounding out of breath.

I increase her speed again and mumble, "You sure you need me?" She laughs as she picks up her pace.

Amy

I drop my phone on my desk in frustration. I can't believe he won't even answer my texts now. I guess I don't blame him, but what was I supposed to do? I pick up my phone to call Bree to ask her advice, when a good-looking older man steps into my line of sight, garnering my attention. I look up and smile at him. He's tall and lean, with a full head of light grey hair. He has blue eyes and a wide smile, as he glances down at me.

"Amy Stone," he announces, "it's so nice to finally meet you," he proclaims. He holds his hand out to me and I stand up, grasping his hand and shaking it firmly.

"Uh, thank you, Sir," I stammer, awkwardly, contradicting my actions.

He chuckles, and introduces himself, "I'm Warren Kirst. Between your father and now Preston, I feel like I already know you," he claims.

I pretend to laugh, slightly puzzled by his comment. I've barely seen Preston since we had lunch last week. I thought he was no longer interested. Then again, maybe he's not and he's just referring to work. "That's very kind," I mumble, robotically.

He releases my hand and informs me, "I have a project for you and Preston to work on together. Why don't you go get him and meet me in my office," he suggests.

"Yes, Sir," I reply. He nods in acknowledgement, before he turns and strides away.

I sigh and stand up, walking towards Preston's office. I stop in front of Polly's desk and smile. "Hi, Polly," I mumble.

Her eyes widen when she sees me, before she covers it with a polite smile. "Hi, Amy. How are things going?" she prods.

"Fine, I guess. How about you?" I ask, politely.

"I work for my brother," she grumbles in response, making me laugh.

"Sorry," I quickly murmur my apology.

She waves it off and mumbles, "Exactly." She sighs and inquires, "Can I help you with something?"

"Actually, I need Preston. Your dad wants to see us," I advise.

She grins wide and taps into the intercom. "Preston, Amy's here to see you," she announces. I hear a loud thump, as she releases the button. "Go ahead," she offers.

I hesitate momentarily, when his door suddenly flies open and a woman with dark wavy hair strides out of his office. She pauses and looks me up and down with clear distaste, but I don't let that kind of shit bother me. I straighten my shoulders and hold myself tall, even though she has at least three inches on me. "Can I help you?" I prod. She rolls her eyes and stalks away, without another word.

Polly laughs, clearly amused and mumbles under her breath, "Bitch." I turn to her, arching my eyebrows in question. "Her, not you," she quickly clarifies. "I'm pretty sure she was trying to seduce my brother," she grumbles and scrunches up her face in disgust. She pales and her eyes widen with regret. "I just mean she only wants to sleep with him for his money. I know her," she blurts out, awkwardly, just as Preston steps up behind her.

"Gee, thanks for the ringing endorsement, Sis," Preston grumbles.

"Ugh," she grunts in frustration. "You know what I mean!" She turns and narrows her eyes at Preston, but he's completely focused on me.

"Can I help you with something, Amy," he offers.

His intense gaze leaves me feeling on edge. "I..." I begin.

"Step into my office for a minute," he urges. He splays his palm on my lower back and nudges me inside. I do as he says and he closes the door behind us, the

105

moment we cross the threshold. He lets his hand fall to his side as he steps around me and towards his desk.

"Are you seeing her?" I probe, even though I know it's none of my business.

He spins back towards me smirking, clearly pleased with my question. "Jealous?" he prods.

I roll my eyes, annoyed with myself for even voicing my curiosity. I shake my head and quickly apologize, "I'm sorry. I shouldn't ask."

"Why not? You know I'm interested in you," he claims. I arch my eyebrows, my doubt clearly visible. "It's true," he insists. "But you were obviously still involved with someone else, no matter what you told me."

I gasp in surprise and stammer, "Wh..what do you mean?"

He pauses, as if deciding what he should tell me. He takes a step closer to me and holds my gaze. "The night of our date, when we went to Bro's," he begins. I instantly feel all my blood drain from my face, afraid I know where he's going with this. "I saw you kiss Matt Young on the pool table," he confesses. "Then you got a huge bouquet of flowers from him on your first day," he continues. I exhale slowly in relief, but I attempt to keep my reaction subtle. "If you're dating him, you're not dating me," he answers simply.

"That's fair," I answer, "but I'm not dating him."

"Could've fooled me," he responds.

I sigh in understanding. "Look, I know how it looks, but Matt has always been one of my best friends." He arches his eyebrows in challenge, but I don't blame him. We never really acted like we were just best friends. "It doesn't matter though, we're not together. We're never going to be together," I emphasize, needing to tell someone. "In fact, I don't even know if we're friends anymore," I claim, my heart aching as I utter the truth.

"Really?" he prompts, taking a step closer.

I nod my head in confirmation and mumble, "Really."

He lets his hands fall to my waist as he looks down at me. "I don't share," he reiterates.

"What about the woman that was just in here?" I question.

He smirks and replies, "Polly's right about her. She's a bitch and I have zero interest in her, but I do have to work with her from time to time." He leans closer to me, his lips hovering above mine as he repeats, "I don't share."

His lips touch mine and I enjoy the feel of him for barely a moment before I quickly pull away, wondering what I'm doing. I didn't come here for this. How did I even get myself into this kind of mess? "Your dad," I blurt out.

He steps back, clearly confused, "What?"

"Your dad wants us to come to his office. He has something he wants us to work on together. I was supposed to come and get you," I quickly explain.

He grins and nods in understanding, "We'll finish this conversation later." He cradles my face in his hands and presses a chaste kiss to my lips, before releasing me. "Let's go find out what he wants," he advises, spinning me towards his door.

I follow him out the door as a fleeting thought crosses my mind. How does he know Matt? I'll have to figure out a way to ask him later, without stirring up any trouble.

Chapter 13

Amy

I'm thrilled Mr. Kirst wants me working on this project for Diana Brooks with Preston. That woman is a genius in fashion, both for people and for your home. She owns several clothing and home décor and design stores along the Northeast. She also has an upcoming fundraiser for a non-profit organization that helps struggling families with everything from building or refurbishing their home to providing them with all new wardrobes, as well as education and services to help them with careers and job placement. I've heard it's an absolutely unbelievable event and I'm going to be there this year representing Kirst Marketing, along with Preston, of course. It's like a dream come true. Diana Brooks is an absolutely incredible woman.

Preston leans over my shoulder, reading the social media marketing outline I'm putting together. "This is looking good, Amy," he murmurs and tilts his head towards me. I feel his hot breath on my neck, giving me goosebumps. My breathing picks up, as he brushes his lips along the curve of my neck and gently nibbles.

"Preston," I gasp, slightly uncomfortable. We're still at work. Anyone could walk in. Plus, I don't really know what I want from him. I know that's never stopped me before, but...I glance nervously towards the door and he chuckles softly in response.

"It's late," he rasps. "We're the only ones still here," he claims.

"How do you know?" I challenge.

He chuckles again and shrugs his shoulders. "I don't, but I can't help myself," he mumbles. He spins my chair around and puts one hand on each armrest, caging me in. He leans in towards me and pauses, just over my lips. "It's been fucking torture holding myself back from you," he rasps. He slides one hand behind my neck and weaves his fingers into my hair. He gently tugs my hair, forcing my head up to meet his gaze. "Watching you strut around here all day in your tight as sin dresses or those low-cut tops and your short skirts," he grumbles and slams his lips down onto mine. He holds me in place with his hand firm on the back of my head. Then he tugs on my hair, tilting my head back further and allowing my mouth to open just enough for him to shove his tongue inside and completely devour me.

I hear the door click open causing me to instantly stiffen. I plant my hand on his chest, pushing him away, but he doesn't budge. He takes his time releasing me and smirks as he slowly stands up. He turns towards the doorway and arches his eyebrow in question. The same woman from earlier stands there with her arms crossed and her eyes narrowed on me. "I was told you were in here and thought you might need some help," she murmurs, seductively.

I fight not to roll my eyes. Instead of answering her, Preston questions, "Why are you still here?"

"I came back for a file I wanted to review," she claims.

He doesn't respond to her statement. He just stares her down, surprising me. She finally grumbles, "I'm leaving now." She changes her tone and purrs, "See you tomorrow, Preston."

"Close the door on your way out," he instructs.

She spins on her heel and mumbles, "Whore," under her breath, just before she slams the door shut.

Preston's jaw clenches in anger and then he takes a deep breath, exhaling slowly, as if trying to brush it off. "Sorry about that," he mumbles.

"It's not your fault she's a bitch," I retort, surprising myself. I instantly feel my face heat in embarrassment. He doesn't seem to like her, but like he said before, he does have to work with her.

He laughs in response and I exhale slowly in relief. "You are too much," he murmurs, his amusement apparent.

"Thanks?" I say as more of a question.

"Do you want to get out of here and go get some food?" he prompts. "Something easy?"

My stomach growls in answer and I feel my cheeks heat in embarrassment. "I think that's a good idea," I mumble.

"Great. Let's go," he encourages. He reaches down and grasps my hand, pulling me up with a gentle tug.

He releases me and I mumble, "Thanks. I'll just go grab my purse from my desk and I'll be ready."

Matt

I sit down at a small black table with my whole grain turkey sandwich, topped with lettuce, tomato, alfalfa sprouts, onion, cranberry, olive oil and vinegar. I take a sip of my super green protein shake and set it back on the table as I look around the café. The floors have a rustic red tile, that doesn't really match the rest of the restaurant, which is mostly black, white and silver. The woman at the counter wears familiar charcoal leggings, but she has a marbled pink t-shirt on top. I stare at her, waiting for her to turn, curious. Vanessa spins, instantly spots me and freezes. I smirk and arch my eyebrow, as I gesture to the seat across from me in invitation.

She takes a deep breath, before she strides towards me and smiles wide. "Well, hello again," she greets me.

"Miss me already?" I tease. She rolls her eyes and turns to walk away. I quickly jump up, chuckling. I reach out for her and gently lay my hand on her arm. "Vanessa, I'm kidding. Please, stay." She hesitates, so I smile wider and urge, "I'd really like your company."

She gives me a shy smile and turns back to me, relenting. "Okay, Matt," she concedes. "We did say we would start over, right?" she prompts, as she lowers herself into the seat across from me.

"Right," I confirm.

I glance down at her small container of salad as she sets it on the table causing my eyes to draw down in concern. "Is that all your eating after that workout?" I prompt.

"Um, no, I just...um...I wasn't sure what I wanted, so I figured I'd start with a small salad and then maybe I'd go back for something else," she stammers awkwardly.

I narrow my eyes and offer her some of my smoothie. "Here, why don't you try some of this? It has almost everything you need in it, plus some extra protein," I murmur. "You need more to eat," I encourage.

Her cheeks turn a deep shade of red and I bite the inside of my cheek, wondering if I overstepped. She's a client, but she didn't ask me for nutrition advice. "You're right," she yields. "I'll get a smoothie after I eat this," she claims.

I breathe a sigh of relief and mutter, "Good."

She takes a bite of her salad assessing me. I watch her, waiting to see if she'll tell me what's on her mind. She finally opens her mouth and prods, "So what do you do when you're not at the gym or out drinking?"

I grin, grateful she's keeping the banter light. We rapidly fall into an easy conversation, talking and laughing for more than an hour. "Well, I should probably head home," she murmurs, as she glances at her phone, checking the time. "I have some papers to grade tonight, before school tomorrow," she explains.

I nod my head in understanding and admit, "I don't know how you deal with middle school kids all day."

She giggles and wipes her mouth with the napkin in front of her. "Sometimes I don't either," she concurs.

I laugh and mumble, "That didn't work out too well for you."

Her eyebrows draw down in confusion and she questions, "What?"

Instead of answering her, I reach over the table and wipe a streak of salad dressing off her cheek. I hold my hand up for her to see and mutter, "See?"

She blushes a deep shade of red and mumbles, "Thanks."

I laugh a little harder, when something suddenly catches my attention out of the corner of my eye. I glance up just in time to see Amy standing inside the café, with that asshole Preston's arms around her. He leans down and kisses her, tightening my chest, but the part that kills me is watching as she kisses him back, with no inhibitions. I flinch and look away. Vanessa turns to see what I was looking at and her eyes widen at the display in front of us. She looks back at me and reaches for my hand, giving it a squeeze. I focus on her as she gives me a look of both understanding and encouragement. A look I appreciate more than I can explain.

"Want to get out of here?" she probes.

"Hell, yes!" I declare, emphatically.

I stand up and take a deep breath, exhaling slowly. Vanessa glances at me and grasps my hand, entangling her fingers with mine in support. I smile down at her, appreciatively, as we stride out of the café, hand in hand.

Amy

"So this fundraiser we have to go to," I begin, curiously, as we step inside the café, "Do we have to bring a date?" I inquire.

Preston halts and I follow his lead, turning to look at him for an answer. He narrows his eyes and plants his hands low on his hips. "What don't you understand about the words, I don't share?" he questions, irritably.

"I...I don't..." I stammer and heave a sigh. I really don't understand how I got myself in this position. Am I really going all in with Preston? He seems like a nice guy and he's definitely good looking. He's smart and he seems to have his shit together. In the past, I wouldn't hesitate with him, just knowing this. And that's not everything. He's also already set for an amazing career. He practically runs his own company that he will eventually take over when his dad retires. He seems to be everything my parents want for me. I gulp over the lump in my throat, feeling torn as my thoughts drift to Matt. No one has ever made me feel like he does.

"Look," he begins, interrupting my thoughts. "I really like you, Amy. I thought we were on the same page, but if that's not the case, I think I deserve to know now."

"Preston, I..." I trail off, not sure how to respond, but knowing he's right.

He huffs a laugh and sardonically grumbles, "There's your friend." He gestures with his chin towards a table to our right.

Glancing up, my heart lurches in response. Matt's eyes shine brightly as he looks across the table at a beautiful brunette. Is he on a date? He bursts out laughing, the sound making my chest ache for him. Then, he reaches across the table and wipes something off her cheek. I close my eyes and mumble, "Yup," popping the p.

Preston puts his arm around my shoulders and pulls me towards him. He looks into my eyes and brings his other arm up to rest on my other shoulder. "Jealous?" he probes.

"What do I have to be jealous about?" I retort, automatically. He's not mine. He never will be. I made sure of that. He moved on pretty damn quickly and he won't even talk to me anymore. I did this. This is what I wanted. Right? My heart clenches at the thought of not having him in my life, but I have no right. I need to start making an effort in someone like Preston. I'm supposed to be with someone like him and he's standing in front of me asking. It's time I do something about it.

Preston's eyes narrow momentarily. Then, he slides his hands up my neck and tangles one hand into my hair, while he cradles my face with his other hand. The corners of his lips twitch up, as his eyes sparkle with mischief, just before he crashes his lips down on mine. For the first time, I kiss him back with fervor, letting my emotions take over. He shoves his tongue into my mouth and I push back, lick for lick and stroke for stroke, hoping to diminish this ache in my chest. He finally slows the kiss and pulls back, a cocky smirk on his face.

"Let's get some food and bring it back to my place," he suggests. "We can talk more about the project and the upcoming fundraiser," he claims.

"Okay," I agree.

"And you're my date for the fundraiser," he emphasizes.

I paste a smile on my face and nod my head in agreement. He keeps one arm looped around my neck as we step up to the counter to order. I point to the first thing on the menu, not even sure what I'm ordering, as I struggle to keep myself in the moment.

Chapter 14

Matt

Vanessa holds my hand as we walk away from the café, while I'm completely lost in thought. What the fuck does she see in him? We turn the corner and Vanessa pries my fingers away from hers, garnering my attention. "You were starting to cut off my circulation," she mumbles, only half joking.

I heave a sigh and quickly mumble an apology. "I'm sorry, Vanessa." I take a deep breath and exhale slowly, before I continue. "Thank you for doing that for me. I can't begin to explain how much I appreciate that," I murmur.

"I guess you could say I know how you feel," she admits, giving me a sad smile.

"I'm sorry to hear that," I softly proclaim.

She shrugs her shoulders like it's no big deal and grimaces. "What are you going to do, you know?" she prompts.

I nod my head, as I look down at her, realizing we have more in common than either of us care to admit. "Yeah," I whisper. I gulp over the lump in my throat and change the subject before this conversation gets any deeper. "Do you want to run with me tomorrow morning?" I inquire.

"I run early," she reminds me. "I have to be at school, so I get up at five and I'm out of my house by quarter after," she enlightens me.

"That sounds perfect," I concur. I need to keep myself busy.

"Okay," she agrees. "Where should I meet you?"

"My place? I live near the entrance to the park trails," I suggest.

She hesitates for a moment before she nods her head in agreement. "Alright," she concurs. "Text me your address," she requests.

I smirk and remind her, "I don't have your number." Her eyebrows draw down in confusion and I reiterate, "You gave it to the gym, not me."

She sighs and holds her hand out without a word. I unlock my phone and hand it to her. She adds her contact info and sends herself a text, before she hands me back my phone. "Don't make me regret that," she mutters.

I chuckle softly as she turns and strides towards a silver Camry in the front of the parking lot. Then I make my way to my bike in the opposite direction, anxious to get out of here. I'm not taking a chance of having to talk to her when she's with him. I throw my leg over my black and chrome Harley, with a few accents of dark red. I sit back, propping the bike between my thighs. I grasp my black helmet off the side and pull it over my head. My thumb flips the switch to turn it on and then I push the one next to it, the low rumble vibrating through my legs and through the rest of my body. I push off the stand and immediately take off out of town, needing to hit some open road. Tonight is a good night to take the long ride home. It won't be nice enough to ride for much longer and I need time and space to clear my head.

The concrete, brick, steel and lights of the small town disappear as trees quickly surround me on both sides of the road. My body starts to relax, as the cool wind whips around me. Cruising through the hills on the far side of town, I make my way around the far perimeter of town, refusing to think about Amy.

Unfortunately, my thoughts soon drift to Grant. His obsession with motorcycles is part of the reason I wanted my own. Memories of him suddenly consume me. Images of him run through my head like a movie; him fixing up his ride, while we talk and laugh about everything, him showing me what to do, the replica he gave me for my birthday, cheering for him at his football games and then he supposedly lets some woman fuck up his head, his life and he's just gone, without a word to anyone...without a word to me. Then the rumors, mom and dad chasing after him and not knowing if he's alive or dead...it's all just too fucking much! I grind my jaw and give my head a small shake, maintaining my focus on the road in front of me. My hands tighten around the handlebars, as I take the curve coming in on the other side of town.

I pull into a dirt parking lot and stop, planting my feet. Sitting back, I look out into the empty dirt and grass lot, imagining everything I want to create. I mumble to myself, "This is what I need to focus on." Fuck everything else, or everyone. I need to take a look at everything again tonight to see where I'll be after this week. It's time to get this project started.

Amy

Standing outside on the balcony at Preston's condo, I snap a few pictures with my phone, with the incredible view of Boston Harbor behind me. Grinning wide, Preston steps out onto the balcony and slides the door closed behind him. "Enjoying the view?" he prods.

I nod my head in response and offer him a smile, as he hands me a glass of white wine. "Thank you," I mumble. "It's gorgeous," I mumble what he already knows. He nods his head, staring at me with raw hunger, leaving me feeling naked.

He takes a sip of his wine and sets his glass down on a small, sleek, silver and black table. He steps closer to me and inquires, "Are those pictures for your blog?"

I shrug my shoulders and regretfully admit, "I'll post one or two. I haven't been doing as much since I started at Kirst." I honestly hate that I haven't had time to stay on top of it.

He steps closer and softly runs his finger along my jaw, before he follows his finger with a trail of kisses, just underneath my ear. "Take one of us and post it," he instructs.

I arch my eyebrows in surprise. He's barely talked to me in the past two weeks and now today I can't seem to get rid of him. I guess he thought me confessing I'm not dating Matt, gave him the green light in our relationship. Do we even have a relationship? I'm so confused. "Don't you have to ask your marketing team or something?" I probe.

He chuckles, the sound vibrating right through me. "I do whatever the fuck I want and that includes you," he declares, smirking at his own joke. I bite the inside of my cheek and fight not to roll my eyes. He may be portrayed as one of Boston's most eligible bachelors, but sometimes his ego is a ridiculous turn-off. "Besides," he murmurs, "wouldn't you rather we put it out there than someone else?"

I heave a sigh, knowing he's right. We have to think about every little thing. Since we both already have a huge social following and because of his company, he's extremely visible in the public eye, we both are. We can control the story if we're the ones who put it out there, but what is our story? "You're right," I concur. We need to talk about this.

He grins wide, obviously enjoying my words. I pull out my phone and lean into him. He drapes his arm around me and we both smile as I snap a picture. Then he turns his head towards me and nudges my chin to face him. He kisses me, holding me in place. He takes my phone from me and snaps another picture, before I have the chance to argue. I feel his smile on my lips, as he pulls away. He looks down at my phone and sends the pictures to himself before he hands it back to me. A cool wind blows through the balcony, giving me a chill and making me shudder. "Why don't we get you inside and warm you up," he suggests, a devilish look in his eyes.

I nod my head and step inside, striding over to my purse and dropping my phone in. "So, what should I expect at the fundraiser?" I question, spinning on my heel to face him.

A gasp escapes me at his unexpectedly close proximity. "Let's talk about that later," he murmurs. "We have time," he reminds me. "Right now, I want my mouth on yours."

He weaves his left hand into my hair, firmly guiding my lips to his. He kisses me hard, his mouth moving over mine with urgency. He pushes his tongue into my mouth and begins exploring. I kiss him back, trying to get lost in the moment. His right hand drifts down my back and cups my ass, giving it a light squeeze. He pulls me into him and groans into my mouth. He walks me backwards until the back of my knees hit the black leather coach and I fall backwards. He follows, his lips never losing contact with mine, as he climbs on top of me. My body finally begins to heat, but I don't know if it's because he's covering me and I can barely breathe, or because I'm enjoying this. Am I? I attempt to stop questioning myself and focus on Preston.

"Fuck Amy," he moans. He slides his hand up my thigh. My breath instantly becomes erratic, while my heart beats rapidly; feeling like it's on the verge of losing control. "I want you," he murmurs. His hand inches closer to my core and I suddenly feel like the world is closing in on me. I rip my lips away from his and turn my head to the side, away from his hand holding me to his lips. Attempting to catch my breath, I stare blankly at the couch cushion. His mouth begins descending towards my chest.

I exhale harshly and plant my hands on his chest, gently pushing him back. "Preston," I rasp.

"Hmm," he murmurs, continuing to maneuver his way down my body.

I push him harder, desperate for him to listen to me. "Preston," I state, with much more force.

He immediately stops and his body tenses at my tone. He slowly lifts himself up and holds his body over mine. He finally lifts his gaze to my eyes and prompts, "Yes?"

I open my mouth to respond, but I quickly snap it shut. I gulp down the lump in my throat and take a deep breath, exhaling slowly. I look him in the eyes, needing him to understand what I'm saying. "This is too much, too fast," I mutter. A flash of hurt and something else I can't quite decipher passes through his eyes. The look alone increases my anxiety, as questions race through my mind. Confusion engulfs me, not knowing why I even said that. The words fell from my lips without my consent. I don't think I've said those words since middle school. I always had a boyfriend or I had Matt. My heart begins to race and I struggle to hear his reply over the vigorous pounding of my heart.

Glancing away from me, he composes himself before answering. "Whatever you need, Amy. I'll be here waiting," he mumbles. He pastes a smile on his face and gently kisses my lips. He pushes up, momentarily hovering over me, before he kisses me one more time. Sighing heavily, he sits up, pulling me with him. He glances down at me, his disappointment evident.

"I'm sorry, Preston," I grumble, a nauseous feeling taking over my stomach.

He shakes his head and forces another smile. "Don't be. I can wait," he claims. "You're worth it, Amy."

His sweet comments only succeed in making me feel worse. The further he pushes, the more this overwhelming sense of guilt overpowers me, clawing at me from the inside, out. "I should go," I mumble.

"You don't have to," he murmurs.

I nod my head and claim, "Yeah, I do." I stand up and grab my purse, slipping it over my shoulder. He follows me to the door. Forcing myself to stop and turn around to face him, I look up into his eyes. "I'm sorry," I repeat.

Ignoring my comment, his lips crash into mine. He moves his lips over mine in a possessive kiss. Abruptly releasing me he complains, "I have to go take a cold shower." He smacks my ass, as he nudges me towards the door.

"I'll see you tomorrow," I reply. The door closes behind me and I exhale slowly, feeling my body relax more with every step I take. "What am I doing?" I mutter to myself. I shake my head in frustration. Disheartened with everything I do or say, I turn towards the stairs. Maybe the exercise will do me good. I grimace and allow my shoulders to sag in defeat. I need to just go home and get some sleep. Maybe then I'll be able to think straight, without Matt clouding my judgment.

Chapter 15

Matt

Pulling my thin gray long-sleeved shirt over my head, I stride out to the living room. I grasp my phone, tugging it out of my pocket as I sit down on the couch. I quickly scan through my emails, making sure I don't have anything I should deal with right away this morning. Just as I close my email, a text pops up from my dad, but I ignore it, not ready to deal with them yet. Then again, I don't know if I'll ever be.

Despite my intentions and my determination, my thoughts inevitably drift to Amy. I really don't understand what it is about that guy. It makes me wonder if it's more about me, or my reputation because of my family. My curiosity takes hold and I hesitate for only a moment before I open one of my social media accounts and search for Preston Kirst. Several pop up for the man I'm searching for, including one with Kirst Marketing, his personal page and even several fan pages because I guess that asshole needs a bigger ego than he already has. His personal page is marked public, so I tap on it. An image of him kissing Amy has me seeing red. My body instantly heats, my stomach knots and my jaw clenches, as anger, rejection and betrayal consume me. I know we've always been casual and she said that's what she still wanted even with me fighting for more, but after the night we had, I never believed she would turn around and do this. Maybe she's as heartless as everyone always warned me. I flinch at my own thoughts, refusing to believe it, knowing I'm just pissed. I read the simple caption, "Enjoying a quiet night at home with my woman."

Standing, I yell, "Fuck!" I pivot back towards the couch and slam my phone onto it, like I'm at the pitcher's mound. Before I have a chance to react, it bounces off the cushion and onto the floor, smashing the screen. I heave a heavy sigh and drop my head to my chest in defeat. When will I ever learn? A knock on my door pulls me out of my dark thoughts before they have a chance to take over. Trudging to the front door, I yank it open.

Vanessa stands on my front porch wearing navy blue leggings with a simple pale grey, long sleeved, V-neck t-shirt. She has her hair pulled up in a high ponytail, with no trace of make-up on her smooth skin. She stares at me as if she's about to spin on her heel and flee. "Um...hi...ah...we can do this another time. I can go by myself. It's no big deal," she stammers, adorably.

Knowing she probably heard my minor freak-out, I force myself to relax, attempting to calm her anxiety. I smile and shake my head, "Nah, I'm almost ready." I take a step back into my living room and glare at my phone. Turning around and strutting right back for the door, I grumble, "Forget it, I'm ready now."

She glances past me, her eyes sweeping over the broken pieces of my phone. She arches her eyebrows in question, "Rough morning?"

"You could say that," I concede, grimacing. I exhale harshly and mumble, "Let's just get out of here. I need this," I add.

She nods her head in acknowledgement and turns, walking out the door, with me on her heels. She gets to the bottom of my driveway before she hesitates and prompts, "So, which way do we go for the trails?"

Nodding my head, I advise, "There's an entrance about a quarter mile up on the right side of the road."

Jogging slowly as we approach the trail, I easily get lost in thought, the thumping of our feet pounding the pavement lulling me into a peaceful rhythm. I turn and begin picking up my pace, but Vanessa meets me nearly stride for stride. "So, what happened to your phone?"

Reflexively clenching my jaw, I grumble, "It's not a baseball."

A laugh slips out before she can stop it and I attempt to ignore it. "Sorry," she mutters.

I shrug and pick up our pace again as we run on the dirt trail between the trees. "As you already know, I thought there was finally a chance with Amy, my ex, but her head wasn't in the same place as mine. Apparently, she moved on pretty quickly after our talk the other night and she's now dating that asshole we saw her with last night," I enlighten her.

"Apparently?" she prompts.

I shrug my shoulders and reply, "He put something up on social media."

She smirks, "Don't you know, you can't always believe what you see on social media?"

I nod my head sadly in defeat, "Yeah, but her words the other night packed the punch, this just sealed the deal."

She nods her head in understanding, not sounding out of breath, so I increase our pace again. "My ex and I broke up because he wanted to take a break, but he still expected me to be around, while he was out doing whatever and whomever he wanted. I'm not doing that," she blurts out, shaking her head defiantly. I notice the hitch in her breath, telling me there's a lot more to the story.

"You deserve better than that," I insist. A sudden wave of guilt washes over me at my words. Amy deserves better than that, yet that's what I've been giving her since we started this in high school. Maybe that's why she won't give me a chance.

"Yeah, I do, she whispers," her voice sounding haunted.

I glance at her out of the corner of my eyes, the look on her face looking a lot more like fear than betrayal or even defiance. I shake off the thought, knowing I don't have a right to even ask her those questions. "It seems we have more in common than I thought," I acknowledge.

She nods her head in agreement, not daring to glance in my direction. "Yeah," she pushes out between breaths, finally sounding slightly winded from our run.

Amy

Stepping through the back door of my parents' house, into the kitchen, I spot my mom standing at the stove with a spatula, and paste a smile on my face. "Hi, Mom," I mumble, announcing with mock glee, "I'm here."

She glances in my direction, her eyes narrowed, assessing me, but I'm not sure why. My stomach begins churning, wondering what this is all about. "Why don't you get everyone something to drink," she suggests.

"Okay," I mumble, dragging out the word. I do as she says, knowing it's more of an order than a request.

"How are things going?" Mom asks.

I shrug my shoulders and murmur, "Fine."

She pinches her lips tightly together and probes, "Do you have something you want to share?" I shake my head slowly and walk over to her by the stove. She grabs a plate and begins dishing food, some type of chicken, carrots and wild rice. I take two plates and walk them over to the table, setting them down for my dad and me before going back for hers. Just as I reach for her plate, she grasps my wrist tightly, halting me in my tracks, her sudden movement causing water from the stove to splash up on the back of my hand. I inhale sharply and bite the inside of my cheek, refusing to even flinch from the pain. She gets in my face looking intently into my eyes, as if trying to read every bad thought I've ever had, causing my heart to beat out of control. "What did you do?" she whispers accusingly.

I shake my head, feeling panicked and confused. Suddenly her grip loosens and her features soften as my father steps into the room. "Hi, Amy! How was your day?" he questions, obviously happy to see me.

I take a deep breath and quickly make my way to the sink, not yet ready to look at him. "Hi, Daddy," I greet him, clearing my throat. I turn cool water on and stick my hand underneath, letting the water run over the small burn. "Sorry, I accidentally splashed some hot water on my hand," I explain, trying not to cry.

"Are you alright?" he asks, taking a step toward me.

I put my free hand up to stop him, nodding vigorously, "I'm fine," I murmur. "Please, sit, eat," I encourage. "I'm just going to run it under the cool water for a minute and then I'll join you." He nods reluctantly, but moves to sit down.

A few minutes later, I'm finally sitting at the table with them. I pick up my fork and push my food around on the plate. "Are you alright?" my mom prompts, as if she truly cares.

"I'm fine," I mumble, knowing she hates that word.

She grimaces. "Then why are you so sad? Did you get into a fight with your boyfriend or something? Treat him right," she urges, pretending to tease.

"He better treat you right," dad grumbles, authoritatively.

My heart soars in response, but I quickly push it away and focus on the conversation. Puzzled, I shake my head and question, "What boyfriend?"

Mom grins from ear to ear and proudly announces, "Preston, of course." My eyebrows draw further down in confusion and she laughs in response. "Did you think you could keep it a secret from your family when you're dating one of the most eligible bachelors in New England?" she challenges. "I have no idea why you wouldn't tell us," she rambles. I bite my tongue, stopping my rude retort, as my stomach suddenly feels like it's on a tilt-a-whirl. I open my mouth to argue when she slides a picture in front of me. I glance down, my eyes widening at the image of Preston and me kissing with the heading, "Most Eligible, No Longer Eligible" written in bold black letters. I take a deep breath and exhale slowly, attempting to regain my composure.

"Is everything alright?" dad probes.

Glancing at him, I smile at the concern in his eyes. "I'm fine, Dad."

"And Preston?" mom prods.

I force a smile and shrug my shoulders, not wanting to talk about it. "I don't know," I grumble.

Dad glances at his phone and then meets my gaze, his apology apparent. "I have to take this," he explains. I nod my head in understanding and watch him walk out of the room, tensing in anticipation of my mother's wrath.

"Did you ruin it already?" mom hisses, bringing my attention back to her.

"What? No!" I insist.

"You are dating him though, right?" she prompts. "You can't just run around with him being a whore," she accuses.

A gasp escapes my lips, but I don't know why it surprises me. She's never truly cared anyway. I just don't want to upset dad. "I..." I trail off, not wanting to have this discussion with her of all people. I've never hated anyone more than her.

"Well, you've been Matt's whore for all these years. I wouldn't put it past you," she grumbles.

My chair clatters to the ground, as I abruptly fly out of my seat. My fists clench at my sides, as I take a threatening step towards her. She flinches away, as if I were going to hit her. And maybe I was. I don't know.

"Amy!" dad yells, as he steps back into the room. My heart plummets to the pit of my stomach. Turning around slowly I meet his gaze with tears in my eyes. "What is going on?" he questions, demanding an answer.

Shaking my head, I insist, "I wasn't doing anything!" Then I spin on my heel and storm out, slamming the door behind me, before anyone can say another word.

I run up the stairs to my apartment, tripping on the step and scraping my knees. I push myself up and keep going. I can't do this anymore. I can't stay here. I don't know what I was thinking. I love my father, but I'll never survive living so close to her ever again. I don't understand why they're still together. Doesn't he know what she's really like?

I push through the door and slam it behind me, collapsing on my bed and curling up under the covers. My whole body aches, feeling as if my insides are attempting to claw their way out through my chest. I wipe the tears from my face, but they continue to fall. I pick up my phone and scroll to Matt's name, needing him more than anything. I tap on his number and then, swiftly hang up, knowing he won't answer my call, not now. It's not even fair of me to want him to talk to me.

I take a deep breath and exhale slowly, attempting to relax to no avail. There's only one other person I can call, but she doesn't know the whole story. She was my best friend growing up, yet I never confessed the deep dark secrets of my relationship with my mother to her.

She just thinks we don't get along. I was too embarrassed for her to see the whole truth and then I let my mother's advice with boys break down my relationship with Bree even further. I'm grateful she didn't give up on me, especially with how I treated her. I hate myself for what I did to her and Christian. I know it's no excuse, but I am my mother's daughter. It's time for me to change that, but I don't know how.

Chapter 16

Amy

"Amy! Hi!" Bree greets me cheerfully.

"Hey, Bree, how are you?" I prompt.

"I'm good. It's been crazy up here recently with all the fall colors almost in full effect. So many tourists, but that's good for us," she adds, referring to Christian's business with his brothers and sister. They have an adventure tourist company. They take people around to various places in the area and do things like river rafting, kayaking, skiing, hiking, camping, climbing and a bunch of other stuff at all different levels of difficulty, but since they know the area, they're able to take people around to do these things at a much safer level than doing it on your own.

"That's great," I mumble. "I love fall up there."

"Are you okay?" she prods. "You don't sound like yourself. You sound...off," she observes.

I heave a sigh and concede, "Not really."

Her voice instantly turns soft, full of concern, "What's wrong? What happened?"

I laugh humorlessly and admit, "A lot."

"Talk to me," she encourages.

"Well, where do I start?" I mutter, defeatedly. I guess I'll start with my job, since that's probably the one thing in my life that's going better than expected. Things are actually going pretty well there, I guess. "It's mostly fine, but I just got a really fantastic assignment this week with Preston from his dad for us to work on together. Have you heard of Diana Brooks?" I inquire.

"Yes! You've talked about her before and shared some of her designs on social media," she reminds me.

"Of course," I mumble at the reminder. "So, I get to work on a project to present to her with Preston. Plus, she has an upcoming fundraiser for a non-profit organization that helps struggling families with everything from building or refurbishing their home to providing them with all new wardrobes, as well as education and services to help them with careers and job placement," I ramble the now familiar information.

"Wow, that's really wonderful." She pauses before questioning, "Why is this a bad thing?"

I shake my head even though she can't see me. "It's not. It's great. It's just," I pause, attempting to come up with the right word, "interesting working with him."

"Interesting how?" she prods, pushing me.

"He likes me and normally I'd say that's a good thing. He's exactly the kind of guy I like," I say, not willing to make him look bad. "And I do like him," I confess.

"I don't understand what you're saying, Amy," Bree informs me.

"I know, I'm sorry. It's just Matt," I begin, taking a deep breath. "I feel guilty."

"Do you want to be with Matt?" she asks, softly.

"We got in a huge fight the other day and he's not even talking to me," I confess, ignoring her question. "I miss him," I reveal, knowing I won't say more than that. "But now that Preston put out there that we're dating, it's made things so much worse," I elaborate.

"What do you mean?" she probes.

"Preston and I were working late last night and he posted a picture of us on social media basically claiming me as his girlfriend. Between the two of us, our following is astronomical and the media picked it up and there are already articles about us out there. My mom and dad saw one of them and said something. My mom was elated," I grumble, shaking my head. "But you know how they feel about Matt. This just makes it so much worse. They've always wanted Matt out of my life and they think this is their ticket. My mom and I were already fighting about it. I think she's told the whole world her daughter is dating The Preston Kirst," I sarcastically proclaim. "She puts so much pressure on me. I hate her, Bree. She acts like everything's my fault and she even fucking burned my hand!" I yell. My eyes widen, realizing what I just said.

"Wait, what?" she interrupts, her anxiety increasing. "What do you mean she burned your hand?" she questions forcefully.

"It was an accident," I blurt out, still not prepared to have this conversation with her. I thought I could, but I can't. The extent of everything that's happened with my mom is too much to deal with right now. "I was arguing with her and she was at the stove and some water splashed on me. I get reckless and clumsy when I'm with her, she just makes me so mad," I attempt to explain.

"Are you sure that's all it is?" she prompts, sounding worried.

"I'm sure, Bree. My stress level is through the roof when I'm around my mother. I just can't deal with her. I don't know why I thought it was a good idea to move above the garage after not living here for over four years. I should've known better," I grumble.

She sighs and suggests, "Why don't you move in with Matt?"

I gasp at the thought. "What?"

"He would do anything for you Amy. You know he would," she encourages. "And you'd have your own room when you want it," she teases.

"I don't know…" I murmur, trailing off.

"I really don't know why you two aren't together. I think you guys belong together," she reiterates the same words she's repeated many times throughout the years.

This time, I flinch at those words, the same words Matt conveyed that caused our fight. I can't. He never used to think like this. My heart lurches painfully at the thought of life without him, but I can't go there. "Bree, I can't," I whimper.

She heaves a sigh and lets it slide. "Even so, you can still move in with him. You can visit your dad when you want and you wouldn't have to worry about them watching your every move or fighting with your mom all the time. Then you can look for a place when you figure out what you're going to do after this internship is over and you know where you're going to settle."

"True," I mumble.

"Besides, you do get clumsy when you fight with your mom," she reiterates in a softer tone, as if she's questioning the reason.

"You're right," I concur, "but Matt isn't even talking to me. He won't answer my calls or even any of my texts."

"What happened with you guys?" she asks. "You were great when we saw you over the weekend."

I sigh heavily and mumble, "It doesn't matter."

"It does, but if you don't want to tell me, that's fine. Why don't you just go over to his house and talk to him. He can't ignore you if you're standing in front of him," she proposes.

"He can," I argue.

"But if he knows you need help, he'll be there for you, Amy," she emphasizes. "Go talk to him, ask him for help," she urges. "I'd offer you a room, but Christian and I live too far away for you to commute to work."

I nod my head in agreement, even though she can't see me. "You're right," I concede. "I'll go talk to him, but I'm not making any promises," I add defiantly.

She chuckles and admits, "I wouldn't expect you to."

"Preston won't like it," I admit.

"Well, he'll deal with it if he really likes you. You need help and you've been friends with Matt your whole life. If he doesn't understand that, he's not the man for you," she advises.

I smirk, thinking about how close she is with Blake. Christian really struggled with it for a while, but he dealt with it for her. "Of course you would say that," I joke.

She laughs and insists, "Well, it's true!"

"Thanks, Bree," I murmur, appreciatively.

"Anytime. I love you, Amy."

"I love you too. I'll let you know what I decide," I tell her.

"Please," she begs.

"I'll talk to you later," I declare, wrapping up the call.

"Bye, Amy."

I disconnect the call, knowing she's right. One way or the other, I have to talk to Matt. I can't live like this anymore. I take a deep breath and exhale slowly. I pick up my phone, my finger hovering over his name again, but my fear of him not answering has me setting it right back down. Bree's right, I should just go over there. Maybe I'll talk to him tomorrow. I should give him a little more time to calm down first.

My phone pings, alerting me to a text and making my heart lurch with hope. I glance at the screen and sigh heavily at the sight of Preston's name. "Go out to dinner with me," he states. I hesitate, tempted to sit here and sulk. Another text comes through from him, "Please? I want to talk to you about the fundraiser next week."

I grimace and relent, "Okay."

"Great! Get ready. I'll be there in an hour," he informs me, not giving me much of a choice. I shove thoughts of my mom and Matt out of my head for now and push up off my bed to get ready. I don't have much time.

Matt

"Yeah, man, it's finally happening," I mutter, hardly able to believe it myself. "I closed on the deal this afternoon," I confirm.

"That's great, Matt!" Blake declares. "You've been working towards this for so long," he acknowledges. I feel a small sense of pride at his comment.

"Yeah, but I still have a shit-load of work to do before it's done," I mumble, reminding both him and myself.

"True, but this is like a whole new chapter now. This is what you've been working for," he adds, encouraging me.

I clear my throat, trying to get rid of the tightness in my chest. I'm finally building my dream. Fuck my family and everyone else. I've worked my ass off for this and I've gotten to this point on my own. I don't need any of them. "Since I already have the architect's plans, I started setting up appointments to meet with contractors next week," I reveal.

"Let me know if I can do anything to help," he offers.

"Thanks," I reply, grateful. "Are you and Liz coming down anytime soon?"

"I'd like to get down to see Aubrey, but my parents are actually heading up this way next weekend with Kari. Liz and my mom are going to do some stuff for the wedding and depending on what they're doing, Kari might be with my dad and me," he explains.

"How is everything going with Kari?" I ask. She's Blake's little sister that he didn't even know about until a few years ago. His parents even split up for a while because of it while we were in high school.

"She's good. She still loves school and she's really into gymnastics at the moment." He pauses, as if wanting to say something.

"Spit it out, Blake. I can tell you have something on your mind," I claim.

Sighing heavily, he admits, "I just wanted to know if you talked to Amy?"

I wince, just hearing her name. "Nope, she's busy working at Kirst and hanging out with Preston," I state, bitterly.

"Really?" he challenges.

Grinding my teeth, I take a deep breath and exhale slowly. "Yup," I confirm.

"She'd have time for you and to hear about this," he insists. "You haven't talked for almost a week," he stresses, making me flinch. I fucking know! I'm the one that's living without her and I miss her every damn day! Even when we were separated by state lines and over a three-hour drive, she was still in my life. We talked and texted all the time, but now...it hurts too much knowing she'll never be mine. I can't do that if I ever want to get over her. "You're the one that said..." he begins.

"I know what I said," I abruptly snap, interrupting him. My stomach instantly flips with regret. "I'm sorry," I murmur.

"I'm just saying, you may want to check in with her," he urges. "It's just, I talked to Bree the other day and she said..."

"Drop it, Blake!" I plead, forcefully interjecting.

"Fine," he relents, reluctantly, "for now."

Suddenly uneasy, I quickly end the call. "Blake, I gotta' go. Give Liz a hug for me," I request, smirking.

"Alright. Later, Matt and congratulations again," he reiterates.

"Thanks," I respond and tap the red button to end the call.

Dropping my phone on the coffee table with a loud thump, I let my head fall into my hands, slightly defeated. She's all I think about, no matter how hard I'm working and how hard I'm pushing myself, I can't get her out of my head. I wish I could, but I can't. I lift my head and swipe my phone off the table. I pull up Amy's name and stare at it momentarily. She's the first person I wanted to call when I closed this deal today. Momentarily hovering over her name, I grimace and pull up Vanessa's name instead. Besides the training sessions she scheduled this week, we ran together three times as well. We get along well and enjoy each other's company. She's beautiful, easy to talk to and she doesn't push me. I tap on her name and send her a text. "Want to join me for a celebratory drink?"

Dancing dots instantly appear on my phone, as she types her response. "What are we celebrating?"

Smirking, I reply, "You'll have to let me buy you a drink to find out."

"Fine," she replies, making me chuckle.

"Don't get too excited. I'll pick you up at 8?" I prod.

"I'll be at your place at eight. I'm still not telling you where I live," she claims.

Shaking my head in amusement, I tap the thumbs up response. Then I sit up and lean forward, glancing over the blueprints for Mindful Advantage Health and Fitness. I'm still playing around with the actual logo, but I did have something simple in mind. I'm just trying to decide if that's still what I want, knowing Amy helped me come up with it. I don't need to be reminded of her on a daily basis when she's not mine and unfortunately, that's not about to change no matter what I do or how I feel.

Chapter 17

Matt

I lean across the small wooden square bar table, staring attentively at Vanessa. She's wearing a simple fitted, dark green t-shirt and black skinny jeans, with short black leather boots. Her hair falls loosely over her shoulders and she quickly tucks it behind her ears as she looks up at me. "I have to ask," I begin, "there's something I just don't understand."

"Okay," she mumbles, anxiously, dragging out the word.

"You're incredibly fit, you keep up with me a lot of the time, you know what you need to be doing, you're not training for a marathon or triathlon or anything like that and you're self-motivated," I declare. "So why the hell are you paying me?" I give her a cocky smile and sit back in my chair. "Don't get me wrong, I'm sure there's more I can teach you," I wiggle my eyebrows flirtatiously. She giggles and shakes her head as if annoyed. "Plus, I could always use more money for my project. I'm not turning you away, but it's pretty obvious you don't need me, Vanessa."

She sighs heavily and bites her lower lip as she looks up at me from underneath her eyelashes, as if trying to decide what or how much she wants to tell me. "My ex-boyfriend was an asshole," she proclaims.

I chuckle and state, "I thought we already established that, explain."

"After we'd been dating for a while, he started putting me down all the time. He made sure I would do things his way..."

"What do you mean?" I interrupt.

She shakes her head, telling me she doesn't want to go there right now and I have to respect that. I'm not the kind of guy that pushes a woman to do something she doesn't want to do. "Sparing you the details, I just mean I ended up with a pretty poor self-image because of him," she confesses, her cheeks turning a deep shade of red.

My body heats with anger. I don't understand how anyone can treat people that way and with the way she's avoiding telling me any details, causes me to believe it's a lot worse than what she's insinuating. She drops her head and stares down at the table, causing me to wince. I reach out to her, placing two fingers underneath her chin, I gently tip her head up to meet my gaze. The raw emotion and vulnerability in her eyes eats away at me. "You're beautiful, Vanessa," I insist.

She smiles softly and nods her head in acknowledgement. Her Adam's apple bobs up and down as she swallows hard. "Thanks," she rasps.

"I mean it, you're beautiful," I repeat. She nods her head, struggling to look at me, but I won't let that slide. I'm going to help her regain her confidence. I stand up and place a gentle kiss on the top of her head. "Come here," I encourage, holding my hand out to her.

She glances at my hand and hesitates before reaching for it. I pull her up and cradle her face in my hands. "What are you doing, Matt?" she prompts.

I look into her eyes and repeat, "You're beautiful, Vanessa. That asshole was obviously a fucking clueless douchebag." She averts her gaze and wraps her hands around my wrists, gently tugging, as if attempting to pull me away. I tilt my head down, waiting until she looks at me again. "You're beautiful," I reiterate, emphasizing the words.

She gives me a familiar look I can't quite decipher; appreciation, pain. I tip my head down and press my lips to hers, kissing her. She opens her mouth, letting my tongue inside and kissing me back. It feels good, different, but good. I let one hand slip off her face and slide around her back, pulling her close to me, hoping to build more chemistry. I know we can get there if we try.

She falls back on her heels, tearing her lips away from mine as she looks up at me with wide eyes, surprised. "Matt," she begins.

I notice them out of the corner of my eye, just before he speaks, "Well, well, well, it looks like you two are having fun," Preston taunts, his arm slung around Amy's shoulders.

I glance at the girl from nearly all of my dreams as she stands in front of me, her piercing blue eyes filled with a range of emotions crashing into mine, causing my heart to skip a beat. I slowly release Vanessa, letting my hands fall to my sides as an overwhelming feeling of guilt suffuses me. I watch as his hands slides down her sides and he pulls her back to his chest, his arm possessively wrapping around her front and falling just under her breasts. I stand rigid, momentarily frozen, glaring at him.

"Hi, Matt," she whispers, timidly, surprising me. My eyebrows draw down in confusion as I look down at her, noticing dark circles under her sad eyes. Amy's not timid. I open my mouth to ask if she's okay, but Preston's devious chuckle, pulls my attention right back to him.

He smirks at me and mutters with displeasure, "It's you again. Every time I see you, you have a different woman you're fucking." Both women instantly heat in embarrassment.

I take a threatening step towards him. "Watch it, asshole," I warn.

He holds his hands up in surrender and proclaims, "I'm just stating facts." I grind my jaw in irritation, seething in anger with every second he stands in front of me, my fingers twitching, begging me to throw a punch, but I'm not letting this asshole drag me down. He quickly looks Vanessa up and down and taunts, "It's good to see you again, Nessa."

My eyes widen and my mouth drops slightly open, I'm confused and pissed and I want to take it out on this prick. I probe, "Excuse me?" I clench my fists at my sides, practically begging him to give me a reason to hit him.

"Come on Matt, we should go," Vanessa urges. I glance at her, her face suddenly pale and her eyes wide, pleading with me.

I glance down at Amy one more time, before I allow Vanessa to tug my arm and pull me towards the door, my eyes remaining focused on them, until the cool air smacks me in the face. "Fuck," I grumble, breathing out harshly. I feel Vanessa looking at me and I turn and face her. "I really fucking hate that asshole! It took everything in me not to punch that smirk off his face and it has nothing to do with her."

Her eyebrows nearly hit her hairline in obvious doubt, as she repeats, "Nothing?"

Chuckling humorlessly, I shrug, "Well, maybe a little bit."

She forces a laugh as we walk to my truck. "You and I are quite a pair, huh?" she prods.

I shrug my shoulders and question, "You want to tell me what that was all about?"

She quickly strides around to the other side of my truck, avoiding my gaze. "I don't know what you mean," she claims.

I climb in behind the wheel, just as she's buckling her seatbelt. I do the same and lean towards her, staring, waiting for her to meet my gaze. "How do you know Preston?" I prompt.

I watch as she takes a shaky breath and gulps down a lump in her throat. "Matt," she begins and then shakes her head. She closes her eyes and sighs in defeat.

Taking another breath, she requests, "Can we maybe get something to eat and go back to your place to talk?"

I give her a firm nod and start my truck. Just as I pull out onto the street, she blurts out, "Preston is my ex-boyfriend."

I gasp and slam on the brakes, grateful there's no one behind me, as we both jerk forward, our seatbelts doing their job. I struggle for air, as my heart sinks to the pit of my stomach. "Fuck!" I yell at the top of my lungs, slamming my fist on the steering wheel. Out of the corner of my eye, I realize Vanessa's whole body has gone rigid. I look over and she's pale as a ghost, her eyes as wide as saucers. I'm scaring her. I know better. I need to tread more carefully. I heave a sigh and quickly apologize. "Sorry, you just surprised me," I claim. She nods and I turn back to the road, anxious to get food and get back to my place for some fucking answers.

Amy

I'm wearing a long-sleeved, russet scooped-neck sweater, with a chocolate brown, knit, mini-skirt and knee-high matching chocolate brown boots. I thought it would be perfect for this cool fall evening, until Preston's eyes land on me, as I meet him in my driveway. His eyes instantly heat with lust as he steps out of his car. Stalking over to me, he wraps his arms around me and pulls me into him. I let my hands fall to his biceps, just before he covers my mouth with his, bending me backwards. He pulls back just enough to speak and groans, "What are you wearing?"

"Clothes," I answer, sarcastically.

He instantly smacks my ass, hard, startling me. "Ouch!" I complain.

"Don't test me," he warns.

He soothes the spot he just hit with one hand, while the other slips under my skirt. My body heats, confusing me, but I also know I'm uncomfortable. I attempt to push him back, but he holds tight. "Preston, we're in my driveway," I emphasize.

He squeezes the inside of my upper thigh and sighs in defeat. He drops his hand and pulls back. "If you don't want me to jump you in public, don't wear this," he stresses.

I grimace and glare at him, he rolls his eyes and guides me around to the passenger side of the car, opening the door for me. I slip inside and he closes the door, before jogging around the front of the car and slipping in behind the wheel. It doesn't take long before he parks his car at the bar. He climbs out and strides around to my side, helping me out.

We walk inside with Preston's arm wrapped possessively around me. He smirks and points to the tables over to the right, "Look who's here," he announces.

I turn in the direction he's pointing and inhale sharply, as Matt pulls the same woman I saw him with last week into him, tenderly cradling her face in his hands. He looks down at her with what appears to be adoration, just before he kisses her. My heart stops. "Let's go say, Hi," he proposes. He tugs me along, without giving me a chance to argue.

Preston says something I'm too numb to comprehend and they break their kiss. They turn to us and Matt's eyes meet mine. I see a flash of something, but I can't register anything except my own heartbreak. I don't have any right to feel this way. I practically pushed him into her arms. "Hi, Matt," I mumble. Not even hearing my own voice, I attempt to focus on my breathing. I stare at Matt, his fists clenched as he steps towards Preston in warning. I have to shake myself out of this daze and figure out what's going on before something happens, but the girl tugs Matt out the front door. I'm finally brought back to the present, as the door closes behind them.

My back is pressed up against Preston's front, as he kisses my neck and his thumb grazes the side of my breast. "Let's get that drink and go back to my place," he suggests. I spin around and look at Preston smiling down at me. He's handsome, smart, successful, rich and obviously wants me. Why am I trying so hard to avoid this with him when it's blatantly obvious Matt has moved on with her? I flinch and Preston's eyes narrow. "You still want him," he claims, glaring. "Are you jealous of her?" he probes, appearing irate.

I gulp down the lump in my throat and vigorously shake my head, wanting to calm his anger. "Nope," I insist, trying to convince us both. I push up on my toes and wrap my arms around his neck, pressing my lips to his. I thrust my tongue in his mouth, pushing the kiss deeper as he cups both of my butt cheeks and pulls me into his hard length. I force out a groan and push back from him. I flutter my eyelashes and paste a smile on my face. "Why don't we skip the drinks and just go back to your place," I suggest, arching my eyebrow in question. I'm never this hesitant. I need to do this and move forward before I change my mind.

He grins, salaciously and instantly spins me towards the door. "Let's go," he announces, blatantly pleased with my reaction.

Chapter 18

Matt

I sit down on the couch next to Vanessa, attempting to appear relaxed and approachable. I need her to talk to me. I can't believe Preston is her ex-boyfriend. After everything she's already told me, which really isn't much, it still makes my stomach twist with anxiety just thinking about the thought of Amy with him. I know I'm pissed she doesn't want to be with me, but I can't let anything happen to her. That would kill me. My foot begins tapping nervously and I bite the inside of my cheek, trying to remain patient, while she gathers courage to speak.

She closes her eyes and takes a deep breath in, before she exhales slowly and opens her eyes, glancing at me. "I'm sorry, this is just really hard for me to talk about," she admits. "I saw him with her the night we ran into each other at the café, but even after your comments about them, I was hoping she was just a fling to him, since it's obvious she means a lot to you."

"Vanessa," I begin, not quite sure what to say. She's right. I'm not about to deny it. I'd do anything for Amy. I just don't want to hurt Vanessa.

She immediately interrupts me, "Don't worry about it. We're both trying to get over past relationships. I'm okay with that. I don't even know what we are, if anything at all, but I don't want anyone else to go through what I went through with him," she confesses. "No one deserves that," she whispers, her voice barely audible.

My chest tightens, making it difficult to breathe. "Shit," I grumble under my breath, my anxiety skyrocketing.

"He started out as a good boyfriend. We went out a lot, he was caring and attentive, but we spent a lot of time with his family, his friends, his work functions, or it would be just us. It was never my family or friends," she emphasizes. "He started buying me lots of gifts, including clothes he expected me to wear. It was nice at first because I didn't have the types of things I needed to go to some of his functions with him, but then things started to change." She pauses, pulling her knees up to her chest and wrapping her arms protectively around them. She rests her chin on her knee, avoiding my gaze.

"Are you okay?" I prompt.

Her Adam's apple bobs up and down as she gulps hard and nods her head automatically. I lean forward, resting my elbows on my knees and clasping my hands tightly together between them, anticipating her confession. "At first it didn't seem like a big deal, he'd tell me my clothes weren't appropriate for where we were going, then it became more accusatory and degrading. He eventually started calling me names, telling me I'm stupid and I'm lucky to have him, or I'd never make it anywhere if it weren't for him. He told me I started gaining weight after dating him and I can't just stop giving a shit about what I look like. He told me I was getting fat and he had me work with his trainer. When I would eat something he didn't approve of, he'd tell me I shouldn't eat like that and compare me to some model-like woman nearby. He started telling me what I should say when we were in public, but again, they were his family, his friends and his business associates, so what did I know?"

I angrily grunt, "Van..."

She holds her hand up, stopping me. "Let me get this out and then you can say whatever the hell you want," she rasps, a tear slipping down her cheek.

I feel like I already know where this is going and I don't know what to do with myself. I'm on edge, shaking, and completely on fire. The more she talks, the more I know this is going to get worse and I'm going to lose my shit. "Okay," I relent, forcing the word out.

She sighs, holding herself a little tighter. She closes her eyes, her agony written all over her face, as she speaks. "When I would do something my way instead of his, he got pissed," she emphasizes. "At first he just got aggressive and I would end up getting hurt, but it was my fault."

"That's bullshit!" I yell, unable to control myself.

"Please, Matt," she begs for me to stop. I'm breathing heavily, feeling as if my world is closing in on me, but I concede, needing to know every single detail.

"I started with bruises and I hit my head a few times, falling backwards, but that was nothing compared to when I would fuck up when he was drinking," she states, sounding hollow. "He...He was so mad at me one night at one of his events. He had been drinking and he thought...he thought I was flirting with this man and he wanted to...to punish me," she stutters on a choked sob.

I stand up, my whole body vibrating in anger and searching for an outlet. I grab a glass still sitting on the table. "Fuck!" I scream. I throw it across the room, like a baseball, letting it shatter against the wall. Vanessa flinches at my action, her eyes wide with fear, afraid of me. I close my eyes and sigh in defeat, feeling overwhelmed with emotion. "Shit, I'm sorry, Vanessa," I ramble. "I would never hurt you. I'm pissed because someone did. I swear," I plead, begging for her to believe me. I cautiously sit down next to her. "I just..."

She shakes her head and whimpers, "It's okay, it's fine, I'm fine," with tears streaming down her face.

I shake my head and insist, "No, it's not. I'm sorry. I'm so fucking sorry." She nods her head, her body seeming so small, curled up in a ball and shaking. I move behind her and begin to wrap my arms around her in comfort, but suddenly hesitate, realizing she might not want that from me. "Is it okay if I wrap my arms around you?"

"Yes," she rasps between breaths, gutting me with her sobs.

I wrap her in my arms, pulling her back to my chest. I hold her, attempting to calm her breathing, as my own becomes more and more erratic. When she calms, I attempt to ask her one of the questions that's eating at my soul. "Did he ever...did he ever force himself on you?" I'm dizzy, holding my breath and awaiting her answer.

She begins crying harder and shakes her head, "Matt, I can't. I signed, I can't. I just can't," she keeps repeating the same words over and over again, causing me to assume the worst.

"Did you ever report him?"

"I just can't, you don't understand, I can't," she reiterates, nearly hyperventilating with clear panic. "I had no chance, I just had to get away. I can't. It was my only way out."

"You have to say something," I beg, desperate.

She pushes her way out of my arms and looks at me for the first time. "No!" she screams, forcefully. Her face is red and blotchy, streaked with tears, still streaming down her face. "You can't tell anyone! Not even her! I wasn't supposed to tell you! Please," she pleads.

My whole body aches, feeling her pain. At the same time, I've never been more livid and terrified in my entire life. I have to get Amy away from him. What the fuck am I going to do? She'll never listen to me, especially now, and when I can't even tell her the truth? This whole situation

149

is fucked. "Okay, Okay," I momentarily placate her, attempting to get everything straight in my head. I pull her back into my arms and hold her. She leans into me and cries on my chest, while living nightmares run through my head on a repetitive reel, taunting me. What the fuck am I going to do?

Amy

The moment we step into Preston's apartment, he pushes me up against the wall and kisses me. I place my hand on his chest and attempt to push him back enough to breathe. "Can I have something to drink first?" I request.

He sighs heavily and pushes off the wall, moving away from me. "Sure," he mumbles. He turns and strides for a cabinet in the corner, where he keeps all his alcohol. "What would you like?" he questions.

I grimace, feeling like I need a little bit of liquid courage or something to dull the ache in my chest. "Maybe a shot of bourbon?" I ask, uncertainly.

He arches his eyebrows and chuckles in response. "That's what you want?" he clarifies. I shrug my shoulders and he shakes his head in amusement. He grabs two low-ball glasses and a brown bottle, pouring some in each. He sets the bottle down and returns to me, with a glass in each hand. He holds one out to me with a crooked grin.

I take the glass and mumble, "Thanks."

He holds his own glass up in a toast, "To finally getting everything we want."

I clink his glass and he downs what looks more like a double shot, before setting his empty glass down on the table and nodding in my direction to do the same. I tip my glass back and swallow it down, the alcohol burning my throat. I reflexively scrunch my face up and mutter, "Ack."

He chuckles and takes my glass from me, setting it down on the table. "Now where were we?" he prods. One hand goes to the back of my neck as his other hand falls to the top of my ass. He pulls me into him, as his lips crash into mine. I kiss him back, feeling like I need something to make me feel good again. I need this.

He pulls his mouth away and tips my head back, kissing and licking his way down my neck, as he slides his other hand up under my sweater and cups my breast. He pulls back and nearly rips my sweater over my head, his eyes filled with lust. He moves one hand back, flicking the clasp open and pushing it away before backing me up to the couch. He starts to unbutton his shirt as his eyes greedily take me in. I feel a sudden wave of unease go through me, as he throws his shirt on the floor and lies down on top of me. He begins kneading my breast, his thumb brushing over my nipple, bringing it to a taut peak as he kisses a path down my neck.

I moan into the kiss, allowing my hands to roam. Matt suddenly pushes his way into my thoughts, taking me by surprise. I jut my tongue out as Preston kisses me harder, while images of Matt kissing her shove their way closer to the forefront of my mind with each kiss, making my stomach turn. My head spins as I struggle, but I'm not able to push Matt from my thoughts. Breathily, I prompt, "Um, Preston?"

"Hmm?" he groans, continuing down his path.

Questions suddenly flood my mind and I need answers now. "How do you know the girl Matt was with tonight?"

I feel him tense above me, as he momentarily hesitates. "She's my ex-girlfriend," he enlightens me, before continuing to kiss me.

"Why did you break up?" I probe.

He groans in irritation and flicks his tongue over my nipple before replying, "It doesn't matter. Relax." He slides one hand under my short skirt to my inner thigh, tracing the edges of my thong. "I'm loving this skirt," he claims, attempting to pull me back into the moment. "You're so gorgeous."

I pause, but I can't get out of my own head. "It does matter," I repeat. He drops his head between my breasts and groans in frustration, one hand tightening on my thigh and the other on my breast, his thumbs digging in. "Ouch, Preston, that hurts!"

He groans again, pushing off me and I flinch back into the couch, covering myself with my hands. He glares down at me and blurts out, "She's a bitch. I found out she only dated me for my money and then she spread a bunch of lies about me when we broke up, trying to make herself look good."

"Lies?" I repeat.

"Lies," he reiterates, not giving me any more. "Are we really going to talk about this right now?" he asks, exasperated. "I thought you were over him. Why should it matter to you who he's with?" he challenges.

"I am over him," I proclaim, my heart skipping a beat with my false statement.

"Well, it sure doesn't fucking feel like it. You're treating me like a fucking yo-yo and I don't fucking deserve that!" he spits out at me.

"I'm sorry. That's not...I'm sorry," I repeat. "You're right. I'm sorry."

He shakes his head in disappointment. Then he leans over, snagging my sweater and bra off the floor and throwing them at me. I pull them to my chest and stare at him, my stomach churning. He's right. "Put your clothes on," he instructs, grabbing his own shirt off the floor and

152

striding for his bathroom. "Since you already ruined our night, I'm going to take a cold shower, and then I'll take you home," he informs me, not giving me a chance to argue.

The bathroom door slams shut, making me jump. "I'm such an idiot," I mumble to myself, dropping my head into my hands. Why would I let Matt and that girl take over my head when I'm with someone else? What the hell is wrong with me? I need to suck it up, put on my big girl panties and go talk to him or I'm never going to be able to move on with my life. I can't move in with him, but I need to make peace with him. I'm not willing to let him go completely. We can be with other people and still be friends. Him and Bree are the only ones who have always been there for me and she lives over three hours away. Maybe it's been long enough that he'll finally talk to me again. I hope so. I need someone in my corner. Plus, I should warn him about the girl he's dating. I hate the thought of someone taking advantage of him.

Chapter 19

Amy

I force myself to get out of my car and walk up to his front door. My stomach twists into knots and I have to focus on slowing my breaths. I've never been this nervous to see Matt before, but I honestly don't know if he'll even talk to me. He still hasn't answered any of my calls or texts. I stand in front of his door and raise my hand to knock, but freeze, uncertain. Maybe I should go home and try calling him again first. He might even be at the gym, why am I already worrying when I'm not even sure if he's inside. I close my eyes and exhale slowly, letting my hand fall on the wood, reluctantly and then harder, before I take a step back and wait anxiously.

I hear his footsteps, just before he pulls the door open and gasps at the sight of me. "Amy," he whispers my name, causing my breath to catch in my throat. He's dressed in white net shorts and a black t-shirt, pulled tight around the firm muscles of his shoulders and biceps.

I gulp down the lump in my throat and paste a smile on my face. "Hi, Matt," I mumble.

"What are you doing here?" he prompts, making me flinch.

"Ah, I need to talk to you. Can I come in? Please," I request.

He hesitates, and I wince in response. Shifting his eyes behind him, before returning to me, he heaves a sigh, and relents, "Yeah, okay."

I breathe a sigh of relief as I step inside, brushing past him. I breathe in his fresh, clean scent, his familiar and comforting presence nearly slapping me in the face. I stride over to the couch and sit down on one end before my shaky legs defy me and give out. I take a deep breath and look up at him, slowly approaching. "I'm sorry I just barged in here, but you weren't answering any of my calls or texts," I begin in explanation.

He sighs sadly and lowers himself down on the other side of the couch, facing me. "What are you doing here, Amy?" he repeats, sounding desperate for my answer.

I honestly don't know where to begin. I should've thought more about what I wanted to say. "I miss you," I blurt out the truth.

His face softens and saddens at the same time. He runs his hand down his face, appearing exhausted. "Amy," he begins.

I quickly interrupt, knowing I need to say more. "Matt, I know I didn't handle things well between us and I regret that. You mean so much to me. I'm sorry," I apologize. He grimaces, but doesn't comment. "I know that might not be enough, but I am sorry," I emphasize.

He nods his head and meets my gaze, his own eyes sad and haunted. "I know," he rasps, his voice gravelly.

I clasp my hands together and begin fidgeting, looking down at my hands as I start to talk. "There's just been so much going on lately, Matt. I'm trying to figure out what I'm doing with my life. My job is keeping me so busy and even though I thought I'd hate everything about it, I'm excited now that I'm working on this project for Diana Brooks. She's absolutely amazing! I'd work with her every day if I could," I admit. "Plus, I knew living above my parents' garage wouldn't be easy, but being so close to my mom every day and having her scrutinizing everything I do," I shake my head and scrunch my nose up in distaste, "it's torture," I conclude, vaguely. I need to tell him more about my mom, but I don't know if I'm ready for that yet.

"I don't understand what any of this has to do with me," he proclaims, making me cringe.

I look up and meet his gaze. I stare into his eyes, my body filling with warmth, calming me. Maybe I can ask him for help. Maybe I can stay here with him. Maybe I can be with him and get away from my mom at the same time. Maybe I can have it all. My heart begins racing and tears well in my eyes. I gulp down the lump in my throat and take a deep breath, still holding his gaze. "I don't want to do this without you," I confess, shocking myself.

His eyes widen at my admission. "What?" he prods. "What do you mean by that?" He stares intently at me, pleading with me for answers, his eyes flickering with hope. "You made it clear I wasn't what you wanted," he states, his hurt obvious. "What about Preston?" he probes, saying his name with apparent disgust.

I shake my head, knowing it's time to admit the truth to both of us. I open my mouth to respond when I suddenly catch movement out of the corner of my eye, just over his shoulder. I lift my gaze and my heart instantly sinks into the pit of my stomach at the sight. The same girl from last night steps into the room with wide eyes, nearly drowning in one of Matt's faded navy-blue t-shirts with Red Sox written in red over her chest and her ass sticking out of her lacy black underwear, and her hair messy from sleep. Feeling as if Matt personally reached into my chest and crushed my heart with his bare hands, I gasp for breath. I look down at my lap and take a deep breath, exhaling slowly.

"Amy," Matt prods. "Are you alright?"

I don't respond. I can't even gather the strength to lift my head and look at him. "Um, Matt," she mumbles.

He turns to face her, "Vanessa," he murmurs her name, making me nauseous. I'm too late. I know I have no right, but my body doesn't seem to care. They exchange a few words, but I don't register any of them, before she spins on her heel and strides back down the hallway towards the bedrooms. "Amy," he calls, trying to get my attention.

I finally lift my gaze back to his, feeling numb. "Ah, yeah, Preston, he's fine. He's the one that suggested I should get closure with you before we try to move on," I claim.

He rears as if I slapped him. "Closure?" he reiterates through narrowed eyes.

"Yeah. I care about you Matt and I hate that we haven't been talking," I insist, knowing I'm not giving him the whole truth.

"Preston is not a good man, Amy. You need to stay away from him," he warns.

"Excuse me?" I question.

"Vanessa was telling me," he begins.

I shake my head in denial. "Vanessa," I repeat.

"Yeah," he mumbles, gesturing down the hallway.

I shake my head and clench my fists in irritation, instantly hating her name. "You shouldn't listen to anything she has to say. She lies," I emphasize. "Preston has been good to me. He's been patient," I state, wanting to make him mad.

He scoots closer to me and reaches out, with pity in his eyes. "Amy," he rasps.

I flinch away from him as if he burned me with his touch. "Don't," I warn. She's in his bed right now, wearing his clothes and he dares to reach for me? To touch me? I know I'm being irrational, but I can't think any other way in this moment. It hurts too much seeing her here, especially when I'm sitting here open and vulnerable, asking for his forgiveness and telling him I need him. How dare he.

He grinds his teeth in frustration and insists, "Preston is dangerous. I don't want anything to happen to you."

I huff a humorless laugh and blurt out, "What? She told you that?" I ask bitterly.

"Yes, she did," he confirms, "and I believe her."

"Of course you do, you're sleeping with her," I mutter under my breath.

"What?" he asks, but I shake my head in response. "This is what you wanted!" he angrily reminds me.

I shake my head in refusal, "No, I never wanted you out of my life!"

"No, you just wanted to use me for sex," he retorts.

"That's not true!" I scream, fighting my tears.

He drops his head into his hands, appearing defeated and whispers my name, "Amy." I glance down the empty hallway and my chest tightens, making it difficult to breathe. "I know I said it's hard to talk to you all the time, but I don't want anything to happen to you. I don't think you should be anywhere near that guy," he gently murmurs.

I nod my head in understanding, my whole body aching, and feeling lost. "Well, I guess it's good you don't have a say in it anymore then, huh?" I retort. I stand up on shaky legs, determined to get out of here before my tears start to fall. "I gotta' go," I grumble.

I stumble towards the door and Matt reaches for my arm, searing me with his touch and helping me maintain my balance. I right myself and quickly shake him off. "Just please be careful," he begs.

"I can take care of myself," I maintain.

"Amy, please, promise me you'll be careful!" he reiterates, stepping into my space.

I look up at him, my heart beating out of control and nod my head in agreement. "Sure," I softly concur.

He relaxes just a little and releases my arm, chills slamming into me at the loss of contact. "Thanks," he responds. "I'm always here if you need me," he emphasizes.

I nod my head and tear myself away from his gaze. I pull his front door open and rush out to my car without looking back. I back out of the driveway and pull onto the street before my tears start to fall, nearly blinding me. "I guess this is how it's supposed to be," I mumble to myself, concentrating on getting home safe.

Matt

"Fuck!" I yell, slamming the door behind her. I fall back against the door and close my eyes in defeat. For just a moment I thought she was telling me she made a mistake and wants to be together, but I was obviously wrong. She's still dating that asshole. I can't believe she doesn't believe me. Is Preston the one telling her Vanessa is lying or was it just jealousy? I shake my head, knowing it doesn't matter. Either way, he still has a hold on her and that scares the shit out of me. I can't let anything happen to her, but how the fuck do I stop it?

"Are you okay?" Vanessa hesitantly whispers, pulling me out of my thoughts.

I give her a fake smile and nod my head, "Yeah, I'm fine." She arches her eyebrows in challenge and I shrug in response.

"Did you tell her?" she questions.

I nod, "Sort of."

"Sort of?" she repeats.

I heave a sigh and push off the door, sauntering back towards the couch and flopping down. "Yeah, I said he was dangerous. I didn't want to tell her anything that might cause you problems, but she doesn't believe me. She said you were lying," I reveal.

Vanessa grimaces and mutters, "Preston."

I look at her in question and for the first time, I realize what she's wearing, making me groan in frustration. "What?"

I run my hand through my hair and sigh, knowing Amy immediately jumped to conclusions about us and in the past, she'd probably be right, but not this time. In fact, after Vanessa finally fell asleep, I spent most of the night worrying about Amy and how I was going to tell her. I just fucked that all up. It's not Vanessa's fault. "How are you feeling?" I question, changing the subject.

She stares at me for a moment before answering, "Better, I guess."

"Good," I reply, nodding my head.

"Do you want to go after her?" she asks softly.

I shake my head, denying myself, knowing there's no point. "Nah, she won't believe a word I say right now. I have to figure out how to get her to believe me."

"Let me know if I can help," she offers.

"Thanks," I murmur, grateful.

She walks around the back of the couch and sits down in front of me. She looks up at me from underneath her long lashes. "Thank you for letting me crash in your room last night."

I smirk and remind her, "You passed out in my arms. Did you want me to throw you out on the street?"

She shakes her head and inquires, "Where did you sleep anyway?"

"After you passed out, I slipped out here and slept on the couch. I don't think either of us are ready for anything," I answer honestly.

She nods her head in understanding, her lips pressed into a firm line. "You're a good guy, Matt."

"Don't tell anyone," I joke.

She rolls her eyes and sighs. "Maybe we can try another date?" she pushes.

I look down at her, her gaze hopeful, but I'm not sure if it's because it's me or because I'm not anything like him. I place my fingers gently under her chin and tilt her head up to mine. I lean down and press my lips to hers in a sweet kiss, intending to give her comfort, before I pull back. "I'm going to jump in the shower. Help yourself to whatever in the kitchen if you're hungry," I offer, without answering her question.

"Thanks," she murmurs, giving me a sad smile.

I stand up and stride down the hallway towards my bathroom. I'm more confused than ever about Amy. I don't believe she came here for closure. Our whole conversation had a different feel until Vanessa walked out in my clothes. I know exactly what she thought, but I wasn't about to have that conversation with her when she's already shattered me. I can't do that again. But did she lie to me because of it? I don't fucking know. I turn on the hot water and quickly strip down, feeling both emotionally and physically drained, yet I haven't done much of anything so far today. I step under the hot water and close my eyes. I have to figure out a way to keep Preston as far away from her as possible, but how do I do that without talking to her and breaking my own heart all over again?

Chapter 20

Amy

I park my car next to the garage and look around. Preston's car is parked at the curb, with no sign of him. There's no light on above the garage and the light by the steps shows me he's not waiting there either. I grimace, glancing at my mom and dad's house. "Great," I grumble. I flip the visor above my head down and glance in the mirror. I wipe my face, attempting to wipe away my tears. I reach for my purse and quickly touch up my make-up not wanting any of them to see me like this. I take a deep breath and exhale slowly before forcing myself to step out of my car. I trudge up the driveway to the back door. I place my hand on the handle and take one more deep breath, anxious about what I might walk into.

I step inside and paste a smile on my face as two heads swivel focusing on me. "It's about time you got home," my mom states firmly. "Where were you?" she challenges.

I bite the inside of my cheek, refusing to let her get to me after the night I've endured. "I stopped at a friend's," I reveal vaguely.

She stands up from the table and pats Preston on the shoulder as she approaches me. "Well, poor Preston here has been waiting for you for quite a while. Your father already went up to bed," she informs me. I nod stiffly and she continues, "He was hungry, so I gave him something to eat while he waited for you."

"Thanks," I mutter, irritably. I glance at Preston, not really ready to talk to him. "What are you doing here, Preston?" I question.

"Amy!" my mother scolds. I all but roll my eyes at her, maintaining my attention on him.

He clears his throat and stands, taking a step towards me. He smiles, his eyes optimistic as he approaches. "I was hoping we could talk," he begins.

"I don't know if tonight is a good time. It's late..." I claim.

He interrupts, "I know, but after I dropped you off, I went home and felt terrible. I turned right back around to talk to you, but you weren't here. I tried to call and text, but you didn't respond," he explains, making me grimace. I haven't bothered even looking at my phone since I got to Matt's earlier. "Your mom found me out front and insisted I come in and have something to eat while I wait for you," he elaborates, reminding me of her presence.

I clench my jaw and glance in her direction, now on the other side of the counter, listening intently to our conversation. I may not want to deal with this right now, but having my mother listen to any of this makes it a million times worse. "Let's go over to my room and talk," I suggest, tilting my head towards the garage.

His smile grows, appearing more genuine, as he nods his head in agreement. "Perfect," he murmurs. He turns towards my mother and grins. "Thank you for the food and the company," he politely states.

"You're welcome, Preston. You're welcome here anytime," she emphasizes happily, irritating me further.

I turn towards the door and tense as Preston's hand falls to the small of my back, guiding me outside. He drops his hand as he silently follows me to my space. I open the door and turn on the light, while he closes the door behind us. I loop my purse on a hook by the door and kick off my shoes, waiting for him to speak, even though I feel like I owe him an apology.

"Are you going to even look at me?" he prompts.

I stop and turn to face him and mutter, "Sorry."

He closes the distance between us and looks down at me. "Listen, I'm sorry for being an asshole earlier." He reaches up and cradles my face in his hands, holding my gaze. "I'm frustrated because I really like you Amy and I feel like you've been back and forth with me and that's kind of a sore spot with me," he claims.

"What do you mean?" I prompt.

He rubs his thumbs along my jaw, and reluctantly admits, "Vanessa used to do that with me. In reality there were times she was cheating on me, but she didn't want me to know because she wanted me to think I was the only man in her life, knowing I won't spend the money on her if we weren't exclusive."

"That's not what I was doing," I insist.

"Well, what were you doing?" he challenges, looking into my eyes and searching for answers. "You seem extremely invested in someone you're not even dating, yet you're pushing me away and we're just getting started."

I grimace and he drops his hands to his sides in defeat. "I'm sorry," I repeat. I inhale, and attempt to explain everything as quickly as possible. "I've known Matt my whole life. He's always been one of my best friends and we watch out for each other." I shrug like it's no big deal.

"You see how that can be a problem for someone like me?" he asks.

I shake my head in denial and remind him, "Relationships are based on trust." That's what Bree has always told me. It's why her and Christian fell apart the first time. It's also why my relationship with her became difficult. She didn't trust me enough to really talk to me about him. Now Matt is doing the same thing and not trusting what I told him, but choosing to believe her instead. Maybe I should trust Preston and give him more of a chance. I don't know.

"And you trust him?" he prods. My stomach flips with anxiety and I don't answer. Usually I'd answer that question without any doubt, but right now, I don't know if I do. He shakes his head and mutters, "Don't answer that."

I shake my head and step towards him. I reach up, placing my hands on each side of his neck and lightly tug to get his attention. "I'm sorry I even brought him up before. I'm sorry I ruined our night earlier. I'm sorry Vanessa was horrible to you, but I'm not her," I emphasize.

"So, what do you want, Amy?" he questions. "Are you going to put a little more faith into me? Or are you going to focus on him?"

I shake my head, knowing Matt can't be my focus, not now. For my sake, and everyone else's, I need to focus on Preston, on us. "I'd like to give this a shot," I claim.

He nods his head, relief flashing through his eyes. He grins and crashes his lips into mine. I kiss him back with all I have, not wanting him to feel rejected again. I know what that feels like. He walks me over to my bed, kissing me until I fall back. He leans down, covering my body with his. His hand skims over my body and he groans in frustration. "I wish you were back sooner," he proclaims over my lips. Pulling back, he regretfully declares, "I don't want to leave, but I gotta' go." I scrunch my face up in displeasure and he laughs. "I know, but after this event is over, I'm not going to let you out of my bed for the rest of the weekend."

I nod in acknowledgement, internally grateful. My whole body is both physically and emotionally exhausted.

"I understand," I murmur, softly. He pushes into me, letting me feel him and I rasp his name, "Preston."

He chuckles and teases me, "Besides, you look like you don't have enough energy to handle me right now. I roll my eyes in response. He leans down and presses his lips to mine again, moving his mouth in a slow, patient rhythm, before rising and hovering over me, reluctant to leave. "Get some rest," he commands. "You're going to need it." He smirks, giving me a chaste kiss, before he pushes himself off the bed.

"Yes, Sir," I murmur, my eyes drifting closed before he even walks out the door. I hear the door close and fall asleep, without even bothering to change.

Matt

After working, I finished up my own workout, before leaving the gym. I walk outside, with Amy still on my mind. I would give almost anything for her to stay away from that asshole, but I don't know how to convince her it's the best thing without proof of him doing anything wrong. I tried searching last night and I didn't come up with anything damning, besides an array of different women on his arm. I did find several with Vanessa from last year, making me more anxious. I need to get her away from him before he has a chance to do anything to her. I feel it in my gut that she's telling me the truth about him.

My phone rings, interrupting my thoughts. I pull it out of my pocket and glance at my screen, seeing the name of the contractor I want to hire. "Matt Young," I answer.

"Hey, Matt. It's Dwayne Thompson. I wanted to see if you could make it a little early. Something came up with another project I already have going and I have a meeting I can't miss this afternoon," he states.

166

I glance at the time and grimace. "I'm just leaving the gym now. I have to stop home quick and I'll be over to your office," I propose.

He hesitates before agreeing, "You got it, but I may have to cut out early."

"Alright, I'll hurry," I reluctantly agree.

"Thanks, Matt, I'll see you soon."

I disconnect the call and reach for the handle of my truck when I hear yelling nearby. I turn around and immediately spot the source of the commotion across the street, a couple deep in their own world, yelling at each other. He's hovering over her, with his back to me and her back against the brick wall behind her. I can't tell who either of them are from this position, but in this town, I'd be surprised if I don't know them. I notice a few other people on the street looking on as he screams at her, "You did this, and you have no fucking right." He takes an intimidating step towards her and I instantly jog towards them, shoving my way into their business.

"Hey, everything okay?" I call out.

Both heads turn towards me and my stomach twists with anxiety at the sight of Vanessa and Preston, both red-faced and angry. "Matt," she rasps.

My eyes flick back and forth between the two of them, attempting to read the situation. "You okay?" I repeat.

She nods and Preston laughs humorlessly. "Why don't you tell your girlfriend to butt out of my life!" he retorts.

"Vanessa," I prod, cautiously, not making an attempt to correct his assumption.

"I don't want anything to do with your life, Preston!" she argues.

"That's not what you just said," he claims, arching his eyebrows in challenge.

She clenches her fists and screams at him in frustration. "That's not true! You're such an asshole!"

He shakes his head in annoyance and mutters, "Excuse me, I have better things to do." He pauses and glares down at her, causing me to take a protective step in her direction. He tips his head towards her opposite ear, and whispers something I can't hear, before taking a step back. She clenches her jaw and narrows her eyes at him. He glances at me and smirks, "And a better woman waiting on me."

I gulp hard and cross my arms over my chest, preventing myself from doing anything stupid. I seethe as I watch him walk away, before I dare glancing in Vanessa's direction. "What the fuck was that?" I mutter.

She shakes her head, obviously upset by their encounter. She closes her eyes and mumbles, "I don't want to talk about it."

"Vanessa," I begin.

She shakes her head, and pleads, "Please Matt? Will you just hang out with me for a while and maybe I'll talk about it later."

"I have a meeting I have to get to," I start to explain.

Her head drops in disappointment and she mumbles, "Oh, okay."

Guilt begins eating away at me. I know I can't walk away right now, leaving her to fend for herself after that. Plus, maybe she'll give me something I can use against him. I heave a sigh, hoping I don't regret this, but I'm probably never going to make it to his office on time now anyway. "Come back with me to my place, so I can shower and then we'll hang out," I suggest.

She breathes a sigh of relief and turns to me with a smile. "Thank you."

"I'll meet you there?" I ask, assuming her car is around here somewhere.

She nods in agreement, "My car is just around the corner."

I nod, staring at her for another moment, still trying to figure out what they were arguing about, but I have no fucking clue. "Okay," I mutter. I stalk towards my truck, pulling my phone back out of my pocket. I dial and wait for him to answer. "Hey Dwayne, sorry, but I'm never going to make it there in time. Can we reschedule for any other day?" I question and wait to confirm a new appointment. I want this guy to build the gym, another day or two shouldn't matter.

Chapter 21

Matt

Almost the moment she walks through my door, I can't stop myself from blurting, "So, are you going to tell me what you were arguing about with that asshole?" My hate for him simmers inside of me and feeds my growing anger towards him. I need proof of how bad he really is so I can get Amy away from him.

Vanessa heaves a sigh and runs her hand through her hair, looking away from me. "We've talked about him enough, don't you think?" she prods, a look of irritation on her face.

I grimace, remembering I'm pushing her to talk about something that's difficult for her. I close my eyes and exhale slowly, attempting to rid myself of all my pent-up stress. "I'm sorry, Vanessa, I know it's not easy for you," I relent. "I'm going to go shower. Make yourself comfortable," I offer.

"Thanks," she replies, still not meeting my gaze.

I take a quick shower and dry off, pulling on a pair of black boxer-briefs and worn blue jeans, momentarily unbuttoned. I stride across the hall to my room, finding Vanessa standing next to my bed. Her eyes widen as she stares at me, taking in my sculpted chest. I arch my eyebrow in surprise and challenge, "Can I help you with something?"

She gulps and shakes her head before answering. "Sorry, I thought I left something in here the other day," she mumbles as an excuse. I give her a look of doubt and she blushes a deep shade of red. "No really, I left my bra here," she adds, embarrassed.

I chuckle in amusement. "I wouldn't think that would be something that's easy to forget."

"Well, no, but I didn't change back into my own clothes. I just pulled a pair of your sweatpants on and a sweatshirt. I was drowning in them anyway, so no one could tell," she claims. I walk over to my dresser and open the drawer, pulling out a navy-blue t-shirt. I shut the drawer just as she wraps her arms around me. Laying one hand over my abs and the other over my chest, I feel her lips press against my back, increasing my heart rate.

"Vanessa," I begin, "I thought we decided this wasn't a good idea."

I spin around, facing her, letting my hands rest on her shoulders, as her hands fall to my chest. "You decided that and I don't agree," she pushes.

I arch my eyebrows in surprise, as she presses her lips to my bare chest. "Vanessa," I repeat. "I don't want a relationship right now," I insist. At least I'm not ready for anything with anyone who's not Amy, no matter how much I try. Maybe if I get her away from this fucker, I can move on.

She flinches slightly, but kisses my chest again, before pausing and meeting my gaze. "It doesn't have to be exclusive, Matt. I just need a release. Don't you?"

I hesitate, believing she's not that kind of girl. "Of course, but..."

"No, buts," she interrupts. "I want this," she claims.

"You're not that kind of girl," I argue.

"What kind of girl is that?" she challenges, annoyed. "Besides, you don't know me well enough to judge one way or another!"

I wince, realizing she's right, but I can't help that I want better for her than some asshole that doesn't want anything more. Everyone deserves better than that, but I guess we can't always get what we want. I grimace thinking of Amy and wondering if she's with him. "Fuck," I mumble as her hands begin trailing the ridges of my chest and I attempt to maintain my focus. "I saw you at the bar with Ember. She was the one that was hitting on me," I remind her, "not you."

She looks at me, unimpressed. "Did you really notice me, Matt? You were more focused on Ember and Amy to even know who I was."

I flinch, knowing she's right. Her hands slide around my back and down to my ass, as she pushes herself into me. "Fuck it," I groan, giving in. I lower my lips to hers, shoving my tongue into her mouth. She pushes as I back her up to my bed. She falls back and momentarily holds me at bay while she pulls her shirt over her head and throws it on the floor. Then, I watch as she shimmies out of her dark blue jeans and kicks them onto the floor. She lies back in her lacy black bra and panties, smirking as I take her in. I hesitate momentarily and question, "Are you sure about this Vanessa?"

She sits up and reaches into my opened jeans, rubbing her hand over my cock, and making it jump under her firm touch. I groan in response. "I'm sure," she confirms. "I want you, Matt." She pushes my jeans and boxers down, pulling out my long shaft.

"Fuck," I mutter as she holds it firmly in her hands, stroking it up and down. I reach behind her and unclasp her bra. She lets go of my cock, allowing her bra to fall off her arms and to the floor. I palm her breasts in my hands as she wraps her lips around my dick and begins to suck, her tongue licking as she goes. It's not enough and I hold myself back from pumping into her mouth. I pinch her nipples and step back, pulling my dick free of her now swollen lips, and she whines in response.

I chuckle and step towards my nightstand, pulling a condom out of the already opened box. I rip it open and toss the wrapper on the nightstand before slowly rolling it on. I reach down and run my fingers over the silky material of her underwear before I tug them off. Then, I run my fingers through her already wet folds. "Matt, please, I want you," she whimpers, desperately.

My jaw clenches, as an image of blonde hair spread out over my comforter flashes through my mind. I remove my fingers from her pussy and tap her hip, needing Amy out of my head. "Stand up, turn around and spread your legs," I demand.

"Wha..." she begins to ask and trails off, before following my instructions. I step up behind her and line my hips up with hers. I wrap one arm around her front, palming her breast and squeezing. With my other hand I line my cock up at her entrance and grip her hip, as I thrust inside her at an odd angle. I groan in frustration and put my hand on her back, guiding her face towards the bed as I release her breast. She falls, and moans my name, "Matt."

"Stay there and stick your ass in the air," I direct. She does as she's told, opening up for me. I instantly grip her hips and readjust before I thrust in and out, making her groan. I do it again and again, Amy's smiling face turning to one of bliss, as she looks up at me with adoration. I shake my head, forcing myself back in the moment, reminding myself who lies beneath me. I begin moving faster and harder, desperate to get Amy out of my head, while I'm fucking another woman, but she's unapologetic, in my mind, showing me how good it can be. I grip Vanessa's hips tighter, thrusting so hard and fast, I'm sure to leave bruises.

"Matt!" she screams my name as her orgasm rips through her, clenching my cock.

I keep moving, closing my eyes as my blonde beauty completely takes over my senses. I groan and bite my tongue, attempting not to utter her name as I release, feeling unsatisfied and completely ridden with guilt. I sigh heavily and slowly pull out of Vanessa. I step away from her, feeling sick as I walk over to the bathroom, carefully removing the condom without another word. I toss it into my garbage and glance in the mirror. My own reflection making my stomach roil. "Fuck," I mutter, with disgust.

I lean against the sink feeling like shit. I had an image of another woman in my head while I fucked this one. I'm not that asshole, no matter what she wants. I couldn't even look at her as I fucked her. What the hell is wrong with me? The worst part is, it didn't help. It only made everything worse. I feel like such a fucking pussy! I heave a sigh and run my hand through my hair in frustration. Why the hell am I still in love with her?

I run my hand through my hair and force Amy out of the forefront of my mind. Then, I trudge back to my bedroom, preparing myself for a difficult conversation, but I find Vanessa already half dressed. She looks up at me and gives me a broad smile. "Thanks, Matt," she murmurs.

I arch my eyebrows and clarify, "You're thanking me?"

She giggles and shrugs before pulling her shirt over her head. "Yeah, I am. I needed that," she proclaims. She zips and buttons her jeans before she steps over to me and pats me on the chest in appreciation. "I have to go get a few things ready for my class this week," she announces. She leans towards me and kisses the corner of my mouth. "See you later," she states, grinning.

"Yeah, bye," I mumble.

I stand momentarily dumbfounded, as I hear her walk out my front door and start her car. The moment I hear her pull out of my driveway, my anxiety floods back ten-fold. The sound of her engine fading into the distance causes reality to finally crash into me like a Mack truck. She never told me what she was fighting about with

Preston. "Damn it, Vanessa!" I grumble, punching the air. I grab my phone and tap her name, but she sends me straight to voicemail and I know she uses her Bluetooth in her car. "Shit," I grumble.

Amy

I bounce into the kitchen, excited to go out with my friends. Brett's having one of his bonfires tonight and Matt's going to come and pick Bree and me up. I hum a dance song in my head I can't quite place as I grab myself a glass of water. I put it to my lips and take a sip, just as my mom steps into the room. "Hi, Mom," I mumble, forcing a smile.

"What are you so happy about?" she questions, glaring at me.

"Ah, nothing," I mumble.

She smiles and proclaims, "Oh, wait! Are you going on your date with that boy Griffin tonight? That's wonderful!" she declares without waiting for a response.

I shake my head, "Mom, I'm not going out with Griffin tonight. I'm going over to a friend's house tonight with Bree," I explain vaguely.

She narrows her eyes and pushes, "What about Griffin? You don't tell a boy like him no."

"Mom," I grumble, irritated.

She pinches her lips tightly together, appearing as if she's biting her tongue. She takes a deep breath and exhales harshly. Then with her voice laced with doubt, she repeats, "With Bree?"

I gulp down the sudden lump in my throat and nod my head, barely able to speak. "Yeah," I whisper my confirmation.

"Whose house?"

"Brett's" I reply.

"And how are you getting there?" she asks, arching her eyebrows. I grimace and she shakes her head before I even have a chance to respond. "You're not getting in a car with Matt Young!" she insists.

"Mom," I argue, "Matt is a good guy! What is your problem with him?"

"I said No, Amy!" she repeats.

"Mom!" I scream, defiantly. I accidentally drop the glass of water from my hand and flinch as it shatters by my feet.

"What did you do?" she yells, stepping towards me. "You're such a fucking klutz!"

My eyes widen in fear and I hold up my hands, attempting to protect myself from her. "I'm sorry it was an accident," I claim.

"Clean it up!" she yells.

I momentarily stand frozen and she quickly closes the distance between us. She grits her teeth and wraps her hand into my hair using it to forcefully pull me to the ground. I put my hands out to keep my balance, my knees and hands slamming to the floor simultaneously right in the middle of the broken glass. I shriek in pain, not able to hold it in, "Ah!"

She tightens her hold on my hair, pulling my head back until I meet her gaze. "You clean up this mess and then, go clean yourself up. You're not going anywhere tonight," she insists. "The next time you want to go to hang out at a friend's house, you call Griffin and ask him to take you," she instructs.

"Okay," I whimper.

She finally releases my hair and I exhale harshly, feeling as if I can breathe again, even with my head pounding. She scoffs, "That's if he'll even want you now." She shakes her head in disappointment and mumbles, "You better get your shit together before it's too late."

I slowly ease out of the glass, blood dripping out of several cuts on my hands. I glance down at my black skirt, wishing I would've gone with jeans instead as blood drips down my legs. I watch the blood fall, my eyes beginning to blur.

I startle awake with a loud gasp, frantically checking my hands and knees for injuries. I thankfully come up empty and breathe a sigh of relief. I look around my small apartment and finally realize it really was just a dream, well this time anyway. I reach up to my face, wiping my tear-stained cheeks as I attempt to pull myself together.

I climb out of bed and peek out the window at the slowly rising sun. "It's so early," I complain, aloud. I glance back at my bed with longing and sigh heavily. I might as well get up. It's not like I'm going to get anymore sleep after that dream before I have to go into work. I don't understand why I keep having these dreams again all of a sudden, but I have to figure out a way to make them stop. I can't live like this again.

Chapter 22

Matt

Vanessa has been avoiding me all week and now she cancelled her personal training session for today. I'm grateful I'm able to get out of here a little early because I have the rescheduled appointment with the contractor today, but I have this sick feeling in my gut about how she's handling this. I don't think she's avoiding me because we hooked up, I think she's avoiding me because I saw her fighting with Preston and she's not prepared to give me answers. The thought that she's in the middle of something with him makes me sick. Then worrying about Amy being caught in that asshole's web feels like a punch to my chest, taking my breath away. I have to know what's going on, but how do I find out if Vanessa isn't talking and I've been avoiding Amy just the same?

I pull into the gravel parking lot, an extended, doublewide trailer set up next to an empty lot and Dwayne's black pickup truck pulled right up to the front door. I park next to it and step out of my truck, the chill in the air reminding me I have to start this project soon if I want to dig the foundation before the cold hits and freezes the ground. I stride up to the front door and knock, the door rattling as I do. "Come in," Dwayne calls.

I step inside the trailer turned office and pull the door shut behind me. He has two desks in an L-shape on one end and a rectangular table in the middle set up with architectural plans spread out over it and a small kitchen on the other side. "How are you, Dwayne?" I inquire.

"Matt! It's good to see you," he declares. Standing, he reaches out and clasps my hand, shaking it firmly.

"You too," I agree. "Thanks for rescheduling."

"No problem," he acknowledges, with a slight nod of his head. "So, I've been reviewing your project and besides specifics, we have to talk about timing. Plus, I do have other projects on the table," he enlightens me, not providing me with further details.

"Of course. I don't know what your schedule looks like, but I was hoping to get the foundation set before the ground freezes," I reveal.

He presses his lips tightly together and nods his head. "It's possible," he murmurs, rubbing his chin thoughtfully. "I have to take a closer look at our other projects, but as long as everything goes smoothly with the permits and the town board, we could hopefully squeeze that in before a deep freeze. Let's go over the details and I'll give you my updated costs. They're almost the same as I originally quoted you, but they have gone up slightly," he admits.

"Okay," I agree. I sit down at the conference table and we take our time going through everything, my excitement growing by the moment. Then he smiles and shakes my hand before we both stand. "Thank you, Dwayne," I state, grinning.

"It's a pleasure," he replies.

Striding out the door, I return to my truck with a smile on my face. I drive into town and park at the end of the block by the grocery store. I need a few things, but I want to grab something to eat first. Before I get out of the truck, I reach for my phone and dial Blake. He picks up on the first ring. "Hey, Matt. How'd your meeting go?"

I grin, proud of finally making it to this point. "Good," I confirm. "We have to finalize the plans and permits and run everything through the town board, but if everything goes smoothly, we should break ground before the holidays," I inform him.

"That's fantastic! Have you told Amy yet?" he questions.

I wince and stammer, "Well, I, um, no. I haven't really seen her lately."

"Well call her then," he suggests.

I rub the back of my neck, hesitating. "Well, I um, I will," I mutter, unconvincingly.

"Still avoiding her?" he prompts. "Call her!" he emphasizes.

I heave a sigh, an image of Preston filling my mind. Thoughts of Amy with him, brings conflicting emotions to the surface. Not even thinking about how much I hate that asshole, I'm afraid he's worse than any of us know. I just don't know how to prove it. But if she's determined to be with him, I want to push her away. I can't do that to myself. Yet, if anything I've heard is true, I want to do anything in my power to protect her from an asshole like him. "I don't know," I mumble.

He sighs heavily and begins, "Listen, I tried to tell you this the other day, but you didn't want to hear it, but I think you need to. I talked to Bree the other day and she had just hung up with Amy. She said Amy doesn't sound like herself, but she didn't tell Bree anything."

I shake my head and attempt to interrupt him, not wanting to hear it. "She's fine. She's just busy with her internship," I claim, unsure if it's true.

"Well, she's also too busy for social media," he proclaims.

"That's impossible," I argue.

"Look," he urges. "I know you've had this agreement with her for years and things are different with you two right now, but you know her better than anyone," he reminds me. "She's all but disappeared from social media and Bree was really worried about her. She said she's quiet and withdrawn, but she didn't have time to tell Bree anything when she started asking questions. We both know that's not Amy," he emphasizes.

My eyebrows draw down in confusion and I bite the inside of my cheek, wondering if it's something with her family or Preston. Then again, maybe it is the internship. "Maybe," I murmur, my head filling with all kinds of explanations.

"The correct response is, 'Yes, Blake, I'm going to call and check on Amy.' This is the perfect excuse to call her, Matt. She would want to know about your project!" he reiterates.

"You're right," I admit.

I hear the grin in his voice as he replies, "I usually am."

I chuckle in response. I glance up and spot Amy stepping out of the grocery store and approaching her car with a cart full of groceries in colorful recyclable bags. "Well, it looks like I might have the chance right now," I declare.

"What? Amy?" he prods.

"Yeah," I confirm. "I gotta' go. I'll catch you later."

I disconnect the call and climb out of my truck as I slip my phone in my pocket. My gaze doesn't waver as I head for her car across the parking lot, watching as she begins loading her groceries into the back. Her legs appearing long in her chocolate brown leggings and oversized cream cable knit sweater, a long brown dress coat hanging open over top. My heart begins to pick up its pace as I approach. I clear my throat and just before I reach her, I rasp, "Hey."

She startles and spins on her heel, her blonde hair flying over her shoulders as she falls back against her car with her hand on her heart. She breathes a sigh of relief as she meets my gaze. A small smile curves her lips as she whispers my name, "Matt." I take a deep breath and

181

exhale slowly. Momentarily overwhelmed by seeing her again. Feeling like it's only the two of us standing in this parking lot, I take my time appreciating her, before returning to meet her eyes and wondering if Bree is right and if she is, why? I *need* to know.

Amy

The sight of Matt causes my heart to skip a beat, while the sound of his voice sends shivers down my spine. I've missed his face, his eyes, his playful smile, his voice, the way he makes me feel and if I'm honest, I miss his touch. I guess I just miss *him*. He looks damn good in black jeans with a few loose strings and a gray long-sleeved thermal. I paste a smile on my face and my voice catches as I ask, "How are you?"

Offering me a crooked grin he answers, "I'm doing alright." He tilts his head to the side and looks at me as if he's trying to make a decision. Then he shrugs and prompts, "Do you want to grab a bite to eat?"

My eyes widen in surprise. He goes from ignoring my calls to this? I don't get it, but I don't care. "I'd love to," I pause and glare at my trunk full of groceries. Of course when I finally decide to get more of my own food so I'm able to more successfully avoid my mother, Matt finally wants to hang out again. "I do have to get all of this home though." I glance at him and back at my food before focusing on him. "Would you like to come over and I could cook you dinner?" I offer.

It's Matt's turn to be surprised. "You want to cook dinner for me?" he repeats, arching his eyebrows.

I roll my eyes dramatically and smirk, "What? Do you think I can't cook?"

"Nah, you do okay, but we both know I'm the master," he teases, making me giggle for real. "Above the garage, not at the house, right?" he clarifies, hesitating.

I grimace, understanding his reluctance. I nod my head and mumble, "Yeah."

I watch as he nods his head, biting the inside of his cheek, considering his response. "I'll follow you over. I can park down the street if you want," he suggests, making me cringe.

"Matt," I begin.

He shakes his head, instantly interrupting me. "Don't," he warns. "I'm pretty sure your mom and I have a mutual dislike for each other," he mutters.

I sigh, feeling the same as him, but she's my mother. I felt like I finally escaped in Maine, but I couldn't get anything more than my job at the coffee shop. I had to come back if I wanted to pay my bills. If it weren't for social media, I wouldn't have the wardrobe I do, but lately even that's too much. I'm barely able to deal with work, Preston and my mom. "I'm sorry," I murmur. A look of irritation crosses his face and I quickly correct myself, knowing he hates when I blame myself for something I shouldn't. "I know it's not my fault, but I'm sorry you've had to deal with her."

He nods in understanding and advises, "I'll meet you at your place."

Vanessa suddenly crosses my mind. I hate that it does, but I don't want to put him in a tough situation. "Will Vanessa mind that you're having dinner with me?" I prod.

He flinches as if I slapped him and then he sighs heavily and runs his hand through his hair. "She doesn't have a say in what I do. She's not my girlfriend," he states, enlightening me.

I feel my whole body breathe a sigh of relief as I do everything I can, not to visibly react. "Oh," I mumble.

"Why do you care?" he challenges, assessing me through narrowed eyes.

I shake my head and attempt to explain myself. "I don't. I just don't want to put you in a difficult situation."

"It never bothered you before," he argues, causing me to wince.

"I guess I'm just protective of you," I claim.

He nods, a smirk playing on his lips. "And jealousy has nothing to do with it?" he dares, arching his eyebrows.

I feel my face heat in embarrassment and I shake my head in denial. "Maybe this isn't the best idea," I begin.

He takes a step closer to me, the backs of my knees tapping the rear bumper of my car. I gasp at his close proximity, my breathing rate increasing as my body heats. "Are you afraid to be alone with me, Amy?" he probes.

I shake my head, knowing it's the truth. I could never be afraid of this man, but I am afraid of my reaction to him. I want him, just as much as I always have, but I can't give in, not now, especially not now. "No," I force out.

He chuckles softly and leans down, placing a tender kiss on my forehead and causing my heart to ache from his sweet gesture. "I'll see you at your place then," he reiterates. Then he takes a step back before spinning on his heel and striding across the parking lot towards his truck before I have a chance to change my mind again.

Chills run through my body, the air suddenly feeling drastically colder. I tear my eyes away from his firm ass and set the last bag down in my truck before closing it and returning the cart to the rack. Then I slip in behind the wheel of my car and crank the heat up. I back out of my parking spot and make my way home as quickly as possible. I went from a night at home going over a few details for the fundraiser before crashing, to eating dinner at home with Matt. The same man my body, my mind and my soul miss terribly. The same man I would do anything for, but also a man I don't deserve. That doesn't mean I'm not going to enjoy every minute he'll allow me to be around him, for now anyway. Sighing, I mumble to myself, "I'm in so much trouble."

Chapter 23

Amy

I can't believe he's here after ignoring me for so long. It feels like it's been forever when in reality it's been maybe a week. I thought he was done with me and I can admit that hurt. Taking a deep breath, I exhale slowly before I stride to the small table and set a plate of chicken bruschetta laid on top of a bed of penne in front of him.

He glances up at me and smiles appreciatively. "Wow," he mumbles. "This looks and smells really good," he praises.

I feel my face heat from his compliment as I sit down across from him. "Thank you," I reply, staring at my plate.

He takes a bite and groans, the sound sending vibrations and heat to my whole body. "This is delicious. When did you learn to cook?"

I stare at my plate, playing with my food as I respond, "Well, um, I ah, I don't want to eat in my parents' kitchen all the time and I can't live on take-out," I stammer.

I hear his fork clink against the plate as he sets it down. I glance up at him through my long lashes, wondering what he's thinking. He leans his forearms on the edge of the table and folds his hands in front of him. He chews the food in his mouth as he stares at me, assessing me, judging me, and making my heartbeat out of control. I drop my gaze, not able to maintain eye contact. "Amy," he prods, slowly pulling my eyes back to his. He stares at me intently, momentarily searching, for what I don't know. I have the strongest urge to either kiss him or walk away; I'm not quite sure. He finally breaks the silence, questioning, "Is everything okay?"

I let out a harsh breath and shake my head, attempting to push away his inquiry. "I'm fine," I blurt out. "I've just been busy," I claim.

"With your internship?" he probes, his eyebrows drawn down in concern.

I heave a sigh and shrug, "I guess." My mind drifts to everything that's happened lately, from my disagreements with Preston, to my fights with my mother, to my sleepless nights filled with nightmares from my past, to stressing about what my parents want for me and what I'm going to do with my life once this internship is over, but most of all I miss Matt and everything about him. My chest aches, once again feeling lost and alone, even as Matt sits across from me. I know he wants to help, but what could he even do?

"Amy, if something is going on with you, I'd like to know. I can help you with whatever it is," he prompts.

His words feel as if he's squeezing my chest. I wish that were true, more than he could even know. I shake my head and paste a smile on my face, "I'm fine, Matt," I claim. "Just tired," I insist, giving him a half-truth.

He opens his mouth to push me further, I just know it, but I don't think I could hold it together talking to him and I have to if I'm going to survive. He won't always be there. I've made sure of it. My chest squeezes tighter, making it difficult to breathe. I force out my breath and quickly interrupt, stopping him. "What's going on with you anyway? It's strange not knowing what's going on in your life," I concede.

He nods in agreement, as his sexy, crooked smile lights up his face. His hand rubs along his jawline, the sound of his scruff from his five o'clock shadow apparent and bringing a smile to my face. "Yeah, it is," he concurs.

"Something is going on. Something big," I claim, leaning towards him across the table. I can feel his

187

excitement increasing just watching his reactions to my comments.

His smile grows and he nods his head in confirmation. "You could say that," he responds vaguely. Then he takes another bite of dinner.

"Matt!" I scold, a genuine grin lighting up my face. I hate when he makes me wait.

He chuckles, careful to chew the food in his mouth. I watch as his Adam's apple bobs up and down as he swallows. He picks up his fork again and I reach across the table, grasping his wrist to stop him, causing him to laugh louder. "Okay, okay," he murmurs, his eyes alight with amusement. He holds my gaze and reveals, "So, I'm finally building my gym."

My eyes widen as his hand slips out of my grasp. I gasp in shock, my heart skipping a beat, thrilled his dream is finally coming true. "Matt, that's incredible!" I exclaim. "When? Where?" I instantly question.

He laughs, his eyes settling on me before he elaborates. "Well, I finally bought a piece of property just outside of town. Then I met with Dwayne today and it looks like as long as everything goes smoothly with the town board, I should have everything in place to break ground before the holidays," he explains, grinning ear to ear.

I stand up and round the small table without thought. I throw my arms around him and he pushes his chair back just enough to pull me into his arms and his lap. My heart thunders in my chest as I squeeze him tight with everything in me. "I'm so happy for you, Matt," I whisper, feeling his happiness nearly vibrating out of his pores. "I'm so proud of you."

"Thanks, Amy," he murmurs, holding me tight. "That really means a lot," he rasps, his emotions causing his voice to catch in his throat.

I let my head fall back, smiling as I look at him. "I remember the first time you talked about building this place and now you're here," I state, as if it's news to him. "You're absolutely remarkable," I compliment, my intentions holding much more meaning than I'm willing to convey.

He looks into my eyes, his holding so many emotions, I'm momentarily overwhelmed. I struggle to breathe, until I know I can't take anymore. I crash my lips over his, wanting to taste him and needing him closer. He barely hesitates before he's pulling me closer. I cradle his face in my hands, the scratch of his stubble on my palms, shooting tingles up my arms and straight to my nipples. I stand up without pulling our lips apart, throwing one leg over his lap to straddle him. His hands weave their way into my hair as he pushes our kiss deeper, his tongue diving in to twist and tangle with mine, each flick of his tongue consuming me. I can't get enough.

Matt

I groan into her mouth, not able to hold back, no matter how much I know I should. She's everything I want, everything I need. She grinds her hips down on me, pulling a growl from my lips. "Amy," I rasp her name in warning.

She whimpers in response and I fist her hair and gently tug her head back, allowing my lips to roam down her neck, towards her chest. I cup her breast with my free hand, feeling her hard nipples through her thick sweater. "Matt," she mumbles breathlessly.

I release her hair, allowing my hands to slide down and slip underneath her sweater, quickly pulling it over her head and tossing it onto the floor. My head falls between her breasts as I slide her straps off her shoulders and push the cups to the side, allowing them to spill free. I turn my head and hum as I take one nipple into my mouth, while I pinch the other between my thumb and pointer finger, rolling it between my fingers.

She groans and tugs on the ends of my hair, pulling me up and I oblige. I look into her blue eyes, darkened with lust, only succeeding in increasing my craving for her. She reaches down and rubs my hard cock, straining to break free from the constraints of my jeans. She pulls the button open, tugging the zipper down. Reaching in, she firmly rubs up and down my dick, bringing a guttural groan to my lips. I can't take it. My whole body feels like it's on fire, filled with adrenaline and ready to burst. "I need you," I mutter desperately.

She breathes what sounds to me like a breath of relief and echoes my sentiment. "I need you, too, Matt."

I grin as I stand up, holding her tight to my chest and twist towards the kitchen counter, even the bed seems too far away, but the small table is filled with our barely touched food. I tug her leggings and panties down over her ass just before I place her on the counter. Her quick intake of breath, reminds me it's probably cold. I lean back and give her a cocky smirk. "I'll warm you up quickly," I claim, just before I run my fingers over her folds. Her head falls back, her eyes nearly rolling back in her head as I push into her wet center. "You're soaked for me," I murmur.

She groans in agreement and I drop to my knees, needing to taste her. I slide my hands up her thighs, my thumbs gently digging into her flesh. Then I lean in and jut my tongue out, licking her slowly up to her clit and then back, pushing my tongue inside as my mouth covers her. I groan at the sounds coming out of her mouth and suck her gently as I release her. I pause, looking up at her.

She stares down at me, her eyes half closed, her lips swollen and parted as she whimpers. "Matt, I want you," she reiterates.

I lick her again before I stand. She greedily reaches for me, freeing my rigid cock and running her hands along the taut skin. "Fuck," I mumble, struggling to last as if it's my first time. I reach into my back pocket, barely hanging off my hips and pull out my wallet. I grab a condom before tossing my wallet on the counter next to her. I pull back and rip the wrapper open, easily unrolling it over my hard dick. I prepare myself at her entrance and pause, searching her eyes for any sign of doubt, but I see nothing but lust and something else I crave only from her.

"Please," she begs, reaching for me. I gladly relent, pushing into her with a hard thrust, making us both gasp. She wraps her arms around my back, slipping her hands underneath my shirt and scraping her nails lightly along my back as she arches her hips into me. I let go of my hesitations, meeting her hard with every thrust. Our bodies slick with sweat, begin slapping together as I pound into her, in and out, harder and harder, needing every inch of her to be mine. She screams my name, "Matt! Yes, Matt!"

I watch her face contort with pure pleasure as her insides clench around me, squeezing me so tight I can't hold on another second. My dick tightens with heat and a shock of energy, making me pause buried deep as I can possibly get inside her, just before I fall over the top with a possessive growl. I pump into her again and again, riding out my orgasm. I finish and let my head fall to her shoulder, wanting this, wanting her, more than I can explain. "I fucking missed you," I whisper inaudibly.

She runs her fingers through my hair and asks, "What?"

I sigh and kiss her bare shoulder. I lift my head and look into her eyes before I place another kiss on her lips. "Guess I was a little impatient," I joke.

She giggles adorably, causing my heart to squeeze. "Help me down," she requests.

I nod and reluctantly pull out of her, before I plant my hands on her hips and lower her to the ground. I momentarily keep my hands on her skin, taking in her rumpled appearance. She's still wearing her bra, her hair is a mess and her leggings and panties hang from her knees. She's absolutely gorgeous. She slips her arms back into her bra, tugging the cups over her breasts. I reluctantly release her with a sigh, watching as she pulls her pants up, before making her way over to her sweater on the floor by the table.

I feel like I need to say something, but I have to get this condom off first. "I'll be right back," I mumble. I quickly make my way to her bathroom, removing the condom, tying it off and tossing it in the garbage before fastening my jeans.

I wash my hands, reminding myself of why I wanted to talk to her in the first place today. There was definitely something bothering her before I let my dick jump in front of my head. I was willing to let it go briefly, hoping she'd open up to me on her own, but I can't seem to control myself around her. Sometimes I feel like she turns back time on my hormones, making me feel like a teenage boy all over again. I have no idea how she fucking does it, but I can't let this go. I have to find out what's bothering her. If it's that asshole, I need to do something. Blake's right though, she's not herself. Even her eyes seemed to be lost at first, almost like she was losing her light, but when I told her about the gym, everything about her brightened immensely, she nearly blinded me. Maybe it is the internship and she's just tired. I sigh and run my hand through my hair and pull the door open, ready to find out.

I smile and take a step towards her, the softness in her eyes taking my breath away. She straightened herself up, but her lips are still swollen from my assault on them and her hair still slightly askew. I close the distance between us, her gaze never wavering from mine. I reach up to her cheek and murmur her name, "Amy."

"Matt," she replies.

"I think we need to talk," I state. She nods in agreement.

A knock at the door causes her to jump, her whole body tensing. I step towards her protectively. She grimaces and steps away from me as another knock comes, harder this time. "Amy, I have a surprise for you. Open up," Preston's muffled voice calls through the door. I watch as Amy's face pales and she sways on her feet, her body stiff as a board. "I know you're in there," he emphasizes.

"Do you want me to get rid of him?" I offer.

She turns to me with wide eyes, and vigorously shakes her head. I swear I see fear in her eyes. I clench my fists and stride towards the door before she can stop me. Preston stands before me fuming and glaring at me. "Well, well, well, this is," he pauses and glances at Amy, before turning back to me and grumbling, "unexpected."

Amy suddenly pulls herself out of her daze and steps between us. "Relax. Matt just came over to catch up," she explains. I look at her with wide eyes, but she's staring at him, fearful of something. Is she afraid of him or is she afraid of him leaving her?

"Well, we have to talk about the fundraiser tomorrow night," Preston states. He holds up a bag in his right hand with wrapped boxes inside. I have something for you too," he advises.

I watch as some of the tension drains from her face and her eyes soften as she looks up at him with appreciation, making me cringe. "I'm just leaving anyway," I announce. I stalk over to the kitchen counter, swipe up my wallet and slip it into my back pocket before I glance in her direction. She's staring at the ground, eyebrows drawn down, not meeting my gaze, but why? Does she want me to stay? Does she want me to go? Does she trust him? I don't know, but I can't stand here like a fool. "I'll catch you later, Amy," I mumble just before I stalk out the door, hearing it close behind me without a response.

"What the fuck?" I mumble to myself as I quickly make my way down the block to my truck.

Chapter 24

Matt

I change into black shorts and a white long sleeved workout shirt, so hopefully cars will see me running by the side of the road. It's either run or drink, or maybe both, I don't know yet. My phone rings and I glance at the screen to see Vanessa lighting it up. "Fuck that," I mumble and toss my phone on the kitchen counter before stalking out the front door. Now she's ready to talk to me. I'm sick of doing things on everyone else's fucking time. What about my time? I slam the door behind me and take off in a run, needing to work out my frustrations before I lose my shit.

I used to not let things bother me and then I had to go and fall for the one girl I knew would wreck me. What the fuck is going on with her? She's never been this way with me, treating me like I'm nothing to her. She wouldn't even fucking look at me! I push myself harder, and faster, not paying attention to where I'm going or the blur of trees and buildings I'm passing. Forcing my legs to quicken, and listening to my feet pound the pavement, hoping it lulls my mind into a content silence. I need to get away from everything hindering me, everything I feel pulling me under before it tears me apart...like Amy.

I grunt and pick up my pace again, punishing myself for my thoughts. I know I'm the one who put myself in this position. We've always been best friends, but with incredible benefits. I've never let it get to me before. If she were dating someone, I'd find someone else. If she needed someone to pull her out of a tough situation, I'd be there, but she'd also do the same for me. I haven't always made the smartest choices when it comes to women and I obviously still can't now, but she's always been there for me when I needed her. She's even gotten rid of a few clingers and stalkers for that matter. I chuckle to myself thinking about how much fear she put into a couple of those women. She can really squeeze a lot of fire into that sweet little body of hers when she wants to.

I sigh again, the cold air beginning to burn my lungs as realization dawns on me. That's the problem. Amy always seems either happy or she's pissed off and ready to take on anyone in her way. No matter what's going on and how she's feeling, she's always full of life. There's never been much of an in between, although I'm one of the few that sees the in between she does reveal. Why did I see something else in her eyes tonight? What's going on with her? And why the fuck don't I already know what it is? Blake's words ring in my ears. Knowing Bree thinks something's up makes me even more anxious. If she can tell being hours away from her, it should be a given for me.

I really wish that asshole didn't show up tonight and not just because I wanted to talk and jump into round two with Amy. I fucking hate that man and the more I learn about him, the more I despise him. Is he the problem? It sure didn't seem like she wanted to see him, but that could be me imagining what I believe. It could be because she didn't want him to know what had just transpired between us too. He's the one there with her and I'm out here freezing my balls off and pushing myself to the edge.

What I don't get is why she's even dating him. I've seen her date guys like him before, hell, Christian was one of those guys when he lost Bree, but there's still something different. Is what Vanessa said about him true or is she fucking with me too? Why were they fighting anyway? I groan in annoyance, pissed at myself for ignoring Vanessa's call when she might've been ready to give me some answers, but will they even be the truth? I've never had so much fucking doubt about things in my life.

I continue to push myself harder and harder with images of Amy's distraught features on my mind, making me wonder if I should've walked away just now. I can't seem to stop second-guessing every little thing. "Fuck," I grumble, my muscles beginning to burn from the strain and the cold.

I look up, taking in my surroundings, and attempt to take a deep breath in, but the cold air causes me to begin coughing instead. I slow, attempting to catch my breath, jogging until I hit a dirt and gravel parking lot. I didn't even realize I had come this far, let alone that this is where my feet wanted to take me without my consent. I look out at the empty lot, not able to see anything, but darkness, but it doesn't matter. The sight of the emptiness that's all mine gives me back my feeling of hope. I need this and I'm finally making it happen. Nothing else matters, I have my future right here.

I know I won't be able to completely let everything go with Amy until I know what's really going on with her and her asshole boyfriend, or whatever the fuck he is to her, but I don't need any of it. I've got all I need right here. If she's just going to leave like my brother did, like my parents did...I don't fucking need her anyway. I run my hand through my hair and drop my arms to my sides. Who am I kidding? I may not need her, but I would never abandon her. I'm not like the rest of them.

I take a deep breath and turn around, ready to trek back home. I need to focus on my project, but I'm not going to stop pushing until I have some answers. Now that it looks like Vanessa stopped avoiding me, she's a good place to start.

Amy

My heart pounds so hard in my chest, I can barely hear over the flow of blood in my ears. I'm nervous as to what he's going to say. I spin around and begin picking up the dishes from dinner, our food barely touched. My face heats, thinking of Matt and what did happen instead. I set the dishes in the sink dreaming of him.

Cold, firm hands fall onto my shoulders making me flinch and spin around. Preston stands, towering over me, pushing into my space, and looking down at me through narrowed eyes. Guilt washes over me as he gives me a hard stare. "I said," he begins leaning even closer and pressing his body into mine, "what was he doing here?"

I attempt to gulp down the lump in my throat, and control my breathing as my anxiety skyrockets. "Um, I told you, he…"

He instantly cuts me off, emphasizing, "You *told* me you two were done. You *promised* me he wasn't an issue. I should be your fucking priority!"

My breaths become heavy as I struggle to find the words I'm looking for. I look up, his brown eyes dark and intimidating as he scans my body. His body tenses even further as he pushes into me. "We just ran into each other and…"

"And what?" he interrupts. He runs his fingers through my hair and yanks it, making me gasp in pain. He holds it up between us, a scowl on his face. "You have food in your hair," he states, accusingly.

I fight to maintain control, but I feel my body heat, betraying me. "Can you move, please?" I beg, suddenly feeling trapped.

He drops my hair and grasps my wrists, pinning them behind me. "Why? You don't want me to smell him on you?" he challenges.

"Preston, stop!" I beg.

"You're intent on making a fool out of me and you want me to stop?" he probes reproachfully.

"No," I argue, vigorously shaking my head.

"I think I've given you enough chances. I think I'm just asking for trouble by keeping you around," he proclaims. He grimaces and lets me go as he pushes away from me.

He takes a step back and runs his hand through his hair in frustration as I focus on catching my breath and gathering my courage to speak. "Maybe you're right. Maybe we're not a good idea," I mumble.

He throws his head back and laughs humorlessly. "So that's it? You make a fool out of me and now you want to end things?" I stare at him wide-eyed, seeing the hurt in his actions. I step towards him and he holds his hand up and shakes his head. "Don't." He takes a deep breath in and exhales slowly. "Maybe you should go take a shower and clean yourself up before I say something I might regret," he mutters with distaste. "I'll be out here. Come talk to me after we've both had a few minutes to calm down," he instructs.

I want to argue, but I don't. I take a few steps towards the bathroom when he reaches out to stop me, grasping my arm. I turn to face him and he lifts the bag he was holding when he walked in and offers it to me. I shake my head and he squeezes my arm tighter. "Just take it. After your shower, open the packages. I bought you some things for the fundraiser tomorrow. If we decide tonight not to do this, I'll take everything with me and bring someone else," he emphasizes.

I hesitate, wanting to ask what he means, but I don't have the energy yet. He's right. I need a few minutes to clean myself up and pull myself together. I nod stiffly and take the bag from his hand before he releases me.

I exhale slowly and make my way to the bathroom. I close the door behind me and turn on the water before I strip down and step into the shower. I quickly wash away the food in my hair along with the smell of Matt, feeling as if a weight pushes down on me. I feel like I can't have what I want, but it may not matter if I ruined everything else, but that's what I do, ruin everything. I sigh heavily as I step out of the shower and wrap a towel around myself, realizing I left all my clean clothes on the other side. I groan in frustration and complain to myself, "I can't believe I did that. Idiot," I grumble.

I sit down on the closed toilet seat and open the card attached with a bright blue ribbon tying the handles of the bag together. I flip it open and read, "Amy, I'm looking forward to a night out with my one and only. Love, Preston." My heart sinks, his sweet words making me feel worse than I already do.

I open the first box, the biggest of the three and gasp as I pull out a royal blue shimmering evening dress. I stand and hold it up, admiring the soft, silky fabric and beautiful lines. It's a sleeveless dress with a deep V, with two shimmering pieces of fabric crisscrossing just above where my breasts would be. Then the back also appears open, with another deep V and similar pieces of fabric crossing at my lower back. There's a long slit on the right, which would allow me room to move and look sexy. It's absolutely gorgeous. I set it down to open the next box, finding brand name 3-inch stilettos in a little bit darker blue. "Damn," I whisper. Finally, I lift the lid on the last box to find diamond and sapphire jewelry, including reverse teardrop sapphires, surrounded by diamonds in both earrings and a necklace with the same design, but slightly bigger than the earrings.

I close my eyes, my guilt again overwhelming. Tears begin to burn my eyes and I take a deep breath in and exhale slowly, attempting to keep my emotions at bay. A soft knock sounds at the door, pulling me from my thoughts. "How are you doing in there?" he prompts.

"Um, I forgot clothes to change into," I begin.

"Well, that's not a problem," he claims.

I roll my eyes even though he can't see me. I look down at all the things he bought for me and I stand, opening the door without thought. His eyes roam over my body greedily and I attempt to ignore him. "Preston, I can't accept all this," I begin, shaking my head.

He cringes and almost instantly pulls himself back together. "Can I ask you a question?"

"Of course," I state, shrugging my shoulders.

"If we don't continue dating, are you going to date him?" he asks.

I wince, knowing that's something I'd want, but also something I don't know if I can ever really have. What if we don't work out? Then I'd be left completely alone. But I don't think I can walk away from him. "I don't know," I answer honestly.

He grinds his teeth in irritation and takes a deep breath, exhaling slowly to regain control. "So, you want to give up your internship, your future, what we have, and what we could be all for something you don't know if you want?" he challenges.

I open my mouth to argue, but I don't know what to say. Instead, I shake my head and insist, "You don't want me."

He slowly takes predatory steps towards me, his gaze insistent. He reaches me and lifts his hand, letting his fingers trail across my jawline, down my neck, towards my breasts, stopping as he reaches the edge of the towel. "On the contrary," he mumbles.

He glances up at me with heat in his eyes, confusing me. "How? After everything?" I question.

The corners of his lips twitch up in amusement. He meets my gaze and admits, "Maybe it's because of everything, but make no mistake," he pauses lifting my chin and holding my gaze on him, "I want you," he rasps.

My heart skips a beat as I feel the heat build between us. I squeeze my legs together, not wanting to go there, my mind still on Matt. He leans in and presses his lips to mine, kissing me. I momentarily freeze before kissing him back feeling confused. He pulls me closer, his hand slipping under my towel and pulling me back to reality. I jump back, planting my hands firmly on his chest. "Preston, stop. We need to talk about this," I claim.

He chuckles softly, his amusement obvious. "Okay. Here's what we'll do. You keep the boxes and you can have tonight and most of tomorrow to decide what you're going to do. I'll call you at four to find out if you're coming with me or if I need to contact a backup." I feel my eyebrows draw down in confusion and he reaches up to smooth out the lines. "Don't worry so much. This is your last shot to make things right between us. I think I've been pretty fucking patient. If you want to come to the fundraiser, you come with me as my date and my girlfriend. If you don't want to go that route, I'd work on finding another internship," he threatens. He takes a step closer to me, his eyes narrowing before he declares, "And Amy, after tonight, I'm warning you now, I'm done waiting."

I gasp at his blatant insinuation. His words make my stomach turn, as I repeat them in my head, trying to decide if he's being real. You can't threaten people like that and get away with it. I open my mouth to argue and he tilts his head to the side, a smirk on his face. "Think about what you say and what you want before you say something you might regret. You might want to fully understand the repercussions of fucking me over," he states as if it's no big deal.

"What's that supposed to mean?" I retort.

He chuckles and kisses me softly on the lips before he mumbles, "Just don't make a quick decision. Give it the night to think about it. I'm just asking for one last chance before you give up on us. It's the least I deserve after all this don't you think?" he retorts.

I wince, knowing I don't even deserve this, but he's right. Is that really all he's asking for? I don't know, but maybe a night to sleep to think will do me some good. "Okay," I agree, reluctantly.

"Good, girl," he mumbles. He pecks my lips slow and sweet before he turns and strides to the door. He pauses with his hand on the door and looks back at me. "I'm not the one in the wrong here and I'm willing to give you one last shot," he reiterates.

My stomach flips, knowing he's right. I don't deserve this, I repeat to myself over and over, so why is he giving it to me? He walks out and closes the door behind him. I crawl into bed with my towel still tightly wrapped around me, not bothering to get dressed. I'm confused, tired and frustrated. What just happened?

Chapter 25

Matt

After I jump out of the shower, I glance at the time. I still have a few minutes before Vanessa shows up. She didn't answer her phone last night, but she texted me to ask if she could come over before lunch today to talk. I unlock my phone as I drop down on the couch, remembering a comment about Amy's social media. She's always been very active and able to work things in her favor, getting free items and commission on products, services and companies she recommends. Normally, I don't pay much attention, but with everything I'm hearing, I can't help but question it.

I pull open one of her social media accounts finding almost nothing in the past two weeks. Opening the next app, followed by another and another, again finding her activity nearly scarce, bringing a frown to my face. I tilt my head to the side, thinking. Why would she let this fall through the cracks?

A knock at the door startles me and I set my phone down on the coffee table as I stand up. Striding towards the door and pulling it open, I find Vanessa on the other side with a hesitant smile on her lips. "Hi," she mumbles. She stuffs her hands into the pockets of her unzipped, quilted, white vest, worn over the top of a fitted, V-neck black sweater, with a pair of dark blue skinny jeans and tall black leather boots.

I muster up a half smile before standing back and gesturing her to come inside. "Vanessa," I whisper her name, disappointment washing over me, even though I'd been expecting her.

Stepping past me, her arm brushes against my chest. She turns and looks up at me, her gaze appearing apologetic. "I'm sorry I've been avoiding you," she begins, surprising me by jumping right into it.

"Have a seat," I offer, not yet acknowledging her apology. I want to know why she was avoiding me in the first place. "Would you like something to drink?"

She shakes her head mumbling, "No, thank you." She lowers herself down onto the edge of the couch and I sit down opposite her, waiting for her to speak. She heaves a heavy sigh and repeats, "I'm sorry, Matt."

"What exactly are you sorry for Vanessa?" I prompt.

She winces and elaborates, "I'm sorry for ignoring your calls and texts after everything that went on between us." She blushes a deep shade of red and turns her head away from me, avoiding my piercing gaze.

I nod my head in understanding, although I'm still confused. "Vanessa, for me it's not about fucking me and then ignoring me. I don't give a shit about that," I blurt out blatantly. She cringes and I continue, "You're obviously avoiding me for another reason and I think it has to do with your ex. Care to share?" I probe.

She drops her head into her hands and grumbles, "I don't like talking about him."

I grit my teeth and ignore her comment. I push, "What were you fighting about when I saw you the other day?"

She runs her hands through her hair and mumbles, "He was being an asshole."

I chuckle humorlessly and retort, "He's always an asshole. What were you fighting about and why don't you want me to know?"

She lifts her head and meets my gaze, "It's not that I don't want you to know." I arch my eyebrows in challenge and she groans and sighs heavily, relenting. "It's because we were fighting about you."

"Me?" I ask, my disbelief clear in my voice.

"Yeah, he told me to stay away from you," she claims. I burst out laughing. I can't help it. He's telling her I'm the problem? I don't know if I believe that. "Why would he care what you do? He's not dating you anymore," I reiterate.

"Yeah, but...he, um...I don't know," she stammers, shaking her head. "He said he does," she argues.

I take a deep breath and exhale slowly, attempting to stay calm. So many alarms are going off inside my head; I don't even know where to begin. "Vanessa," I growl. She flinches and fear instantly rises in her eyes, reminding me what she said about him the first time. I wince, knowing her reaction is genuine and shake my head, instantly apologetic. "I'm sorry. I'm just pissed. I would never hurt you," I proclaim, knowing she needs to hear the words.

She grimaces and nods her head slowly. She takes a deep breath and lifts her gaze to meet mine. "Look, Matt," she begins, "He liked to control me when we were dating and he wants to control me now, even if I won't let him. He told me I should stay away from you and I yelled back at him. I told him no and I said something about Amy. He got really mad and that's when you showed up," she rambles, trying to get everything out all at once.

"What did you say about Amy?" I question.

She shakes her head, mumbling, "I don't know."

"You have to at least have an idea," I insist.

She opens her mouth to respond, when my cell phone rings, vibrating on the coffee table I glance towards it and see Dwayne's face lighting up the screen. "Excuse me, I have to get this," I mumble. I swipe my phone up from the table and put it to my ear. "Hey Dwayne, what's up?" I ask.

I hear his heavy sigh through the line and my stomach instantly stirs with unease. "Matt, you're not going to like this," he claims.

I stand up, pacing towards my kitchen. "What's going on? What am I not going to like?" I probe. I can practically feel his hesitation through the phone and I blurt out, "Just tell me, Dwayne! What's the problem?"

"We have an issue with the town board," he states.

"What kind of issue?" I ask. My heart stops and restarts, beating out of control.

"Someone on the board doesn't want you to get your project approved," he declares.

I feel dizzy as I continue to pace, breathing heavily and begging for more information, "Who? Who's standing in my way Dwayne?"

Someone from the Kirst family," he reveals.

"Shit," I grumble. I take a deep breath, barely able to control my rage. Is he fucking kidding me? He thinks he's going to control me? "Thanks, Dwayne."

"I would contact them about your proposal and see if you can change their minds," he suggests, not realizing that's not the issue.

"Thanks. I'm on it. I'll get back to you," I mutter, barely able to hold myself together.

"Great. We'll talk soon," he replies and disconnects the call.

I drop my head back and yell, "Fuck me."

"Everything okay," Vanessa calls from my living room.

I shake my head and trudge out to the living room, needing her to leave. "Vanessa, I'm sorry, but I have something I have to take care of. We'll have to finish this conversation another time," I inform her.

"Okay. Is everything alright?" she repeats.

"Fine, fine," I mumble unconvincingly. "I'll catch you later," I state, pulling her to her feet and guiding her towards the door. I don't have time for any misunderstandings.

"Okay, I think I'm going out for drinks with a couple friends if you want to join us later," she offers.

"Thanks," I mumble, pulling my door open and nudging her out.

"Bye," she responds. I nearly slam the door behind her, my phone still clenched so tightly in my hand; I'm surprised I haven't crushed it. He's fucking with my life now and I'm not putting up with that shit!

Amy

I pack up the dress, the shoes and the jewelry and slip it back in the bag Preston brought everything over in, the moment bittersweet. It's all incredibly beautiful, but after sleeping on it, I do have clarity. I can't go with Preston to the fundraiser, no matter how hard I've worked. I would give almost anything to meet Diana Brooks and after working so hard on this project, I think that's what I've been looking forward to the most. But I can't go as Preston's date, or be his girlfriend for that reason alone. I like him, but it feels like Christian all over again, except I slept with Christian on day one and look where that got me. Now, I'm doing the same thing. I'm going after a man, dragging my heart along for the ride and hoping it catches up with my brain and my actions. I want my happily ever after more than anything, but to get it I'm listening to what my parents want for me or what they think is good for me and not what I really want or what I need. I need to put myself first for once.

I do like Preston, but I started dating him for my parents, not for me. And why? Because my dad and his dad have business deals together? Or maybe it's because my dad respects their family? Or maybe because my mom thinks I need to be with someone of a certain status and she doesn't want to settle for any less? She still scares the crap out of me, but that's no excuse, not anymore. She doesn't have a choice this time. I'm not going to let her manipulate me anymore. If I have to be a barista for the rest of my life I will. I can't live under her thumb anymore. I feel like I'm losing myself a little more every day. I just hope my dad understands. I have to tell him without putting any fault on her, or it won't turn out well for me. I know it. I don't believe she would really do anything in front of him, but living on edge, anticipating her anger gives me constant anxiety if nothing else. I feel like I've reverted back to doing everything my parents want me to do just by living here again and then acting out to spite them. I'm so messed up, but I'm done pretending.

This would be so much easier if I could move out, but I don't have anywhere to go. Now that I won't have a job or an internship, I definitely can't afford to go anywhere. I have to find something somewhere, anywhere.

My thoughts stray to Matt. I can't seem to stay away from him. I feel full of life when I'm with him. Nothing feels forced or fake between us. We've known each other for what feels like forever, but no one knows me like he does, not even Bree. I've been keeping him at a distance for so long, I didn't realize he'd already built a permanent home inside my heart and I can't seem to get rid of him no matter how hard I try.

I realize I shouldn't have done anything with him last night and I feel guilty for what I did because of Preston. He doesn't deserve this, no one does, but it's like I couldn't stop myself. I'm so happy for him. I felt driven to show him just how proud of him I really am. I can't be with Preston when I don't *want* to stay away from Matt. It's not fair to any of us. I don't know if he'll be willing to take a chance on me again after everything I've put him through, but I have to try. If I have to give up everything else in the process, well, I've been in much tougher situations before. I'll figure out a way to come out of this smiling.

My cell phone rings and I glance down at the screen, smiling as Matt's crooked grin lights up my screen. It's like he read my mind. I tap answer and put my phone to my ear, a bright smile on my face. "Hi, Matt, I was just thinking about you," I cheerfully greet him.

"Were you?" he grumbles irritably, making me flinch.

"Um, yeah, I was going to call you," I begin.

"Why?" he spits out, interrupting me, sounding disgruntled. My heart begins to pound, suddenly uncertain where this conversation is going.

"I, ah, wanted to talk to you and tell you about Preston," I quietly admit, hoping my confession will turn his attitude around.

He chuckles humorlessly. "Well, isn't that ironic? That's exactly who I wanted to talk to you about!" he declares vehemently.

"Why?" I ask, suddenly anxious about his response.

"You need to tell your boyfriend to get the fuck out of my life!" he demands.

"What are you talking about?" I challenge, confused.

"He's fucking with my project Amy!" he yells.

"What?" I gasp in shock.

"He won't even take my calls, but he's already making my life a living hell. Tell him to back the fuck out of my business!" he orders fiercely.

"I don't understand," I mutter, tears building in my eyes. Breathing becomes difficult and my hands begin to shake as he elaborates.

"He's on the review board for new buildings, businesses and projects. He alone has my project on hold, impending further board review," he explains bitterly. "Putting it simply, if he wants to stop me from building my gym, he can make that happen and he's already started the ball rolling in that direction."

I shake my head in denial as my heart sinks into the pit of my stomach, praying it's not true. "No, no, no," I repeat, feeling myself begin to panic.

"Yes," he confirms. "Tell him to back the fuck up," he repeats slowly for emphasis.

"Matt, I'm so sorry," I murmur.

He huffs out a harsh breath and grumbles, "Yeah, sure." He sighs in defeat and mumbles, "I gotta' go. I'll catch you later." He disconnects the call before I have the chance to respond.

Tears run down my face, as my heart seizes in my chest, but I'm still breathing, struggling to comprehend what just happened. I feel as if my insides work to tear through my body from the inside out, piece by piece, until there's nothing left. I finally get the courage to go after what I really want, but I should've known better. I'm not meant to live a life with pure love. I can't have it; I can't have him. Matt was never meant to be mine.

I refuse to be the one to take away his dreams. No one has worked harder than him to get here. He deserves his gym. I will do whatever I have to do to make sure it happens. No one will take this away from him.

I pick up my cell phone and tap Preston's name. He answers almost instantly. "Amy," he greets me happily.

I gulp down the lump in my throat and force out the words. "Leave Matt alone."

"I don't know what you mean," he claims with mock innocence.

"You do!" I insist, attempting to maintain my composure. "You're holding up his building project."

"Oh, that," he mumbles, sounding bored. "If you want me to put in a good word for him with the board, I'd be happy to do that for my beautiful girlfriend," he offers.

My whole body tenses before I slump in my seat, knowing I've lost. "Okay, Preston, you win," I mumble, fighting back more tears.

"I'm not the one who's been playing games," he claims.

I shake my head in frustration, ignoring his comment. "Why do you want me? I ask the same question I did last night. Is it because I haven't been throwing myself at him like most women? Is it because I'm a challenge? Is it because he's used to getting what he wants?

"What matters is that I do want you and I can't wait to show you how much," he growls.

Gulping down the lump in my throat, I force happiness into the sound of my voice. "I'm looking forward to it. I'll be waiting for you to pick me up at seven," I inform him.

"Be ready a few minutes before. I'll be picking you up in a town car tonight. We can't be late," he asserts. I nod even though he can't see me. "Oh, and Amy," he prods.

"Yes?"

"I'll take care of the board for your friend on Monday. It's nothing you need to worry about tonight. We've worked too hard to let something like this get in the way, don't you think?" he challenges.

"Yeah," I quietly concur. I wipe away my tears; grateful he can't see my face at the moment. "I'll see you in a few hours," I murmur before disconnecting the call. I take a few moments, allowing myself to fall apart, knowing I'll have to spend the rest of the night holding myself together with a smile plastered across my face, just like I've always done. No one will notice my devastation or my heartbreak. I won't let them. The only thing they'll see will be my dedication to my work as well as my love and devotion to my adoring boyfriend. After all, I'm really good at pretending.

Chapter 26

Amy

"You look exquisite," Preston compliments, eyeing me hungrily. I'm wearing the blue dress as well as the shoes and jewelry he bought me. The dress fits my curves perfectly, like it was made for me. I pulled my hair up on top of my head in a fancy up-do, looping a few curls and lightly pinning them down, while leaving a few loose tendrils on each side above my ear.

"Thank you. You look handsome yourself," I murmur, taking in his black tuxedo with a deep blue tie and vest underneath, almost matching my dress perfectly. I take a deep breath and exhale slowly. Pasting a smile on my face, I push the last of my emotions away, refusing to let him see me suffer.

He reaches towards me and tilts my chin up until I meet his gaze. He searches my eyes and smiles, placing a sweet kiss on my lips. Holding my gaze, he murmurs, "We're going to have fun tonight."

I smile and nod my head in confirmation. "Let's go," I suggest.

He grins and takes a step back. "We don't want to be late." I grab a small silver clutch and shawl, pulling it over my shoulders. Preston grimaces and mumbles, "I'm sorry I didn't get you something to help keep you warm. I figured you'd have me," he teases.

I want to roll my eyes, but I refuse. I need to get over my annoyance fast or I'm never going to survive. I do like him; I'm just pissed at him because I can't stop wishing he were someone else. That's not fair to him. I step out the door, ignoring his comment and make my way down the stairs. I grimace, noticing my mother peeking out the window, but keep my gaze focused on the black town car at the end of the driveway instead. An older gentleman steps out as we approach, opening the back door. Thank you," I murmur my appreciation.

"You're welcome, Miss," he replies politely.

I sit down on the black leather seat, Preston sliding in right beside me. I buckle my seat belt and glance out the window, hoping my mother minds her own damn business. I can't deal with her on top of everything else. We back out of the driveway and Preston's hand falls to my upper thigh, pushing the fabric away at the slit. He caresses gently, sending uninvited goosebumps throughout my body, but I do everything I can to ignore them. Glancing at Preston, I remind myself of everything I like about him; he's obviously handsome, intelligent and successful. Most of the time he's a gentleman and he's made it abundantly clear he likes me, doing nice things for me. So many women want him, but I'm the lucky one, I remind myself, attempting to believe it's true. What he did to Matt was only out of jealousy and how can I blame him for that when I gave him every reason to be jealous?

He gives my leg a squeeze, pulling me out of my thoughts. I turn my head towards him, arching my eyebrow in question. "Something on your mind?" he challenges.

I shake my head in denial, answering, "Just thinking about how wonderful you are and the fundraiser tonight. I hope Diana Brooks is happy with everything."

He smiles and nods in approval, before he begins going over everything we need to do when we arrive. I relax back in my seat, gladly falling into work mode. I've let a lot of other things slide, but all the time and effort I've put in with Preston doing this project for Diana Brooks has been worth it. I'm excited to see everything fall into place and finally be able to meet her!

It feels like almost no time at all before we arrive at the venue in downtown Boston. Preston escorts me into an elegant ballroom at the K-Elite Hotel. Just before entering, a beautiful woman in a long, sleek white dress with a scoop neck, silky smooth ebony hair, golden eyes and flawless chocolate brown skin smiles brightly, greeting us. "Good evening. Do you have your tickets?" she requests.

Preston nods and hands her our two tickets. "Right here," he acknowledges.

Her eyes widen and her smile broadens as she grins at him. "Oh, thank you Mr. Kirst. Josef here," she gestures towards the tall bald man with broad shoulders behind her wearing a black tuxedo with a white vest and tie before continuing, "would be happy to take your picture."

"Thank you," Preston mumbles and smiles in acknowledgement. He nods for me to walk in front of him as we approach the photographer.

Josef smiles and instructs, "Step onto the platform and face me."

The platform has an elaborate arch covered in lilies with a wall mural behind including a small community of homes, stores (several clothing stores) and parks, with Diana Brooks Projects written in the center in a beautiful scroll. Preston guides me atop the platform and spins me around holding me close. "Now smile," Josef suggests. He snaps a few pictures before he advises, "The pictures will be up on the fundraiser website tonight and you can download them from there."

"Thank you," I murmur. We step away and I can't stop the giggle from slipping through my lips.

"What's so funny?" Preston asks.

"It's just strange, it almost feels like prom or something," I admit.

216

He purses his lips and grumbles, "I think this is a little more refined than a high school prom, don't you?"

"Of course!" I concede, "It's just," I trail off and mumble, "never mind." He eyes me quizzically and I shake my head and push up on my tiptoes, placing a kiss on the corner of his lips hoping to placate him. "Let's go inside," I prompt.

"Okay," he agrees. We step into the ballroom and my eyes widen in awe. Gorgeous gold and crystal chandeliers hang from the ceiling, light jazz music plays through the speakers from a small band at the front of the room near a large stage. Tall round tables draped with a white tablecloth and topped with either a tall, thin vase with silver and white stones and a white pillar candle, or a small fishbowl with the same stones, but a white tiger lily instead sit as a centerpiece. They're scattered throughout the room with two or three mahogany and black leather stools at only half the tables, encouraging people to mingle. On each end of the ballroom, there's a strip of long tables, decorated the same, but filled with food for nibbling, while the wait staff wanders around the room in white suits with black aprons around their waists, offering hot food fresh from the oven. Most of the decorations around the room are connected to the tiger lily, Diana's favorite and one of the symbols for her organization. Elegant boards with pictures depicting some of her most incredible projects sit around the room, along with a video playing near the large bar, opposite the stage, depicting some of her most incredible projects.

We smile greetings at various people as we stride across the room with his hand firmly on the small of my back. Peeking into a smaller room connected to the main ballroom, we find several people weaving through the tables and bidding on various items as part of a silent auction. A second bar sits in the back of the room, making sure people walk by the items up for bid. I breathe a sigh of relief; grateful everything seems to be set in place.

We step back into the main ballroom and begin looking around. I must admit I'm a little blown away by the people entering and milling about. They all seem to have one thing in common, dressed in their best dresses, suits and tuxedos. Top executives from the fashion industry, home décor companies, as well as other elite stores and brands at all levels stride in, wanting to be a part of this event. Models and a few well-known celebrities wander around the room. Then on the other side of things, I spot government officials, and individuals who run companies dealing with building and construction, reminding me of Matt's project, which causes my heart to drop into the pit of my stomach.

Pulling me closer, Preston's hand slides down, resting just over the curve of my ass. "Are you alright?" he questions.

I nod my head and instantly plaster a smile on my face. If Preston is asking if I'm okay, I'm doing a terrible job of holding myself together. I turn towards him, letting my head fall to his chest. "I'm great. I'm just taking everything in," I mumble.

He eyes me skeptically before nodding his head and placing a chaste kiss on my lips. "Let's get something to drink," he suggests. "It will help you relax," he adds in encouragement.

I nod my head in agreement; thinking a little bit of champagne might be good to help me settle tonight. "Alright," I concur.

"Then we can make our way around the room and I'll introduce you to some key people," he offers.

"We should find Diana early," I emphasize.

"We will," he acknowledges.

We make our way over to the bar in the main ballroom, Preston keeping his hand possessively on my hip at all times. We step up to the mahogany bar and he orders champagne and whiskey. I take the stem of the champagne glass and spin on my heel, turning right into Diana Brooks. She's standing alongside a good-looking man about two inches taller than her with light reddish-brown hair, green eyes, pale skin and broad shoulders wearing a classic black tux, making me wonder if he's her security guard, her assistant or her date. My smile broadens, completely genuine for the first time tonight as I look up at this incredible woman. She's about three inches taller than me, with wavy dark brown hair, olive skin, and mesmerizing coffee-colored eyes. She has a slim build, but holds herself with a power and confidence I try to emulate on a daily basis. "Ms. Brooks," I greet her cheerfully. "It's so wonderful to finally meet you in person," I proclaim.

Glancing from Preston to me and down to his free hand, wrapped possessively around my waist, she grins and holds out her hand. "And you must be Amy Stone," she declares. My mouth drops slightly open in surprise, as my eyes widen. "I've heard so much about you," she proclaims, shocking me even more. She nods at Preston and adds, "It's good to see you again, Mr. Kirst."

"Preston, please," he requests.

She nods her head in affirmation focusing her attention on both of us. "I'm thrilled with the job the two of you and your team have done on the marketing for this event. It looks to be our most successful fundraiser yet," she states.

"Thank you," I murmur appreciatively.

Thank you," Preston echoes. "We have really enjoyed doing everything for this event. Plus, it's been fun being able to work so closely with Amy," he comments. "We would love to work with you again in the future."

She smiles in acknowledgement and admits, "I didn't realize you two were a couple. You kept everything so professional." She nods approvingly, as Preston squeezes my hip in satisfaction. Glancing at me, she advises, "I was extremely impressed with what you did with the social media side of the fundraiser, Amy. I know you worked closely with Preston, but I've seen your other accounts,"

I gasp, her admission taking me by surprise. "Oh, um th...thank you," I stammer, excitement building in my chest.

She finally turns to the man beside her and gestures to him. "This is my assistant, Aidan," she introduces him. "Let him know if you need anything and if you want to find a new place to land after your internship, call me," she teases. I feel Preston instantly tense tugging me even closer to him. I watch as she grins playfully at Preston, her long fingers delicately falling to his chest before she gives him a gentle pat. "See you two later," she murmurs, as she walks away, her assistant trailing behind.

I momentarily watch after them and mumble, "Well, that was interesting."

Preston grunts in response. My head snaps over to him, just as he downs his liquor and turns back to the bar, requesting two more. He tips his head back, allowing the amber liquid to slide to the back of his throat. He swallows and returns his gaze to mine before he gulps another drink from the glass in his hand. I bite my tongue, wondering if I should say something to him. I'm not really sure how much he can handle, but I don't see the point of more alcohol already, not when there're so many eyes on both of us. He leans in and presses his lips firmly to mine before pulling back and giving me a salacious grin. I force a smile as we grab our drinks and make our way through the growing crowd, preparing for a long night.

Matt

"Brett, are you telling me I'm fucked unless I can get this asshole to drop it?" I question, running my hand through my hair in frustration.

"Not exactly, but you're going to need a lawyer like your dad to pull you out of this if Kirst keeps pushing," he advises.

"I'm not fucking calling him!" I snap.

"Okay, okay," he quickly responds. "I just don't want you missing out on building your dream gym because you were too stubborn to suck it up and call your dad."

I heave a sigh and drop my head into my hands, knowing he's right, but I can't do it, not yet. "I'll think about it," I grumble.

"Good, good," he mutters, placating me. "What did Amy say about it?" he prods curiously.

"I didn't really give her a chance to say anything, at least not to me," I admit.

"Seriously?" he questions. "You really are an asshole," he chuckles.

I heave a sigh. He may be joking, but I know he's right. I feel guilty as hell for calling her and blowing up on her. I want to call and apologize, but then I remember that asshole and I don't even bother to send her a text. I'll wait to see what happens. If I don't have any answers a few days into this week, I'll have to find a way to get them and I'll have to do something about it. "So are you going to meet me for a beer or are you too busy sulking to make time for that?" he retorts.

I grimace and glare at the phone, even though he can't see me. "How about tomorrow night instead?" I suggest. "There's a few more things I want to go over tonight," I reveal.

"Sounds good. It's probably better for me anyway," he concedes. "Later, asshole," he taunts.

I grunt and disconnect the call. I open my laptop and find the town by-laws. Then I pull out my paperwork again, hoping to find something I didn't see before to prevent Preston from taking this away from me. I can't fucking let that happen!

Chapter 27

Matt

"Would you get that look off your face?" Brett grumbles, glaring at me across the table at the pub. I glower at him and take another gulp of my beer. "You need to relax and enjoy tonight," he advises.

I huff a laugh and arch my eyebrows in challenge. "Yeah, how the fuck am I supposed to do that?" I question, not really wanting his answer.

"Look around, there's a lot of beautiful women in here tonight," he suggests.

I don't bother lifting my gaze to look around the room. It doesn't matter. I can't get my mind to stop turning. How the hell did my life get so entangled with this asshole? He doesn't even know me, yet he's doing everything he can to fuck up my life. I run my hand through my hair in frustration and tip my stein back, downing my beer quickly. Shaking my head, I finally respond, "I can't."

He heaves a heavy sigh. Folding his arms on the table in front of him, he leans towards me. "Matt, there's nothing else you can do tonight anyway. It's not worth stressing about right now," he reiterates. It's the same thing he's been saying since yesterday when I told him about the board.

"That's not true, I could be doing more research and working on a plan to meet with each of the board members to garner support," I begin.

He gives me a look, reading me well. "I know, I know," I mumble.

"You've been looking at those papers non-stop and I'm pretty sure you already planned out exactly what you could say with every single board member," he claims.

My shoulders slump, knowing he's right. "But it feels pointless to sit here on my ass not trying to do something about it."

"You are doing something about it! You've been working on it non-stop since you found out and I'm pretty sure if you keep pushing yourself like that you're not going to succeed. You need a break before you fall over the fucking edge!" he declares.

Vanessa steps up to the table with two beers in hand, followed by a friend of hers with another two beers. They're both dressed in dark blue skinny jeans with a few strategically placed rips, a body suit, Vanessa's black and her friend's white, with flannel shirts over the top, unbuttoned, but tied at the waist. Vanessa's shirt is colored in a small black and red pattern, while her friend has one with blue and white, matching her blue eyes. Vanessa smiles down at me. Holding the beers up, she offers, "We thought you guys could use another beer."

"Well, thank you," Brett agrees. He immediately scoots over, making room for the curvy blonde woman next to him in the booth, before I have a chance to respond.

She smiles shyly and sits down next to Brett, "Hi, I'm Jade," she says introducing herself.

"Brett," he announces, grinning wide. He gestures towards me, mumbling, "And the grumpy one over there is Matt."

She nods in acknowledgement, "I know." His eyes widen and he glances over at me for further explanation.

Instead of answering his question I introduce him to the woman still standing next to the booth and waiting patiently with beers in hand. "Brett, this is Vanessa."

"Oh, Vanessa," he taunts, causing me to roll my eyes. "It's nice to finally meet you."

I heave a sigh and scoot over. I glance down at the space next to me and up at her, gesturing for her to sit down, but she still hesitates. Forcing myself to say the words, I mutter, "Vanessa, have a seat." She smiles and lowers herself into the booth. "And thank you for the beer," I acknowledge.

"You're welcome," she replies. "So you're still pissed at me," she mumbles, regretful.

I reach for the beer and down half of it before I answer. "I honestly don't get it. I feel like you're only telling me half truths when it comes to him, so I guess I'm not sure how to be around you," I attempt to explain.

She grimaces and apologizes. "I'm sorry. That's not my intention. I just don't like to talk about him, but I know you two have things you need to deal with," she begins.

I interrupt, "Why?"

She looks at me slightly startled, "What?"

"Why do we have things between us that we need to deal with? What possible issue does he have with me besides," I gasp, feeling like a fucking idiot. Is he fucking with me because of Amy? What the hell? How much does she really have to do with this?

"Besides what?" she prompts.

I shake my head, not wanting to talk about it anymore. "Nothing, thank you for the beer," I repeat, changing the subject.

"You're welcome," she repeats, settling against the leather booth. She scoots a little closer, placing her hand on my thigh. "I really am sorry."

Turning my head, I gulp hard and nod. "I know," I mutter. I sigh and lean back, extending my arm across the back of the booth feeling drained in every way. Brett's right, I need to try to relax.

Amy

I wash my hands as I stare into the mirror, appearing exhausted. I'll admit I'm grateful the night is nearly over, although I'm happy with the results. Someone walks out of another stall and steps up to the sink next to me. My eyes meet hers in the mirror reflexively and I smile at her kind eyes. "Hello, again, Ms. Brooks."

"Amy," she acknowledges, grinning. "Have you seen the numbers after the live auction?" she prompts. I nod my head, smiling proudly. "Those numbers already beat last year and we still have to put everything from the silent auction through. Well done," she praises.

"Thank you," I reply as I dry my hands.

"I meant what I said earlier," she begins. "I'm really impressed with you and I'd love for you to come take a look at what we have to offer after your internship," she reiterates.

My heart beat pounds rapidly in excitement. "Thank you," I repeat. She dries her hands and steps towards the door, glancing back at me just before she steps outside. "Have a good night!"

"You too," I call. I glance in the mirror again, suddenly appearing energized. I'm practically giddy with anticipation. Working with her would be like a dream job. I would love to learn from her. She's an extremely talented, strong and independent woman. I glance at my phone, wanting to call Matt to tell him about it. My shoulders sag almost instantly, knowing I'm probably the last person he wants to hear from right now. Well, besides Preston.

I glance towards the door, knowing I better go back out there. I take a deep breath and exhale slowly, smoothing down my dress before I step out of the bathroom. I lift my head, as the door swings shut behind me, nearly hitting me in the ass as my eyes lock with Preston. I step out of the doorway and he pushes off the wall he's leaning against, with his body tense and his jaw twitching. He holds my gaze, and stalks towards me with a predatory gleam in his eyes. I back up reflexively, backing into the wall right next to the bathroom door. He plants his palms on the wall, just above my shoulders and presses his body into mine, caging me in.

"Did you have a meeting with her in the bathroom?" he probes.

My eyebrows draw down in confusion. "What?"

He laughs humorlessly and the scent of alcohol permeates my nose. He tilts his head down and begins kissing me on the neck. "I just saw Diana leave," he mumbles and kisses me again, making a trail to my collarbone.

"It's a women's bathroom," I sarcastically state the obvious.

"I thought you had a thing for bathrooms," he taunts, chuckling softly.

My heart thunders in my chest, feeling my whole body heat at his insinuation, hoping I'm misunderstanding the situation. One hand slides down to my waist, pinning me in place as he grinds his hips. His other hand slides to the back of my neck, gripping it tightly as he forces my head up until I meet his gaze. He smirks, just before his lips crash down on mine. He shoves his tongue into my mouth devouring me and tasting of whiskey. He groans into my mouth and I slide my hand down, placing my palm on his chest, attempting to push him back. He releases my lips and narrows his eyes in question. "Preston we're at work," I remind him.

He heaves a sigh, relenting and slides his hand down, clasping my hand in his. "Fine! Let's go talk somewhere else then," he concedes. He turns the opposite direction from the ballroom and tugs my hand, pulling me along.

"Where are we going?" I ask, puzzled.

Instead of responding he quickens his pace and tightens his grip on my hand. He reaches a set of intricately carved silver doors and presses the button to the right. I gulp down the sudden lump in my throat as the elevator doors slide open. He pulls me inside and taps a hotel card over a black knob, lighting up the button for the penthouse. My eyes widen in disbelief and I blurt out, "You got us a room?"

His jaw ticks in annoyance, his patience with me seeming to wear thin. "I own this hotel," he declares in response.

"Oh," I mumble. I had no idea. The elevator flies to the top floor, without stopping. The doors slide open and we step right into the penthouse. Ivory colored tile floors, cream-colored walls and intricate white moldings surround us. The first room holds a white couch and two matching armchairs with a glass coffee table and end tables, all with black iron pedestals. Just beyond the living room sits a large dining table and high back chairs in a dark cherry wood overlooking part of Boston Harbor with its floor to ceiling windows. On the left is a beautiful kitchen with white cabinets, stainless steel appliances and a white and black granite countertop, accompanied by a small island in the middle with four cherry barstools matching the dining furniture. "Wow," I murmur.

Preston tugs my hand and pulls me into him kissing me. He cups my ass with one hand and folds the hand he's holding behind my back, causing my back to arch in response. "Preston," I mumble against his lips. He deepens the kiss and pulls me even closer. "Preston," I repeat.

He groans in frustration as his head falls back. "What Amy?" he snaps. "You didn't want to kiss me downstairs," he reminds me, as if I don't remember. "So now we have all the privacy in the world," he claims. "All for you."

"Um, I...I," I stammer, not sure how to respond.

He heaves a sigh and releases me completely, taking a step back. "I had a bad fucking night. Okay? I have shit coming at me from my dad, from investors, from the board and the town," he states, reminding me of Matt. "Diana Brooks tries to poach my fucking girlfriend right in front of me and you acted like she just gave you the fucking moon. She's never looked closely at interns before, but she even checked out your other accounts," he reiterates. "I swear you went behind my back to talk to her," he grumbles.

"Preston, I didn't," I insist.

He huffs a humorless laugh and shakes his head in disappointment. "And now, I just want to forget for a little while and you're still holding me at arm's length. What are you doing here Amy? Are you fucking using me?" he challenges.

"No!" I yell defensively. "I haven't talked to Diana except through the things we sent over from the whole team. You were the one who talked to her, not me. And I'm not using you," I argue. "I do like you, Preston," I claim. I do, I repeat in my head over and over again, attempting to believe it. I'm not crazy about him yet, but I've always been able to change that by throwing myself into the relationship. I can do it again. I don't know why I'm struggling to fall for him. Why is it so hard for me to do this time? I grit my teeth forcing the reason, forcing him, out of my mind. That doesn't matter. *He* can't matter in this scenario. I just need to make it work...at least until Matt's project is in the clear. Maybe then I can rethink things, but not until then. I will not be the reason he loses everything.

"Then show me," he dares, narrowing his eyes at me. "Show me you actually give a shit about me and fucking kiss me back."

I hesitate his eyes sparking with anger. He's in front of me before I have a chance to react. He pins my hands behind my back and clasps them with one of his large ones. Then he takes his other hand and grasps my hair on top of my head and yanks it back, making me gasp. He covers my mouth with his and forces his tongue into my mouth again, causing me to whimper. I close my eyes, attempting to relax into his kiss, but I can't seem to catch my breath. Fortunately, or unfortunately, he misreads my reaction as desire. He releases his hold on my hair and slips his hand down to my breast, squeezing hard, making me flinch. He releases my hair and my lips at the same time, kissing down my neck. "Preston that's too hard," I whimper.

He squeezes even harder, making me cry out before he releases me. He pushes the straps of my dress off my shoulders and lets the dress fall to my waist as much as it can with my arms still pinned behind my back. He rips off the pasties covering my nipples before he bites down and sucks hard on the same breast he just squeezed. "I've been so patient, waiting for you. I need you to understand that you're mine," he mumbles.

"I do," I claim a tear escaping.

He pulls the skirt of my dress up to my waist, revealing my black thong and stockings. He yanks off my thong, snapping the elastic strap against my skin and tossing it to the side. Then he walks me backwards until my knees buckle and I fall back onto the couch with him falling right on top of me. "Ugh," I grunt, my arms aching with the awkward position I fell in. "Please let my hands go," I request.

He ignores my plea and continues to move, pulling a condom out of his pocket before he releases his hard length, not even bothering to remove his pants. Ripping the condom open with his teeth, he quickly rolls it onto his dick with one hand. I shake my head, knowing I'm the kind of girl who usually has sex long before this and I don't blame him. I've made him wait. Without even checking to see if I'm ready, he thrusts inside me. I cry out in pain, feeling like it's my first time. "I'm done waiting. I need everyone to understand you're mine," he emphasizes. He thrusts in and out, my head banging on the armrest, with each thrust. I close my eyes and stop resisting, no longer caring what else happens. It doesn't matter anymore. "You don't fuck anyone, but me. You're mine," he repeats possessively over and over again, digging his thumb and fingers into my hip. He thrusts hard, picking up his pace and releasing, before finally collapsing on top of me and letting go of my hands.

He heaves a sigh and mumbles, "Fuck, I needed that." He kisses my lips and grins, claiming, "I'll make it better for you next time." He slips out of me and pushes up, sauntering towards the bathroom.

I smooth down my dress as I sit up, feeling a little dizzy. I hear my mother in my ear, telling me I did the right thing, making my stomach flip with disgust.

Preston stalks back into the room, looking perfect. "You need to clean yourself up," he advises. I nod my head, knowing it's true. He closes the distance between us and tilts my chin up to meet his gaze. "Maybe now you can stop being so shy with me," he suggests.

My eyebrows pull together in confusion. "What do you mean?"

231

He arches his eyebrows in challenge. "You can make out with your *friend* on a pool table when you're on a date with me." My body heats and anxiety pricks at my insides as he continues. "You can even fuck him in the bathroom, but you're hesitant to kiss me in public," he states. He pauses, letting his words sink in. "That changes now," he demands. Tipping his head down, he kisses my lips tenderly before he steps away and turns towards the front door. "Clean up and meet me downstairs in ten minutes. Don't be late," he instructs leaving no room for argument.

I sit frozen, not breathing, processing his words, his demands, what just happened and feeling as if my world is ending. "Shit," I mutter as reality crashes into me. "What the fuck have I gotten myself into?"

Chapter 28

Amy

Matt backs me up against my house, right next to my front door. He looks down at me, his gorgeous green eyes bright with his intent as he plants a hand on each side of my head, caging me in. My breathing picks up its pace as I get lost in his gaze. The corners of his mouth curve upwards just before his lips brush against mine, hesitant at first. He pulls back, searching my eyes before his mouth crashes down onto mine. Pushing his hard body into mine, he slips his tongue past my lips. I push forward, greedily meeting him with mine, licking, probing, exploring and tasting each other. His hand slides down my arm, finding purchase at my waist, tightly gripping my hip and holding me close. "Matt," I gasp his name.

He deepens our kiss making me moan in pleasure. I grasp his black t-shirt in my hands, gripping him and holding myself back at the same time, wanting to climb him right here on my front porch. He pulls back and gasps for breath. "Amy, you're driving me crazy," he claims.

I tug him back to my lips, licking his lips for entry he gladly gives. He groans into my mouth, causing my whole body to burst into flames. I let my hands slide down his chest, over his shoulders and down his ridged back, my heart beating out of control. I can't get close enough. He does something to me that tips me over the edge. "I want more, Matt," I whisper desperately.

"What the hell do you think you're doing?" my mom demands, stepping out onto the front porch. We both gasp and jump, the sound of her voice startling us apart.

My body instantly feels cold and I push my shoulders back, glaring back at my mother defiantly. "I was out on a date, Mom," I proudly announce.

Her eyes narrow and her lips twitch in both anger and annoyance. She doesn't even bother glancing in Matt's direction, maintaining her focus on me. "Mr. Richardson is here with his son to see you!" she emphasizes.

"Why?" I ask both confused and irritated.

She takes a deep breath and grits her teeth. She barely opens her mouth as she fumes, "Get in the house, Amy!" I cross my arms over my chest and glare back at her, refusing to move. "Now!" she demands angrily.

Matt begins slowly backing away, pulling my eyes to him. "Um, I should go," he mumbles. "We can catch up later, Amy," he offers.

My mother finally spins on her heel, giving Matt her full attention. She plants her hands on her hips seething as she glares at him. "You will do no such thing! You will stay away from my daughter, you worthless piece of shit," she yells in warning. "It's no wonder your parents left you here all alone to go after your brother. He's obviously the only one worth it!"

Matt gasps, his mouth dropping open and his eyes widening in shock. "How dare you!" I retort. He takes another step backwards, as if attempting to maintain his balance. "Matt," I call taking a step towards him, knowing how much those words would hurt him.

I watch his Adam's apple bob up and down as he gulps hard. He looks at me, his eyes pleading with me to let him walk away. A tear escapes out of the corner of my eye and I reluctantly nod my head, knowing I'll be calling him as soon as I get to my room. He shouldn't have to endure my mother's wrath. He doesn't deserve it. "I'm sorry," I mouth the words, not able to speak.

He nods almost imperceptibly, before spinning on his heel and stalking back to his motorcycle. He grasps his helmet and pulls it on as he throws his leg over, straddling the bike. He leans back and starts it up, revving the engine *just before he pulls away from the curb, escaping as quickly as possible while I watch him drive away.*

Before he even rounds the corner, my mother grasps my arm and yanks hard, pulling me towards the house. "Ah," I yelp in pain. She practically throws me inside, making me stumble over the threshold. "What were you thinking?" she questions, her disbelief clear. "What if they were still here and saw you acting like...like...like trash on our front porch?"

I do a double take, realizing what she just said. "You mean they're not here?" I probe.

"They were. They just left," she informs me. "And you're damn lucky they did!"

"Mom! You lied! I was on a date with Matt and you ruined it!" I reiterate.

"Acting like a whore on your front porch with that boy is not a date," she claims, with blatant disgust.

"I'm not a whore! I just kissed him!" I scream, defensively. "I like him!"

"You will not go out with him again, Amy," she insists, her underlying threat apparent. "Do you hear me?"

"I hate you!" I scream, tears burning my eyes. I spin on my heel and stalk towards the stairs, needing to get as far away from her as possible. I barely get to the third step before my head snaps back as she yanks my hair, pulling me backwards down the stairs. I twist my ankle trying to catch myself, as my hands desperately reach for my head, trying to get free. I fall backwards, my head slamming into the wall by the stairs with a loud crack, everything around me instantly becoming blurry, as I gasp for breath.

I try to pull my focus to something, anything, only to have my mom standing over me and pulling my head back again, waiting until I look in her direction. "You are such a disappointment," she mumbles, shaking her head. "But you will not embarrass this family," she claims.

"Mom," I cry, begging for her mercy.

She tightens her hold on my hair, making me whimper, but I quickly snap my mouth shut afraid of what she might do. "You have a date with the Richardson boy tomorrow night," she informs me.

I shake my head in refusal, "No, I don't want to go out with him."

She laughs humorlessly and insists, "This isn't about what you want. Stop being so selfish and think about other people for once in your life! This is about what's best for you and for this family. You will go out with him and if you want to be a whore, do it with him," she states. I gasp in shock. She smirks innocently and shrugs her shoulders. "I'm so disappointed in you, Amy," she mumbles, shaking her head sadly. My chest aches imagining the same look on my father's face. After everything your father does for you, going out with this boy and making sure he has a good time is the least you can do."

"Dad would want me to be happy," I claim defiantly.

She sneers at me as she releases her grip on my hair. "Your father set the date up for the two of you. He wants you two to meet and hit it off. He thought you would be perfect together," she announces, her voice almost giddy.

"If he knew how much I like Matt," I begin arguing.

She laughs and shakes her head, stopping me midsentence. "He hates Matt's family. He wants you nowhere near any of them." My heart feels like it's breaking with every word she utters. "And if you try to get out of this, I will make you pay for it. You need to act like a grown-ass woman and do everything you can to make sure it goes well. You have some of my genes, do something useful with it for once and flaunt yourself for the right man."

I shake my head, tears streaming down my face and whisper, "But I want Matt."

She grips the same arm as before and jerks me towards her, causing me to cry out in pain. With her face barely inches from mine she commands, "You will do what's right for once in your damn life and go out with this boy. You will smile, have fun and do whatever you need to do to make him happy."

I whimper, staring at her firm stance, knowing I can't wait to get away from her. If it wasn't for Bree and Matt, I'd never make it through high school. "Okay," I reluctantly concede, too sore and exhausted to argue anymore. Right now, I think I'll do whatever I need to do to make this stop, to make her stop.

She gently brushes my hair out of my face and smiles in approval. "That's my girl. Go clean yourself up. You're a mess."

I stand on shaky legs, my body swaying and my stomach turning as I stand up. I quickly reach for the banister to hold myself up, desperate to escape to my room and hoping my shoulder isn't dislocated again. There's no way I'm going back down stairs for an ice pack, but I need to pull out my lavender, frankincense and myrrh oils and heating pad to get rid of the inevitable bruising quickly. At least that's something I've become really good at.

I blink awake, feeling heartbroken and sore as if the fight with my mom just happened, instead of being a dream from the weekend before my sixteenth birthday. I attempt to sit up and pain shoots through my arm, reminding me of a different altercation that did happen just last night, but with Preston. I quickly check over my body for pain and bruising. I find some on my arm, my hip and even my breast, causing me to close my eyes as an overwhelming ache slams into my chest. I don't know if I can do this, but I won't be the reason Matt doesn't get his dream. I take a deep breath and exhale slowly, pushing myself up through the pain.

My phone rings and I reach for it, Preston's face lighting up the screen. I sigh and paste on a happy face, hoping it transfers to my voice. "Hello?"

"Good morning, beautiful," he declares cheerfully. "How are you feeling this morning?"

"A little sore," I answer honestly, knowing he probably won't take it the way I mean it.

"I hope I wasn't too rough on you last night," he responds.

I laugh humorlessly and mumble, "I'll be fine."

"I was thinking I could come and pick you up and we could grab some breakfast before I take care of everything with the board for you," he suggests.

I hold back a groan, not wanting to do much of anything, but I need to do this, even if it's only to make things better for Matt. I owe him that much. "Sure. Just give me an hour to get ready," I request.

"I'll be there in forty minutes," he states and disconnects the call.

"Fan-fucking-tastic," I mutter and toss my phone on my bed. "I've got this," I reiterate to myself. I've always been really good at pretending and I'll do anything to make things right.

Matt

I leave work and drive the few minutes into town, heading towards the grocery store. I need to pick up some food for dinner. I have to do something to keep me busy, so I figured it's a good time to try out a new recipe. I park my car just as my cell phone rings. I glance at the screen and have a quick intake of breath seeing Dwayne's name, I instantly tap answer and murmur, "Dwayne? You have some news for me?" I ask without preamble.

He chuckles humorlessly. "You sound anxious," he teases me.

I sigh heavily and run a hand through my hair. "Please," I plead, struggling to breathe.

"Right, sorry," he mutters. "I imagine how stressed you've been," he adds. I bite my tongue, not trusting myself to say something I won't regret. "Well, you don't have to worry about it anymore. It's all taken care of," he announces.

"What do you mean?" I question, demanding an explanation.

"Just what I said. It's all taken care of," he repeats. I grimace, waiting for him to continue, needing more. "I guess whatever the issue was, the board has the answers they were looking for," he elaborates. "We can go ahead with the project."

I heave a sigh of relief. "Thank fuck," I mumble, feeling as if a weight has been lifted from my shoulders. My mind momentarily flips back to his words and I can't stop myself from questioning, "What was the issue anyway?"

"They never disclosed that information to me," he admits. "They would have to if it went further, but I guess they figured it out without having to do that."

"Thank you," I mumble and set up another meeting with him before disconnecting the call. My stomach churns anxiously, Amy crossing my mind and guilt attempting to strangle me. I hate what I said to her. She's not responsible for that asshole and it feels like I'm suffocating knowing I accused her of exactly that. If that doesn't make me an asshole, I don't know what does. I need to apologize.

I back out of the parking lot without stepping foot outside my truck pulling onto Main Street. I park along the side of the road and jump out, striding towards the coffee shop, hoping she still follows her Sunday routine. I pick up my pace, hoping to get there before I have a chance to change my mind. I stuff my hands into my pockets and pick up my pace, the cool air giving me a chill. I look up just as the woman I'm thinking about steps out of the shop, a small coffee in hand. She wraps her arms protectively around herself and walks briskly in my direction, not paying attention to where she's going. She looks tired, but as gorgeous as always, nearly taking my breath away in a long-sleeved black shirt and rust orange jumper with thin straps. Black leggings wrap around her legs, adorned with short black leather boots with a one-inch heel and accented with three round buttons on the outside of her ankle.

"Amy," I murmur. She keeps walking and I call her name a little louder, "Amy." She maintains her focus on the sidewalk in front of her, ignoring me. "Amy," I repeat one more time a little louder. I gently reach for her arm, trying to stop her.

"Ah," she gasps at my touch, instantly spinning away from me.

I hold my hands up as a peace offering. "I'm sorry, I didn't mean to scare you," I apologize.

She pastes a smile on her face and proclaims, "You didn't scare me."

I nod my head slowly as she edges even further away from me, making me wince. "I just wanted to apologize for acting like an asshole the other night. You didn't deserve that from me. I was pissed and I took it out on you," I concede, regretful.

"It's fine. It's no big deal. I hope it all works out for you," she adds, her fake smile still plastered on her face.

"It's fine, everything is moving forward," I mumble quickly answering her question. I see relief pass through her eyes, but I brush my project to the side, not caring with my attention solely on her. My eyebrows draw down in concern as I take in her pale skin, the dark circles under her eyes and something else I can't quite pinpoint. "Are you alright?" I implore, worried. I reach towards her, needing to help with whatever she's going through.

She backs away shaking her head and contradicts the movement insisting, "I'm fine. I'm just in a hurry. Plus I forgot a coat and it's cold," she rambles. "I'll catch up with you later."

She spins on her heel, rushing away from me as if she's scared. A sick feeling creeps into the pit of my stomach while I watch her hips sway as she walks away from me. She can be pissed at me all she wants, but I don't think that explains what just happened. She seems more skittish than pissed. What the fuck is going on with her? It almost reminds me of the way she used to be around her mom. I gulp down the bile creeping up my throat at the reminder. I hate that fucking woman with a passion, but the feeling is mutual. I wonder if she has anything to do with how she's acting now?

I stare after Amy, my heart aching for her, even when I know I can't have her, but that won't stop me from trying to help her when something goes wrong. I always said I would be there for her and I'm not about to let that change now. I don't give a shit what her boyfriend has to say about it either.

Chapter 29

Amy

I'm tired. I'm on edge and I don't feel like myself. It's been three weeks since the fundraiser and I'm incredibly grateful it's Friday. I need a fucking break. I'm done with constantly grinning and laughing, attempting to portray the happy persona everyone expects from me. I'm tired of nodding in agreement with whatever Preston says when at least half the time I'm not even listening. I'm tired of his protective demeanor and his patronizing bullshit, thinking he can smile, kiss me, buy me flowers, or take me shopping and get his way. I'm tired of the derogatory comments on social media due to jealousy over him. I'm tired of hearing how happy my mom and dad are that I'm dating Preston and how fucking lucky I am to be with someone like him. I'm tired of sleeping at his place, even though being at home isn't any better. I'm even tired of the sex. We haven't been together for long, but it suddenly feels like an eternity. I don't know how much longer I can do this. It's all bullshit. Matt is usually the only one who sees through my facade, but since Preston doesn't like me being around him, avoiding him works best for now. I don't think I've felt this alone since I shut Bree out because of everything with Christian and I never regretted anything more in my life. Is this what I deserve? Is this where I'm supposed to be?

I glance at my phone, checking the time and admittedly wanting to know if Matt sent me any more messages, but I'm not that fortunate. He's been busy, but he keeps texting to check in, even though I haven't been responding. I can't, not right now. I want to make sure everything for his gym goes through first. I'm grateful to Bree for keeping me updated, although she thinks it's because I don't want to cause problems with my new boyfriend. If she only knew half of it, she'd already be in the car on her way here. Luckily Matt already has everything set in place. I've never been happier he's so organized. He'll be breaking ground on Monday. After that happens, I'll feel so much better. Hopefully he'll still talk to me by then.

I can't wait to finish up this internship. I'm ready to move on and find something I really can put my heart into, both personally and professionally. Sometimes I regret coming back home. I know I made a deal with my parents and I had to come home if I wanted to pay my rent, but has it really been worth it? I feel like I'm back to where I was in high school, back to doing what's expected of me, back to pretending, back to being controlled and I fucking hate it. I wouldn't even care if I had to go back to being a barista, but then I think about being so far away from Matt and my heart aches at the thought. I can't imagine knowing I have no chance of running into him, let alone not living in the same area as him again. Last time I left, I knew I'd see him again, I knew I'd be back. Plus, we visited one another all the time; even if sometimes Matt claimed he was there to see Blake.

The phone rings on my desk, startling me out of my thoughts. I take a deep breath and exhale slowly before reaching for the receiver and answering the call. "Good afternoon, Kirst Marketing, this is Amy, how may I help you?" I ramble, overdoing my enthusiasm.

"Amy, it's your mother," she informs me, like I wouldn't recognize her voice.

I keep my smile on my face, hoping some of it transfers into my tone, so I don't sound like I want to strangle her. "Yes, what can I do for you," I formally reiterate.

She actually has the audacity to laugh at me. My hand tightens on the receiver as I glare at the phone, even though she can't see me. "I just hung up with Preston and his father dear and they transferred me over to you. I'm impressed you're there so late. Preston seems to be a good influence on you," she claims, making me grimace.

"What did you do, Mom?" I ask without preamble, instantly dropping my act.

"I didn't do anything a normal mother wouldn't do!" she insists, vehemently. "I just invited your boyfriend and his family to join us for Sunday evening dinner."

My heart drops into the pit of my stomach. I don't want to eat with my mother or Preston. But how can I refuse? "Mom, I don't know if Sunday is a good time for me. I have a lot of things to do,"

She interrupts, "Whatever your other plans may be, cancel them! If Preston can make it, so can you. We've talked about this, Amy. You need to make more of an effort to make Preston happy and show him you want to be a part of his life. Plus, your father will be home this weekend and you'll finally have a chance to do something good for him for once."

"What's that supposed to mean?" I retort.

"Suck it up and do what you have to do!" she reiterates. "Act like an adult for once in your life," she pleads sounding exasperated. "Do you always have to be so selfish?"

I wince, her comment feeling as if she punched me in the stomach. I open my mouth to argue, but immediately snap it closed, imagining the consequences. "Okay, Mom. I'll be there," I concede. "I have to go," I blurt out and hang up before she has a chance to say another word. I groan in frustration, much louder than necessary, grateful almost everyone already left for the day.

Suddenly, arms wrap around me from behind, causing my whole body to stiffen. Preston presses his face into my neck and takes a deep breath. Forcing myself to relax as he kisses my neck, I mumble a greeting, "Hi."

He spins my chair around so I'm facing him and jokingly questions, "Hi? That's all I get?"

I shrug and huff my response, "Hi, Preston."

He grits his teeth in annoyance and leans towards me, bracing his hands on the arms of my chair. "You've been staring at the same screen for nearly an hour. Daydreaming about me?" he prods, playfully.

I bite the inside of my cheek and paste a smile on my face as I nod my head in agreement. "You know me so well," I tease, barely hiding my sarcasm.

He grins and presses a hard kiss to my lips before straightening and smoothing out his black suit jacket. He looks around the office as he speaks to me, "I bought you some new clothes for this weekend. You're coming home with me tonight and spending the weekend," he instructs, leaving no room for argument.

"I have to go home," I begin.

He interrupts, "I just had a chat with your mom. She knows you'll be with me this weekend. Then we're having a family dinner at your parents' house on Sunday. As for you, I have everything you need at my place," he insists.

I shake my head, slightly dumbfounded. He chuckles, clearly amused as I try to figure out how to get out of this. "I can't...I um...I..." I stammer.

"You're adorable when I take you by surprise. Don't worry, I'll make it worth your while," he claims. He kisses me again and pulls back, grinning down at me. "We'll leave in five minutes," he announces, before he spins on his heel and walks away.

My stomach twists into knots and I drop my head into my hands. "Fuck," I mutter under my breath.

"I have to ask," a soft feminine voice begins, startling me. I snap my eyes up to find the dark-haired woman I've seen hitting on Preston a few times standing over my desk with her arms crossed as she glares down at me.

I don't remember her name, but I don't really care. I force a smile and implore, "Ask what?"

"Is it the money? The job? The fame of dating one of Boston's most eligible?" she grumbles, irritated.

I arch my eyebrows in surprise. "Excuse me?" I challenge.

"Well, he buys you designer clothes, shoes, jewelry, takes you out to fancy restaurants, elite events, introduces you to some really important people and what do you do besides cater to him and fuck him?" she prods.

I stand up, clenching my fists and narrowing my eyes at her. I don't know why her words bother me so much, but they do. Usually, I'm able to let things like this roll right off my back, so why am I letting it get to me? "You don't know what you're talking about," I seethe, attempting to control my anger.

She chuckles humorlessly, "Oh, really? Then why do you put up with Preston's shit? I saw how rough he was with you after you misspoke in the meeting. Is that the way you like it? Rough?" she smirks. I gasp, not even sure how to respond to her, making her laugh harder. Her eyes sparkle in amusement knowing she's getting to me. She leans closer to me, taunting me. "You're not good enough for a man like Preston," she insists, hitting me where it hurts. I've had too many people in my life tell me those same spiteful words over and over again. I'm never good enough. My breath hitches and I struggle to breath, as my heart races, my blood pounding in my ears. "You're nothing but a common whore," she sneers.

I can't take it! I'm not a fucking doormat! Reflexively, I reach up and slap her hard across the face, her head flinging to the side with the force. Her hand flies up to her cheek, as she gasps in shock. "Bitch!" she yells, grabbing Preston's attention as he strides out of his office.

He rushes over and stands between us holding his arms up to stop us, but neither one of us even attempts to move. "Preston," I whisper, anxious for his reaction.

"Your little bitch hit me!" she reiterates.

Preston looks at me and arches his eyebrows in question, keeping his expression neutral. I gulp over the lump in my throat and force out a confession. "I did," I confirm. He gives me a look, urging me to continue. "She was harassing me," I add.

He steps towards me talking softly, "What do you mean harassing you?"

There's no point in staying quiet. Either I've fucked everything up or I tell the truth and hope he takes my side. "Well, for starters, she called me your whore," I blurt out casually.

Preston's whole body tenses and he clenches his jaw. His face turns red and his nostrils flare as he slowly turns to face the woman. "Is that true?" he challenges, his voice deep and threatening.

"I um, no, I, it's not that, it's just that, um…" she stammers, shaking her head.

"Leave," he declares.

"What?" she asks with wide eyes.

"Leave now!" he repeats harshly.

"You're firing me? You can't fire me," she argues. "She hit me!"

He pauses and looks around, not seeing anyone except his sister. "Polly," he calls.

247

She looks up and Preston motions for her to come over. She stands and approaches us with a polite smile and questions, "Yes?"

"Did you hear or see what happened here?" he probes, knowing she was within earshot.

"Yeah, Tia was being appalling to Amy. She basically accused her of using you, called her a whore, said she wasn't good enough for you and hit on her, refusing to back down," she rambles.

"I did not hit on her!" Tia screams, shocked and offended.

"Oh, I'm sorry, I guess I misunderstood." Tia smiles triumphantly and Polly continues. "She propositioned her, asking her if she liked it rough. I guess not long after that is when Amy slapped her," she finishes.

Holding back a laugh, my eyes widen in shock, but I keep my mouth shut tight, not daring to argue while Tia, stands in front of us fuming.

"If you'd like I can call security," Preston calmly threatens.

She spins on her heel and stalks away without another word, an imprint of my hand prominent on her cheek. I glance at Polly barely muttering, "Thank you."

She grins and winks, "She's been harassing me and any woman that comes near Preston for a long time. It's about time the circumstances worked out where we could get rid of her without consequence." She spins on her heel and walks away as I slowly turn to face Preston.

"Thank you," I whisper, quietly, barely able to look him in the eye.

His fingers tilt my chin up to meet his gaze. He looks me over before softly asking, "Are you alright?"

I nod my head and rasp, "Yeah."

The corners of his lips twitch up in amusement and my eyebrows draw down in question. "I saw you hit her and it was kind of hot," he admits.

I laugh and push up on my tiptoes, pressing my lips to his. It's the first time in a while my heart's beating fast for him. I feel a little giddy because of him. I'm even hot because of him. "I want you," I mumble. I weave my hands into his hair and deepen the kiss. He wraps his arm around my waist and picks me up, striding back to his office without breaking our kiss.

"Good night, you two," Polly calls as she walks towards the front of the office, leaving for the day.

Waving as Preston kicks the door closed behind us, he flicks his tongue inside my mouth, demanding more and I willingly give it to him. Maybe this is what we needed, a way for me to see why I liked him in the first place. Maybe this is a good thing.

Matt

My cell phone rings and I dive for the table, snapping it up, holding my breath in anticipation. I glance at the screen and exhale harshly in disappointment at the sight of Brett's name. I answer and put my phone to my ear. "Hey, Brett," I mutter.

"Don't sound too happy to hear from me," he jokes.

I sigh heavily and admit, "I was hoping you were Amy."

"Still haven't heard from her?"

I run my hand through my hair in frustration and grumble, "Nope."

"I'm sure she's fine, man," he proclaims in encouragement.

"Yeah, I know," I mumble, not believing it. I know something is going on with her or she wouldn't be trying so hard to avoid me.

"Listen, I wanted to see if you wanted to grab a beer with me tonight?" he proposes.

I hesitate, not sure if I'm in the mood to go out, knowing he's going to be hitting on anyone with a skirt. "I don't know, I have a lot of shit to do," I claim.

"No, you don't," he argues. "Not until you break ground on Monday, then you can kick your ass in gear."

"I'm not celebrating until that happens," I emphasize. I can't stop stressing, worrying something could still go wrong.

"Who said anything about celebrating? Come on man," he pleads. "It seems to me you need a distraction for a couple hours. It's just a beer and I need a fucking break from studying."

I sigh, conceding, "Okay, but let's meet at nine. I have a few training sessions lined up tomorrow," I explain.

"Great, see you then," he adds and disconnects the call before I have a chance to change my mind.

I check my messages and missed calls one more time before I set my phone down, glaring at it. Brett's probably right. A couple beers could probably do me some good right now before I lose my fucking mind.

Chapter 30

Matt

Brett slides a pint of beer across the table towards me and grasps another in his own hand holding it up in a toast. I pick up the glass, hesitating momentarily. "I told you I'm not celebrating until it's done," I insist.

He scoffs and waves me off, "Not what this is about," he claims. "I swear," he reiterates. I nod in acknowledgement and he continues, "This is just a toast between friends to the week being over and to being my wingman."

I shrug, expecting as much and tap his glass with mine. Pulling it to my lips, I take a long drink, letting the cool liquid ease down my throat. "Ah, that tastes good," I mumble, returning the glass to the table. "So how are classes?" I prompt.

Brett groans and requests, "Don't fucking talk about classes, don't talk about the L-SAT, don't talk about studying. I need to forget about it tonight," he emphasizes.

I nod my head in understanding and chuckle to myself. "We sure have a lot of shit on the do not talk about list tonight," I mutter.

He laughs and nods in agreement, "True, but there's a lot of women here we could talk about or talk to instead," he proposes. I don't even bother looking around. I don't care. The one woman I want to talk to isn't here, I already checked. I don't even know if she would talk to me if she showed up. "But, speaking of assholes and the law," he mumbles.

"What?" I prod. "Are you calling yourself an asshole?" I joke.

He shrugs, the corners of his mouth curling upwards as he concedes, "If the shoe fits." He laughs and I shake my head in amusement. "Not the asshole I'm talking about though," he amends, nodding his head towards the front door behind me.

"Who?" I mumble and peak over my shoulder. My heart sinks and races in the same beat. Amy walks in looking hot as sin in a short black skirt molded over the curve of her ass, a black top coming down in a V connecting with a button at the bottom of her full breasts and a silver belt separating the two, making me wonder if it's one piece or two. She's wearing knee-high black suede boots with a two-inch heel, showcasing her calves. A man's arm wraps around her waist, pulling her close, forcing me to tear my gaze away from her to find that asshole Preston by her side. I clench my jaw and grunt in irritation as I turn back to Brett grumbling, "Fuck."

"I'd stay clear of him until you're up and running," he advises.

"I don't want to be anywhere near him," I concur. I order another round of beers, as two women approach our table.

Brett grins and asks, "Would you like to join us?"

I force a smile in greeting, not even hearing their names, my mind on Amy. I drink my beer and pretend to listen as I keep sneaking glances at her. That fucker keeps a hand on her at all times making my blood boil, hating every second of it, but I can't do shit. I glance across the table at Brett and confess, "I have to bail, man."

He nods in understanding and reaches his hand out, tapping mine and pulling back. "I'll catch you later," he acknowledges.

I nod to both of the women, offering a polite smile and turn towards the exit just as Preston walks outside with his phone to his ear. I slow, approaching Amy instead, her eyes focused on her phone as I sit down across from her.

She looks up, her eyes widening at the sight of me. "Matt, what are you doing here?" she questions.

"Out for a drink," I answer vaguely. "You look gorgeous," I compliment.

She gives me a genuine smile and I breathe a sigh of relief at the beautiful sight. "Thank you." She warily glances towards the door before looking back at me. "I'm, ah, here with Preston," she stammers.

I give her a tight smile and nod my head. "Yeah. I just wanted to see how you were doing. Last time I saw you, you seemed off and you've been avoiding me since," I tell her something we both know.

She bites her lower lip as she stares at me, her nerves showing. "Yeah, I just thought after what happened with your project, it would be better for both of us if I stayed away."

"If that were the case, I would leave you be, but my life would never be better without you," I emphasize. "Plus, there's something bothering you and I want to know what," I declare, feigning confidence.

She shakes her head in denial, "Nothing is bothering me now that everything worked out for you."

"Bullshit," I retort. "Is it your mom? Him?" I push, attempting to read her reaction.

Her eyebrows draw down and she bites her bottom lip as her eyes flicker back to the door. She opens and closes her mouth, unsure how to respond. "Matt, I..." she begins and trails off.

Preston walks back through the door, his body going rigid the moment his eyes land on me sitting with Amy. She straightens and puts on her fake smile, "Thanks for stopping to say, hi. It's been a while. It's nice to see you again. You remember my boyfriend, Preston" she rambles, awkwardly, dismissing me.

Ignoring me, he sits down, grasping the back of her neck and kissing her hard, claiming her. My stomach turns as she returns his kiss. He pulls back, his hand clamping down on her upper thigh. I don't want to walk away from our conversation, but she turns away from me, focusing all her attention on him with her fake smile.

"Yeah," I mutter. I stand and walk to the bathroom at the back, needing a minute to make sense of this. We've disagreed before, we've fought before, but she's never stepped this far back from me. I run my hand through my hair in frustration, knowing I won't get anywhere tonight with Preston glued to her side. I need to go home and try again tomorrow.

I walk out of the bathroom and look over the growing crowd just as Preston grips Amy's arm and seems to pull her up from her seat, rougher than necessary as she stumbles into his chest. His jaw twitches as his arm goes tightly around her, guiding her towards the exit. I quicken my pace, making my way through the crowd and towards the exit.

"You're still here," the woman who sat next to me calls out.

I nod my head and force a smile as I point towards the exit. "Yeah, I ran into a friend," I claim, the words sour on my tongue. Amy is so much more than that to me and always will be. "I'm leaving now, though. It was nice meeting you," I add. I step past her before she attempts to drag me into a conversation I don't want to have and make my way towards the door.

I step outside, the cool air crashing into me. I turn towards the parking lot and hear yelling. "I said, get in the fucking car!" I'm sure I know that voice, making my heart stop. I round the corner, only seeing red at the sight in front of me. I barely comprehend what I'm doing before I'm on him.

Amy

The moment Preston walks back through the door his body goes rigid as his eyes land on Matt sitting with me. His steely gaze meets mine causing my heart to sink into the pit of my stomach making me sick with anxiety. I instantly sit up straight and force myself to smile. "Thanks for stopping to say, hi. It's been a while. It's nice to see you again. You remember my boyfriend, Preston," I emphasize, hoping my words will appease Preston. Plus, I hope Matt won't push it; that wouldn't be good for me.

Before I have a chance to register what's happening Preston sits down next to me and crashes his lips into mine. I gasp in surprise, before kissing him back, not wanting to cause a scene. I'm not naïve. I know what he's doing. His jealousy is shining through, but I'll deal with it for now. He pulls back and smirks as he licks his lips, hungrily. His hand clamps tightly down on my upper thigh and I grit my teeth, trying not to wince in response. I focus all my attention on Preston, hoping to ease his worry.

"Yeah," Matt acknowledges bitterly. Out of the corner of my eye I see him stand and walk away.

Preston grips my jaw hard and kisses me again, thrusting his tongue into my mouth. He deepens the kiss as he loosens his hold on my face and slides his hands down the front of my body. He grasps my thighs, his thumbs digging into me and pinning me to my seat. He finally pulls back and I gasp for breath. Keeping his face close to mine, he glowers, his gaze like ice. "First, you make a scene at the fucking office," he grumbles and takes a deep breath before continuing, "and I stand up for you," he reminds me. "Then, you turn around and make a fucking fool out of me with him?" he challenges, his voice a deadly calm.

"That's not what happened," I argue, shaking my head in denial. "He was just saying hi," I claim.

He laughs humorlessly and proclaims, "He was fucking you with his eyes. He was probably remembering the time he fucked you against the door in the bathroom!"

"Preston," I gasp his name in shock. Tears sting my eyes and I gulp down the lump in my throat as I shake my head in denial.

"Let's get the fuck out of here," he declares. "We'll have a drink at my place."

I nod my head in agreement and he rises. I reach for my purse and barely grasp it before he grips my arm, roughly picking me up and pulling me out of my seat. I'm obviously not moving fast enough for him. Then again, I don't think I can get out of here fast enough either.

He clasps my hand, pulling me along towards the exit. The moment we walk out the door he quickens his pace. "Preston, you're walking too fast," I claim, attempting to pull my hand away from him. I stumble at the same time he jerks my hand harder. My heel catches on the cracked pavement and I can't stop my forward momentum, crashing to the ground. I put my free hand out to brace myself from impact. I hit the ground hard, both knees and my right hand hitting first, making me cry out in pain. "Ah!"

He turns and looks down at me, shaking his head in annoyance. "What the fuck is wrong with you?" he yells. He reaches down and picks me up, wrapping his arm around my waist and nearly carrying me the rest of the way to his car.

I hold my breath, attempting to keep my tears at bay, but an unwanted whimper escapes. He growls and sets me down on my feet next to his car. He pulls the door open and I look up at him, wondering if I should just call a cab instead. I look at the fire in his eyes as he stands, impatiently waiting for me to get in the car. "Um, maybe I should go home, so I can clean up and you can calm down," I suggest.

He hisses through his teeth and closes the distance between us. I step back, bumping into his car. He presses his body into mine, holding me in place. He grips my hip tightly with one hand and weaves his fingers into my hair with the other, tugging until I'm looking into his cold, hard eyes. My heart begins racing and I focus only on my breathing and his words. "You will clean yourself up at my place and I will calm the fuck down when you make it up to me at home."

I feel the blood drain from my face and I stammer, "Wh...what do you mean?"

He tightens his hold on me and spits out, "You will not make me look like a fool!" He huffs and pushes away from me, returning to the open passenger door of his car. He's fuming, clamping the door so tight, his knuckles begin turning white. He takes a deep breath and speaking each word slowly for emphasis he states, "Get in the fucking car, Amy!"

I stand staring at him with my mouth hanging open, telling myself I need to do as he says, but I can't seem to move a muscle. "I..." I begin. He reaches for me attempting to push me into the car, but I grip his hand, trying to pull him off me. "You're hurting me!"

"I said get in the fucking car!" he yells. He pulls me towards him and shoves me back, the side of my head slamming against the top of the doorframe as I fall into the car. I groan in pain as he lifts my feet off the ground and places them gently in his car, confusing me.

"You fucking asshole!" I hear the sound of Matt's guttural scream. A moment later, Matt charges Preston, slamming him into the side of his car and knocking the wind out of him. "I'm going to fucking kill you!" he threatens. Then his fist flies at Preston's jaw, followed by his whole upper body flying back in reaction.

Preston holds his hand up defensively, taking a swing at Matt with his other hand. The movement finally shakes me out of my stupor. "No!" I scream. "Stop!"

Matt grips the front of Preston's shirt with one hand holding him in place and swings at him with another, hitting his jaw again and again, Preston barely able to hold his hands up in defense. He's no match for Matt and I'm terrified Matt really will kill him. I attempt to stand up out of the car, instantly feeling dizzy and falling back. "Matt, please, stop!" I plead, tears streaming down my face.

His eyes flick over to me, immediately turning soft, full of concern. "Amy," he mumbles, his hold on Preston loosening.

"Fuck you!" Preston yells, landing a hit straight to Matt's cheekbone, his head snapping to the side with the unexpected blow.

Matt spins back towards Preston with a feral growl, punching him in his gut with an uppercut and knocking the wind out of him, before coming at his face with a left hook. Preston falls to the ground and Matt hits him again. "This is for hurting her! You will never lay a fucking hand on her ever again!" he yells, punching him again and again.

Sirens wail in the distance making my heart jump into my throat. "Matt, you have to stop! Please! Please, stop!" I beg anxiously, my voice already hoarse.

He grasps Preston by the shirt and pulls him up, shoving him up against his car. "Stay the fuck away from her," he warns.

Preston laughs, taunting him as the sirens approach, "You can't fucking touch me." He tilts his head to the side and spits blood out of his mouth right at Matt's feet, but Matt doesn't even flinch.

Two police cars followed by an ambulance pull into the parking lot, their lights shining on us. Matt releases Preston and takes a step back, while Preston smooths down his shirt, now torn and stained with blood. The sound of silence fills my head as I take a moment to look around, finally realizing the growing crowd in the parking lot around us. I don't even comprehend someone kneeling in front of me, attempting to get my attention, to check me out. She must be an EMT, I think to myself, everything about this moment feeling surreal. "I think we need to take her to the hospital," I finally hear her say.

"No!" I rasp, pulling myself out of my daze. "I'm fine," I claim. "What's happening to them?" I probe, glancing towards Matt and Preston. Preston stands at the front of a police car, talking with two police officers and an EMT checking out his wounds. I look inside the open back door of the same police car finding Matt sitting inside, with his hands behind his back, locked in handcuffs. He drops his head forward, leaning against the back of the seat in front of him in defeat and shredding my heart to pieces.

She glances in their direction before looking back at me without answering. "You have a pretty bad cut on you head," she reveals.

"How'd it happen?" another woman asks.

I tilt my head up noticing a police officer standing next to her. I glance up at both of them, confused. Then I reach up and pat my head, wincing at the movement.

Lowering my hand in front of my eyes, I wiggle my fingers, now wet and sticky with blood. "I just fell. I'm okay," I mumble, reflexively. "I don't need to go to the hospital," I insist. "What's happening?" I push.

"We're talking to some of the witnesses to find out what happened," the police officer reveals. "You can give your statement to us after you're fully checked out."

Her words, talking to witnesses, rings in my ears, the reality of our situation slamming into me hard. I have no way to protect Matt if there are witnesses. What am I going to do? I feel my anxiety rising as I notice movement out of the corner of my eye.

Preston, looking pretty badly beaten, but still walking approaches us cautiously. He's escorted by a tall, broad male police officer. "Babe, are you alright?" he prompts, sounding concerned.

I shake my head, confused. My eyes veer back to the EMT as my breathing quickens and my heart rate picks up. I don't want to go home with him. My eyes flick back and forth between Preston and the EMT before I mumble, "They're taking me to the hospital."

"I can meet you there," he offers.

"No, go home. Get some rest. You're hurt," I emphasize. "I'll call my dad," I insist.

He nods reluctantly and steps towards me, crouching down in front of me and kissing me softly on my lips. "Call me when you wake up," he requests. "I need to know that you're okay."

I nod in acknowledgement, knowing I can never go back to him and afraid of what that means for Matt. I glance back over at Matt, terrified for him and unsure what to do. He turns his head, his gaze meeting mine looking pained, just before the door slams shut, closing him in. I stare at him through the window until I'm loaded into the ambulance. Laying back I close my eyes letting my tears flow as the EMT cares for me. This is all my fault. I thought I could handle him, but I ruined everything just like I always do.

Chapter 31

Matt

The moment I'm released from the holding cell at the police station, I gather my wallet, my keys and my cell phone at the desk before I walk out with Brett by my side. We step outside into the cool, crisp, clean air and I halt. Taking a deep breath in, I sigh heavily, momentarily relishing the feel of the sun shining down on me. I run my hand through my hair in exhaustion and frustration, feeling overwhelmed with everything that happened since last night. I glance at Brett as we walk to his car; a silver Mercedes Benz C-Class his parents gifted him for his college graduation. "You look like shit," he smirks, attempting to lighten the mood.

I nod in agreement. He's right. I have Preston's dried blood all over me, a bruised cheekbone and jaw, my bloodshot eyes look dead from lack of sleep, my mouth tastes like ass and I probably smell like shit too, but I don't fucking care, not when she's in danger. "Thanks for bailing me out," I grumble.

He chuckles humorlessly and shakes his head. "Words I never thought I'd hear you utter," he admits.

I pull the door open and slide into the passenger seat of his car. I buckle my seat belt and mutter, "You and me both."

"I thought you were going to stay away from him," he probes. He starts his car and backs out of the parking spot, pulling out onto the road.

I grind my jaw and nod my head, recalling the way he pulled her out of her seat and then the way he attempted to shove her into his car, slamming her head on the roof. Plus, I noticed her knees covered in blood, giving me reason to believe I missed more of the traumatic scene. I gulp down the lump in my throat that refuses to go away. "He put his fucking hands on her, man," I rasp, barely able to get the words out.

He hits the brakes hard, glancing over at me in astonishment. "What the fuck did you just say?" I turn my head, glowering at him, not able to repeat the fucking words. A tear escapes and slips down my cheek, as I struggle to hold myself together. "Fuck," he acknowledges in complete shock.

I huff at his response, his reaction barely a fraction to how I'm feeling. I feel like I'm being torn apart from the inside out, as I watch her head slamming into the car on repeat. It's my own personal nightmare. I can't stop my mind from wandering, wondering if she's okay. I grab my phone and attempt to turn it on to no avail. "Shit."

"I have a cord in the glove box if you want to charge your phone," he offers.

"Thanks," I murmur and do as he says.

He glances in my direction and briefly hesitates before suggesting, "You need to call your dad for help on this one."

I wince, knowing he's right. "I know," I concur.

"I heard some of the people talking to the cops and they were all saying it looked like you started it," he enlightens me.

"Of course they did," I mumble.

He smirks and adds, "Well, either way, he looked like shit." A small smile of satisfaction curls my lips, but it quickly falls away, knowing what he did to her. "I should also let you know I called the gym to let them know you wouldn't be able to come in today. They said they'd cancel your training sessions for you and to call them later."

"Thanks," I mumble. Work is the last thing on my mind at the moment. At least someone is thinking straight.

"I also talked to Blake last night. I'm almost positive he left Maine early this morning. He said he'd text when he got in, but I didn't want you to have to wait longer than necessary in that concrete shithole," he reveals.

I force a smile and mumble, "Appreciate that. I'll give him a call."

He drives the rest of the way to my house in silence as I stare out the window, watching the blur of brightening fall colors pass by in a blur, feeling completely wrecked. I have to figure out a way to help her, even it's not me who does it. Maybe Bree is the answer. Talking to Blake will be a good thing. Brett pulls into my driveway and I unplug my phone turning to him, not sure how to thank him for this. "Thank you, Brett," I mumble. The words feel inadequate and I open my mouth to say more.

Shaking his head, he quickly interrupts, "No worries, Matt. I know you'd do the same for me." I pinch my lips tightly together and nod my head in agreement.

With a lot more effort than should be necessary, I climb out of the car and close the door behind me. Trudging up to my front door, I try to prepare myself for what I need to do. My phone vibrates and pings several notifications as it comes to life. I unlock my door and step inside, feeling the weight of the impending phone call I know I have to make. I stride to the counter, dropping my keys and wallet, as I plug my phone in to further charge.

I quickly scroll through all my missed messages and calls, hoping to see Amy's name, but I'm not that fortunate. My heart sinks further and I drop down onto the stool at the end of my kitchen counter, letting my head fall into my hands. I stare off into the distance, wondering how the fuck I let everything get so out of hand. I take a deep breath and exhale slowly, attempting to pull myself back together. I stare at my phone trying to get the courage to dial when Blake's face pops up on my screen. I breathe a sigh of relief at the momentary reprieve and tap to answer the call. "Hey, Blake," I mumble.

"Thank fuck. Are you home?" he questions.

"Yeah, Brett just dropped me off about ten minutes ago," I acknowledge.

"Excellent. I'm coming by," he states, not giving me a chance to refuse.

"Alright. Give me a little time though?" I request. "I really have to shower and I have an important call to make real quick.

"Got it. I'll be over in about a half hour," he concurs.

"Sounds good, thanks," I recognize.

"Later," he mumbles and disconnects the call.

I stare at my phone knowing I can't put it off any longer if I'm going to make it through this mess to the other side. I close my eyes, take a deep breath in and exhale slowly, attempting to relax as much as possible. Then, I click on my contacts and pull up his name. I tap on it before I have a chance to change my mind. It barely rings once before I hear his deep voice on the other end of the line. "Matt? Is it really you? Is everything okay?" he prods.

I shake my head even though he can't see me, feeling my anxiety growing in my chest, feeling as if tiny little spikes surround my heart as it bounces throughout my insides. I gulp hard and force out the words, "Dad, I need your help."

Amy

I blink my eyes awake, squinting at the light with my head pounding as the nightmare of last night comes crashing back down on me. My dad brought me home from the hospital about seven o'clock this morning and tucked me into bed. I reach for my cell phone and glance at the time, 1:07pm. I slept for six hours and I feel like I have the hangover from hell. I scroll through my missed texts and calls, Preston three of those, but not a single one from Matt. I hope he's okay. I have to find out what's happening with him. I send a text to Brett, knowing he was there last night. Hopefully he knows what's going on with him. My stomach turns and I attempt to gulp down the nausea. Maybe eating will help, but I know I don't have anything here and if I want to eat, I need to make my way across the driveway.

I move slowly, glancing down at my pale blush pink sweatpants and oversized chocolate brown sweatshirt. I run my fingers through my hair, wincing as I near the cut on my head. I ended up with seven stitches last night. I didn't even realize I cut my head at first. It's definitely not going to be easy washing my hair. Stepping into my brown fuzzy slippers, I cautiously make my way out the door and down the stairs, clinging to the handrail for support. I amble in through the back door, stepping into the kitchen.

My mom looks up from the sink and meets my eyes. "It's about time," she announces, making me grimace. "How do you feel?" she asks, just a touch softer.

"I'm doing okay. I'm hungry," I admit.

My dad steps into the room, his whole face lighting up before instantly flooding with concern at the sight of me. "Amy, sweetheart, should you really be walking around? You should be resting. I could've brought you some food," he offers.

I give him a grateful smile, "Thanks, Dad. I'm doing okay. I actually think eating something might help me feel a little better," I admit.

He approaches me and wraps his arm protectively over my shoulders. "Why don't you go lay down on the couch and I'll bring you something," he proposes.

"Okay," I relent. "Thank you," I mumble as he guides me towards the living room. I sit down on the ugly floral couch my mom loves so much, but I have to admit it has always been comfortable.

Dad grabs the remote for the TV and sets it down on the coffee table, scooting the table closer. Then, he covers me up with a light gray blanket. "How's that?" he prompts.

"I'm fine, Dad," I proclaim. He hesitates, trying to decide if he should believe me. "I promise," I add.

He nods his head and kisses me gently on my forehead. "What would you like to eat?" he asks.

"I think I just want a bagel with cream cheese and some berries if we have it," I tell him.

"I believe we have blueberries," he acknowledges.

"Perfect," I murmur, the corners of my lips curving up in appreciation.

He turns around and I close my eyes, but I don't' hear his feet retreating to the kitchen. I open my eyes to find him staring at me. "Sweetheart, you know you can tell me anything, right?" he gently prods, looking hopeful.

I nod my head in agreement, at the same time, my head and heart fighting about my response. "Yes, Dad, I know."

He gives me a tight smile and turns towards the kitchen, returning only a few minutes later with a bottle of water, along with my bagel and fruit. "Thank you," I mumble, grateful. I immediately start nibbling on the bagel, my stomach beginning to settle the more I eat.

"I have to get some work done, but I'm working from home today, so I'm right here in my office. Call me if you need anything," he advises.

"Okay," I agree. "Thanks, Dad."

He places another kiss on my forehead, murmuring, "I love you."

"I love you too, Dad," I murmur, before he retreats to his office.

A few minutes later, my mom strolls into the room, her eyes narrowed. "You're really loving this aren't you?" she questions.

"Yeah, I love getting my head smashed so hard that I have to have stitches," I respond sarcastically.

"Watch your tone with me young lady," she warns. I force myself not to roll my eyes, so I don't hurt myself. The doorbell rings and she glances at me with her lips pursed and her body rigid. She heaves a sigh and strides towards the door as my phone beeps with an incoming text.

I quickly snatch up my phone and hold my breath, preparing for news at the sight of Brett's name. "We were able to get him out late this morning. I just dropped him off at home. I know he'd like to hear from you. Are you okay?"

I quickly type my response, "I'm fine. I'm home resting. What's happening with him?"

"If you're asking if he's hurt, not really, just a couple minor cuts and bruises, mostly on his knuckles. If you're asking if he's a mess, my answer is yes. He's really worried about you...so am I. If you're asking what's happening with being arrested, well, that's another story," he responds.

My stomach twists into knots and I set the bagel down on the table, no longer able to put anything into my mouth. "What do you mean?"

Instead of answering he asks, "Are you still dating Preston?"

Technically, I am, but I have to figure out a way to deal with him. "Yes," I answer simply.

"Well, then maybe you should ask your boyfriend to drop the charges," he states.

My eyes widen in surprise and I clarify, "What are you talking about?"

"He's the one who had Matt arrested for assault and with all those witnesses, it's a slam-dunk," he enlightens me.

I feel my panic escalating, knowing I can't let this happen. This is all my fault and Matt was only trying to protect me. On top of that, I have no idea what kind of influence this could have on the construction of Matt's new gym.

I look up as my mom walks back into the room with a huge smile on her face, causing me to arch my eyebrows in surprise at her one-eighty. "Amy, look who stopped by," she croons, stepping to the side revealing Preston with a huge bouquet of fall flowers in his hands. My whole body goes rigid. I sit up quickly, instantly regretting the movement. "He was worried about you," she acknowledges, with an adoring look in his direction.

I bite the inside of my cheek, holding back my laugh and contemplating how to approach this situation. "How are you feeling?" he prompts.

I appraise him, remaining silent as my mom reaches for the flowers, giving me a look of warning. "Here, let me take those. I'll put them in some water for you," she offers.

Chapter 32

Amy

I slowly let my eyes run over Preston, taking in his appearance. His face swollen and bruised almost everywhere, leaving him with two black eyes, bruised cheekbones and jaw, his nose slightly crooked and a cut lip, contradicting his pulled together attire. He's dressed in a light blue button-down shirt and dark blue jeans, with dark brown loafers. "How are you feeling?" he repeats, as my mom walks out of the room.

"Okay, but I'm sure I look better than you," I joke, confident he won't do anything in my parents' house. He cringes and I ask, "Can you even see? How did you get here?"

He laughs humorlessly and lowers himself onto the couch next to me. "Not really," he admits. "I took a town car. I may be using it for a while," he concedes.

"Does it hurt?" I probe, more curious than anything.

He nods and admits, "I took some pain killers to help." He leans over and places a gentle kiss on my forehead, reminding me of what he did to me. Tears spring to my eyes, not able to hold them back. "Does it hurt?" he repeats my question.

"Yeah," I croak. "They had to give me stitches."

His head drops, his whole demeanor appearing crushed. "I'm sorry, Amy. I'm so fucking sorry," he apologizes and softly kisses my lips, but I don't react. I can't.

"I have bruises on my arms, my hips and my thighs. My knees and hand are scraped and sore. I feel like I have a hangover to rival all hangovers, but I didn't drink and I can't even wash my hair normally because I have seven stitches in my head," I emphasize, making him flinch.

"I'm so sorry, baby," he croons, placing soft kisses on my face. "I swear I never meant to hurt you. I will make it up to you. I would never hurt you on purpose," he claims.

"You're pressing charges against Matt?" I question, ignoring his plea.

He stiffens and sits back glaring down at me. "Did you see what that asshole did to me?" he seethes, gesturing to his face. "I have more underneath this," he reveals, gesturing to his ribs under his shirt.

"He was protecting me," I remind him.

He cringes and takes a deep breath, pulling himself together. "Baby, I didn't mean to hurt you. It was an accident," he reiterates, gently tucking my hair behind my ear. "What he did to me was intentional," he insists.

I laugh humorlessly and shake my head in denial. "I told you, you were hurting me," I remind him.

He clenches his jaw in both anger and irritation and then flinches from the movement. He takes another deep breath, attempting to settle. Then, he looks into my eyes and confesses, "I don't want you to hurt, ever! What happened with you was an accident. I want to do everything I can to protect you and take care of you. I love you," he declares.

My eyes widen in shock as he cradles my face in his hands, gently pressing a kiss to my lips. I carefully pull back, shaking my head in refusal. "No, you don't. I can't have any part of that kind of love anymore. Not ever again," I emphasize.

"Amy, don't do this," he cautions.

"We're done," I whisper, fearful for the repercussions as the words leave my mouth.

I see the instant flash of anger in his eyes. I brace for impact, knowing my dad is close if I need him. "Well, if that's what you believe, then you and that asshole are both fucked," he states, revealing his true colors, yet again.

There's no way in hell I'm allowing him to do this to Matt. I take a deep breath, pulling strength from anything I can grab onto. His words confirm for the first time in my life I *know* I'm about to do the right thing. My lips curve up in a smile and I taunt, "Are you sure about that?"

He hesitates, taken aback by my question. "There were witnesses all saying the same thing; he started it. He's fucked," he emphasizes.

I nod in agreement, "True, but there were also a few witnesses who saw what you did to me. The police asked me if I wanted to press charges," I claim.

"No," he mutters, shaking his head.

I smirk and nod my head in confirmation. "Yup," I mumble, popping the p.

"Then why haven't they done anything?" he challenges.

"I'm supposed to contact them today since I was in the hospital all night and in too much pain to talk. They'll be over later to take my formal statement," I explain, giving him a partial truth.

He stands, scowling down at me. "You aren't going to do anything," he warns.

I huff a laugh asking, "What are you going to do about it?"

I watch his chest rise and fall rapidly as he attempts to contain is anger. "What the fuck do you want, Amy?" he spits out.

"I want you to drop the charges against Matt and leave him and his project alone," I instruct, feigning confidence.

"And then you won't press charges?" he clarifies.

"Right," I confirm.

"If you want me to back off him after what he did to me, you're done with the internship. You will not talk about this ever again. You will never speak a bad word about me. You will just be the ex-girlfriend that things didn't work out with," he pauses an adds, "You will sign a non-disclosure agreement including your agreement to never press charges."

"You want me to sign a non-disclosure agreement?" I repeat.

He grins and nods his head, "Yeah. I'll have it drafted today. You sign it and send it back and all charges will be dropped. Then you'll be free to fuck up your life all on your own."

"How do I know you aren't lying?" I push.

"I'll add it into the agreement," he answers.

"You've got a deal," I reach out, flinching as he shakes my hand.

He stands up, wincing as he shakes his head in distaste. "I can't believe I fell for your bullshit. I should've known you were a just a whore. Like mother, like daughter," he mutters with disgust.

"What the hell are you talking about?" I inquire, more confused than insulted.

He smirks and taunts, "Don't you know about your mom? I thought everyone knew about her."

"Just spit it out, Preston!"

"Maybe you should ask mommy dearest?" he suggests. "Or better yet, ask the guy it seems you will do anything to defend, even throw away the best thing you will ever have," he proclaims.

I roll my eyes and pinch my lips tightly together, refusing to respond. He's just trying to piss me off. "Goodbye Preston. I'll be waiting for those papers," I mumble, dismissing him.

"You don't fucking talk to him until you sign and return those papers, or the deal is off," he asserts. I nod my head in acknowledgement and watch as he huffs and stalks out the door, slamming it behind him.

I can wait a few hours to check on Matt. Hopefully, this will all come to an end quickly. I don't know if there were any witnesses to what Preston did besides Matt. All I know for sure is the hospital has my injuries on record, but my bluff will be worth it to get Matt off the assault charges and for him to get his dream gym. I may not always know the right way to handle things, but this time I have no doubt this is the way it should be. I'd do anything for him.

Matt

Pulling my gray long sleeved shirt on over my head, I stride for the door. I pull it open to find Blake holding up a brown paper bag. "I brought food," he announces.

"Good. I'm starving," I admit. I turn and walk back towards my couch, flopping down, expecting him to follow.

"Well, I have to say, you look better than I expected," he concedes, closing the door behind him.

Arching my eyebrows, I challenge, "What did you expect?"

He shrugs his shoulders and admits, "I don't know. You look tired as shit, but..." he trails off shrugging again.

"I guess the shower helped me look human again," I mumble. "What did you bring?"

"Just a couple Italian heroes. I didn't want to make things too complicated," he states.

"Thanks," I mumble as he hands me a hero wrapped in white paper. We eat for a few minutes in silence before I begin talking, repeating everything that happened last night.

"He fucking hit her?" he reiterates, appearing livid.

I nod my head and probe, "Has Bree said anything?"

He shakes his head, "No and she would've said something about this. This isn't something she'd keep quiet because there's no way in hell she'd just let it happen."

I sigh and nod my head, knowing he's right. "She would want to know."

"I'll call her when I leave," he offers. "You don't need to repeat any of this shit again."

I give him a grateful smile, hoping it doesn't look fake, but he'll understand my intention. "Well with the way things are, I'm lucky if Amy talks to me. Someone needs to be there for her. I have to tell her dad," I mumble.

"Speaking of dads," he begins, trailing off. I glance at him and he arches his eyebrows in question.

I take a bite of my sandwich, gathering my thoughts as I eat. I set my sandwich down on the table and clasp my hands anxiously together. "Yeah, I called him and told him I needed his help," I concede.

"And," he prompts.

"And he should be here tonight," I reveal.

"Thank fuck," he mumbles. I arch my eyebrows in challenge and he quickly brushes it off. "You know you need him on this one."

"Yeah," I concede, "but it doesn't make it any easier. They've been so worried about Grant, they forgot

275

they have another son trying to make it on his own. Giving me their house does nothing to make up for it," I bitterly declare. He nods his head in understanding. Blake was here for me when they weren't. He also met them a few times when they stopped home so my dad could work a big case or something, always claiming they wanted to see me. If that were the case, they would've been there for me a lot more than they ever were and not out chasing the fucking golden child.

"Where are they now anyway?" he questions, curious.

"North Carolina or something like that," I mumble. I shrug my shoulders, indicating it doesn't matter. "He seems to have privileges up and down the east coast and as far as Texas," I mutter.

Blake's eyes widen in surprise, "That's a lot of fucking bar exams!"

I shrug and amend, "Well, not all of them, but quite a few. I have no idea which ones. He may be an asshole, but I'll admit he's smart and if anyone can get me out of this it's him," I claim, hoping it's true.

"Is your mom coming?" he prods.

"I don't know," I admit. "I didn't ask."

"Alright, so what can I do for you? Do you want me to go check on Amy?" he suggests.

Just then a text comes through and I glance at the screen seeing Brett's name. I open it and read, "Amy just texted checking on you. She said she's okay and she's home," he informs me.

I breathe a sigh of relief, incredibly grateful for the information. "Thanks," I quickly reply.

"Brett heard from her," I rasp, feeling as if a weight has somewhat lifted. "I just need to know she's not alone and I pray she's not with him." I hold my phone up and murmur, "I'll try her dad at his office."

I find the number for his direct line and tap to call. A woman picks up and prods, "Jim Stone's office, may I help you?"

"Yes, is Mr. Stone available?" I question.

"I'm sorry, but he's not available right now, may I help you with something?" she offers.

"No, thanks, I'm actually a friend of his daughter and," I begin.

Interrupting, she rambles, "Oh, a friend of Amy's. He's working from home for a couple days. You can find him there."

I feel all the tension leave my body knowing her dad is home with her. I'll have to go talk to him before he goes back to work, but at least this gives me a little time knowing she's safe. "Thank you," I murmur, more than grateful. "I'll do that. Have a good day," I add and disconnect the call. I glance at Blake with a small smile on my face and emphasize, "She's safe." He grins, his own relief obvious. "How's Elizabeth doing?" I ask, changing the subject, needing some form of normalcy.

He hesitates and then nods his head in understanding, knowing I need to talk about something else if I'm going to keep it together before my dad comes home. Just having him here is exactly what I need. I may not have a normal family like most, but I would do anything for my friends and they do the same for me. Blake, Brett, Amy and even Bree became my family when Grant left and my parents chased him, abandoning me. Now with Bree married to Christian and Blake engaged to Elizabeth, I have two more people I know I can depend on because with us, we don't only protect and stand strong for each other, we do the same for those we all love. That's more than family to me; that's everything.

Chapter 33

Amy

My cell phone rings and I cautiously reach for it, my whole body still aching. Bree's face lights up the screen and I groan, already knowing why she's calling. I paste a smile on my face and tap answer. "Hey, Bree, it's so good to hear from you! How are you?" I ask, keeping my tone cheerful.

"Stop, Amy," she pleads. "I just hung up with Blake," she reveals and my body instantly sags with relief and exhaustion. "Are you okay? How are you feeling?" she stammers.

I sigh and concede, "I could be better."

"Oh, Amy," she rasps, her voice shaky, "I'm so sorry."

"It's fine, Bree," I murmur, attempting to ease her worries.

"It's not fine!" she argues. "Something like this is never fine!" she reiterates. "I can be there tomorrow to help," she offers. "I'm sorry I can't get there sooner."

"Bree, you don't have to come down. I'm okay. Well, I'll be okay," I correct.

"I know I don't have to, but I want to be there for you! That's what friends are for," she insists.

"Bree, I love you for that, but you just got married. I'm not alone," I proclaim, still more concerned about Matt then myself. "Did Blake say anything about Matt?" I ask, hoping to redirect the conversation.

"Yeah, but why haven't you talked to him?" she probes.

I groan in frustration knowing that's exactly what I want, but I can't call him yet. I take a deep breath and grumble, "I can't."

"What do you mean, you can't?" she retorts. "Of course you can!"

"No, I really can't," I repeat.

"Okay, explain," she asserts.

"Well, what did Blake tell you?" I prompt, not wanting to repeat anything I don't have to.

"He told me about your asshole boyfriend, you going to the hospital, Matt going to jail and Brett bailing him out. Blake is at Matt's house now," she enlightens me, knowing it will calm my anxiety.

I exhale a sigh of relief and declare, "First of all, he's my ex-boyfriend."

"Thank God!" she exclaims.

"Yeah," I rasp over the sudden lump in my throat.

"You're pressing charges against him, right?" she urges.

I feel a sudden flash of guilt, my stomach churns and sharp pinpricks poke my insides. I shake my head, even though she can't see me. "I can't," I whimper.

"Amy, we'll all be there for you," she begins.

I instantly interrupt, not able to listen to her trying to convince me to press charges and knowing it will never happen. "That's not it. I can't!" I repeat, vehemently. "He threatened Matt! I can't let anything happen to him."

"What are you talking about?" she inquires, her voice on edge.

"I mean Matt finally has everything in place to build his gym. He's supposed to break ground and Preston had it put on hold because he has the power to do that. I just got him to let that go and leave Matt alone when this happened. Every single witness there saw Matt beat the shit out of Preston. No one saw what happened to me and me telling them won't make a difference when I've been friends with Matt my whole life. The only thing it will accomplish is pissing Preston off even more," I adamantly proclaim. "Matt's the one that's fucked, not Preston," I emphasize. "I can't let anything happen to Matt. This is all my fault," I claim, my voice barely above a whisper.

"Amy, none of this is your fault! It's that asshole's fault! Every single part of it," she emphasizes. "And you got badly hurt and had to go to the hospital," she attempts, hoping to change my mind.

"It doesn't matter when there's nothing proving he did anything and he has so much fucking power behind him," I repeat, sounding defeated. "Even if I could get someone to believe me, which is doubtful without proof, Matt would still end up being charged for what he did to Preston."

"Shit," she mumbles, groaning in frustration. "I know you're stubborn and when you have your mind made up, no one can change it, but I really hate this. He should pay for what he did to you! Matt would want that too."

I smile to myself, appreciating her words. My thoughts briefly drift to his beaten and bruised body and I reiterate, "Well, Matt kind of did make him pay. He really did beat the shit out of him."

She chuckles humorlessly and heaves a sigh, relenting. "Okay, so what can we do to help Matt?"

"Well, that's what I'm trying to do. I told Preston there were witnesses saying they saw what he did to me," I admit.

She gasps, "What if he finds out your lying?"

"I'm hoping it will be too late. I told him the police were coming today to take my statement. He's putting a contract together for me to sign saying I'll never say anything bad about him, that we're just ex-boyfriend and girlfriend who didn't work out," I begin.

"Don't sign that!" she interrupts.

"Give me a minute to explain," I plead. She groans in agreement and I continue. "Basically, if I agree to pretend it didn't happen and stay clear of him, he won't press charges against Matt and he'll leave him alone. He also said I can't contact Matt until after I sign the papers or the deal is off."

"Amy, you can't trust him. He could be lying to you and put something in the contract that you don't understand. You have to have your dad with you or something," she insists.

"I can't tell my dad what really happened, Bree," I quietly admit. "Please, I just can't," I beg. "I just need this to all be over with!"

She sighs heavily and hesitantly concedes, "Well, you can't go into this alone."

"What else can I do?" I ask, believing there's no other option.

"What about Brett?" she suggests.

"What about him?" I prod.

"Ask him to come with you and look over the contract before you sign. He's almost done with law school and should be taking the bar soon," she reminds me.

"I don't know," I hesitate, "Preston won't like that."

"Who cares what the hell that asshole thinks!" she seethes, surprising me. Bree isn't normally the one to swear, yell or say bad things about anyone. "He can sign something too saying he'll treat it as attorney, client privilege or something," she adds.

"You know, that might be a good idea," I mumble my agreement.

"It is! Please, call him when we hang up!" she begs.

I sigh heavily and relent, "Okay, Bree. I will."

"I really wish you'd reconsider telling Matt or your dad about it," she prods. "Christian would kill me if I kept something like this from him."

"You did keep something like this from him and me," I claim.

"Blake knew and it's not the same thing!" she argues.

"Close enough," I mumble.

"Fine, but call Brett. I'm going to text him to make sure he's on his way to help you," she reiterates, making me laugh.

"I got it. I promise," I agree, feeling slightly better about the situation. She's right Preston could really screw Matt and me over in this contract. I should have someone look at it who knows the language. I know Brett's not done with school, but right now, I think he's my best option.

"Okay, I'll be down tomorrow," she repeats.

"No!" I argue. "Bree, I'm fine. How about this," I begin, "if in 48 hours you hear otherwise, be my guest, I'd love to see you. Just give me that time to deal with all this bullshit," I request.

"Fine," she grumbles. "Wait! You don't have to go back to work for him, do you?" she questions, sounding panicked.

"No, don't worry, that's part of the contract. My internship is over." I hear her sigh of relief and whisper, "Thank you, Bree."

"For what?" she blurts, confused.

"For always being there for me. I can't even explain how much it means to me, especially after everything that happened," I start, choking with emotion.

"Don't," she urges softly. "I don't even think about it anymore. I'm happily married to the man I love and we're talking about starting our own family. Things couldn't be better, Amy," she prompts, comforting me like usual.

"I'm so grateful to have you in my life," I claim, needing her to know the truth in my words.

"I feel the same way," she agrees, making my heart clench. "I love you, Amy. I'll give you forty-eight hours, but I'm checking in with Brett tonight making sure he's helping you," she repeats.

"Got it and I love you too," I whisper. "Bye, Bree."

She sighs again as she replies, "Bye."

I disconnect the call and immediately pull up Brett's number. I barely hesitate before I connect the call, knowing I don't have a lot of time. "Amy, how are you feeling?" he prompts, his voice full of concern.

"I'm okay, but I think I need your help," I confess, my chest aching with my admission.

"Anything," he concurs.

Matt

"Are you sure you don't want me to stay?" Blake prompts, obviously taking note of my increasing anxiety.

I shake my head, but contradict my actions saying, "I'm sure. You should go home and see your family since you're here." He hesitates and I reiterate, "Go on, Blake. I'll be fine and I'll keep you updated on what's happening as long as I'm able to." He gives me a look, telling me not to go there and I chuckle softly, needing to entertain myself somehow. "I'll be fine," I repeat.

He groans as he stands, stepping towards me. I rise and he gives me a one-armed hug with a firm pat on my back, which I return, grateful to him for so much. He's my family. "Okay," he relents, stepping back. "Call me and let me know how it goes with your dad," he requests.

"You got it," I agree. "And thanks for calling Bree. I already feel better knowing she'll be checking in on Amy." I just didn't think I could repeat the story again. I need to pull myself together enough to explain everything to my dad and that's going to be hard enough.

"She wouldn't forgive me if I didn't," he mumbles, offering me a tight smile as he steps towards the front door. He reaches for the knob and turns back to me. "I'll see you later, Matt," he states. I nod my head and choke down the sudden lump in my throat, anxious for what could happen. I watch as he walks out the door, closing it behind him before I begin to pace, waiting for my dad.

It doesn't take long before a knock at my door causes my heart to stop and restart again at an accelerated rate. I trudge woodenly to the door and pull it open, looking into eyes mirroring my own green ones. I have about an inch on him now and I'm definitely firmer and broader, but his dark hair now has grey peppered in, along with a few wrinkles around his eyes. "Matthew, you look good," he acknowledges, but I don't react. Instead, I stand frozen, staring at the man who's supposed to be my father, but I've barely seen since I started middle school. Yeah, when I was younger, my aunt stayed with me while they chased Grant, but by the time I hit high school, I lived almost completely on my own. "Are you going to let me in?" he prods, pulling me out of the past.

I nod stiffly and take a step back, watching as he walks through the door into the house that once was his home, our home. Everything about this moment feels surreal as I close the door behind him. He places a black suitcase next to the door, I didn't even realize he was holding as he looks around the living room nodding his head in approval. "The place looks good, Matt." I grunt in response and he sighs heavily. "You know, you're going to have to talk to me if you want me to be able to get you out of this mess you've gotten yourself into," he proclaims.

His words have my insides burning, my stomach roiling, my muscles tensing and my jaw clenching. I take a deep breath in and exhale slowly, attempting to calm myself down. "It took me getting thrown in jail for you to actually show up here," I blurt in almost a growl.

He grimaces and looks away. He walks to the coffee table and sets down his briefcase, flipping it open as he sits down on the couch. "I understand where you're coming from," he starts.

I instantly interrupt, "No, you don't! You don't understand anything about me! You don't know me! I'm the child you didn't want, the afterthought," I emphasize, wanting him to know how much I hurt.

He shakes his head in denial, "That's not true. We didn't want you to have to move all over, trying to help your brother. We wanted things to be more stable for you."

I huff a humorless laugh and bitterly spit, "How'd that work out for you? I got your house and you're still chasing the golden child."

He flinches as if I punched him. "We found him," he quietly admits.

I gasp, my mouth dropping open in shock. I stare at him, stunned. "What?" I prod, needing to hear the words again.

"We found him," he repeats.

"When?" I ask.

I see his cringe before he has a chance to hide it, making me stiffen again. "A few months ago," he enlightens me.

"A few months ago," I reiterate, agitated. "And you didn't think I'd want to know?"

He stands back up and steps towards me. I reflexively take a step back and he stops. "You wouldn't answer my calls."

I wince, remembering all the recent missed calls from him and know he's telling the truth. Defiantly I respond, "Well, maybe this news is worth a trip home."

He sighs heavily and nods his head in acknowledgement. "You're right," he concedes, surprising me. "And it also deserves more of an explanation."

I laugh without humor and concur, "Yeah, it fucking does!"

"Look, I need you to go over everything that happened and I don't want you to leave anything out," he requests. "Then, we can talk about Grant," he proposes.

I nod in agreement and push, "I just need to know one thing first." He nods his head and I continue, my voice cracking with emotion. "Why did he leave?"

My dad swallows hard, his Adam's apple bobbing up and down, as he appears to be blinking back tears. He takes a deep breath and exhales slowly before he returns his gaze to mine. "To escape," he mumbles, his voice barely above a whisper.

"What?" I question, confused.

He straightens his shoulders, staring out the window appearing distraught. "He was in a relationship with a woman he didn't tell anyone about and it wasn't good," he pauses, clearing his throat. "The rumors held some truth. He turned to alcohol and then to drugs when he couldn't get away from her. Then he left without a trace thinking he was protecting everyone involved," he enlightens me.

My whole body feels weak and I drop down into the armchair, my head falling to my hands as my heart drops into my feet. "What the fuck?" I groan, feeling as if

I'm looking down on someone else's life. This can't be real. "Explain!"

He shakes his head, refusing. "I'll tell you everything after you confess every little detail about what happened with you, Amy Stone and Preston Kirst." I open my mouth to argue and he shakes his head, firmly repeating, "Details, Matt. I'm not about to lose another son!"

I gasp in surprise, suddenly completely confused and overwhelmed. I shake my head, attempting to clear the fog and refocus on Amy, unexpectedly desperate to confess everything to the man sitting in front of me.

Chapter 34

Amy

It's late. I fight to keep my eyes open as I sit with Preston, watching as Brett goes over the contract line by line with Preston's lawyer at the small kitchen table in my apartment above the garage. They both pause, asking us questions as needed and make adjustments. "I can't believe you brought your own fucking lawyer," Preston grumbles for what feels like the hundredth time.

"What did you expect me to do? Whatever you told me to?" I retort snidely.

He clenches his jaw and shakes his head in frustration. "I expected you to act respectful, professional and loyal. You not only worked for me, you were my fucking girlfriend and the only time I see you put effort into anything is when it has to do with that asshole!" I grimace, knowing he's right, but keep my mouth sealed tight, knowing anything I have to say will only fuel the fire. He takes a deep breath in, exhaling slowly, attempting to get his anger under control. "Why are you fighting so hard for an asshole that's been fucking someone else anyway?" he prods.

I shake my head defensively and mumble, "You don't know that."

He smirks and claims, "Actually, I do. Vanessa confessed everything to my sister." He leans closer to me and whispers in my ear, emphasizing each word, "And I heard every...dirty...filthy word."

My chest tightens and my stomach twists as I struggle for breath. I have no right to be mad, but my head, body and heart don't give a shit. He watches me closely waiting to see how I react.

"You were mine, not his, why should it matter who he fucks?" he questions. I bite the inside of my cheek, trying not to react. "They're getting close too, they run together most mornings after they wake up in his bed together," he taunts. His words remind me of the day I saw her at his house wearing nothing but his shirt. Then he shrugs like it's no big deal. "He's pretty happy fucking someone else," he claims.

"Fuck you!" I retort, no longer able to hold back.

He chuckles softly and leans towards me again, squeezing my upper thigh. "You already did that," he murmurs, his amusement clear.

I seethe, barely able to see straight. "You fucking..."

His eyes widen and he reiterates, "I can still cancel this deal."

"So can I," I retort. I see him flinch, quickly covering it up. His reaction reminding me he no longer holds all the power, at least he doesn't think he does. "Get your fucking hands off me," I grit out.

He clenches his jaw and pulls back.

"Everything okay, Amy," Brett calls from across the room.

I look up to find Brett's concerned gaze on me, reminding me no matter what happens with Matt, I'm not alone. I straighten and square my shoulders. "I'm okay," I answer, with a small smile on my face. "Let's just get this done," I prompt.

He grins and nods his head firmly. "You got it," he mumbles.

Preston's lawyer glances over to the two of us and back at the table. "Would the two of you join us again?" he requests.

I stand and walk over, lowering myself into the chair next to Brett. He smiles and gives me a nod of encouragement in support. They both go over everything one more time, making sure we both understand the entirety of the contract. So, everything to do with both work, as well as personally up until the moment we both sign the contract is included," I repeat, needing to be clear. "That includes everything with Matt," I restate.

"Yes," both of them nod their heads in agreement.

"So you can't press charges against Matt or do anything to mess up his new build," I clarify, glancing at Preston.

"And you can't press charges against me," he emphasizes.

I gulp down the lump in my throat and nod my head in affirmation. Looking at Brett I inquire, "Okay, where do I sign?"

He smiles sadly, repeating, "Are you sure this is what you want? Matt wouldn't want you to protect him. He's more concerned about you."

"That's why you're here. This is what I want," I reiterate.

He nods his head, relenting as he hands me a pen, guiding me through each place I need to sign and date, as well as the few spots I need to initial.

I finish and hand the pen to Preston, watching as he does the same. As he finishes, he slams the pen on the table and mutters, "Good riddance." I barely restrain myself from rolling my eyes. He leans in close to me and whispers in my ear, "A bit of advice." I tense, waiting for him to continue. "Instead of spreading your legs in the bathroom at the bar like a two-bit whore, I'll fuck that loose pussy anywhere." I instantly lift my arm, fuming, ready to slap him across the face. He catches my wrist and holds it, looking down at me in warning. "You're no longer under protection of me or any contract," he reminds me, a small smile tugging at the corners of his lips.

Breathing heavily, I snap, "Neither are you and this is harassment."

He smirks, knowing I was the only one who heard him, so for now, he's right. "Leave," I grit out.

He pastes a huge smile on his face and nods. "Have a good night," he taunts, waving over his shoulder as he walks out my door with his lawyer following after him.

I feel my whole body collapse into the chair the moment the door clicks shut. "What did he just say to you?" Brett asks.

I shake my head and mutter, "It doesn't matter. I don't ever want to see that asshole again!"

Brett sighs in defeat and squats down, wrapping his arms around me. "Are you okay?" he prods.

I nod my head, returning his hug. "Thank you, Brett."

"You don't have to thank me, Amy. That's what friends are for," he claims. "Besides, I'm happy I could help you both."

"Well, thank you anyway," I repeat, pulling back.

"When are you going to talk to Matt?" he prompts.

I force a fake smile at the thought of him with Vanessa. "It's late. I'll talk to him tomorrow."

"He wouldn't care about the time," he claims.

My stomach twists, imagining interrupting something with her. "I promise I'll call him tomorrow," I insist. "Just let him know he's safe," I request.

He nods, relenting. "Will you be okay on your own?"

I nod, "Yeah. My parents are just across the driveway if I need anything," I remind him.

He nods and glances towards the main house before bringing his gaze back to me. "If you're sure, I'll go then and I'll get you a copy of the contract tomorrow," he advises.

"I'm sure," I confirm. I nod my head and watch as he walks out the door, waving goodbye.

I stand and trudge to my bed, carefully dropping onto the mattress, so my head doesn't spin. I'm relieved, but my heart feels heavy as worry consumes me, hoping Matt can forgive me for the situation I got him into. I close my eyes, yearning for some sleep.

Matt

I watch my dad, waiting to see his reaction. Hopefully, he can get me out of this mess, but more than anything I just want Amy safe. He tents his fingers, staring at them in thought. "Dad?" I prod. He looks up, meeting my gaze, and arching his eyebrows in question. "I don't regret what I did," I begin. "I would do it all over again to protect her," I emphasize.

He groans and runs his hand down his face in disbelief. "But why does it have to be Amy Stone?" he questions.

"What the hell is your problem with Amy?" I retort defensively.

He grimaces and concedes, "Well, it's not exactly Amy, it's her family."

I shake my head, not understanding what he's talking about. "What do you mean?" I probe.

He releases a heavy sigh and inquires, "What do you remember about the time before Grant left?"

I shrug, and run my hand through my hair feeling exhausted. "I don't know, what does it matter?" I mumble.

He cringes and emphasizes, "It matters, Matt. It matters so much more than you realize."

"What the hell are you talking about?" I question, irritably.

"Amy's mom is part of the reason your brother began getting into trouble," he begins.

My eyebrows draw down in confusion and I ask, "I don't understand. You said it had something to do with a secret relationship." My stomach begins churning in fear of where this conversation seems to be going.

His whole body sags in defeat as he closes his eyes with worry lines etched into his forehead and corners of his eyes. He slowly opens his eyes, glancing in my direction, before leaning back and staring at the ceiling. I open my mouth to try to get an answer when he starts talking. "Grant should be the one telling you this, but with everything going on with Amy, I don't think this can wait," he claims.

"Dad," I prod.

He maintains his gaze on the ceiling, informing me, "He had an affair with Amy's mom." My eyes widen and I gasp in shock. Quickly covering my mouth, I remain silent, waiting for him to continue. "Amy's dad was gone for work a lot and she hired Grant to help with some of the work around the house. Your mom and I knew that," he mutters, shaking his head in disbelief. "We didn't think anything of it. He needed income to save for college." He pauses, momentarily lost in thought. "Anyway, she seduced him," he grunts, his face scrunching up in pain, disgust and regret. "I'll let your brother tell you most of this, but she would get jealous of her own daughter and punish Grant for it by hurting him."

"What do you mean hurting him?" I ask, needing clarification.

"She hit him with whatever she could find. Her being a woman he didn't fight back and he didn't tell anyone. Everyone assumed it was due to football, even us," he claims, closing his eyes as his agony and guilt nearly eats him alive. "He stopped going over there and then she began threatening him in other ways, until he went back, but it only got worse. He started drinking and smoking pot and I don't know what else. And you know the rest, eventually running away when he fucked up the game with the scouts."

"Holy shit," I mumble in complete shock.

"There's more, but Grant will talk to you," he mutters.

"Why didn't anyone tell me?" I ask, feeling the panic creeping in.

"We didn't know the whole story," he insists. "Grant took off and we didn't know until we found him a couple months ago and even then, it took a long time for him to open up to us."

"Fuck," I grumble running my hand through my hair. "But you suspected something with the Stones didn't you?" I demand, my heart beginning to race with fear.

He opens his mouth and closes it, shrugging his shoulders. "It doesn't matter, you can't do anything with assumptions."

"But what about Amy?" I yell.

He shakes his head in confusion, "What do you mean?"

"What if Grant wasn't the only one she hit? What if she hit Amy too?" I challenge.

His eyes widen and I see in his gaze the moment it clicks. "We just thought it was Grant and the Kirst boy before him. I didn't even think she would hit her own child. Amy was always so happy," he claims.

"She's really fucking good at pretending," I grit out. I can't help but think about all the times she's gotten hurt and blamed it on cheerleading or her clumsiness when she was fighting with her mom. She'd tell me the truth about fighting with her mom, but was she telling me the truth about the rest? My hatred for her mom increases, causing my insides to feel like they're on the verge of erupting. My whole body begins to shake with rage.

"How is Amy doing with all this," he gestures to his notes spread out in front of him regarding what happened last night.

I glance at my phone, uneasy and admit, "I don't know. She hasn't been talking to me lately." At that moment my phone beeps and I nearly breathe a sigh of relief at the sight of Brett's face.

I press the green button to connect the call and bring my phone to my ear. "Brett?" I prompt, hopeful.

"Matt, the charges were dropped against you," he states without preamble.

"What? How? Why?" I blurt out in astonishment.

"I can't really answer that, but let's just say, she will do anything for you, too," he comments vaguely.

My heart drops into the pit of my stomach, terrified for what he means. "She can't owe him anything. She has to get away from him. I don't care what happens to me," I proclaim.

He chuckles, realizing his mistake. "She's safe and she will remain far away from that asshole. Talk to her," he encourages.

I sigh in relief and mumble my agreement, "I will." She better not put herself at risk with him to protect me. "Thanks, man," I mumble.

"Yeah, I'll talk to you later," he responds and disconnects the call.

I set my phone down, feeling the tension release from my head and shoulders almost instantly. "She's okay," I murmur.

I hear the relief in my dad's reply, "Thank God."

"And Preston dropped the charges," I reveal.

I see my dad's whole body sink into the couch at this unexpected reprieve. He drops his face into his hands as a tear slips from the corner of his eye. "Thank you," he whispers, but not to me, causing my heart to clench. For the longest time, I've thought they didn't give a shit. Knowing they do, I can't imagine what they would've done if Preston went through with the charges. I would've made it as long as I know Amy would be okay.

"Dad," I prod, wanting to ask more about Grant. Maybe this information will tell me more about what's been going on with Amy and why she insists on pushing me away. Suddenly, I process what he said before and I gasp, freezing with my dad's words coming back to me as if on replay. "What do you mean the Kirst boy?" I inquire slowly. "Preston Kirst?"

He shakes his head, "No, not the one that's been involved in this mess with you. The older one, Prescott."

Chapter 35

Matt

I sit down on the couch, freshly showered. Last night, dad and I stayed up talking about a bunch of shit, good and bad. We talked more about Grant and how they finally caught up with him after all this time. I told him about the gym I'm building and even touched a little more on why there was no way in hell I would back down when it comes to Amy. If there's something I can do to help her, I will, even if she still doesn't want to be with me. I don't need to think about that right now with all the other shit on my mind. My phone pings, pulling me out of my thoughts and alerting me of a text. I hold my breath hoping to see her name, but no such luck.

Opening the message from Vanessa, I read, "Are you okay? Are you home?"

"I'm fine and home," I reply.

"Can I come see you?" she requests.

I sigh heavily and immediately respond, "Not today. My dad's here."

She sends a response, but I ignore it, laying my head back on the couch. I'm still reeling from everything that's happened in the last couple days, from seeing what that asshole did to Amy, to ending up in jail, to asking my father for help. Then when he gets here, the shit he told me about Grant and Amy's mom blows my mind. Plus, I'm sick knowing my brother wasn't her first victim, but Preston's older brother took that honor. I didn't even know he had an older brother. Then again, I never had a second thought about the Kirst family until Amy started working for them.

"Amy," I mumble to myself, running my hand through my hair in frustration. More than anything I want to talk to her to make sure she's okay. I'm sick just thinking about how evil her mom has always been and terrified to learn I'm right about her. I've never wanted to be more wrong about something than I do right now. Thinking back to all the fights she had with her mom over the years makes my stomach roil, knowing it may have been many more times and I believe that's true. Did I do even more damage, letting her come to me to blow off steam and forget about it? I thought it was typical family shit, she seemed so fucking happy. Yeah, I knew when something was bothering her, but was it really that much more than she shared with me? "Fuck!" I yell in frustration, throwing a couch pillow across the room.

Standing, I dial her number again, praying she picks up, but I hear the cheerful greeting of her voicemail, "Hi, it's Amy..."

Groaning in frustration, I disconnect the call. Attempting to figure out what the hell I'm supposed to do from here, I begin pacing from my living room to my kitchen and back. My dad strides into the room with his suitcase rolling behind him, stopping me in my tracks and I narrow my eyes in response. "Leaving so soon?"

He grimaces as he meets my gaze. He releases the handle of his suitcase and approaches me. My whole body tenses, preparing for what I'm sure he's about to say. He holds his hand up in apprehension, as if to calm me down, but the action just makes me shake my head in disbelief. "It's not what you think," he begins.

I arch my eyebrow in challenge and prompt, "Really? And exactly what do I think?"

Sighing heavily, he mutters my name, "Matthew."

"It doesn't matter. I should've known," I grumble. "Did you just come here to protect your reputation?"

"Matt!" he warns, attempting to stop me. "I realize I deserve this from you, but just listen," he pleads.

I grind my teeth, breathing heavily through my nose, my nostrils flaring. "Fine," I grunt, crossing my arms over my chest.

"I wasn't planning on going anywhere until we got this taken care of, but now that everything seems to be working out," he shrugs and I laugh humorlessly. He continues, ignoring my bitterness. "I'm going to go back down to hopefully bring your brother home, at least to spend some time with the four of us," he explains.

"Why would he come now?" I question, feeling hope, anger and resentment.

"He says he's ready to make amends," he informs me.

I gulp down the lump in my throat and let my hands fall to my side, clenching my hands into fists. "Are you sure that's what he wants?" I push, fearful of the reality.

"No," he answers honestly. My eyes widen in surprise. "But he's trying and after everything, I can at least give him the benefit of the doubt now," he mumbles, his guilt weighing heavily on his chest. I nod my head in understanding and turn my head to look out the window, trying to see things from their perspective. I only succeed in making myself feel worse. He breaks the silence, adding, "Besides, your mother can't get all of our shit together on her own."

Returning my attention to him, I nod my head in understanding. I'm not ready for any of them to truly be in my life again, but I'm not about to push them over the edge of the cliff to get rid of them for good either. "I guess I'll see you when I see you," I mumble.

"Soon," he claims.

I nod my head in acknowledgement, refusing to believe it until it happens. "Just give me a heads up when you figure out when you're coming back," I request.

"Of course," he instantly concedes. He fidgets in front of me awkwardly, before stepping towards me as he brings his arms around me in an awkward hug. He gives me a firm pat on the back and rasps, "I know this might not mean much coming from me, but I'm proud of you, Matthew." I gulp down the lump in my throat as he releases me and steps back, turning towards his suitcase.

"Dad," I begin. Stopping, he spins back towards me and arches his eyebrows in question. "Thank you," I murmur, my voice hoarse. He gives me a tight smile and a firm nod. I clear my throat and add, "And thank you for coming to help with this," I put my hand up and shake my head, not having a clue how to sum up the last couple days and still in disbelief he dropped the charges.

"If you need me, just call," he urges, "I will be here," he emphasizes. In the past I've doubted his words, but I guess he's proven me wrong.

I nod my head in acknowledgement and watch as he grasps the handle of his suitcase and rolls it out the door behind him. He stops on the front stoop and glances at me over his shoulder. "And Matt, please answer your phone," he begs.

The corner of my mouth twitches up as I nod in agreement. "Keep me posted," I reiterate. He nods and walks towards his rental car as I close the door behind him.

Now I need to talk to Amy. Then again, I don't think I'm going to feel better until I see her face to face, but I have to get her to talk to me first.

Amy

Glancing at my reflection in the bathroom mirror, I grimace at the discoloring on the side of my head near my temple and then wince at the movement. The

300

discoloration and swelling spreading and now covering more space than it did yesterday. My hips, thighs, hands and knees don't look much better. I slowly and carefully pull soft, olive green, loose fitting pants on, along with a baggy cream sweater with a wide neck. Having anything too close to my skin just makes me ache even more. I should be used to this by now, I've had so much worse, but I don't want to. I inhale deeply and exhaling slowly I mumble to myself, "I can deal with this."

My phone pings with another message from Matt. Now that I know he's safe and I don't have to think about Preston anymore, I really need to talk to him, but I don't want him to see me like this. I look like the walking dead. I trudge out of the bathroom and pull up the last text I sent him, considering what I should say to him. Will he even forgive me for all this? It's my fault he almost lost his business before it even began and ended up in jail. At the same time, I'm the bitch who's been avoiding him. I hate myself for what I've done to him.

I think about all the times Bree, Blake, Brett and all our other friends have tried to push us together and I don't allow it because why? My parents? My mom? My dad? Fear? I shake my head in defeat. I don't think my dad ever realized what Matt means to me. I no longer believe he would want someone else for me if he did. Maybe I can talk to him first. I know he's staying home this week to make sure I'm okay. Suddenly determined and wanting to talk to Matt, I grab my phone. I don't want to ignore him any longer, I never did. Besides, I don't have to stay away from him now with the contract signed and filed. I start by texting him a simple, "I'm sorry." Then I slip my phone in my pocket and slide on my black indoor/outdoor fuzzy slippers and carefully make my way over to my parents' house.

Sneaking through the house in hopes my mom doesn't realize I'm here, I make my way to my dad's office. Softly knocking on the door, I hold my breath in anticipation.

"Looking for someone?" my mother's voice comes from behind me, startling me. I spin towards her with wide eyes, wincing at my movement. Her shirt hangs untucked and wrinkled, her hair sticking out at all angles and her eyes appear red and glassy.

"Hi, Mom," I mutter. "I was just looking for dad."

She crosses her arms over her chest, wobbling on her feet as her eyes narrow on me in suspicion. "He went to his office to pick up some files to bring home. He wants to be here to take care of his precious Amy," she grits bitterly. "Why the hell is he always so worried about you?"

My eyes narrow in confusion and I give her a snarky reply, "Because I'm his daughter and that's what good parents do."

"How dare you," she warns, stepping closer to me. "After everything I've done for you!"

"I should hope you do something, even if you don't act like it, you are my mother," I retort, knowing I shouldn't, but I can't seem to stop myself. I'm done being manipulated and abused by her.

"You little bitch!" she yells. She reaches up and slaps me hard across my face, my body in its weakened state, too slow to react until after she makes contact. My head whips to the side, my ears ringing. My hand reflexively goes to my cheek, attempting to protect myself as I sway on my feet, dizzy and trying to catch my balance. "How the hell do you do it?" she demands.

My eyes widen, taken aback. "What are you talking about?" I question.

"You get more and more of his time and attention, while I get less and less," she complains irrationally.

"Who, dad?" I prompt, puzzled.

She narrows her eyes and grits her teeth, looking at me like I'm stupid. "Yes, your father! He's my husband," she emphasizes.

"And he's my father," I snap. "I don't understand what you're talking about," I reiterate. "You're not making any sense."

"You always want to be the center of attention, with your father, with all the boys, you always want to be the only woman in the room. You need everyone looking at you, especially when it means taking it away from me," she seethes.

"So, you hit me because you're jealous?" I question aloud, trying to piece everything together.

She slaps me again, the sound echoing in the hallway and I grip the wall for support feeling dizzy. "I'd never be jealous of a little slut like you, but why couldn't you obey me? Obey Preston? He was perfect. You could've had everything you ever wanted with him and everyone would stop looking at me like I was some kind of pariah!"

"Wh...what?" I stammer, and begin backing away towards the back door, using the wall as support.

"I never wanted kids, but I love your father and he would've left me if I didn't give him a child. So I did and he slowly stopped paying attention to me anyway, focusing most of his love and devotion on you," she mumbles, shaking her head as if ridding herself of the thoughts. "I was trying to help you. All you had to do is be with a man like Preston and everything would've been fine, but you had to go and break up with him! Why would you do that? You think going back to Matt Young will help? That will just make everything worse! His family is poison! But you have to go and ruin everything!" she yells, stalking towards me.

"Mom, what happened with Preston has nothing to do with you," I argue defiantly, confused by her rant.

"It has everything to do with me!" she retorts.

"I don't know what you're talking about," I mumble, backing up slowly.

"You always have to have your way! You're so fucking selfish! We could've had everything back to how it should be," she proclaims.

"Don't you care that I don't want to be with him?" I probe.

"You don't know what you want," she claims. "You're too weak to stand on your own!"

Not able to take anymore, I step forward and slap my mother across the face without a second thought. Her head whips to the side as she gasps. Her hand comes to her face protectively, while I stand frozen and wide-eyed. I've never retaliated before, not like that. She growls as she lunges for me, knocking me off balance. I stumble back into the wall, and weakly try to scramble away as she claws at me. I push away and make it out the door, stumbling to my car, grateful I left the keys in it.

Squeezing my eyes shut to clear my vision, I start the car and pull out as she comes running out, unsteady on her feet. I back out of the driveway, praying no cars cross my path. I drive barely seeing the road as tears run down my face. I don't think about where I'm going, my body on autopilot, getting me to the one place I know I'll be safe.

Pulling into his driveway, I scramble out of the car and to the front door as if I'm still being chased. I ring the doorbell and breathe a sigh of relief as he answers the door and I fall into his arms. "I'm sorry," I whimper and close my eyes.

"Amy? What the fuck happened?" Matt questions sounding panicked. I feel my feet leave the ground as I let go, sobbing into his chest and knowing he'll take care of me. "Did he do this to you?" he spits.

"No," I stammer, not able to say anymore.

Chapter 36

Amy

He cradles me in his arms as I finally begin to catch my breath, letting the reality of what just happened sink in. As I attempt to pull back to look in his eyes, I wince in pain, my head throbbing as if being attacked by a jackhammer. "Ouch," I grumble.

"Are you alright? What can I get you?" he prompts softly.

I attempt to swallow, but my throat feels dry and scratchy. "Could I have some water and some aspirin?" I rasp.

"Of course," he mumbles and carefully gets out from under me. I slowly try to sit up, placing my feet on the floor. He's back moments later handing me a glass and some aspirin. "Here," he offers.

I quickly gulp down both, finishing the water without a breath. "Thank you," I mumble.

He takes the glass from me, asking, "Do you need more?" I shake my head in response. He takes the glass from my hand and sets it down on the coffee table, before carefully sitting down next to me. Wrapping his arm around my shoulders, he cautiously urges me back. "Please talk to me," he begs, as he rubs my back in a soothing motion.

"My mom and I got into another fight," I declare without preamble.

I feel his whole body tense at my admission. "Your mother did this to you? After you were already hurt?" he probes with barely concealed anger.

I nod my head, afraid to look at him, guilt for what happened to him suddenly stifling. "I'm so sorry, Matt," I whimper.

"Amy, look at me," he urges, but I don't move. "Please," he pleads, his voice cracking with emotion. He tenderly cups my chin, guiding it towards him until I meet his concerned gaze. My heart clenches inside my chest and I struggle to breathe looking at him. "Do not fucking apologize for that asshole, ever!" he emphasizes. "None of it was your fault. He made his choices and I made mine. I will always choose you and I'm not about to let you or anyone else stop me," he declares, sounding determined.

I inhale a shaky breath, overwhelmed with how he makes me feel. My insides feel like a tornado has been let loose, while my outsides feel so much pain. "Matt," I whisper.

"Your head," he murmurs softly. "Should you go back to the hospital?" I shake my head and wince at the quick movement. He sighs heavily and informs me, "I'm going to start looking you over to make sure you're okay. Alright?" I nod my head feeling dizzy as he slowly inspects my body, unable to hide my pain anymore. He starts at my feet, making his way up my body. I wince when he reaches my knees. He slows and I feel his lips tenderly brush my skin. He lowers my pant legs and running his fingers along my upper legs and hips he asks, "What about under here?"

"I have some bruises from the other day," I concede.

He grimaces and moves my arms and shoulders around. I wince feeling pain where I hit the wall earlier. His eyes narrow as he watches me closely. He questions, "What about under your shirt?"

"I don't know," I grumble. "Can we just do this later? Will you just hold me?" I request. I need to feel his arms around me.

He gulps down a lump in his throat and pulls me close to him. I lay my head on his chest as he cradles me in his arms. I take a deep breath and exhale slowly, as another tear escapes. "Do you know my mom never wanted kids? She only had me to keep my dad?" Feeling his mouth open to respond, I shake my head, stopping him before he starts. "I don't want your pity, Matt. I just need to confess the truth before it completely destroys me," I admit.

"It's not pity, Amy," he grits through his teeth. I lean back, looking up at him and see the pain in his eyes. He takes a deep breath and softly relents, "But please talk to me."

I return my head to his chest before continuing. I'm afraid to look him in the eyes as I confess the truth about my family. "I went over to the house to talk to my dad, but he ran into the office to bring more work home so he could take care of me and I ran into my mom instead. I think she might've been drinking..." I trail off, wondering if that's been the case in the past. I'm honestly not sure. "Anyway, she said the normal hateful things," I mutter, grateful I don't have to repeat that part because he at least knows that much about her. "Then, she told me she hates all the attention I get from my own father, like I was trying to steal him away from her or something." I shake my head in disbelief. "She started ranting, saying I always had to be the center of attention. She claimed I would steal all the boys attention too," I shake my head, confused. "I don't understand why she'd say something like that," I admit, puzzled.

"Fuck," Matt mutters under his breath. "I think I do."

I pull back and look up at him in surprise. "What do you mean?"

"Exactly as it sounds," he grumbles. He sighs heavily and runs his hand through his hair with incredulity on his face. "My dad said," he starts.

My eyes widen in shock and I cut him off, "Your dad? You talked to your dad?"

He grimaces and concedes, "Yeah, I needed his help for my arrest. Blake and Brett convinced me to call him. He came up right away."

"Holy shit," I mumble, stunned. He huffs a humorless laugh and nods his head. "I'm so sorry," I repeat, my guilt again consuming me.

He shakes his head and arches his eyebrows in challenge. "I told you not to apologize for that. It's not your fault!" Giving him a sad smile, I nod my head, even though I don't agree. "It worked out anyway. With my dad, I mean," he amends. "We had a chance to talk and it went better than I ever thought it could." He shakes his head and takes a deep breath. "Anyway, I'm getting off track. They found Grant a couple months ago. It took them a while to find out, but your mom is the reason he left."

I gasp, feeling as if my heart stopped. "What?" I probe.

"To keep everything simple for now, she seduced him, manipulated him, threatened him and abused him. He wouldn't fight back because he won't hit a woman and didn't think anyone would believe him. The one time he tried, no one did. That's when he started getting into trouble and then eventually took off. I guess before him, she did the same thing with Preston's older brother."

"Preston has an older brother?" I blurt.

"That's what you ask?" he prods.

I shrug, "I think it will take me time to process everything else to be honest."

"You don't seem that surprised though," he observes.

I bite the inside of my cheeks, knowing this will be everything. If I say this, I will be laying myself out utterly

309

bare for this man, but he's the only one I could imagine opening up all my vulnerabilities to. "Yes, and no. I'm surprised she sunk to seducing someone so young."

"I think he was seventeen at the time it started," he informs me. I nod my head and he probes, "And the part you're not surprised about?"

I grimace and another tear slips down my cheek as I lean back on his chest. His hand immediately begins moving up and down my back, comforting me and giving me courage to speak my truth. "All the times I got into fights with my mom, they weren't just verbal like I led you to believe. I'm not as clumsy as everyone thinks," I mumble, my voice barely above a whisper.

I know he heard me though because I catch his shaky exhale with a softly muttered, "Fuck!"

"The first time she hit me I was only twelve years old," I reveal. "Then tonight, for the first time, I hit her back," I confess. "Just once, but...it felt good to finally stand up to her."

Matt

I hold her in my arms, almost afraid to let go as I continue running my hands up and down her back, attempting to comfort her. My mind drifts back to earlier when she showed up at my door. I've never been more grateful and scared at the same time. I've never seen her so broken both inside and out. She crumbled in my arms, finally allowing all her walls to come crashing down, while trying not to get crushed, the moment of finally having her in my arms again, bittersweet. For the longest time I just held her and rocked her before she finally calmed down enough to confess everything to me. I struggled to control my anger, but I needed to do

310

everything I could to be what she needed. She's my priority.

She finally passed out from complete and utter exhaustion, both physical and emotional. She may not know it yet, but I'm not letting her go back, not with her mom in that house. She can take the spare room here permanently. Fuck, I want her in my bed, but I'm not an asshole. I'm not going to push her. I'll never push her. I realize I'm setting myself up for another heartbreak, but maybe in the long run she'll change her mind about us. I know we're perfect for each other. I just wish she would believe it too.

I'm so fucking grateful she never has to go near that asshole Preston again, either personally or professionally. I can't believe how much he manipulated her. I wish she didn't sign that fucking contract, but then I wouldn't necessarily be able to be there to protect her from her mom or him. If I say something now, I not only screw myself over, but I put her at risk for breach of contract. I would never do something that could get her in trouble, but I wish I could do more. I'll always protect her at all costs. I'm glad she at least allowed Brett to help. I just wish I could've helped her sooner. If I ever have a chance to take him down, I won't fucking hesitate.

I think hearing the whole story about her mom hurt the most. I've always fucking hated that woman knowing how she treated her, yet I didn't even know half of it. Finding out what she did to my brother only solidified my hatred, but what that evil woman did to the incredible one in my arms, her own daughter, absolutely crushed me more than anything. I'm devastated and heartbroken for her. I can't stop thinking about all the broken bones she's had, all the times she needed stitches, or didn't come to school because she was supposedly sick or had some kind of accident. I think about every injury or wound I remember on her body and wonder if her mother might've been the cause of every single one of them. I feel sick every time I think about it.

I can't help but wonder how her dad didn't know? I realize he traveled a lot for work, but how could he be so blind? Sighing heavily, I berate myself. I'm her best friend and I didn't fucking know! I feel my body tense, pissed off at myself again. How can I blame her father, when I probably saw her and talked to her more than him? My stomach twists into knots and my heart clenches, my whole body taut with tension. I feel my guilty conscience weighing me down and shoving me into the ground. I should've fucking known!

Taking a deep breath and exhaling slowly, I remind myself to get away from my destructive thoughts, knowing they won't help her right now. I need to focus on her. I know I'm desperate to care for her and help her heal, but I have no idea where to begin. I shake my head and admit to myself, that's not true, I do know. I need to talk to her father and find out if he will do what he has to do to protect her. I think I need to do it tonight.

I glance down at her, sound asleep in my arms and carefully brush her hair out of her face. I internally cringe at every cut, lump, bump and bruise, but at the same time, my heart skips a beat at her undeniable beauty even with her injuries. No one deserves to go through everything she's endured, yet she's not only survived, she's become one of the strongest and most courageous women I know. I lean down, placing a soft kiss on her forehead, enjoying the feel of her skin on my lips. "I love you, Amy," I murmur softly. "I'm so fucking sorry. I'm here for you. I'm right fucking here," I emphasize, watching her sleep.

Placing another soft kiss on her forehead, I carefully get out from under her, and lay her back down on the couch. She rolls over onto her side, facing me and curls herself up into a ball. I grab a dark blue fleece blanket and shake it out, laying it over her to keep her warm. She looks so small, as if she's trying to protect herself, even in sleep.

I grab her phone and turn it on silent, hoping she'll be able to get some rest. Striding into the kitchen, I open my junk drawer. I pull out a notepad and pen, writing her an old-fashioned note to let her know where I am, in case she wakes up while I'm gone. I make my way back over to her and set the note right next to her phone. Crouching down next to the couch, I tuck a loose strand of her long, blonde locks behind her ear and gently caress her cheek, promising, "I won't let this happen ever again. No one will lay a hand on you ever again." My heart clenches and I softly press my lips to her temple. Closing my eyes briefly, I pray my words hold true. I need her to be okay.

Standing, I grab my wallet, my keys and my phone and quietly slip out my front door, determined to make things safe for her, how it always should've been.

Chapter 37

Matt

Parking my car along the curb in front of Amy's house, I walk up the paved walkway to the front door, something I haven't done in years knowing how much her mom hates me. I didn't want to get her in trouble, but I no longer need to worry about her mother's wrath in the same way, Amy's safety now my only concern. I hear muted arguing inside, but I can't decipher a single word. I hesitate for only a moment before raising my hand and pounding my fist on the door, bypassing the doorbell to release some of my anger.

It's only a moment before the door flies open revealing Amy's dad, his eyes immediately scrunching together in confusion as his shoulders sag in disappointment at the sight of me. "What are you doing here?" he snaps, irritably.

I grind my teeth together and take a deep breath, exhaling slowly, attempting to remain calm. "Mr. Stone," I grit out, "I'm here about Amy."

He gasps, his eyes widening. "Do you know where she is? I went to the office to get some more files and I came right home, but I guess she got in a fight with her mom and took off. I'm really worried about her and she's not answering her phone," he rambles.

I huff a humorless laugh and shake my head in disbelief. With a touch of disgust, I repeat, "A fight with her mom?"

His eyes narrow and he replies slowly, dragging out the word, "Yes."

"Do you have any idea what kind of fight they were in? Do you know what really happened? What has been happening for years with your wife and daughter?" I emphasize my question, my anger rising.

"What are you talking about?" he asks. "Do you know where she is?" I attempt to control my breathing and reign in my fury. Impatient, he yells, "If you can't tell me where my daughter is, leave! I need to find her!"

He moves to shut the door and I put my hand up, stopping him. "I know where she is," I state before he has a chance to do or say anything else.

He stares at me wide-eyed, waiting for an answer. "Well," he prompts, cantankerously.

"She's safe," I respond vaguely.

"Tell me where my daughter is, so I can bring her home. She'll be safe here," he insists.

I laugh, even though I don't find anything about this situation funny, I can't help myself. "That's where you're wrong!" I retort.

He gasps, taken aback by my comment. "I think it's time for you to go," Mr. Stone declares, taking an intimidating step closer to me.

Ignoring his remark and his implicit threat, I continue. "Did you know your wife hit your daughter?" I inquire, watching him closely for his reaction.

His whole body sags in defeat as he shakes his head in disappointment. My body begins shaking with anger, believing the worst with his reaction. He sighs heavily, claiming, "She told me Amy hit her tonight and she reflexively hit her back. She feels terrible."

"That's what you fucking believe?" I shake my head, my blood boiling like an inferno, feeling as if I'm about to lose it. "That's so far from the truth," I mutter. "She's been hitting your daughter for years! Beating her into submission at times. All the cuts, bruises and broken bones Amy's had since she was twelve-years-old were all because of the woman you married."

315

"What?" he gasps, shaking his head in disbelief. "That can't be true," he denies.

"Tell me this, did you ever wonder why she was always hurt when she was such a phenomenal athlete? Did you really think Amy was that clumsy when it came to cheerleading? She was the fucking captain of her squad for a reason! She ran the camps all through high school and college, she was the one everyone went to for help and modeled themselves after because she was that fucking good," I emphasize.

I see doubt flicker in his eyes as he scans through his memories and he returns my gaze appearing unsure for the first time. So, I keep pushing, "But she broke her arm, her leg, her ribs, even her fucking collarbone when she was home with her own mother, while you were gone traveling for work. I don't know what she told you, or even what she told the doctors to get away with it, but she wasn't practicing cheer, not even one of those times."

At that moment, Amy's mother steps into the doorway, and my chest burns as if it's on fire as my body vibrates. She holds a frozen pack of vegetables to her cheek, glaring at me. "What is he doing here?" she spits with disgust. "If Amy is anywhere near you, no wonder she's resorted to being so violent," she mutters. "You're trouble!"

Mr. Stone puts his hand up, holding her back and maintaining his focus on me. "Why wouldn't she talk to me?" he questions.

"Because you kept pushing her to be a certain person, get a certain job, date certain people, like Preston Kirst and all the ones before him. Her own mother made her think she's not worth anything if those things don't happen. She believes it's what you expect from her," I reiterate.

"How dare you!" Mrs. Stone warns.

"She just wants to get rid of me because of what happened with my brother, "I claim, gesturing to her, "but it's never okay to hit someone or manipulate them to do what you want."

"You're such a liar! I never laid a hand on your brother! He got those injuries in football! Get off my property!" she screams.

For the first time I look at her, giving her my full attention. My eyes go wide with incredulity and disgust. "Lies? You want to talk about fucking lies?" I challenge. I see the hesitation in her eyes before I continue. "You singlehandedly tore my family apart and yours, spreading lies about Grant and our family when it was all about you and protecting your fucking image." She swings her hand at me and I grasp her wrist to stop her before it makes contact with my face, shaking my head in revulsion. "You're supposed to fucking protect her and instead you do everything you can to bury her alive."

"Jim, make him leave! Stop letting him stand here spewing lies about me!" she demands, while glaring at me.

Ignoring her, I release her hand as Mr. Stone pulls her back out of my reach. I glance at him, and inform him, "I don't know if it was Preston's abuse that put her over the edge, or me going to jail trying to protect her, or maybe it was her deciding she'd had enough and she wasn't going to do it anymore, but I will do everything I can to protect her. That includes letting her come home. She's not coming anywhere near this house when the woman who claims to be her mother abuses her in every fucking way. I can't let it happen. I won't let anyone hurt her, no matter who they are," I reiterate, my voice breaking. I reach up and wipe the tears away I didn't know had fallen, while ignoring her dad's tears of

317

disbelief, confusion and devastation. He deserves to feel even a little bit of what she's gone through all these years.

"How do I know you're telling the truth?" he probes.

"You don't! He's a lying piece of shit, just like his brother," her mom proclaims, vehemently.

"Like Prescott Kirst?" I taunt with loathing.

She gasps in shock. "How do you know about Prescott?" she questions, her eyes wide with terror.

I shake my head, refusing to answer her question, instead focusing on Mr. Stone. "Don't take my word for it. Talk to your daughter. She's staying in the spare room at my place. I'm still in my parent's house," I reveal, letting him know where to find me. "Come talk to her," I urge. "She shouldn't have to lose you too, but if you even think about bringing her," I pause gesturing towards Mrs. Stone, "I'll call the police and I won't allow you to come back. I won't let anyone hurt her ever again."

I spin on my heel and stalk away, hoping I just did the right thing. I hear them yelling as they shut the front door, but I ignore it all, going over the conversation in my head. The fact that Mr. Stone actually listened to what I had to say has to mean something. If he believed his wife without a doubt, I don't believe we would be in this situation. I'd probably be sitting in the back of a cop car again or he would've slammed the door in my face, but neither of those things happened. I just hope it means he'll come for her. In the meantime, I won't leave her side. I hope she forgives me for confronting him and sharing her truth, but she's more important than how pissed at me she might be for speaking up.

Amy

Slowly fluttering my eyes open, it takes me a moment to realize I'm lying on Matt's couch, but Matt's body heat no longer assists in keeping me warm. I attempt to stretch, my body feeling tight, stiff, and sore. My headache doesn't feel much better than when I went to sleep, but I guess it's tolerable, now. I prop myself up just a little bit and look around the room, wondering where he might be. "Matt," I rasp. I clear my throat and with no response, try again. "Matt," I call. Sighing heavily, I drop back down on the cushions. Glancing over at the coffee table, I notice a bright yellow note sitting next to my phone. Reaching over, I grab my phone and the paper, smiling at the sight of my name in Matt's messy scrawl.

"Amy,
I hope you slept okay. I'm hoping I'll be back before you wake up, but just in case, I didn't want you to think I just took off. I promise I'll be back soon. I just had something to do that couldn't wait. I hope you're feeling a little better. By the way, I put your phone on silent, and please help yourself to anything in the house.
Love, Matt"

I smile to myself, loving the fact he left me such a sweet and simple note. Rolling over, I stare at the ceiling, thinking about everything that happened with my mom. I still can't believe I slapped her and finally confessed everything to Matt. I drove here without even thinking. I knew I'd be safe here. I knew I'd be safe with him. I can't go back home, not after hitting her.

I can't help but wonder what I would've done if Vanessa had been here. The thought makes me sick to my stomach. I need to stop pretending. I don't want him with anyone else, but I'm the one who pushed him away and into her arms. I know he'll always be my friend and he'll always be there for me, but why would he bother trying for more after how I treated him? I need to confess I want more with him. I don't want to be with any guy my parents want me to be with, no matter what. I want to be with Matt. There's no one better than him in my eyes and there never will be. No one else matters, just him. I've always loved Matt, but I think I can finally admit I'm in love with him and I've been in love with him for a long time. I don't want anyone else, even if he no longer wants me.

My mind wanders back to Vanessa, wondering if he really likes her. I don't want to ruin anything for him. He deserves to have everything he wants and be happy. I groan, hating myself for pushing him away in the first place, but I not only pushed him away, I practically shoved him out the door. If he really likes her, I won't say anything. I may not like her with Matt, but Vanessa deserves better than Preston too. No one deserves someone like him. If she's the one who makes Matt happy, I could never take that away from him, but I'm not going to pretend anymore. I won't date someone I don't want to be with anymore. It's not worth it. I've ended up alone, homeless, unemployed, beaten and battered both emotionally and physically. I'm scared, but I can't go back to living like that, that's why I went to Maine for college and fought so hard to find what I wanted there, but it didn't work out for me there and I almost ruined everything for Bree as well as myself. I wish I could go back before I met Preston and before he met Vanessa and open my eyes to what I should've known all along, but it's too late for that. I need to focus on figuring out what I really want to do with my life and go after it. As for Matt, I need to find out what he's thinking and go from there. That's all I can do right?

The sound of the door opening has me lifting my head and smiling at the sight of the man in my thoughts walking in the door, running his hand through his messy hair. He's wearing dark blue jeans and a dark green, thermal, long-sleeved shirt with the sleeves pushed up. He closes the door behind him, his eyes instantly falling to me. He sighs in relief, smiling as he walks towards me. Crouching down in front of me, he reaches up, pushing my hair out of my face. "Hi," I murmur.

He grins wider in response. "Hi. How are you feeling?" he inquires, his eyes full of concern.

"I'm doing okay," I claim.

"Good," he mumbles. "Did you eat or drink anything yet?"

"No, I...um...I was wondering if we could talk?" I stammer anxiously. I need to get this over with before I lose my nerve.

"Of course," he replies. My stomach growls in response and I wince as he chuckles in amusement. "Why don't I get you something for dinner first. It's late. I nod in acknowledgement as he makes his way into the kitchen, giving me a few more minutes to gather my thoughts and my nerve.

Chapter 38

Amy

I pop the last bite of the turkey sandwich Matt made for me into my mouth. "Mm," I moan. "That was delicious. Thank you."

"You're welcome," he replies, before taking a drink of his water.

"I guess I was hungrier than I thought," I admit.

He chuckles softly and prompts, "So you wanted to talk?"

I take a deep breath exhaling slowly, as I nod my head in confirmation. "Yeah, I do." Sitting back, I turn, facing him, waiting until he leans back and meets my gaze. "First, thank you for letting me barge in here and thanks for taking care of me," I emphasize, needing him to know how much it means to me.

He shakes his head and proclaims, "You don't ever have to thank me for that. I want to be here for you. I just wish you would've told me sooner."

Glancing down at my lap, I begin fidgeting with my fingers. "I know," I concede.

I open my mouth to continue when a knock sounds at his front door. "I'm sorry, let me see who it is," he mumbles. Forcing a smile, I watch as he stands and strides for the door.

He pulls it open and I gasp at the sight of my dad standing nervously on Matt's front stoop. "Dad?" I rasp, confused. "How'd you know I was here?"

He glances in Matt's direction and reveals, "He came over to see me."

I have a quick intake of air and look at Matt with wide eyes. Biting the inside of his cheek, he anxiously looks to me for approval. "I told him I wouldn't let him in if your mom came with him. I thought you might be ready to tell him the truth after talking with me last night. You said you didn't want to lose him. You can be pissed at me all you want, but he needs to know what she's done to you Amy," he states, pleading with me through his eyes.

Tears begin running down my face, my heart clenching in fear, regret, and anticipation. Matt rushes to my side, immediately apologizing. "I'm so sorry. I shouldn't have done that. I was absolutely livid and wanted him to know. I had no right. I'm sorry. I'll ask him to leave, just please stay here with me. You can't go back there," he begs.

Looking into his eyes, I see his fear and know he did it for me. "I'm not mad," I rasp. Ironically, I think this push is exactly what I need to confess everything to my dad. He wipes my tears away and I let him, as my anxiety consumes me. Taking a deep, shaky breath, I whimper, "Matt, I'm scared."

Seeing pure devastation on his face, he clasps my hands tightly and looks into my eyes. "You're one of the strongest people I know, Amy. I know you can do this, but if you're not ready, I'll send him away. I just can't let you go back," he repeats.

Shaking my head, I concur, "I'm not going back." I gulp down the lump in my throat and concede, "No, I'll talk to him. I don't think it's something I'll ever be ready for and you're right. He should know."

Smiling down at me, he looks at me with both relief and pride. He wipes my tears and brushes his lips gently across my temple. Leaning back, he offers, "I'm going to go for a walk and give you two some privacy."

"Thank you," I rasp. Nodding his head, he steps towards the door passing by my dad as I call to him, "Dad."

He cautiously steps into the room, sauntering over to me as the door closes behind Matt. His eyes roam my body, wavering at my temple, visible pain washing over him. "Are you alright?" he asks cautiously.

"I'm okay. I've had worse," I admit.

His whole body flinches at my simple admission, just before he nearly collapses onto the couch next to me, making me wonder how much Matt told him. My stomach churns anxiously as I wait for him to say more. "Your temple looks worse," he observes, making me grimace. "Do you have other injuries I don't know about from earlier?"

Afraid of his reaction, I stare at my lap, watching my tears fall like raindrops. "Yeah," I croak. "My shoulder, side and hip are already bruising from when mom shoved me into the wall."

He gasps in horror and I finally lift my head, meeting his teary gaze. "It's true?" he cries. I hold his gaze, staring at him through my blurred, teary eyes and nod my head in confirmation. I don't need to bother asking what he means. "How long?"

Taking a deep breath and then another, I close my eyes and finally admit, "She was always cruel when you weren't around, especially when you left for your trips, saying a lot of mean things, but the first time she hit me, I was twelve-years-old. After that, she never stopped. Today is the first time I fought back."

"Shit," he gasps, attempting to steady his own breathing. "Why didn't you come to me?" he pushes, sounding desperate and defeated.

I shrug my shoulders, and open my mouth, attempting to explain, but I feel at a loss for words. "I...I just..." I stammer. Taking another steadying breath and exhaling slowly, I try again. "She always made me feel like it was my fault and I deserved everything she did to me.

She reminded me over and over again that you wanted me to listen and do what I was told. Then when you talked to me either before you left, on the phone, or even after you got home, you emphasized her point by telling me to be a good girl. I believed it's what you wanted," I confess.

He shakes his head, his own tears falling freely as he looks at me, fraught and full of guilt. "Never! I can't tell you how many times I almost left to come home when you were hurt just to see with my own eyes that you were okay, but your mom told me you were fine or you saw the doctor." Shaking his head in disbelief he adds, "She convinced me you were just clumsy and I believed her. I should've never listened to her. She's your mother. I thought she would take care of you!"

I scoff and probe, "Did you know she never wanted kids?"

"What?" he questions wide-eyed. "How do you know that?"

"She told me," I state, grimacing.

I watch his face contort with anger, pain, devastation and guilt. Shaking his head he mumbles, "She was never like this before we had you, but I saw glimpses of it. I should've listened to my gut." Focusing on me, he inquires, "All your broken bones?"

Nodding my head in confirmation, I start to list a few of the ways she'd find to hurt me. "She pushed me down the stairs, into the kitchen counter, threw me into walls, breaking mirrors, picture frames, or dishes and then tossing me into the glass on the floor. She pulled me dislocating my shoulder, she yanked me out of the shower by the hair and slammed my head into the bathtub or sink. My hair was one of her favorite things because she could yank me to where she wanted me to fall, keeping most of my injuries below the neck. I missed more school than she probably told you and she didn't take me to the doctor if she didn't think she wouldn't be able to explain it away," I ramble.

"Oh, my God. What have I done?" he gasps, frantic. "I'm so sorry! I should've never let her come back," he proclaims. "My poor baby girl!" he sobs. "I'm so sorry, Sweetheart!" Wrapping his arms carefully around me, I fall into his embrace, both of us in tears, while he apologizes over and over again. "I'm sorry. I'm so sorry!"

As we both begin to catch our breaths, I process his comment. "You said you should've never let her come back. What do you mean?" I prod, needing clarification.

"When you were little, she had a torrid affair with a young man. He was only eighteen at the time," he mutters with disgust. "I came home one night and saw her hit him, probably thinking I would think he came on to her, but I stood in the doorway stunned for a while before she noticed me. I told her to leave and you would stay with me. I let her convince me to give her one more chance because I didn't want you to have a broken family," he enlightens me, his words full of regret.

It hits me hard, knowing our family ended up not just broken, but completely obliterated. Momentarily ignoring the part about taking her back, I wonder aloud about her affair, "Do you mean Prescott Kirst?"

He gasps, his eyes widening in shock. "You knew?"

I shake my head, "No, Matt told me some things earlier and I remember waking up to you and mom fighting when I was little. There's one time I never could forget," I admit. "I heard you say you were leaving her and she begged you to give her another chance. You finally agreed for my sake."

"You heard that? And remember it?" he prods in surprise.

I cringe and grumble, "It's burned into my memories."

If possible, his shoulders sag even further in defeat. "I'm so sorry, Amy," he repeats.

"Why didn't you leave when it happened again?" I question.

Sighing heavily, he divulges, "I don't know. I guess I could never prove it really happened then or if it was just a rumor. She claimed the boy was obsessed with her and she was afraid of him. I didn't know what to believe, so I didn't want to break our family up over something that might be true and end up losing you."

"The boy, you mean Grant? Matt's brother?" I prompt.

He winces, nodding his head. "Yeah," he confirms.

"Is that why you guys hated his whole family?" I push, heartbroken for everything that could've been if I didn't have such a horrible mother.

"With Prescott, everything remained relatively discreet with him and his family, but it was different with Grant. We were all better off staying away from each other with so many accusations flying around," he claims.

I shake my head in refusal, "No! We all would've been better off getting her out of our lives! She never cared about anyone, but herself! Matt is my best friend and you both tried to rip him away from me!" I exclaim, a feeling of betrayal overwhelming me.

"I know and I'm sorry," he repeats. "He's a good man."

I scoff and shake my head, arguing, "You should've known it then!"

He nods his head, his Adam's apple bobbing up and down as he swallows the lump in his throat. "You're right and I don't think I'll ever be able to forgive myself for everything that's happened to you. I just hope you will consider keeping me in your life. I know I don't deserve it, but I love you so much, Amy. I promise to be a better father to you if you'll let me try. I don't expect your forgiveness, I'm just hoping you'll give me a chance to earn it."

"It's going to take me some time, Dad," I mumble. "I'm trying to figure out what I need right now."

Nodding sadly, he grumbles, "I understand."

"Why do you believe me?" I probe. Shaking my head I add, "It's just, you don't even seem to be hesitating...I thought..." I trail off, not sure how to explain it.

"I guess I've had enough indications over the years, but I never had proof. I thought the doctor would say something if it were more," he admits, his whole body cringing with shame. He opens his mouth, but hesitates before asking, "What do you want to do about your mother? She should pay for what she's done," he seethes. "Do you want to press charges?"

I feel a weight return to my chest at the thought. I just want to move on. I don't ever want to deal with her again. "I just want her out of my life," I whimper, my breaths unsteady. Clenching his jaw, he nods in understanding. "Will you...will you leave her?" I rasp.

Glancing at me, I see my own pain reflected in his eyes as tears stream down his cheeks, his emotions overwhelming me. I don't know if I've ever seen my dad cry. "I would never wish I didn't marry her because I wouldn't have you, but if I could go back and leave her the first time, I would in a heartbeat. There's no way I'm going to hesitate now! I love you more than anything I could possibly imagine. I'll never be able to apologize to you enough."

He holds his arms out and I fall into his chest, wincing at my sudden movement, but I ignore my pain. "I love you, too, Daddy," I whisper, feeling like a little girl again, full of hope. I'm so grateful he believes me. I can do this.

Matt

Stepping outside, I close my front door and pull my phone out, double-checking the ringer volume. I don't want to miss her call if she needs me. I slip my phone back in my pocket, just as Vanessa pulls up and steps out of her car. I saunter over to her and stuff my hands into my pockets. "Hi," she greets me cautiously.

"Hi. What are you doing here?" I ask without preamble.

"Are you still mad at me?" she probes. I narrow my eyes and cross my arms over my chest, waiting to hear why she's really here. She sighs and runs her hand through her hair before meeting my gaze. "I'm here for two reasons. I heard what happened the other night and I wanted to check on you, but all you give me is a short response telling me nothing," she complains. "I was worried about you."

"Well," I shrug, "as you can see, I'm just fine. Preston dropped the charges, so it all worked out," I announce, pasting a fake smile on my face.

"I had nothing to do with that!" she insists. I nod my head in acknowledgement, not able to give her more. "I would have done something if I knew," she claims. "I really do like you," she reiterates.

"What's your other reason for being here?" I prompt, ignoring her comment.

"I want to apologize for what I did do," she concedes.

My eyes widen in surprise and I question, "What?"

Sighing heavily, she repeats, "I want to apologize for what I did and for not being completely honest with you about everything." I stand mute, waiting for her to elaborate. Looking away from my gaze, she begins fidgeting. "I feel sick after everything that happened. I just need to tell you what I couldn't before," she mumbles, uncomfortably.

She obviously wants to ease her guilty conscience and I need to know the truth. "Okay, do you want to take a short walk?" I suggest.

"If you have time," she replies, hopeful.

Glancing back at the house, I nod my head in agreement. "A short one," I confirm.

Chapter 39

Amy

My dad releases me, tears lingering in his eyes. He makes his way to the door and turns back towards me with a look of determination. "I realize I will never be able to make up for what she did to you," he concedes, his voice cracking. He clears his throat and adds, "But I'll keep apologizing for the rest of my life. I will do everything in my power to stand by you, support you and give you whatever you need from me, while you choose what path is right for you in your career, in life and love. I don't want you to ever settle. You deserve to have it all."

I smile, glancing at him through more tears, as my chest tightens. I don't know if he even realizes how much his words affect me. I've been trying so hard to live up to certain expectations. I've never felt good enough, but I pushed through, pretending to be what I thought he wanted me to be. "Thank you," I rasp.

"I love you," he reiterates.

"I love you, too," I reply, just before he walks out the door.

I wipe the tears from my face, as I reach for a Kleenex, thinking about the conversation I just had with my dad, a conversation I didn't know if I'd ever have the courage to have, but Matt gave me the opportunity, giving me the push I didn't know I needed until it was right in front of me. I feel overwhelmed. My body still hurts, I've lost so much the last few days, but I don't think any of the things I've lost are needed, except for maybe a place to live and Matt did say I could stay here. I want to take him up on that, but I need to know where his head's at before I get too comfortable. I want to be proud of who I am and I know it will take time, but I think I'm finally ready for it.

I've found my strength and I'm not turning back. It feels like I'm starting over, but I'm restarting with so much; a great education, experience, my dad, my friends, and Matt. How much Matt wants to give me, my only question. A new beginning is exactly what I need.

The front door opens and Matt walks in, a smile lighting up my face at the sight of him. "You're back," I happily state the obvious.

"Ah, yeah," he stammers awkwardly, giving me an apologetic smile.

My eyes scrunch together in confusion, but then Vanessa steps inside behind him with a tentative smile on her face. She holds her hand up and waves as she greets me, "Hi, Amy."

I quickly force a fake smile onto my face as my heart drops into my stomach, my hopes of a future with Matt sinking. Taking a deep breath to calm the butterflies that have taken over my insides, I gulp down the lump in my throat and politely reply, "Hi, Vanessa." I'm suddenly unsure what to do. Do I sit out here with them and intrude, hanging out with them? I can't handle seeing them kiss. It will hurt too much. Maybe they'll go to his room so they can be alone? I can't handle that either. I feel sick. I begin scrambling to push myself up. I'll just go to the spare bedroom to be alone; that's all I can muster at the moment. I can cry in peace in there. I hate myself for waiting too long. It's too late. My heart hurts worse than my broken body.

I attempt to ease to my feet and Matt's instantly at my side. He wraps his arm around my waist, and grasps my elbow to help keep me balanced. "What are you doing?" he questions.

I feel my face heat and I look around as if searching for something. "I uh, just thought I'd go get some rest," I claim.

He chuckles and reminds me, "You just spent half the day sleeping."

My cheeks turn an even deeper shade of red. "Yeah, well," I mutter, uncomfortably.

"Well, I was just talking with Vanessa," he begins, making me wince, "and now she would like to talk to you."

My head snaps up to meet his gaze. He looks down at me, his sexy, irritating smirk in place and arching his eyebrows in question. I narrow my eyes at him and hesitate for a moment before I agree, puzzled and clueless, "Um, okay."

"I'll grab us some water and maybe a snack," Matt offers. "Do either of you want anything to eat?"

I return his smirk, reminding him, "I just ate." He shrugs and turns towards the kitchen, leaving me alone with Vanessa.

"What do you want to talk to me about?" I question awkwardly, sitting back on the couch.

She takes a deep breath as she lowers herself into the chair near me and begins fidgeting, nervously twisting her fingers together. "How are you feeling?" she asks, ignoring my question.

I grimace and admit, "I've been better."

"I'm sorry," she apologizes.

My eyebrows draw down in confusion and I blurt out, "Why? You didn't do this to me."

She flinches and nods her head in acknowledgement. "Yeah, but I knew what Preston was capable of," she states.

"That doesn't make you responsible for him being an abusive asshole," I state blatantly.

Her eyes widen and she laughs. "True, but..." she begins trailing off. She sighs, her gaze returning to her lap. "I do have something I have to confess."

"Okay," I prod, dragging out the word.

"I'm sorry, this is really hard for me to confess, especially after everything I went through with Preston and knowing at least some of what he did to you," she begins. I clench my jaw at the reminder and pinch my lips tightly together as I nod in acknowledgement, keeping my lips sealed.

"Well, you know I dated Preston and I'm not really supposed to talk about our relationship, but…"

"I understand that," I grumble under my breath.

She offers me a sad smile, before returning her gaze to her hands. "Well, he kind of kept me under his thumb," she mumbles.

"Well, I'm sorry to hear that, but I don't understand why you're telling me this. I really don't want to know anything about him," I retort.

She flinches and glances up at me with apologetic eyes before averting her gaze once again. "Well, um, I um did something that involves you," she stammers.

"What do you mean?" I probe as my heart begins racing.

Her face scrunches up with anxiety as she continues. "Well, Preston knew I really liked Matt," she admits, making me wince, but I quickly try to hide my reaction. "And Preston wanted you and he wanted you away from Matt. So, he bribed me to help keep you guys apart."

My mouth drops open and my eyes go wide at her admission. "Excuse me?" I respond in utter disbelief.

"I didn't really do anything I wouldn't have done already, except maybe," she pauses, her Adam's apple bobbing up and down as she gulps down the lump in her throat, "make it seem like we were more than we were to you, and push Matt into more than I knew he wanted."

"I don't understand," I mumble in shock.

"I just wanted you to know Preston was doing everything he could to keep you away from Matt and control you, and I was aware of it. After I found out what happened with you in the hospital and Matt ending up in jail, I never hated myself more. I just thought you should know the truth," she reveals.

I feel sick hearing her confession, but I also want to ask if that means her and Matt aren't together, but instead I blurt out, "Did you sleep with him?" She opens her mouth to answer and I put my hand up and shake my head vehemently to stop her. "Forget it. Please, don't answer that. It's none of my business."

"I don't know about that," she mumbles, "but maybe you should talk to Matt about that. I just want to say I'm sorry. I never should've agreed and I should've told Matt everything right from the start." I nod my head, processing her information. "I'm just really sorry," she repeats.

Matt steps back into the room and places three waters down on the table. Vanessa stands up and shakes her head, "No thank you. I have to go. I have some papers to grade," she explains. She steps towards Matt and wraps her arms around him, giving him a hug and whispering in his ear, as he returns the movement. I quickly avert my gaze, my chest clenching with heartbreak at the intimate gesture. "I really am sorry, Amy," she repeats.

I look up and paste a fake smile on my face, nodding my head in acknowledgement. "Bye."

She turns and walks out the door, pulling it closed behind her as Matt sits down next to me, watching me closely. Glancing over at him, I meet his intense gaze, my heart skipping a beat. I don't know if I can do this. I can't lose him.

Matt

I stare at her, the look on her face tense, distraught and hurt. I need to know what's going through her head. I appreciate Vanessa's apology, but I can't imagine the feelings it's brought up with Amy. "Amy," I prompt, but she continues to stare at her lap. "Amy," I repeat, scooting a little closer to her on the couch. "Would you look at me, please?" I urge. Reaching over, I place my fingers under her chin and gently nudge until she meets my gaze. "Are you alright?"

"Yeah, I'm okay," she maintains, sounding almost defeated.

"Please, talk to me," I plead. "I need to know what's going through your head right now."

I watch as she takes a deep breath and exhales slowly, gathering her courage to talk to me and I fucking hate it. Talking to me should be easy! "Okay," she mumbles. "I know you don't want me to apologize, but after hearing her confession, I have to tell you I'm sorry again. I feel like if I wasn't so stupid in the first place," she begins.

I drop my hand from her chin and run it softly down her arm, until I reach her hand. I clasp our hands together and give her an encouraging squeeze. "Please don't say that," I prod. "You're not stupid and now that you've told me everything, I understand where your feelings come from and why. I just wish I would've known sooner so I could really help you."

"You've always helped me," she emphasizes.

"I could've done more," I claim, feeling guilty.

She huffs a humorless laugh and insists, "You're the last one who should say that. You've done more for me than anyone in my life and I appreciate you more than I can even begin to explain."

I cringe knowing she appreciates me, but I'm still not enough for her to love. I can't hear that from her. My grip on her hand loosens and I sit back. "Glad I can help," I mutter feeling defeated.

"Are you and Vanessa together?" she blurts out.

My gaze snaps to her, taken aback. I have a sudden burst of hope seeing her brows pinched together while she bites her lower lip anxiously. A small smile pulls at the corners of my lips. Keeping my eyes on her, I watch her reaction, as I answer, "No."

She arches her eyebrows in surprise and pushes, "Were you?"

I wince, knowing I need to answer her honestly. "Not exactly," I mumble. She arches her eyebrows waiting for more. Sighing heavily, I run my free hand through my hair and admit, "We hung out a lot and we went out a few times, but you were with Preston."

She flinches and shakes her head. "I know I have no right to ask, but I hate the thought of you guys hooking up. In the past I pretended it didn't matter, but it does, even more now."

"You were with Preston," I emphasize, giving her the answer she's looking for without saying the words, "and I was trying to get you out of my fucking head."

"You're right," she concedes, her whole body tensing as pain flashes through her eyes. "I'm sorry, but that doesn't make me hate it any less."

"Why?" I prod.

"I made a mistake by pushing you away in the first place. Something like this shouldn't have had to happen to make me realize how it always should've been, but it did," she explains, giving me hope.

"And how should it have been?" I probe, still needing more.

She shrugs and admits, "I miss you, Matt."

I drop my eyes to the couch as my heart plummets along with it, disappointment overwhelming me. She misses me. I'm still in love with her and she fucking misses me. "That's fucking great," I mutter under my breath.

"It's more than that though," she elaborates. My breathing and heart cease simultaneously. I lift my gaze, anxiously waiting for the words I need to hear spill from her lips more than I need my next breath. "I'm in love with you," she proclaims with a confidence I need to hear. I feel my whole body relax as if I've been pushed to my limits my whole life and for the first time, I'm finding a release. My heart restarts at a rapid pace, as my breath whooshes out of me, making me dizzy. "I've always been in love with you, Matt. It's just..."

Taking her injuries into account, I crash my lips onto hers, stopping her from saying anything else, those three simple words the only words I've ever needed to hear from her luscious lips. Sliding my hands up, I cradle her face in my hands, as my mouth moves in a slow rhythm with hers, my whole body tingling and reveling in her response. Pulling back, I stare into her eyes and clarify, "Are you sure you want this? Us?" She nods her head in acknowledgement, happiness shining in her eyes. "I can't go back, Amy, I won't," I insist.

"I don't want to go back. I want to love you and only you," she reiterates. "If you'll still have me, I want us to be my reality," she proclaims.

My heart jumps into my throat and back into my stomach like a ping-pong ball, the moment between us surreal. "I love you so damn much!"

"I love you too," she repeats. A smile consumes my features, my whole body engulfed instantly by an inferno as I kiss her again.

Chapter 40

Matt

I pull back, afraid I'm going to hurt her. She's been through so much. I don't want to push her. She leans forward, searching for my lips. Cradling her face in my hands, I emphasize my thoughts, "I don't want to hurt you."

"I need to be close to you, Matt. I'm feeling better, I promise. I need you," she proclaims.

I look into her eyes and brush my lips across hers. I pull back and wrap one arm around her back and the other underneath her legs, scooping her up into my arms as I rise. She squeals at the unexpected motion and wraps her arms around my neck as she settles into my chest, my erratic heartbeat thumping against her cheek. I carefully carry her back to my room, gently easing her down onto my bed. I stand for a moment looking down at her, appreciating her beauty and seeing a light in her eyes I'm not sure I've ever seen before.

I lay down next to her, cupping her face with one hand and pulling her close to me with the other, pressing our bodies together. "I've missed you so damn much," I admit, my chest aching. Reaching for her hands, I hold them momentarily between us, feeling the power of our heartbeats, finding their rhythm together. I feel as if all my senses have been enhanced, electrifying every nerve ending in my body. Brushing her hair back from her eyes, I kiss her softly, my lips tingling with the slightest brush of our lips. She whimpers, the sound making my insides ache. I wait until her eyes flutter open and hold my gaze before I speak. "I'm going to make you mine, but we're going slow tonight. I want to cherish you," I reveal, her blue eyes instantly darkening to a deep ocean blue.

Her Adam's apple bobs up and down as she gulps down the lump in her throat and nods her head in acknowledgement. Pressing my lips to hers, I move them matching the rhythm of our heartbeats. I lick her bottom lip, begging for entry, her mouth parting almost instantly. I lick, twist and dance with her tongue, enjoying her sweet taste. Pulling back, I trail kisses along her jaw, my tongue sweeping up towards her ear, tasting the salt on her skin. I kiss and nip at her neck as my hand slides down her arm and along her hip. Slipping my hand under the hem of her shirt, my heart skips a beat at the feel of her soft, velvety skin.

Leaning back I give the bottom of her shirt a gentle tug and she moves, making it easier to pull it over her head. I toss it onto the floor as I take her in, my stomach clenching as my anger returns and I struggle to tame it. "It's fine, I'm fine," she claims, attempting to reassure me. She places her hand on my chest, trying to calm me down. "It's really not that bad," she mumbles. I suddenly have immense pressure on my chest, my heart aching with her claim. How could someone hurt her like this? But this isn't caused by just one asshole, but also her mother. Her whole left side, from her shoulder down to her hip, looks like one big bruise. Then, both arms have bruises that look like where he grabbed her, one more faded than the other as if it might be a few days older.

"Fuck," I murmur, tears springing to my eyes. I can barely breath, my chest feeling like it's about to collapse. "I need to see all of you," I state, desperate. She nods, giving me permission. Hooking my fingers into her waistband, I gently tug her pants down, pulling them off and adding them to our growing pile of clothes. The bruise on her left side continues down just past her hip. Her right hip and both her thighs appear to have faded finger marks, causing me to begin shaking. Her scraped knees seem to be healing, but it's not enough. I hate that I couldn't protect her from this. "I'm so fucking sorry," I apologize, feeling as if I've failed her.

"It's not your fault," she mumbles.

I move up her body and look into her eyes, firmly declaring, "It's not your fault, either." She nods sadly and I repeat, "It's not your fault!"

She looks into my eyes as if begging for my words to be true. "I know," she concurs. I arch my eyebrows, making sure she believes it. She nods her head, the corners of her mouth curving up in a soft smile. "I know," she reiterates, with a little more confidence.

"No more pretending, Amy. I want to hear the words," I plead. "I need to hear you say it."

"It's not my fault," she affirms.

"I'm going to remind you of that every single day until I'm sure you believe it," I inform her. I kiss her lips and mumble onto them, "I love you," and then kiss her again, not giving her a chance to respond. I slip her bra off with one hand and see a little more bruising on the side of her breast. I gently cup her breast and brush my lips over the bruising. Then, I softly place a few kisses along her side. A few tears escape and drop onto her belly as I kiss a path, making my way down her body. She weaves her fingers into my hair as I lick her, kiss her and whisper, "I love you," over and over again.

"Matt," she whimpers.

I tug her underwear down, hating the faded mark on her pelvis, another tear escaping as I brush my lips over it, my heart feeling like it's shattering and being put back together at the same time. "Fuck," I mumble. "Can I taste you?" I request, not wanting to assume anything.

"Please," she rasps. I brush my lips over her core, and flick my tongue out, licking her seam, a groan escaping me at her sweet taste. I lick her slowly, pushing

341

my tongue inside and sliding up to her clit. Circling my tongue around, I gently suck as I curve one hand under her ass and with my free hand, I slip a finger inside her already soaked pussy.

She releases a loud moan, her insides already swelling and tightening around my finger. Adding another finger, I continue licking her slowly, savoring her taste and the soft sweet moans she's making as she arches towards me. Her breathing begins to pick up, her body heat burning as my name escapes her lips, "Matt!"

"I've got you," I whisper over her folds. I gradually increase my pressure on her clit, while my tongue swirls faster. Keeping my eyes on her face, I watch her reactions and listen to her sounds as a feeling of pure nirvana consumes my soul. She whimpers as her insides begin clenching my fingers curled inside her over and over again, while my tongue continues its slow and sensuous attack on her clit, riding out her orgasm.

She falls back with a satisfied, heavy breath. I lick my fingers clean, and make my way back up her body. She pushes up and presses her lips to mine in an all-consuming kiss. "You never go slow like that. That was..." she trails off and kisses me again, at a loss for words. Moaning, she pulls at my shirt causing me to pull back from our kiss. "You're overdressed," she states the obvious.

I smirk and reach back with one hand, pulling my shirt over my head and tossing it on the floor. Her eyes pool like liquid sapphires as I stand and kick off my jeans. Then, I reach into the nightstand drawer and grab a condom out of the box, before I slip out of my underwear and join her back on the bed.

Her eyes widen and her lips curl up in a smile as she takes me in. "That looks painful," she observes, nodding towards my fully erect, hard cock.

"That's because of you," I reply, grinning as I roll the condom on. My hand brushes over her nipple before it curves around her back, pulling her flush. Looking into her eyes I murmur, "Every part of you is so incredibly beautiful. I've been in love with you for so long." I kiss her tenderly and roll her onto her back as I move my body over hers, keeping my muscles taut so I don't crush her. "I want to make you mine," I repeat my words from before.

"I'm already yours, Matt," she responds, filling my heart. "Make love to me," she requests.

I grin, and mumble, "My pleasure." I move myself to the edge of her entrance and hesitate. "Please tell me if something hurts."

"I'm okay," she reiterates. "Please, Matt," she urges desperately.

Obeying, I thrust inside, both of us gasping. I give us a moment to adjust before I begin to move, feeling like I'm already about to explode. "You feel so fucking good," I mumble.

"I've missed you so much," she replies, breathily.

I kiss her and look into her eyes, feeling so much more than I've ever felt. "I'm not going to last," I admit.

"That's okay," she rasps. "We'll just go again. I did sleep all day," she reminds me. She pushes up to kiss me as her hands run up and down my back.

I grin and press my lips to hers as I move with her in a slow, rhythm, thrusting in and out. Breaking from our kiss, we both gasp for breath. I tilt back, slightly, hitting her insides at a perfect angle, as I maintain our slow and steady pace, relishing every sound leaving her kiss-swollen lips. Her breathing becomes heavy and rapid, mine matching hers with every breath.

"Matt," she rasps, her hips meeting mine. She begins clenching around me, milking my dick as her eyes roll back into her head as another orgasm wracks her body and a loud moan leaves her lips.

I push in and pause, my own body filling with heat, as my balls tighten. Pulling out, I thrust back inside her warm, tight, slick center as she squeezes me. I push in as far as I can go, my body falling over the edge and I release, groaning with pure ecstasy. I slow down and stop inside her, covering her mouth with mine, trying to pour all my love for her into this kiss. Pulling back, I drop my head to her shoulder, sighing heavily with satisfaction. "Yeah, we'll definitely have to do that again, but first I need to get rid of this condom," I joke. I kiss her again before pushing off the bed and making my way to the bathroom to dispose of the condom and grab a warm, damp cloth to care for her.

Amy

My thoughts continue to wander as I relish being wrapped in Matt's arms, my back to his front. Something about this felt different. I don't know if it's because I finally feel free, or because he went excruciatingly slow, or because we confessed our love to each other. Then again, maybe it's just because it's him. How did I think this wasn't an option?

"You've gotten quiet," he murmurs, tracing his fingers mindlessly across my bare belly. "What are you thinking?" he asks, tilting his head to better see my face. "I still can't see you," he claims. Then he easily moves us around, readjusting us so we're lying face to face with his arms wrapped around me.

I giggle and sigh happily. "You, me, us," I mumble. He arches his eyebrows in question, asking for more. "I didn't think I would ever have this," I confess. "Not really. I started believing I didn't deserve real love."

"You deserve so much more than love. I'm going to try to show you how much I love and adore you and what it should always be like when someone loves you with every part of them. I wish I could give you everything you deserve..." he mumbles.

I interrupt him, insisting, "You are everything I could have ever dreamed of, Matt."

Tipping his head forward, he kisses me slow and sweet. His forehead falls to mine as he looks into my eyes. He slides his hand up, cupping my cheek and caressing my jaw with his thumb. I see the hesitation in his eyes just before he blurts, "I hate asking, but I need to know...Did he force you?" he asks his voice cracking.

I attempt to pull my gaze from his, but his grip on my face tightens just enough, begging me to stay. My stomach twists as I take a shaky breath in. "I...I didn't say no," I softly admit, as more tears slide down my cheeks. "I didn't know how," I whimper, barely getting the words out. I hate myself in this moment as agony flashes through his eyes. Clearing my throat, I continue, "I was afraid of the consequences." I watch as he briefly closes his eyes, breathing in and out. "I'm sorry," I rasp.

His eyes fly open and he clenches his jaw. "Don't ever apologize for anything that happened with him or your mom ever again," he emphasizes. "I just hate that you went through any of it. I wish I could've done something to protect you. It kills me! But you are not to blame," he reiterates.

"But," I attempt to explain myself.

He stops me, pressing his lips to mine and then pulling back and cupping my face with both hands. "I don't give a fuck, if you didn't say the words. I only care about what you wanted. I want to fucking kill that asshole," I grumble.

"Matt, we can't do anything," she reminds me.

Nodding my head, I take another calming breath. "I know," I seethe. Sighing, I proclaim, "I know all this shit will take a lot of time for us to work through, but I don't care how long it takes or how hard it might be, I want to do all of it with you. We will climb out of this pit together. Please, just talk to me. Tell me what you need. I'm terrified I'm going to do or say something that reminds you of him or your mom." I pause, shaking my head in concern. "Your bad days are my worst days and your good days are my best days. We've got this as long as we do it together," I insist.

"Together," she repeats for emphasis.

A smile tugs at the corners of my lips. "I love you," I state. "I've wanted to say those words for a long fucking time, so you may be hearing them a lot," I tease, attempting to lighten the mood.

"I don't mind," she giggles. The sweet sound sends goosebumps all over my body. "I love you, too." I kiss her, but she pulls back, the look she gives me causing my heart to skip a beat. "Thank you," she rasps.

"For what?" I prompt, puzzled.

"For never giving up on me. I don't know if I would've ever made it to this happy place without you," she claims.

I shake my head in denial, "No way. I don't know a soul stronger, or more courageous than you." Her eyes sparkle a little brighter and I press my lips to hers, no longer able to hold back, my hand traveling back down her creamy skin and pulling her close. "Hope you're ready for round two," I taunt, smirking at my girl. "My girl," I repeat the words from my head. I again cover her mouth with mine, putting every part of me into loving every part of her.

Epilogue

Three months later...

Amy

After work, I quickly make my way over to Matt's new gym. He's been so gentle with me, worried about how I'll react because of everything that happened with Preston. I need him to understand it's not the same thing, not with him. Now that we're really together, everything feels so much more electric and I love his tender side, but I don't want him treating me as if I might break. I want both sides of us and after everything we've been through, I've started believing we deserve it. With the grand opening tomorrow, I want to surprise him in his office. Maybe the red, lacy teddy with perfectly placed little black bows I'm wearing underneath my black dress and red blazer will help ignite the fire under his sexy ass. I need to be the wild side of us again.

He grins as I walk in, my red heels clicking on the tile floor. "Hey, this is a wonderful surprise!" he states. Striding over to me, he instantly presses his lips to mine.

"Mm," I moan. "I love you."

He takes a deep breath, steadying himself. "I love hearing those words out of your mouth," he murmurs. He kisses me again and replies, "I love you too." Clearing his throat, he prompts, "So, how was work?"

I feel my face light up as I admit, "Incredible. I love working for Diana Brooks!" I'm thrilled to be working in her corporate office promoting all kinds of fashion, home décor and even some community programs I truly believe in. I'll never forget the day she contacted me because she heard I'd left Kirst. I've already learned so much working for her and I'm proud to be a part of her team.

"Good," he replies, a touch of satisfaction in his voice. He's been so supportive about my new job, always asking me for details. He opens his mouth to probably do just that, but I stop him, laying my hand lightly on his chest.

"I have a surprise for you," I announce, playfully.

The corners of his lips twitch up in a smile. "You do, huh?"

"Yeah, can we go into your office?" I request.

"Sure," he easily agrees. "Hey, Kim, why don't you head home," he suggests. "We have a big day tomorrow."

"Yes, we do," she agrees. "I'm excited." She turns to me and inquires, "You'll be there, right?"

"I wouldn't miss it for the world," I confirm.

"Excellent! I'll see you both tomorrow!" she proclaims. "I'll lock the doors on my way out," she informs Matt. She turns and begins gathering her things as we step into his office.

"Bye," we both call as he shuts his office door behind us.

"It's going to be so incredible to have a physical therapist on site here when she's done," Matt claims. I'm thrilled Kim took Matt up on his offer to join his team.

"You're lucky," I concur.

"What's my surprise?" he prods.

"Well, close your eyes and I'll get it out," I mumble, as I slide my blazer off my arms and lay it over the back of a black leather chair. I'm a little nervous which is ridiculous. He's seen me naked so many times since the first time back in high school, but now he's mine. My heart skips a beat at the reality.

"Okay," he agrees, closing his eyes without argument.

Reaching behind my back, I slowly unzip my dress, wondering if he hears the sound. I let my dress slip off and fall to the ground, pooling at my feet. I step out of it, leaving my heels on. Taking a deep breath, I stand proud in front of him and command, "Okay, open your eyes."

I watch as his eyes flutter open and his chin drops to his chest with a gasp. "Fuck, me," he mutters.

"That's exactly what I plan on doing Mr. Young," I reply, a smirk on my face.

He stalks towards me, his gaze burning into mine. He stops in front of me, leaving just enough space for his eyes to roam my body from head to toe. My knees feel weak from the heat of his stare, but he grasps my hips and pulls me close holding me up. "You're so fucking gorgeous," he rasps over my lips, just before his mouth comes crashing down on mine.

I suck his lower lip into my mouth and then release it with a groan. "Please don't hold back on me anymore. I need you to devour me like you can't get enough," I plead.

"Amy," he mumbles my name with a desperation I hope he's feeling for me.

"Please don't worry about hurting me. You can only hurt me if you break my heart. I need you to claim me like you did before we were together," I declare.

He lifts me up and places me on the smooth, cool surface of his new black desk. He cradles my face in his hands and looks into my eyes before he growls, "You are mine, every single piece of you and I will never get enough."

He covers my mouth with his, his tongue pushing its way inside and playing with mine. Placing his hands on my knees, he nudges my legs apart and steps between them. He presses his body into mine and I automatically react, grinding myself into his still covered cock. His hands begin roaming my body, one hand cupping my breast as he tears his lips away from our kiss leaving me breathless. He tips his head down and kisses my hard nipple through the lacy material, before nibbling it with his teeth. My breathing picks up and I moan in pleasure. I arch my back towards him, needing more and begging to get closer. "I need you," I rasp.

"You're sexy as fuck in this thing, but I'm about two seconds away from tearing this off you. How the fuck do I get it off?" he complains.

I giggle in response and reach for him, slipping my hands inside his waistband. "I'll help you after I get these off."

"No," he smirks, as I arch my eyebrows in surprise. He pulls his shirt over his head, the sight of his hard abs taking my breath away. I lick my lips as I tug his pants down, barely getting them over his ass, before he pushes me back on his desk, stopping me from going any further. He pushes one side down, revealing my breast and immediately covering it with his mouth. His other hand travels around to the top of my ass. Finding a clip, he flicks it open, giving him access to my heated core. "Found it," he announces with a proud grin.

That's not the only one," I retort, as I reach up and wrap my hand around his cock.

He hisses a harsh breath and admits, "That's the only one I have the patience for."

My heart flip-flops, loving what I do to him. He pushes the fabric away and slides his fingers along my folds with a groan. "Fuck, you're wet."

"Always for you," I confess. He grips my hips and kisses me desperately. My heart beats rapidly as my body tingles craving him. "Matt," I rasp, gasping for breath, "I need you."

He places himself at my entrance and growls in frustration. "I don't have a fucking condom."

"You don't need one. I have an IUD and there's no one, but you," I proclaim.

"There will never be anyone but you," he insists. Pausing, his piercing gaze assesses me. "Are you sure?"

I nod my head in confirmation. "I'm positive. I love you, Matt, but more than anything I need you right here, right now."

His lips crash into mine as his fingers curl into my pussy, my swollen insides ready to erupt with pleasure. Tearing his lips away, he leans back and flips me over. "Put your palms on my desk and put your head down. I want your sweet ass in the air with those heels," he instructs.

I do as he says, placing my cheek on the surface between my hands. "Like this?"

"Fuck, yes," he replies as his fingers dig into my hips. Suddenly, he thrusts into me, pushing my body into his desk and making me gasp in pleasure as he fills me up. "Amy, you feel so fucking good," he groans.

I moan my agreement. Feeling like I'm already there, my insides squeeze him, skin to skin. He pulls out and thrusts into me again. "Harder," I beg, needing more.

He does as I say, pushing into me harder, deeper and faster, hitting my spot over and over again. My whole body feels like it's on fire. My eyes close involuntarily as flashes of white stars flicker behind my eyelids and I gasp for breath. He thrusts into me, the feel of him becoming overwhelming. I can barely breathe. I begin to tremble. I don't think I can take anymore. "Matt," I whimper, desperately, not even sure what I'm asking. He thrusts hard, again and again, easily pushing me over the edge. My insides clench, squeeze and milk him as he falls over the cliff right behind me with a guttural moan. He slams into me one more time, momentarily remaining deep inside me. Exhaling, he collapses over my back to catch his breath. I sigh, blissfully happy.

"I'm going to claim you on every surface in this place," he announces between ragged breaths.

"That will be fun," I concur, peeking up at him.

He kisses my jaw as he lets his hands run along my sides to my ass, tapping it lightly. "Damn, this was my kind of surprise." He pushes up, taking me with him, his hand snaking its way around my waist. I wobble, slightly dizzy on my feet, but quickly regain my balance in his firm grip. I turn around, leaning back on his desk and look up at him. He reaches for a few Kleenexes and inquires, "Is this okay? It's all I really have unless you go to the bathrooms." I nod my head in confirmation and he reaches his hand between my legs, gently cleaning me up, his fluids dripping out of me. "Is it fucked up that I like this?" he asks.

My eyebrows draw down in confusion. "What?"

"Leaving a part of me inside you," he mumbles. He turns, keeping one hand firmly on my hip as he tosses the Kleenex into the garbage can next to his desk.

"You already live inside me without this," I claim.

He grins, tilting his head down and guiding my chin up with his fingers until I meet his gaze. He places a tender kiss on my lips and pulls back, murmuring, "I love you so fucking much and I'm going to find a way to prove it to you every day."

"Marry me," I blurt without thinking.

"What?" he asks, his eyes widening in surprise.

I gulp down the lump in my throat, shocked by my own words, but also knowing that's exactly what I want the moment the words leave my lips. "Marry me," I repeat with a little more confidence. "I don't want a big wedding, Matt, I only want you," I claim.

"You're proposing to me?" he reiterates.

"Yes," I confirm, shrugging and smiling wide. "I know I've made a lot of mistakes, but when it comes to you, the biggest one I ever made was letting you go. I don't know what I would've done if you hadn't forgiven me."

"There's nothing to forgive," he begins.

Ignoring his comment, I continue, "There's no way I'm ever making that mistake again. I know what I want, Matt and that's you. It will always be you."

He grins wide, the love he has for me shining bright in his eyes. He tips his head down brushing his lips over mine. "Don't worry, there's no way in hell I'm ever letting you go now that you're mine." He kisses me again and mumbles over my lips, "I love you, Amy."

"I love you, Matt," I whisper. The most unbelievable part of this is how loved and cherished he makes me feel. I've never felt more special or treasured than I do with this man. He makes me feel as if my heart might burst out of my chest. Everything about it feels pure. I've never had that with anyone except maybe Bree, but best friends are different than the man I'm in love with, although, I finally truly understand what Christian means to Bree, giving me a sudden wave of guilt. I will do everything I can to repair the damage I've done.

"Are you okay?" Matt prods, pulling his shirt on over his head.

"Yeah," I confirm. He arches his eyebrows in challenge and I explain, "I was just thinking about Bree and Christian. I'm really happy they were able to work everything out."

He gives me a knowing look and nods his head in understanding. "It's been years and she loves you," he reiterates my thoughts.

I nod my head, feeling overwhelmed with emotion. "I'm going to be better," I claim.

"I just want you to be you, Amy. You're the one I'm in love with, not the version you think you need to be. Embrace who you are and trust in our love, I do," he states. I push up on my tiptoes, pressing my lips to his and quickly fall back on my heels.

"You need to get dressed so we can go home before we get something else dirty. I have to leave this place ready for tomorrow," he reminds me.

"Are you nervous?" I question.

"I think I'm more nervous knowing Grant will be here for it. It's been a long time, but I'm excited to see him," he admits.

"I'll be right by your side when you need me," I insist.

"I always need you and yes, I will marry you, but I'm asking you," he claims. "I want to give you the proposal you deserve."

I giggle, not surprised by his response. "I love you, Matt," I reiterate.

He leans down, pressing his lips to mine with a sudden urgency. He pushes his tongue inside my mouth and I open for him, lifting my legs and wrapping them around his back to pull him close. "Fuck it," he mutters over my lips. He slips his arms around my back and holds me close to his chest as he turns and walks out of his office. "Let's go break-in our first piece of equipment."

The End

Acknowledgements

I'm not sure if it gets easier or harder to write the acknowledgements. I feel like I'm not able to do justice to how appreciative I am for all the incredible people in my life who help with my books and support me in some way. This time I want to start by thanking my fans. Afterall, this is a book that would have never existed without you. Countless times over the years I've been asked why Amy is the way she is and this book was my opportunity to finally share it with everyone. Along with all of you, I'd like to thank Nancy and Kelley and all my Beta readers, I appreciate you more than I can express. I'm thrilled you enjoy my books and fall in love with the characters just as I do as I'm writing their stories!

I would like to thank Jessica Scott of Uniquely Tailored for the gorgeous digital and paperback book covers as well as The Unforgettable Series logo included on the cover. With Amy's story being a little different, I knew it was time for a facelift for the series and you gave me even more than I was hoping for. Thank you so much!

Thank you to my friends and other incredible and talented authors and bloggers from around the world who brought me in to collaborate with them and encouraged me to write this story too. I do have to name a few of you who have continuously stuck by my side encouraging me, inspiring me, making me laugh and being the best friends including Vaya Thorn, Ali Lee, Jessica Lou, Jensen Kristyne, Wesley Parker and Natasha of Sinful Desires Book Recommendations. All of you have been incredibly supportive and I'm truly grateful to have all of you in my life! There's so many other amazing authors and bloggers I've gotten to know who have supported me and my writing and I'm happy to call my friends. Although, I'm not naming all of you because there's so many, I do want to say thank you!

Thank you to my friends and family for always being there. I know sometimes I can get lost in my writing, my stories and my characters and forget about the real world. I want to thank you for both understanding and encouraging me to continue doing what I love. I love you all!

Connect with the Author

For more Adult Contemporary Romance, read more by Nikki A. Lamers. Connect with her here:

Official Author Website
www.nikkialamersauthor.com

Amazon Author Page
https://www.amazon.com/Nikki-A.-Lamers/e/B00NU1VU8M

Author Facebook Page
www.facebook.com/pg/NikkiALamersAuthor

Follow Me on Instagram & BookBub
@NikkialamersAuthor

Author Goodreads Page
www.goodreads.com/author/show/8451774.Nikki_A_Lamers

For Clean Contemporary Romance, read books by Nicole Mullaney. Connect with her here:

Follow Her on Instagram
@nicolemullaney

Author Facebook Page
www.facebook.com/Nicole-Mullaney-Author-103006415283835/

BookBub
@NicoleMullaneyAuthor

About the Author

Nikki A Lamers has always had a passion for reading and writing, especially romance. She grew up in Wisconsin with her sister, mom and dad. She always loved reading romance books and watching romance movies with her dad, something they both enjoyed. After college she lived in Florida for a few years working for the, "Happiest Place on Earth," where she met her husband. She now lives on Long Island in New York with her husband and two kids. She spends her free time reading or hanging out with friends and family. She would love to spend more time traveling, visiting new places and meeting new people.